Originally from London, husband in a Surrey villag and she acts as her husbai her fourth book, is her sec novella, *A Bottle of Plonk*. and short stories. Having studied with The Open University and Surrey University, she gained a degree in 2002 with a dissertation on the Harry Potter series and other children's books. However, she prefers to write for adults. *Tainted Tree* was awarded Second Prize, Novel Section, at the 2007 Winchester Writers' Conference.

.

… an engaging narrative voice … I was immediately drawn
into the story.
Donna Condon, editor, Piatkus Books

The atmosphere is skilfully built, humming with suspense …
evocative images and well-chosen vocabulary … a page-turner
Adrienne Dines, author

love from,

Pauline

Also by Jacquelynn Luben

Fiction
A Bottle of Plonk

Non-fiction
The Fruit of the Tree

TAINTED TREE

Jacquelynn Luben

Goldenford Publishers Ltd
Guildford
www.goldenford.co.uk

First published in Great Britain in 2008 by
Goldenford Publishers Limited
The Old Post Office
130 Epsom Road Guildford
Surrey GU1 2PX
Tel: 01483 563307
Fax: 01483 829074
www.goldenford.co.uk

Cover design by Janice Windle, based on her original painting

Printed and bound by CPI Antony Rowe, Eastbourne

ISBN-13 978-0-9531613-8-6

Contents

1.	The Old Man's House	1
2.	The Benefactor	10
3.	Tea for Two	17
4.	Pandora's Box	27
5.	The Housekeeper	34
6.	Pieces of the Jigsaw	44
7.	Addie goes West	54
8.	The Schoolmaster	68
9.	Researching the Tree	77
10.	The Paper Trail	83
11.	Unfair Dismissal	95
12.	Happy Families	100
13.	Rodney's Wife	111
14.	Act of Faith	126
15.	New Friends	143
16.	Summer Storms	160
17.	Visitors for Addie	174
18.	Addie goes back	191
19.	Lost and Lonely Years	207
20.	The Power of the Press	214
21.	A Door to the Past	230
22.	Adrienne's Diary	238
23.	Adrienne at University	250
24.	Adrienne in Love	271
25.	Son et Lumiere	286
26.	Dirty Weekend	305
27.	Exits and Entrances	317
28.	Family Business	329
29.	Orphan in a Storm	341
30.	Survivors	350

Addie's Russell's Family Tree:

24th June 1991

Dr Rodney Heron = Dorothy

|

Adrienne Penelope Heron, born 1943 = ?
                    (died 7th February 1965)

|

Addie (Russell) born 6th February 1965
(Adopted by Joan and Tony Russell)

Part 1

Chapter One: The Old Man's House
24th June 1991

Addie saw the child's photograph on the hall table as soon as she walked through the door. The schoolgirl in the picture was around ten or eleven, with blue eyes, uneven teeth and fair hair in braids. Addie felt a momentary sense of shock, followed by elation. The resemblance to herself was strong - the same oval shaped face and wide mouth - but the girl's bright blue eyes bore no resemblance to her own green ones and her hair was much fairer than Addie's. Even so, there could be no doubt they were related.

'My mother,' she breathed.

The last few days waiting for information, the sleepless nights and then the flight from Boston - they had all been worth it for this moment. She felt tears start in her eyes.

If anyone had told her a month ago that she would inherit a house in England, she would never have believed it. To take it even further into fantasyland, it was one of those mock Tudor places that showed up in English detective thrillers, with black painted timbers and leaded lights. She'd fallen in love with it as soon as she saw the name, *Tamar*, carved on to a timber signboard, and seen the sun's reflection twinkling on the latticed windows. But all that paled into insignificance - it was just a property after all. Just bricks and mortar. Finding out about her mother, Adrienne Heron – that was the important thing. That was all important.

Addie hadn't known the late owner of this house, James Buckley. He'd willed *Tamar* to her mother, but she'd died 26 years ago – when Addie was born. Addie kept asking herself

1

why he didn't know her mother was dead, and what could be the connection between them. If only she'd known about him earlier. Now he was dead too, and couldn't answer her questions, but surely, coming here was going to give her the chance to find out. About himself, about Adrienne - and all the other family that must exist.

The young lawyer from Palfrey, Willow and Amery, the firm administering James Buckley's estate, had followed her into the hall. He closed the door behind him and put his briefcase on the woodblock floor. She turned her gaze away from the picture, and, trying to look unmoved, walked into the living room. The lawyer trailed after her. Did he think she was going to steal something? It belonged to her now anyway. Irritated, she turned. 'Would you mind? I'd like to be alone for a moment.'

He looked surprised, but retreated to the hall.

The sun was shining through the window, giving a warm glow to the elegantly furnished room, and outside, she could see the summer colours of an unexplored garden. She couldn't believe her good fortune. There would be so much to see and discover. But above all, finding out about her English mother was something she had dreamt of for many years. She turned and walked back through the doorway to look again at the photograph. She still couldn't resist gazing at it, even though she had returned over and over again, in the last few days, to the blurry newspaper replica, which had been responsible for her coming from Boston in the first place.

The lawyer had been standing quietly waiting. Now he gave a polite cough, no doubt to remind her of his presence.

Trying to stop her voice from shaking, Addie said, 'You don't know what coming to his house means to me. And to see my mother's photo here.'

'Well, perhaps you'd like to go upstairs and look around on your own. I'll wait down here for you.'

She liked the sound of his voice and the English accent, and she could see he was trying to be kind, but he looked as though his mind were elsewhere – to judge by his unsmiling face, somewhere rather unpleasant. What was wrong with him? He seemed irritated or angry about something. Still, that was not her concern today. *Her* interest was here, in the house – in *Tamar*.

She walked up the stairs, trailing her fingers lightly along the highly polished banister rails. Someone loved and cared for this house or for its late occupant, James Buckley. And he – James, who only on his death had entered her life - he had lived here for twenty years or more; his hand had brushed this banister; his feet, too, had climbed these stairs. Her discovery of him had brought in its wake another unsolved mystery.

Upstairs, Addie found two large bedrooms and a smaller one, all with pink floral covers on the beds and matching curtains. They didn't fit in at all with her mental picture of James. But the fourth bedroom had been converted into a study, the walls adorned with prints of ships at sea. Somehow, here, she knew she had found the essence of the man. It was filled with sober masculinity. She could see James in her mind's eye. A formal man; a very English man, like the pilots and naval men in old black and white war movies.

A large mahogany desk took pride of place, the scars and scratches of years imprinted into the wood. For a moment, she could almost imagine James sitting there, his back straight, writing his letters with an old-fashioned fountain pen and a bottle of ink. But now the desk had been tidied up and was bare, with the exception of one or two ornaments. A faint scent of furniture polish lingered in the air, and there was none of the mustiness associated with an empty house. She wondered who it was that looked so carefully after the home of a dead man.

Above the desk, a rectangular wall map showed the dragon nose of the west of England, pointing into the sea. And next to it were six small black and white photographs in oval frames.

3

These, surely, were photos of people he had loved. She moved closer to examine the pictures and her eyes were drawn to two shots of a teenage girl. She couldn't miss the resemblance to herself, and she knew that they were photos of her mother. These, and the other younger version of Adrienne, must mean that James had kept in contact with her, after all.

What about the other photos? What clues would they provide? As she moved for a better view, she heard another contrived cough from below. The lawyer was hovering downstairs; she could imagine him pacing, even though she couldn't hear his footsteps.

Addie knew she would come back to this room to find out more about James Buckley and how he was connected with her mother, Adrienne Heron. But this wasn't the moment.

She was more composed now. She went down, feeling already as if he were an outsider, and she the gracious hostess. She could see from the speed with which he picked up his briefcase that he was impatient to leave.

'Right, Miss Russell.'

'Thank you so much for bringing me here,' she said. 'There's really no need for you to stay any longer. Perhaps you could just bring in my suitcase from your car.'

'Didn't you book in at the hotel my uncle suggested?' he asked, frowning.

'I decided I'd stick around here. I'd like to enjoy my little bit of British real estate.'

He put the briefcase down again, his face tensing up. She could see he didn't want complications; he wanted to wrap up this job.

'You can't stay here, Miss Russell. It's probably damp. No-one's slept here since Major Buckley's death.'

Why didn't the man understand how important this place was to her?

She touched him on the arm and smiled.

'Don't you worry. I'll be fine,' she said. 'I've got my

sleeping bag. I've camped in places all over the States, and I've got warm clothes specially for England.'

He stepped backwards as she touched him. Was there some almost imperceptible spark between them? More likely embarrassment. Everyone said that Englishmen were so reserved. Anyhow, his voice was still cool.

'Surely, you'll want to create a good impression for estate agents. I'd have thought you'd want to get a good price for the place, and get back to Boston. Property values here are down at the moment, and they could drop further.'

He didn't seem to realise that momentous things were happening to her and the value of the property was trivial by comparison. She wondered fleetingly if these English lawyers ever behaved like human beings. The senior partner of Palfrey, Willow, etc. had already talked at her for more than forty minutes on her arrival at the office, right after the flight, in such incomprehensible jargon that she felt her eyelids weighing heavy even as she sat there. Surely he should have known she wasn't taking it in. Perhaps he was deliberately trying to confuse her.

She'd woken up a bit when this other lawyer appeared; he was younger; he looked attractive. She'd noticed he was about thirty, with grey eyes - yes nice eyes - and fairish brown hair. And she'd had to look up at him as they walked from the office to the car, so he was quite tall - probably six foot. But it seemed he was no better. Maybe they were both trying to keep something from her.

She interrupted him. 'Mr uh…' She realised she'd forgotten his name. Unforgivable. She was normally so good about that.

'Amery. Jonathan Amery.'

She was more tired than she'd realised; she couldn't remember if the older man had already introduced them. She bluffed.

'Oh, I'm sorry, I thought the other lawyer was Mr Amery.'

'As I said, he's my uncle. The other partners left the

5

business years ago. We just kept on the name. My father was the only other partner.'

'Oh, your father is in the business, too,' Addie said. 'So there's even more Amerys.' She joked, 'I guess there was no room left for Mr Palfrey and Mr Willow.'

She saw that the lawyer's face had stiffened again. 'My father died a couple of years ago. It's just my uncle and myself now.'

'Oh, I'm sorry,' Addie said and there was a silence.

She started again. 'Mr Amery, the value of the property is not a priority for me. There's just one thing I'm interested in - why this James Buckley should leave me this house. I guess what I want to find out is whether he could be related to my mother. Do you know anything about it?'

'I'm afraid I never actually met Major Buckley. He's always been my uncle's client.'

She interrupted him, trying to explain, wanting to share her feelings with another human being.

'You see, I don't know anything about him at all - except that my mother was important to him in some way. Most of the time, I didn't even think about her being English.'

His voice now had an impatient edge to it. 'I'm sorry, but my uncle hasn't really filled me in with any details about your family. He simply asked me to bring you here and make sure everything was all right. It's not the sort of thing I normally deal with.' He was still not smiling and she realised now he had been irritated by the errand. But she couldn't let him go - not without trying to find out more.

'I appreciate that, and I'm really sorry to have taken up your time. But your uncle spent most of the time I was with him explaining some of the legal stuff that was in the will. I guess I'm still a bit jet-lagged, because I couldn't really follow what he was saying.'

She was aware she was putting on a 'little girl lost' routine, hoping to win around this man - get some warmth or reaction from him, even if she didn't gain any information. She wasn't used to this lack of response from a man. But the lawyer didn't say anything. She wondered again if he was deliberately hiding information from her.

She went on desperately, 'This Major Buckley has left me nearly everything he owned and I never even knew him.'

'I wouldn't get too excited about it. The property market is so bad at the moment. In fact, what I would recommend …'

Addie, irritated with the lawyer's apparent incomprehension, tried to provoke him into a different sort of response. 'I guess lawyers are always recommending things that will provide them with business,' she said.

'I can assure you, I don't believe in behaving unethically,' he said quite sharply. 'I don't know what sort of lawyers you've mixed with, but I hope I would never recommend anything that was not beneficial to my client.'

Well that had certainly achieved the desired effect. There was a human being behind the legalistic front, after all. It seemed as if she'd hit a raw nerve.

'I certainly didn't mean to upset you, Mr Amery,' she said, though she had.

'It just so happens,' he replied, 'I've had my fingers burnt with a property purchase. My own flat's lost several thousands of pounds in value.'

'Really? Well can't you just hold on till things improve?'

'It's not as simple as that,' he said.

'Oh, why is that?'

He glared at her. 'What was it you were asking me before?'

She had a feeling that despite having annoyed him, she had somehow penetrated his armour.

'What I wanted to know was whether James Buckley had any children. I mean adult children that would be my mother's age now, if she were alive – say, late forties.'

He thought for a moment. She could tell he had relented a little; perhaps he was embarrassed at snapping at her.

'Look, Mr Amery, your uncle told me that my mother was Major Buckley's goddaughter. And he said the same thing to my Mom - my adopted mother, that is - when she called him. But in the newspaper clipping it said "daughter." And that's really what I want to get straight. It's very important to me.'

The tiredness was getting the better of her. She tried to control the tremor in her voice. 'I - I never knew my mother.'

A look of sympathy came over his face. 'I'm sorry. How very sad for you.'

He was quiet for a moment, then said, 'As a matter of fact, I do remember my father talking about Major Buckley a few years ago, when he met him at the office. He said something about the Major's child dying in tragic circumstances.'

'Well that would be it. My mother died when I was born. She was in her twenties. Did he say her name? Adrienne?'

'I don't remember him mentioning a name. I thought he said "wife and child". I may have mixed it up with another case. I only remember his name because he got an OBE at around that time, and my father showed me a write up in one of the papers. And that's all I know.'

The statement was pretty final. She wasn't going to make any more progress now. She didn't even understand what he was talking about - the write up in the papers - this OBE - whatever it was, didn't help at this moment. Tiredness washed over her again and with it a feeling of deflation. The previous forty eight hours had been hectic and she had barely slept on the flight. She had come all this way, not just to see a house she'd inherited, but, above all, in the hope of finding out about her mother and an extended family that she had never met. But now, suddenly, she just wanted to sleep.

She heard a clock strike, and the lawyer glanced down at his watch. Then he found a business card, and handed it to her.

'Don't be too disappointed. These things take time to find out about. Give me a ring after a few days, and I'll try and clarify things for you.' He walked over to the telephone on the hall table and picked up the receiver. 'Yes, the phone's still connected, so you can dial out, if you need me - or anything else. In the mean time, I'll look over his papers.'

'Thank you,' she said, and suddenly she was on a high again. Anything was possible if she had a little support. Perhaps this guy was okay after all.

Jonathan Amery turned and picked up his briefcase, and she walked to the door and waited till he returned with her suitcase.

Her eyelids were drooping, even as she stood there. If she could just sleep for an hour or so she'd be fine.

'You look as if you need a rest,' he said, placing the suitcase on the floor. 'We can talk about putting the house on the market in a day or so, when you've had time to think.'

Her own words surprised her. Two hours ago, she had not known she would make such a decision.

'I'm not going to sell *Tamar*. I'm going to keep it.'

Chapter 2: The Benefactor

'*DID YOU KNOW THIS GIRL?*' read the caption above the picture, just under the unfamiliar name of the British newspaper, and the day it was published - 12th June 1991. In smaller letters, lower down in the article, was the name of the English lawyers to contact - Messrs. Palfrey, Willow and Amery of Guildford, Surrey.

Addie, sitting on a dark wooden chair at the kitchen table in her very own house in England, stared at the photo in the two week old newspaper.

The schoolgirl - Adrienne Heron - sat formally at a desk, a poster behind her commemorating the coronation of Elizabeth II in 1953. Addie looked down at the newspaper clipping for at least the twentieth time and felt again that surge of excitement. In her head, she could hear Mom's voice, as she said, 'It could have been you, when you were that age. You are so much like her.'

It must have been hard for Mom - Joan – not being her real mother, not her *blood* mother. Addie smiled a little as she remembered Joan's comment on another occasion. 'Even as a baby, we could see Adrienne in you. That's why we named you Adeline - after her. I'd gotten so fond of that girl. I couldn't believe she was gone.'

And Addie had seen her lips tremble, as she held out the clipping and said, 'Yes, it could have been you, say, fifteen years ago. But of course, it isn't - it's your mother.'

Seeing the photo, hearing the story, Addie felt as excited at that moment as she could ever remember. It was better than graduating, as good as sex. She had to fight not to show it. And she thought she'd managed. Because she'd spent her life not showing Joan how important her real mother was to her. But Joan herself was enthusiastic. 'You gotta go to the UK, honey. This guy's left a house and some cash. And it belongs to you. Maybe if you go over, you'll find out more about her - about Adrienne. I know how much that means to you.' Addie had smiled a rueful smile. So she hadn't hidden it too well, after all. She gave Joan a big hug then. Sure she longed to know about her real mother. It was part of her identity, wasn't it? But Mom was pretty hard to beat, just the same.

Now here she was, sitting at the kitchen table in a strange house, in another country, drinking black coffee and eating a stale airport sandwich. The unexciting meal didn't dampen her elation. After a good night's sleep, she was back on a high. This is the most important trip of my life, she thought. I'm not going to waste a second. I'm going to find out what the link is between Adrienne and James Buckley.

The kitchen itself was welcoming and bright, though rather old fashioned; dark oak table and chairs with padded cushions. A red check plastic cloth was folded up on one of the work surfaces. Willow pattern china was displayed on an open dresser, though Addie chose not to spoil the display and had taken a plain white plate from the cupboard. Like the bedrooms upstairs, the kitchen did not have James's imprint upon it. This was a room organised by a woman.

Addie got up and wandered out to the hall to look again at the original colour photo on the hall table. She picked it up and, right at the bottom of the photo, saw the date written in a child's rounded hand - 'June 1953' - and underneath, 'Adrienne Heron' - her mother's signature.

Replacing it on the table she looked at it again. The girl's pale face contrasted with the uniform blue cardigan, the colour echoed by her eyes. She remembered Mom commenting once about Adrienne's bright blue eyes, saying they were her most noticeable feature.

It was difficult to think of the little girl in the photo as her mother. Adrienne was neither a child nor a mother figure. She was forever marooned in her twenties - fixed at the age of her death. Addie thought of her now as a contemporary, a woman with whom she herself could identify. There was, she suspected, a streak of rebelliousness and independence in her that was part of Addie herself, and she could see that even in the photo.

In her career in advertising, she liked to think she'd developed an additional layer of skin, the necessary toughness to cope with her world. But sometimes she was almost embarrassed at her own inner core of softness - of occasional sentimentality about this unknown woman. She didn't want a replacement mother. She just wanted to know - what was Adrienne Heron really like?

In the past, finding out about Adrienne had just been an idea - something that flitted through her head periodically. Now she had an opportunity to make that idea reality. This was not the time for daydreams. She had to have a plan of campaign. Well, she had a base. No rent to pay. This was her own place. How surprised the lawyer had been when she'd said that yesterday about keeping it. She didn't care how much it was worth. She wasn't interested in making a fast buck.

But to live here, she'd need to get organised; get in food; get a car; set up an English bank account for when her travellers' cheques ran out. That was the easy part. But how was she going to find out more about Adrienne? She took a sip of her bitter coffee. The first lead to follow was not Adrienne, but James. Maybe he would guide her to Adrienne. But where to start?

She thought back to the meeting with the lawyer, Amery Senior, the previous day. He'd made it so complicated. But she remembered he'd been quite dogmatic. The will didn't say James Buckley was Adrienne's father. That was disappointing - because she'd hoped that's why he'd left her the estate. It was the impression the newspaper article gave. But the lawyer - Mr Amery senior - he'd been pretty disdainful about the article. 'You can't believe these tabloids,' he'd said, 'They're always looking for a story.' Then he'd read out from the will, '*The main beneficiary is to be my goddaughter Adrienne Heron or her heirs, legitimate or otherwise'.* Somehow, the papers had translated that into 'illegitimate daughter'. Addie listened, but she didn't want to hear this rational version of events. Illogical or not, she preferred the romantic story put out by the newspapers. Maybe she'd find some evidence that the old man *was* her grandfather. Perhaps it was the lawyer who'd gotten it all wrong.

One thing was certain. Amery Senior wasn't going to give her any help. There was something about his smooth manner, and the way he dogmatically closed off all possibilities that irked her. For whatever reason, she wouldn't get any more information out of him.

What about the nephew - Jonathan? He was as tight as a clam too, but in a different way. Perhaps he genuinely didn't know much about James Buckley. If that was so, whatever was bugging him was nothing to do with James, and nothing to do with her. He just didn't want to get involved. That was a shame. Because, actually, he was quite attractive and she wouldn't have minded getting to know him better.

She was going to have to ask around. That was an idea - try the local store and see if they knew him. Shopkeepers always knew everything there was to know. And the food store was a good idea anyway, because one sandwich wouldn't keep her going very long. She went out to the hall, picked up the keys from the dish on the hall table and addressed the photograph of her mother.

'Bye, Adrienne,' she said, and turned towards the door. 'I'm going to look at your country.'

As she walked down the road, moving through passages of shade and sunshine she glanced back at the red-bricked house, with its gabled roof, black beams contrasting with white painted walls. It was very different from the timber frame houses you'd see at home in Boston, and she smiled back at it. It's mine, she thought. Surrounding the house, there were shrubs, in various shades of greens, neatly clipped and blending into each other. Some sort of clematis spread up the walls, covered with large half open pink buds.

Her journey took her along a spacious road and past a screen of mature trees and shrubs that protected the various detached houses from prying eyes. It was an affluent area, the sort of place where each property would probably have two cars, but they were hidden in integral garages, not marring the tree-lined road. On the corner, there was a smaller more homely cottage, probably left over from some earlier development. If she'd hoped to ask anyone about local stores, she was disappointed. No-one was to be seen; it was almost as if they didn't want to spoil the picture.

She walked along, rejecting turnings that looked too residential, before finding the sort of food store she was looking for, fortunately, not too far away, in a row of shops about ten minutes from the house. Seeing an Asian woman behind the counter, she thought she might discover some interesting delicacies, but there were no scents of spices to suggest that. The shop obviously only dealt with the local people's basic needs. Addie filled up her wire basket with milk and eggs, cereal and orange juice for breakfast, fresh fruit and vegetables, a couple of frozen pizzas and some biscuits, to keep her going over the next few days. At the counter, she took a couple of notes from her purse, and offered them to the woman.

'Is this enough? I'm sorry, I guess I'm not familiar with the money yet.'

'You are on holiday here?'

'I'm visiting from the States. I'll be sticking around here for a few weeks.'

'Well, we'll try to help you. If you want to order anything, let me know. If I'm not in the shop, just ask for me - Meera.'

'I'd really love some bagels,' Addie commented. 'I'm missing them already.'

Meera smiled. 'I will see what we can do.'

'There was something else,' Addie began. 'Something I wanted to ask.' How do I start, she thought; I don't want to sound like a private detective. 'I haven't got a car yet. I wondered if you do deliveries - for big stuff.'

Meera looked doubtful. 'Occasionally, to help people out, but it's quite difficult to arrange when there's only me. Whereabouts do you live?'

'I'm staying in Woodvale Close. The house is named Tamar.'

'But isn't that where Major Buckley lived?' the woman said, looking at her with curiosity.

'Did you know him?' Addie asked, surprised and pleased to find the line she'd taken was so successful.

'Yes I did. He used to walk down here sometimes, when he could. We talked a lot about India. He was there for some years, during the war and later on. I have many relations there. I was sorry he died. Are you related to him?'

'My ..' Addie hesitated, reluctant to go into the complications of the relationship. 'Not exactly. He knew my mother. I've come here to look things over.'

'He was a kind man. I liked talking to him a lot.'

Addie was still reserving judgement on James Buckley. Off the top of her head, she ad-libbed, 'I thought maybe he was rather cold.'

'Not at all. He was very kind. Very good looking for an old man - wonderful blue eyes and silver hair - and very charming. You ask the Graingers. They will tell you. They worked for him for years. You know them, I suppose.'

'No. Who are they?'

'They live on the corner of Woodvale Close. Mrs Grainger used to cook for him.'

'Oh, so he had servants - sounds pretty high class.'

'No, not like that. He was an old man - and a widower. He had arthritis. He couldn't walk properly and he couldn't use

15

his hands. Mr Grainger used to go in and do the garden and Mrs Grainger did his cooking. Sometimes I delivered his order, if I had time.'

'I'm glad I've found you,' Addie said. 'and I'll be back here again when I've run out of food. Perhaps, if you're not busy then, you can tell me anything else you remember about James. And I'll talk to the Graingers, too.'

'Maybe it would be better to talk to Mr Grainger. You might find Mrs Grainger less forthcoming.'

'Why is that?'

But Meera had returned to the back of the shop without answering.

Satisfied with her expedition, Addie started back to the house. This woman, Meera, and the Graingers would all be able to provide more information about James Buckley - who was not, after all, the rather cold blooded man she had envisaged. Buckley the buccaneer, she thought smiling to herself. Charming, good looking. I think I'm quite glad to have had him for a benefactor.

When she got back, she would make some notes. She was going to collect the evidence piece by piece, and somehow she was going to get the answers to all her questions. A moment of doubt crept into her mind, as she remembered the unfathomable expression on Meera's face. Was there something about this Mrs Grainger she should know? Was she going to discover a relationship between James Buckley and his housekeeper? Something that would tarnish the image she had created in her mind? Then she cast aside her misgivings. Whatever guilty secrets there were to unearth, nothing would stop her in her quest.

Chapter 3: Tea for Two

Addie ran up the stairs and made straight for the study. She was convinced she would get to know more about James Buckley here. This was the room that attracted her, and this was where she would work. She wanted to look more closely at those oval framed photographs, too.

First she examined again her mother as a teenage girl. In one photo, Adrienne was holding a silver cup aloft and, in the other, she stood with a tennis racket in hand, in tennis whites. So she was sporty. They had something in common.

The remaining pictures meant nothing to her. There was a shot of a mother with her baby, and another of the baby on its own. The glass could not hide the frayed edges and creases on these obviously well-travelled pictures. Could this baby be Adrienne too, Addie wondered. If so, she was a much loved goddaughter. The remaining two photos were of another woman, on her own in one, and with a man, presumably James, in the other. These two were in better condition - probably taken much later - and judging by the couple's clothing, in a much warmer climate. Both in their thirties or forties, the man - presumably James - was good looking and very erect, and the woman elegant. So there was more than one woman in James's life. As her mind wandered off, testing possibilities, she heard the sound of the telephone coming from the hall.

She rushed down, excited by the prospect of someone wanting to speak to her.

'Addie Russell,' she said, picking up the phone.

'Oh Miss Russell, it's Jonathan Amery.'

'Hi, Jonathan.'

'I've found something that'll interest you. There's a deed box here at the office. I don't think there's anything valuable in it - just papers and letters, but by rights it's yours, and it might give you the sort of information you're looking for.'

'That's great,' Addie replied. 'Thank you so much. I'm just looking at James Buchan's photos. Seems like he had more than one wife. Does that tie up with what you know?'

'I don't know much of his history at all, Miss Russell. He was my uncle's client and my father's before that. I thought I explained that.'

Addie couldn't remember what he'd explained. Only that he'd been prickly. Seemed like nothing much had changed.

'So about this deed box,' she said. 'Do you want me to collect it?'

'No. I'll be happy to bring it over. Would you mind if I come round this afternoon? I'd like to fit it in with another appointment.'

Addie agreed on four o'clock, and returned to the study.

Now she took her notepad from her bag, and sat at James's desk. She'd scribble a few notes down and, when she was sure of her facts, she could add them to the family tree she'd already optimistically started on the flight over. For now, there wasn't much on it - just the names, Dorothy and Rodney Heron - and the line that linked them to Adrienne and then herself. Was it possible that James was connected to her father? The only other way he could be related to her was through some liaison with Dorothy - either before or after her marriage to Rodney Heron.

In the notebook, she scribbled, *Women in James Buckley's Life?*, and underneath wrote, *Dorothy*, followed by two question marks, leaving spaces for the names of the two women in the photos. Of course, Dorothy - the cold English woman who had rejected her grandchild - could be either of these unknown women. She could be the young mother in better times, or she might be the elegant woman of the other two photos.

The questions nagged at her. Why did James keep photos of Adrienne as she grew up, but hadn't been in contact since her death? Even if he was only Adrienne's godfather - not the mythical grandfather that she had hoped for - where had he been for the last twenty six years - and why wasn't he interested in Adrienne's child?

Maybe it shouldn't have surprised her, for her known grandfather had behaved in much the same way. He was the person that Joan had written to when Adrienne died. Rodney Heron - grandfather by title, but quite unprepared to take on the role. Was James Buckley preferable to Rodney Heron? Well, of course. How could anyone *not* be preferable to Rodney and Dorothy Heron? What sort of people could shrug off their daughter's death with polite regrets and, at the same time, reject their tiny premature granddaughter?

For as Joan had reluctantly told Addie when she was old enough to understand, the Herons had shown no interest when they received the news of Adrienne's death and the birth of their granddaughter. Joan had even written her own separate letter to the English family, when she and Tony had decided to adopt the baby. She had received a chilly reply from Adrienne's father, Rodney, saying that he and his wife much regretted the death of their daughter, but they had no wish to have anything to do with the child.

Addie didn't hear the details till she was a teenager, plaguing Joan with questions, so that Joan was finally pushed into telling the full story. Questions like 'Didn't my mother have any relations?' 'Didn't you try to contact them?' eventually brought forward the unwelcome answers. Addie found them almost unbelievable. They brought forward a second set of questions. 'Didn't they love my mother?' 'Why did they hate me?'

At first Joan waffled a bit. 'It must have been difficult for them,' she said. 'They were probably old - they were shocked.' But when Addie finally asked, 'Would you have done the same thing?' Joan had to admit that she wouldn't. 'Not in a million years,' she said. And when they discussed it again, a few years later, Joan didn't hold back her dislike of Rodney Heron, for he was the one who had written that cold, uncaring letter. 'There's only one name for him,' commented Joan, muttering through her teeth, 'Bastard.'

The truth was unpalatable, but Addie had to face it. When she had explored James's links with her mother, she was going to have to follow up the real grandparents - Rodney and Dorothy Heron. They were the people who would provide the truth about Adrienne. If James were the godfather with just a distant interest in his goddaughter, who perhaps had become his heir purely by default, he should be exonerated from blame.

In the hall downstairs, a clock struck once. It brought her back into the present. She still hadn't eaten.

She got up from the desk and walked out of the room. As she descended the stairs, she said aloud, 'First James and his women; then Rodney Heron.'

She thought about the women, as she prepared food. Now that she knew about the housekeeper, it was obvious that the light feminine touches she'd noticed must have been provided by this Mrs Grainger who ran James's household. So no mystery there, then – apart from the way that Meera in the shop had looked when she mentioned her. Surely not an illicit affair, with Mr Grainger so closely involved in the household. But there was certainly no wife on the scene. Marriage, it seemed, had belonged to the past.

How about the name of the house? *Tamar*. It sounded like a Russian dancer; or a spy. Perhaps she was one of James Buckley's former lovers. Perhaps Adrienne was not really Dorothy Heron's daughter at all; she might have been the product of a liaison with an exotic Russian spy from a James Bond movie. No. Addie chuckled to herself - now she really was letting her imagination run riot.

Once she'd eaten, she felt drowsy again. It was no use people saying you should stay awake to counteract the effects

20

of jet lag. Her body clock was telling her she'd been up long enough. She considered going up to the bedroom for a nap, but, with the sunshine streaming in through the windows, it seemed such a waste of daytime. The back yard was tempting - all the more so, compared with her city apartment in Boston, with its single window box - and she wandered outside.

There were roses in abundance – massed white and yellow blossoms contrasting with brilliant pinks and reds, and she strolled from one bush to another, admiring the plants and inhaling the faint fragrance. Addie often dreamed of her mother carrying roses and she was glad that James had liked them too; it seemed a thread, linking herself, her unknown mother and her unknown benefactor.

Tucked away at the end of the garden was a small wooden summerhouse, and inside it she found a chair and a rickety table. She dusted them down, placed them in a sunny spot and sat down with a cold drink. Her eyes closed and she felt the sun drifting warmly over her eyelids. Soon she was in another world, where somehow her dream mother carrying a basket of roses was mixed up with an old man carrying a deed box.

A shadow flitted over her face, and she felt chilly. She struggled to open her eyes. Jonathan Amery stood above her, blotting out the sun.

'I'm sorry to disturb you. I rang the bell several times, but I couldn't make myself heard. I came down the side of the house. The gate was open.' He looked around. 'It's lovely out here.'

'Is it four already?' Addie asked, still only half awake.

'Yes. Spot on.'

She jumped up. 'I didn't realise. I must have been out here longer than I meant to be. Won't you come inside?'

She led the way into the kitchen. 'Would you like a cup of coffee?'

He glanced at his watch and then smiled apologetically. 'I'm sorry Miss er Ms Russell - as I told you, I'm trying to fit in another appointment this afternoon. I'll just go and get the ...'

From his pocket came the birdlike trill of a mobile phone. He extracted it and pressed the talk button, saying, 'Excuse me a moment.'

Addie put the kettle on anyway, wondering briefly whether her hair was all mussed up, and, if she could do anything about it. At the same time, she listened shamelessly to the one-sided conversation.

'Hallo. Jonathan Amery.

'But I'm on my way now. Tomorrow's not convenient ...

'No, she didn't tell me she had another son. Tomorrow's impossible. Make an appointment next week; that'll give time for consultations with any daughters and grandchildren that might crop up.'

He seemed unnecessarily tetchy to the person at the other end of the phone, Addie thought. Just like yesterday. Yet he didn't really seem an unpleasant person. Just someone with too much on his plate, taking life too seriously.

He put the phone back in his pocket. 'I'm sorry about that.'

'Do I take it your appointment's been cancelled?'

'That's right.'

'Well, would you like some coffee, now?'

He looked at his watch again. She could see he was tempted. Then he sighed and said, 'I really ought to get back to the office.'

The bleep of the mobile interrupted again.

'Excuse me - Jonathan Amery. Oh; Tabitha.' (Secretary, wondered Addie.) He half turned away and walked back towards the kitchen door. (Girlfriend perhaps.)

'An offer. Well that sounds promising. That's very good. Yes, I can be there at five thirty. No problem at all.'

He replaced the phone, and, quite suddenly, he relaxed. Whatever it was that Tabitha had said, it seemed to have transformed him, at least temporarily. He smiled at Addie. 'There's no point in my going back now. New arrangements.

So if your offer's still open, I'd love a cup of coffee, or better still, tea, if you don't mind.'

Beginning to feel quite at home in the kitchen, she dropped some tea-bags into a small brown teapot which was on the worktop and poured in some water. 'Is this okay?' she asked, taking some mugs from the cupboard.

'With milk, please.'

'Oh, sorry. I'll get it from the fridge.'

'Can I take this outside for you, Miss Russell?' he asked, picking up the tray.

'Addie,' she corrected automatically. 'Do you get paid extra for this service?' she added, with a grin.

'We get paid for *every* service,' he said, 'as I think you implied yesterday, but I'll make an exception in this case. It's not often I get the opportunity of sitting in the sunshine. I'm normally stuck in the office.'

He carried the tray out into the garden and set it down on the table. Addie found another chair in the summerhouse and they sat together on the patio.

He looked around again. 'It's a really beautiful garden,' he said.

Addie smiled in response. He was still so very polite and formal, with only the occasional glimmer of a real personality peeping through. They say the Chinese are inscrutable, but just how do you get through this British politeness?

She followed his lead and settled for ritual small talk. 'You must tell me if I've got this tea right. I know it's your English tradition. Are we supposed to have something with it? Cake or cookies?'

'I don't usually have much time for traditions.' he said, picking up the cup. 'I generally throw a tea bag into the cup. It's just another way of getting a quick boost of caffeine. And milk of course. That's very British.. My grandmother always makes a fuss about warming the tea pot, and so on. I suppose if you wanted to be really traditional, a cream tea, with scones and jam or strawberries, would be the right thing for this time of year. Wimbledon week's practically an orgy of strawberries and cream.'

'We'll have to take a rain check on that, Mr Amery.'

Straight faced, he said, 'On the strawberries?'

She could tell he was letting his guard down again. He'd practically fed her the line.

'On the orgy.'

They both laughed, and once more she saw that as he relaxed, his whole personality seemed to change. She got up and went back to the kitchen and brought out a pack of digestive biscuits. 'Next time I'll have something better.'

He smiled and said, 'I'll look forward to that.'

She noticed again his nice grey eyes. If she hadn't had enough of men for the moment, she might be quite attracted. On second thoughts, she was attracted. He was the first man she'd really noticed, since Lloyd. And now of course, except for pure business, Lloyd was out of her life. But on the other hand, though this guy appealed to her, particularly now he wasn't being so straight-laced, she was here for a reason.

'Could I ask you something?'

'Of course.'

'Do you know anything about the name of the house? *Tamar*? I thought maybe it was a name - an old girlfriend, perhaps?'

'As I said, I don't know anything about Major Buckley's personal life,' Jonathan Amery replied.

'I can't wait to find out everything about him,' Addie said enthusiastically. 'And about my mother. She was English, you know.'

He nodded.

'I want to understand what being English is all about. All my life I've been reading English books; watching English films. I can't get enough of them.'

'Well, you mustn't believe in all the stereotypes, you know.

We've moved on since *A Room with a View* and that stiff butler in *Remains of the Day*.

'Well, can we move on then?' Addie said. 'I really hate this formality. Can we drop the Miss Russell and start all over. I'm Addie, short for Adeline. But no-one ever uses that. Three syllables are just too much. Am I allowed to call you Jonathan, or do you get shortened to Johnny?'

'I'm afraid my three syllables don't get shortened to Johnny, for anything. Not even for a valued client. Most people call me Jonathan - even my friends.'

'Well that's okay by me then,' Addie said, taking a sip of tea. She noticed he had reminded her she was a client. She carried on anyway, 'I guess the only way I'm going to find out about you Brits is by going out into the country. What I really need is an escort. You don't know someone who wants a job?'

He was looking embarrassed again. She really shouldn't flirt with him.

'Much as I'd like to oblige, you're practically an heiress, and I'm merely your solicitor - an impoverished and very junior solicitor in the present scheme of things, who does not in any way want to rock the boat and get further demoted. So until we have your estate well and truly sorted out, I think I shall have to resist the temptation.'

So she was right - he was putting up a barrier - giving her a coded message, though delivered in a slightly flippant manner, in order, presumably, not to offend her. She made a mental note to keep the exchanges playful.

'But of course, I shall be happy to call on you to deal with any of your legal problems,' he added.

'Well that's all very fine and dandy, Jonathan' Addie said, wearying of the verbal games. 'This is the opportunity of a lifetime for me. If my aunt hadn't spotted that piece in the paper, when she was visiting the UK, and recognised my mother from the picture, I might not be here.'

Jonathan frowned as if he had suddenly thought of

something unpleasant, but then turned his attention back to her.

'I want to make the most of the place,' she said, 'but how am I going to get to see this country? It'll take me a while to learn to drive on the wrong side of the road - I haven't got a car reserved anyway. And I don't want to miss out on anything.'

'I'm sorry, but I can't really help you; I'm under a lot of pressure at the office, at the moment. If you really want to get around, you're going to have to visit a travel agent. Although,' he paused, 'Now I think of it, I have got one idea.'

'What is it?'

'I won't raise your hopes. I'll check it out and give you a ring in a couple of days.' He finished his tea, and got up. 'Now, I'm sorry, but I've spent as long as I dare, sitting in the sun. I've got an important appointment at five thirty.'

She followed him round to the garden gate, puzzled and irritated in equal parts, as he resisted her enquiries.

As he reached his car, he exclaimed, 'Oh, sorry, I nearly forgot. The deed box.'

He opened the boot, extracted the box, and carried it back into the house for her.

'He was very methodical. Everything's tied up in date order, and it says quite clearly on the outside that it contains personal letters. So - have an interesting evening.'

He took her hand in a formal handshake.

'Goodbye, Addie.'

Despite the earlier banter, the use of her name for the first time, and the light touch of his hand gave the moment a feeling of intimacy.

She let go of the hand quickly, 'Goodbye Jonathan. Thanks for the deed box.'

She watched him from the window as he got into the car, reversed skilfully and drove off towards the main road.

Then she picked up the box.

Chapter 4: Pandora's Box

The deed box was quite heavy, considering it contained only letters. Reading through them all might take a long time, if she was going to find any useful information. Addie decided to make use of the study where she could spread things out, and, in addition, not be disturbed by any callers, such as there might be.

She carried the box upstairs - the washing up could wait - and settled herself down at the large mahogany desk. She took out her notebook and pen. For a moment she was apprehensive. Perhaps she was wrong to go looking in hidden places? What would she find? Wonderful secrets, or disappointments? Would she destroy the dream and then find that, after all, reality had nothing to offer? What was the appeal of this unknown family?

So she was adopted; so what? If you had to lose your parents, you couldn't be with better people than Joan and Tony Russell. Joan Russell was the sort of person who believed in being straight with a child from the outset. Addie could remember no occasion when the realisation that she was adopted had burst upon her. No revelation. It was simply information she had grown up with, like the knowledge that she was a girl. But periodically, as if she thought Addie might doubt her love, Joan had reiterated like a mantra the fact that Addie was a wanted baby. Wanted by Joan and Tony Russell, and wanted by her real mother, had she lived.

Only her grandparents, Dorothy and Rodney Heron, hadn't wanted her, and that was hard to forgive.

Her reverie came to an end. Perhaps, even now, she was sitting looking at a photograph of Dorothy Heron.

She took the framed photos from the wall, once again. Could the sympathetic woman holding the baby possibly be Dorothy?

Realising then that there might be inscriptions on the

27

photos, as there had been on Adrienne's, she examined them in more detail; then she turned them over and unclipped the frames, one at a time, to reveal the backs of the photos.

In faded writing, the mother of the baby had written on one, '*Darling James, Our wonderful baby. Come home soon, Pen.*' On the other, most of the words had been obliterated, and all that Addie could see was, '*Penny and baby, 194*'. Of the other two, only one had an inscription and that said, '*Lillian and James, 1954*'.

Far from solving the puzzle, there were even more questions. And more names to put alongside the two question marks. Penny. Undoubtedly James's wife. Presumably with his baby. The other woman. Lillian. But still no sign of Dorothy. What sort of a man was James? A philanderer? Well she had met enough of them in the advertising industry. Men were men, in the forties, the eighties, the nineties. She was disappointed nevertheless. She had begun to elevate him in her mind to someone special.

Maybe the answers were waiting for her in the deed box - amongst James Buckley's letters. At least she knew he cared about Adrienne, and it was just possible that she was the baby in the picture, since Adrienne was born in 1943. That, at least, was definite - one thing that Addie knew about her mother, for Adrienne had told Joan how old she was. What would Addie find in the box - letters from Penny, perhaps James's first love - or from his lady friends - Dorothy, Lillian or any other women in his life? How would they read? Would they be passionate love letters? Or stiff cold little notes saying, 'My dear, the garden is lovely at this time of year ...'

She couldn't wait any longer. She opened the box.

As Jonathan had said, the letters were parcelled up into chronological batches, either tied with string, or with elastic bands. She looked at the addresses and though some were marked with the already familiar address of the house in which she stood, others were faded and had been sent to

British Forces' addresses in different parts of the world. So James was away from home. Of course - it was war time in Britain. The early forties; even before Pearl Harbour.

At the top of one pile was a telegram, and she made this her starting point, remembering that telegrams were invariably tidings of important news. She opened it carefully to reveal three strips of telegraphed words: *'Congratulations, Old Father Time. Penelope and baby David doing well. Peter.'*

This Peter, whoever he was, was clearly having a joke at James's expense, for James couldn't have been more than thirty at the time. It threw up more questions. Even so, one important question appeared to have been answered. James was the father of a baby boy - the baby in the photograph - and this seemed to be a legitimate and celebrated birth. But the other question was still unanswered. If James was not Adrienne's father, what was the link between the Herons and James Buckley?

Addie continued looking through the box. With so many letters, there were bound to be some more clues. There would be letters from a loving wife missing her husband, she felt sure. She fidgeted to get into a more comfortable position, then taking careful note of postmarks, addresses and dates of each letter, she started to read them. But she could find no letters from Penelope, only some friendly but impersonal letters from the writer of the telegram, Peter Grey, from somewhere called Marsh House.

It was, at first, difficult to work out the relationship between Peter Grey and James Buckley and she assumed that they were friends, perhaps brother officers, although Peter mentioned Penny a few times and confirmed that she and the baby were well. Addie began to wonder if Peter was having an affair with Penny, since he apparently knew so much about her. Then there was the allusion to 'Old Father Time' in the telegram. It seemed to suggest not just that James had become a father, but also that he was somewhat older than Penny, or perhaps, older than Peter.

She had ploughed her way through three of Peter's letters and gained some insight into the war as seen from the home front - for Peter seemed to be obsessed with battles and strategy and had written nothing about his own circumstances - when she found one letter headed Marsh House School. If he was not a teacher, then he must be a pupil. When she came to a mention of Peter's parents, she realised that Peter was almost certainly Penny's younger brother. And now it seemed clear from his letter that he was impatient to move on to the next stage of his life.

Penny's been a brick. She's come here a few times, and saved my sanity. People aren't encouraged to travel around too much, and the train journey's tiring for Mum and Dad.

We hear about what's going on out there, on the BBC, and I can't wait to get there. I thought the war would be over before I could join up. It's been bloody irritating being stuck here at school, like a child, when I wanted to be part of the action.

Anyway, I'm off soon and I'm going to Plymouth to see the parents with Penny and the enfant terrible next week. They're dying to see him, as I expect you can guess, as he's nearly a year old now. Let's hope it takes the pressure off me - you know all the fond farewells and tears from Mum. I expect you wish you could get to see little Davy too, but anyway you've got the snaps. Fat little thing, isn't he?

So if Peter was Penny's brother, the baby David now had grandparents too. What a wealth of relations, thought Addie. And though there were no letters from James himself, he was, nevertheless, being revealed to her through Peter's attitude to him. When Peter wrote 'It's all very well for you to say "Be patient", but you're out there in the thick of it', she could imagine that James must have tried to damp down the boy's enthusiasm for the battle. And it seemed, too, that James engendered respect and affection from his young brother-in-law that was not just to do with the hero-worship of an older man and an officer. He was a good man, she now felt sure. But wasn't it just wishful thinking to believe he and all these other people could be related to her? Still, it was early days in the war; only 1941 - there was still time for another baby to be born. Ploughing on to see how things developed she found that Peter hardly mentioned family matters. He was far more interested in the battles raging.

It was still light outside, but Addie realised she felt hungry again. She glanced at her watch. It was past eight o'clock already. In her trek into the past, she had completely lost track of time, and it took quite an effort to bring herself back into the present. She felt as if she had been watching an old war film, and had walked out of the cinema, surprised to find herself in completely different surroundings.

She was not behaving like her normal self at all. She hadn't even unpacked her suitcase. But when you work, you have no choice but to be organised, she thought. You plan your appointments, your budget, your meals, your social life. Here she was letting events influence her as they occurred.. In some ways, the spontaneity really suited her. Even so, she would have to have some basic food planning, and a structure to her day. Otherwise, in a few weeks, they would find, not her, but her skeleton sitting in James's study.

In the kitchen, she took out a pizza which she'd bought on her shopping trip and put it in the oven, while she made some coffee. She made a mental note to get in some more ready meals on her next outing. Out of respect for the past traditions of this room, she washed the tea cups, placed the red check cloth on the table, and tried to imagine James Buckley sitting there. While she waited for her meal, she turned on the kitchen radio and twiddled the dial until she found some music. But she could not erase the wartime events from her mind and, as soon as she had finished eating, she couldn't resist returning upstairs to the deed box, and the letters lying open on the desk.

Flipping through to see if there were any more letters from Peter, Addie's eyes were drawn to another telegram. Another baby? She opened it and her hands shook as she read it. A bombing raid on Plymouth later that month had demolished Penny's parents' home. Penelope Buckley, Peter, their parents and baby David too, in Plymouth for the christening, had all been killed.

Addie swallowed a lump in her throat and wiped away the tears that came unexpectedly to her eyes.

'The poor man. The poor man,' she murmured. 'He had nothing left. How could he carry on?'

It took her a few moments to compose herself. She realised now that this was the tragedy that Jonathan had mentioned - the terrible loss of wife and child, at home, where James must have thought them safe. And now that she was getting to know James, she could imagine the pain that he must have felt when he received the news, so far away on some battle front. Alongside the name Penny in her notebook, she sombrely wrote, '*Killed in the Blitz, March 1941.*'

The Second World War had always seemed a very remote piece of history. America had been involved in numerous other wars since that time. But America had not suffered bombing raids at home, and now for a moment, she thought about the families who had lived through that, their vulnerability, their lack of any certainty during that six year period. Just as Penny and the women like her sat at home waiting fearfully for the telegrams, so the men too might return home to a bomb-site where their home had once been. As for the names on the list in front of her, well no wonder there were other women in James's life; surely he deserved to find happiness with someone else eventually. She picked up another letter and then replaced it. The correspondence which appeared at first to hold so many possibilities now seemed filled with despair. Even the room seemed darker, as the long English day drew to a close. It's time to stop, she thought.

She went back to the bedroom next to the study; she'd noticed this morning that the bed had been made up. The room was cool now, but she had been warned about the cold, damp, English climate, and had packed pyjamas, which were near the top of the suitcase. She pulled off her clothes, leaving them where they fell and struggled into the unaccustomed jacket and trousers. Then she dived between the sheets. As her mind drifted almost immediately into sleep, she had a vision of the letters soaring upwards, filling the sky, like swifts and swallows on their way home.

Chapter 5: The Housekeeper

'Is anyone there?' The sound broke into Addie's dream, assimilating itself into the story. She was walking along the sidewalk with people who moved, as one body, to their destination. Those who were coming from the opposite direction barged through the oncoming crowd, with no apology, no thought. Addie moved amongst the throng with an invisible aura around her. She was with them, yet totally alone. To anyone else's eyes, she was a part of them. Only she knew that however much she was surrounded by others, she was alone and different.

She longed to confide to someone that part of her was missing. It was as if she were born without a limb, as if her past had been amputated. As she walked along the sidewalk and stopped obediently and automatically at the 'Don't Walk' sign, she heard herself shout to all her lost relatives, 'Is anyone there?'

The shout echoed in her ears, causing Addie to jerk into wakefulness. She opened her eyes, stretched and remembered where she was. She tried to identify the sound, which seemed to have come from the kitchen below. But there was no-one in the house but herself. The dream still hovered over her. Of course it was exaggerated. Even so, it was true that recently, she'd become increasingly aware of the importance of the genes she'd inherited from people who'd always seemed totally beyond her reach.

But now the sun was shining through the lead light windows, making patterns on the floral curtains. I am not alone, she thought. I am not a lost soul - I have Mom and Pop, and a new home now too. This is where I will find my other family - and myself.

Another sound from below. It was not her imagination. Someone was moving china and cutlery. Did burglars do the dishes? Jumping out of bed, feeling suddenly vulnerable, she pulled open the mahogany wardrobe and grabbed a thick, navy blue bathrobe. The she went to the top of the stairs and called, 'Is someone down there?'

'It's Mrs Grainger,' came the reply.

Mrs Grainger. Not a burglar after all. The mysterious woman who had cared for James. This would be interesting. She ran down the stairs.

A plump grey haired woman in an apron, looking remarkably at home, was indeed washing up the dishes. All Addie's ideas about an affair evaporated. She had gained a false impression from the inscrutable expression on Meera's face. This woman did not have the look of a mistress; she looked more like a school matron.

'Mrs Grainger? I wasn't expecting you. How did you get in?' Addie asked.

'I've got a key, of course,' the woman said, and her tone was defensive. 'I called up the stairs, but no-one answered. I come in and clean every Wednesday. For the Major.'

'But Major Buckley's been dead for six weeks. I didn't realise you still came in. I'm Addie Russell. I ... '

'Yes, I know,' the woman interrupted. 'But it was all arranged. The Major left us some money - my husband and me. And some extra to keep the place nice till someone takes over. Part was a gift and part was wages, you see.' She emphasised the last sentence, as if Addie was a child with limited understanding. Then she continued, 'There hasn't been a lot to do - until this morning.'

Addie flushed, 'I'm sorry. I guess I shouldn't have left the dishes. I was very tired last night.'

'It makes extra work if you leave things overnight. The food's all caked on. I've been standing here scrubbing for ten minutes.'

'I'm really sorry, Mrs Grainger. But I didn't know someone else was going to be doing the work.'

'Didn't that solicitor bloke tell you? He's a dozy character. He knows I get wages from the estate. He told me *you'd* be here shortly. I made up the bed in case. He should know I've been coming in to clean. You sure he didn't say?' She glared at Addie, who had already begun to revise her earlier impression.

'He didn't say a word about it. I guess I'd better get some clothes on. Is there hot water for a shower?'

'The Major used to have the water on first thing in the morning.' She looked at the clock pointedly. 'I expect it would have gone off by now.'

'Surely it wouldn't have been left on after the Major's death. It was nearly cold yesterday.'

'It comes on, on *my* day.' said Mrs Grainger. 'But it would be off by now.'

Addie, trying to keep her patience, asked to see the heating controls. Mrs Grainger, pursing her lips in disapproval, showed her the programmer in a cupboard, next to the boiler. It was obvious to Addie that she felt the programme was writ in stone, and that changing it was like changing the storyline of the Bible. Addie set the hot water to come on again, and since Mrs Grainger had made it her business to go upstairs, abandoning the projects in the kitchen, Addie had no option but to follow her.

The bedroom door was open, Addie's clothes lying accusingly on the floor, where she had dropped them.

Her lips clamped together in a thin, disapproving line, Mrs Grainger picked them up and put them on a chair.

'There's no need to do that, Mrs Grainger. I'll tidy up myself.'

'The Major wouldn't like the place in this state.'

'Mrs Grainger. I own this place now. The Major has left it to me. I guess we can come to some arrangement. But please leave my clothes alone.' She remembered the deed box. 'And don't tidy the study. I have papers laid out there.'

'You mean, not today?' said the plump woman, her lips tightly clenched.

'I mean not till I say so. That is, of course, *if* we arrange for you to carry on here. The study's to be left. I shall work in there.'

Mrs Grainger's florid face flushed all the more, and she folded her arms across her chest in a way that was somehow defiant.

'And now,' said Addie, 'if you'll excuse me, I'm going to the bathroom. And then I'm going to have some coffee.'

So this was the motherly soul that cared for James, she thought, as she locked the bathroom door. Now she could understand the inscrutable expression on Meera's face when she spoke about her. They've re-invented Mrs Danvers, she thought. But at least there's no Mrs de Winter.

She washed her face, cleaned her teeth and flicked a comb through her hair. In spite of the Major's wrap-around robe, which did nothing to flatter her, she felt at less of a disadvantage with her mouth and face freshened.

Arriving once again in the kitchen, she found Mrs Grainger replacing pans in the cupboard.

'Would you like some coffee?' Addie asked by way of an olive branch, as she put the kettle on.

'No thank you. I don't want to be here all day,' the other woman replied.

Addie poured herself instant coffee, and sat at the kitchen table, sipping slowly, determined not to be intimidated out of the kitchen. She turned her attention to a shrub in the garden, managing to keep her gaze on it, even when Mrs Grainger passed in front of it.

When she had drunk every drop, as unhurriedly as she could manage, she got up.

'I'm having my shower now, Mrs Grainger. I'll let you know if I want you to call in next week.'

Some sort of emotion - what, it was impossible to say -

passed across the other woman's face.

'About my husband...'

'Your husband?

'Do you want him to come tomorrow, like he usually does?'

'What does he do?'

'He does the garden.'

Addie recalled then her conversation with Meera. She liked the artistry of the garden. Perhaps she would get on with the husband, even if she couldn't manage the wife. She was tempted to repeat, 'I'll let you know,' but Meera had said the couple had worked for James Buckley for years. They would know all about James. They might even have heard mention of Dorothy or Lillian. It would be foolish to sever her links with them out of dislike for this woman. On the other hand, she could not at this moment bring herself to ask any questions.

'He can come tomorrow,' she conceded. 'Then we'll see.'

Addie stayed in the shower a long time, washing her hair, and enjoying the feel of the even warmth on her skin. Through the sound of rushing water, she could hear the vacuum cleaner, first near at hand, then further away downstairs. She dried herself on a hand towel that had been left in the bathroom, then returned to the bedroom in James's robe. Belatedly, she tidied up her clothes and rummaged through her suitcase to find some clean things. Further sounds from below suggested movement of furniture, dusting or polishing, and possibly a show of activity to demonstrate the value of the operator.

She went to the study and sat down at the desk again. Overnight, the sense of loss that she had felt on reading of the death of James's family and in-laws had abated. They were, after all, strangers. As for finding out about Adrienne, there was plenty of time; she was only at the beginning of the trail. She was ready now to continue to explore James's life.

She picked up a letter written in a precise and fussy hand, which followed the telegram, noticing at once that it was sent from Marsh House School. She read:

4th April 1941

My dear Lieutenant Buckley,

It is difficult for me to express my feelings at the loss of your family, in such tragic circumstances, in particular, your wife, whom I found to be a fine woman and who was always so concerned with young Peter. Naturally, it is a great sadness to me that one of our young men should be killed in this way, even before he had the chance to fight the enemy himself, as I know he would have wished.

The letter continued in similar formal vein and then Addie turned over the page, and gasped at the name at the end of the letter. 'I remain, Sir, your humble servant, Rodney Heron.'

'My real grandfather,' she said aloud. That old bastard who'd wanted nothing to do with her. So he was a schoolmaster or even a headmaster at some fancy private school. Well that figured. But was that the only contact between the two of them? How did James fit into this picture?

She felt exhilarated and almost light-headed at finding that there had at least been contact between Rodney Heron and James. She noticed absently that the vacuum cleaner had started up again, but she was too involved in the letters to care too much about Mrs Grainger for the moment. If half a dozen letters could provide so much data, then surely the complete box would provide a whole family history. Somewhere in there, was the truth about her own family background - a past which had been missing all her life.

The hum of the vacuum cleaner below ceased and, after some more cursory thumps, the front door banged loudly, and then there was silence.

Addie looked out of the study window and saw the retreating form of Mrs Grainger making her way down the road. She breathed a sigh of relief, and ran downstairs to the telephone.

'Jonathan Amery, please. It's Addie Russell.'

She waited for the receptionist to put her through.

'Mr Amery Junior for you.'

What an introduction, Addie thought. He must absolutely hate that.

'Hi, Junior,' she said.

'Good morning, Ms. Russell,' he replied in a cold, irritated voice.

'Addie,' she reminded him. 'Look, why didn't you warn me about the housekeeper from hell?'

'Sorry?'

'What's with this Mrs Grainger? She invaded this morning? And I was as unprepared as Pearl Harbour.'

'Ah, the Graingers.' replied Jonathan slowly. 'I thought my uncle had filled you in about them.'

'Well he didn't. So what's going on here?'

'Well, first of all, they received a bequest from the estate of ten thousand pounds, as thanks for their help. That was to be made before any other payments.'

'Have they had that?'

'Yes, they have indeed.' He was back in formal mode, Addie noted. 'And Major Buckley also left instructions that they should continue to be employed and keep the house and garden in order for a minimum of eight months, paid for by the estate. If the main beneficiary - that's you, of course - were to be found, and wanted to dismiss them - perhaps because you wanted to sell the house - they would still receive eight months' salary - both of them, of course, in lieu of notice. That's all there is.'

'It seems quite enough to me, Jonathan.'

'I'm sorry I didn't give you warning. I really thought you knew. You were ensconced with my uncle for quite a while when you came to the office yesterday, and I thought he'd spelled everything out.'

Addie thought back to the meeting with Mr Amery Senior and couldn't remember a great deal about it.

'So either I pay them to come, or I pay them not to come.'

'That's about the size of it.'

'I don't have to make a decision right away, do I?'

'No. Provided they get paid up to December, you can ask them to go at any time. Or you'll have to come to some agreement with them, if by any chance you want to keep them on after that.'

'Fat chance of that,' murmured Addie. As an afterthought, she said, 'I guess you'd better tell them to come, if I'm paying them.' That at least would save her the embarrassment of calling Mrs Grainger herself.

She replaced the phone, and pondered on why Mrs Grainger was concerned about her husband coming on the following day, if they were both going to be paid anyway. Perhaps the answer would be revealed when she met Mr Grainger, no doubt a hen-pecked and humble person, only used to kow-towing to his overpowering wife. She felt vaguely irritated with James for putting her in this position, and with Jonathan for not spelling it out. And come to that, why was he so unfriendly, after that cosy little tea party?

She returned to the bedroom, thinking about it, deciding then to attend to the rest of her unpacked clothes. She checked for creases, and hung up those that passed muster, wondering what occasions might be forthcoming and whether or not she had sufficient range. Her mood of anger and irritation abated quickly. Such moods rarely stayed with her for long, and she was often able to recover her equilibrium by some useful occupation. She wondered if the desire to be organised was inherited from James. But I haven't proved to myself he's related to me, she reminded herself.

She pushed the deed box with its treasures to the back of her mind. She could not spend all day every day poring through the papers. There had to be a form to the day - food and drink, tidying, keeping James's home in the way he would have wanted it, mainly for his sake, but partly too, in order to achieve some sort of truce with Mrs Grainger.

She couldn't live in an atmosphere of constant antagonism. She was stuck with the wretched woman for the next six months. If she stayed that long herself, she'd have to get along with her somehow.

She made herself a brunch of French toast and salad and decided to replenish her food stocks at the Indian grocery. Back home, she hardly walked at all. She jogged and worked out regularly, but never did anything in a leisurely manner. There were always urgent calls on her time and the pace of life was too fast. So the walk to the shops was a kind of luxury her newfound life afforded her.

With the lunch pans and dishes returned to their homes, she marched off to the grocery store. The sky was grey now and the summery optimism of the morning and the previous day was damped down in Addie, as well as in the weather. She had left behind her jacket and shivered as she walked. Meera was serving another customer when she arrived. Stereotypically, they discussed the weather, as Meera filled the woman's carrier bag.

'They said it'll be better again at the weekend,' commented Meera soothingly. She smiled at Addie.

'Hello again.'

'Hi, Meera,' said Addie. 'How are you?' She didn't wait for the other girl to reply. 'My taste buds are getting awfully bored - I had pizza last night and eggs in twenty different combinations. Now I fancy a two-inch thick steak.'

'I am sorry,' Meera said, smiling, her correct, formal accent sounding strange even to Addie's ears. 'As I told you, we only have the basics at the moment. You would have to go to the supermarket for steak. That's about two miles away. Or you could have something from the frozen cabinet. We have burgers and chicken legs.'

Addie sighed. 'I guess burgers and French fries might be an improvement. But, in any case, there's some other things I want. Just in case I have company.'

'So you are settling in?' said Meera.

Addie didn't answer directly. 'You know Mrs Grainger?'

'She comes in for bits and pieces. And she pays for the newspapers sometimes. Though of course, she does most of her shopping at the supermarket. She always complains about the price of things when she comes in here.'

'So you don't get on with her.'

'No, no,' replied Meera. 'I get on with everyone. We are running a small shop here. It's up to me to get on with people.'

'But do you like her?'

Meera avoided the question. 'Major Buckley had a lot of respect for Mrs Grainger. He said she was a good, kind woman. I expect he knew her better than me. Sometimes I find her a bit sharp.'

'Sharp. Yes, you could say that.'

One or two customers had walked in and were taking things off the shelves. Meera immediately changed the subject, telling Addie that her uncle would be bringing some bagels to the shop next week. Then she turned her attention to her new customers, exchanging pleasantries, answering queries and, with a subtle change of expression, showed that she would not gossip whilst there were others around.

Addie made her purchases and started off back to the house. The plastic bag cut into her fingers and the fine drizzle chilled her. I'm going to have to organise myself a car, she thought. The novelty of walking along English streets was already beginning to pall.

Chapter 6: Pieces of the Jigsaw

It was after two o'clock before Addie settled herself in the study again and revisited the moment of the revelation of James's loss of his wife, Penny and son, David. How did he feel at that moment, she wondered. Not like me, for I always knew I'd lost my real parents. There was no sudden catastrophic pain, just a gentle sorrow - a wish that I might have known them.

On balance, she decided it was not even fair to compare James's possible emotions with her own. After all, she had had the love of two good people and the happiness of a normal childhood, which could easily not have been the case.

Her emotions now were in fact not very different from those on one occasion in her childhood, when she wanted to try the fancy foods at a party Joan and Tony were having. The table was covered with dishes of all shapes and colours. There were cheeses and sausages, salads and fruit, cheesecake and other delicious foods that were familiar to her. But there were also foods she had never tasted - olives, green and black, asparagus tips in butter, smoked salmon and anchovies. She asked excitedly if she could have some and was overwhelmed with disappointment when she was refused.

'Not tonight, honey,' Joan had replied. 'I don't want to spoil the table. Tomorrow, I'll let you try some of the bits that are left over.'

Addie went to bed mollified by the prospect of trying out the unknown flavours on the following day. And Joan was as good as her word. The next morning, Sunday, she produced a plateful of the leftovers and allowed Addie to try them out. But she had forgotten to include the olives. Addie was too young to know the name and asked for the cherries. Joan produced strawberries and Addie stamped, shook her head and shouted, 'No. No. Cherries. Green cherries.' Joan patiently found some

grapes and presented them to t[...]
rage and frustration, and the tantru[...]
to her room and a cessation of any fur[...]
couple of years before she discovered [...]
her first taste of an olive was a great disa[...]
had expected it to be sweet. But the bitternes[...]
a minor disappointment compared to the ban[...]
room without knowing the taste of the unknown f[...]

And for a moment, now, Addie smiled at the [...]
the triumph as she held the olive in her hand, her e[...]
old mind thinking - now at last I shall know.

The letters that followed the deaths of Penny and baby Davi[...]
were mainly expressions of sympathy, as might have been
expected. The formal statement from Rodney Heron was
reiterated in similar ones, for James and Penny, it seemed,
came from a background of upper class people. Addie pictured
James at his home in Surrey, on his brief compassionate leave,
trying to extract some crumb of comfort from the stiff
condolences. Then came a letter with a different tone, and
Addie was once again exhilarated to see the name Heron - this
time, Dorothy.

At last, there was proof that Dorothy, too, had been in
contact with James Buckley. As Addie started reading the
letter, she remembered that though Rodney was the
spokesman, Dorothy was an accomplice in the rejection of
Addie; but as she progressed through the letter, it was difficult
to retain the picture of a cold-hearted woman.

My dear Lieutenant Buckley, Dorothy had written.

*I cannot let the tragic death of dear Penny pass, without writing
to express my grief, both for you, and on my own behalf. I met Penny
many times when she came to visit Peter at the school, deputising for
her parents. Because of the difficulties involved with travelling with
the baby, she stayed overnight here on several occasions, and I did*

...everywhere else, the school has ...ained, and as we shared the ...selves laughing over the ...ng in this rather masculine ... the company of another ...e. As you will no doubt ... to those men who are ...e, and there are times ... Naturally, I do not ...te Penny's company ...ne to make a fuss of ...nd I have not been

... rambling on. I had cast my mind back ... ways we shared. She talked so much of you and I ...u for her sake that you would be kept safe. I am devastated at the loss of a good friend and good person. But how immeasurably small is my loss compared to yours.

If I can ever be of any comfort to you, please contact me.

Yours ever,

Dorothy Heron

It was a much nicer, much warmer letter than Addie had expected. This was a different Dorothy from the one that had rejected her. So what had happened to change her? And no clue, yet, as to the connection between James and Adrienne. Logically, it would seem there should be an association between James and Dorothy, continuing on and beyond the birth of Adrienne. And for James to leave his house to Adrienne would suggest that there was some sort of special relationship between them, once she was born. The obvious conclusion was that the birth was as a result of a liaison between James and Dorothy, but this first letter could only be the start of any relationship. Addie looked carefully through the letters that followed, but for the moment there was no sign of Dorothy's handwriting.

She continued working her way through the letters, lost in a time half a century before. Her head was still full of the war, of the officers and men, some going off to die, and naïve young boys eager to join them, of the women who waited, and sometimes met their own tragic end at home. Of shortages and rationing. It was a different world. Suddenly, she spotted another letter from Dorothy. Dated July 1942, it was more than a year after the letters of sympathy which had followed the death of Penny and her family. Its brevity was disappointing, but its content was significant.

> *Marsh House School,*
> *Long Barton,*
> *near Bath.*

Dear James,

I have so enjoyed meeting you, but I have to tell you that my husband and I are expecting a child, and I have been advised to take things very carefully over the next few months. You will appreciate how much this means to me, and that I will follow this advice scrupulously in order to ensure the safety of the child.

It does mean that I must restrict travelling to a minimum and may not have the opportunity for meeting you, as I have in the past.

Yours ever,

Dorothy Heron

So meetings had taken place between them. Yet the tone of this letter was very cool. It left so much unsaid. What had taken place at these meetings? Was there a deliberate ambiguity about some of the phrases - *'the safety of the child'* - almost hinting at some veiled threat. Not to know - not to have any means of knowing - was so frustrating.

But she had found evidence of communication between Dorothy and James. That at least was satisfying. In fact, she felt like sharing the information with someone. She went downstairs to the phone and dialled home. The phone rang and rang. Joan was obviously out for the day. Absently, Addie put some water in the kettle. Some tea would be nice. And perhaps one of the scones she had bought earlier. But all the time, the questions, the theories were encircling her mind. Who else could she talk to? Who could act as a sounding board?

There was only one other person she could think of. 'Mr Jonathan Amery,' she said aloud. 'I am going to invite you for tea.'

She went into the kitchen, and looked out at the calm of the garden, luxuriously sprouting its flowers and shrubs, instead of war-time cabbages. She thought again of the womenfolk making do, experiencing many hardships, without all the conveniences she herself was used to, imagining herself for a moment as Penelope or Dorothy. Then she got changed, put on some makeup, and picked up the phone.

'Jonathan. It's Addie, Addie Russell.'

He took the cue from her.

'Hallo, Addie. What can I do for you, this time?'

'I want to discuss the letters in that box. Do you think you could come round?'

He sounded doubtful.

'Look, Jonathan, I'm not at all sure I'm the rightful beneficiary of this money and I need to clarify some things.'

'All right,' he said, in a resigned tone. 'I'll come over.'

She arranged the cups and saucers, put cream and jam in separate dishes, and the scones in the centre of the table. As she heard Jonathan's car in the driveway, she brought the kettle to the boil again, and poured the steaming liquid into the tea-pot. Then she went to the door and let him in.

'Hi, Jonathan. How are you?'

'Fine. Look is this really urgent, Addie? I was in the middle of some important conveyancing.'

He glanced at the table.

'English tea, Jonathan.'

He didn't smile.

'Addie, I'm working. I can't stop everything to take tea with you. You may be practically an heiress, but I'm a working man. I have to charge you for visits in office hours.'

Her smile faded a little.

'A typical lawyer, huh?'

'I haven't the time to play games, Addie. Your legacy will be eaten up in no time, if you keep ringing me and asking me to come here. I have to book down every phone call, you know.'

'I'm not playing games, Jonathan.' Addie was suddenly irritated. 'You're my lawyer, aren't you, and James's executor. You might put yourself out to do the job properly. If I was home in the States, my lawyer would come over to wipe my nose if I sneezed. I need to know why this guy left me his money. What was the relationship he had with my grandmother? Did he ever meet my mother? Why didn't he leave his money to the Graingers? He thought well of them, so I hear. Is that why she dislikes me? Who was Lillian? I have to talk to someone about these things. I don't know anyone else in this Goddam country.'

Jonathan looked surprised and somewhat embarrassed at the outburst. 'I'm sorry. I'm sorry. I didn't mean to make you angry. I'm under a lot of pressure at the moment.'

He sat down at the table and picked up a scone.

'I can answer one of your questions straight away. I checked with my uncle and it seems that Major Buckley had some association with Plymouth before the Second World War. The Tamar is a river in that region. Probably not an old girlfriend.'

Addie smiled to herself.

For a moment she was moved as she thought of the old man coming back to England, still remembering happy times in his first brief marriage, and naming his house in memory of those days. And it was nice to know he wasn't a philanderer.

'I realise I haven't been making allowances for you,' Jonathan went on. 'I keep forgetting how isolated you are here - you'd have been much better off in a hotel, as I suggested. Let me think what I can do.'

Addie glared at him. 'Don't treat me like a kid who needs someone to play with.'

'Sorry,' said Jonathan again. He passed his cup to her. 'Why don't you pour the tea? What I'm thinking is that though I'll do my best to answer your queries, I just can't be around to chew them over, as you might feel is necessary.' He accepted the tea and took a sip.

Addie, feeling that she had seriously misjudged the friendliness of the previous day, merely nodded.

'Anyway, don't worry, we'll sort something out. I can spare half an hour or so. Just go through your questions again, one at a time.'

But the conversation revealed nothing more of explanation. Jonathan reiterated that, irrespective of any relationship to James, Adrienne Heron, or in the event of her death, her heir, was the main beneficiary of James's will. The other beneficiaries, the Graingers, would (and had) received ten thousand pounds from the estate, a guarantee of eight months' work by the estate or cash in lieu of notice, and further provision at the end of that time.

Addie, who didn't remember hearing the last bit before, pricked up her ears, but Jonathan could not expand on it. His uncle knew more details of the further provision, but he did not.

'Maybe some small annuity,' he suggested.

Absently buttering another scone, he said to Addie, trying, she thought, to sound kindly and avuncular, 'I know you're disappointed that he doesn't appear to be your grandfather. And despite what you say, I think two days stuck here with just the letters is bound to make you a bit tense. Perhaps you'd like a trip somewhere different to see some of the tourist spots.'

Was he offering to take her?

'I thought you were busy,' she commented.

'Yes, I am, but my sister's not. I thought of her when I spoke to you yesterday.'

'Your sister?' Addie, irritated with herself, realised she was disappointed.

'Yes. She's a student - but not much younger than you and she's home from college. She hasn't been able to arrange a holiday job, yet and I'd like to suggest that she contacts you. She could help with research and act as your guide - you could come to some arrangement about petrol and it would probably help her to keep her car on the road.'

'That sounds like a good idea,' Addie said, thinking that, after all, it would be fun to get out and about. 'But it's not much of a job.'

'I'm sure she won't mind helping you for a couple of weeks. I'll probably be able to get my uncle to agree to some modest payment that doesn't affect your inheritance.'

When he had gone, Addie returned to the letters. She felt better already at the idea of telling someone else about her discoveries. Almost immediately, she came upon a second envelope in Dorothy's handwriting. It contained a formal printed card.

To Dorothy Ann Heron, and Dr Rodney Heron of Marsh House, 20th May, a daughter, Adrienne Penelope.

Reluctantly, for it seemed to prove what she had hoped to disprove, Addie felt a frisson of excitement at this confirmation of her mother's birth.

Only a scribbled note on the back relieved the card's formality – *Rodney and I both hope that even though you are so far away, you will consent to becoming Adrienne's godfather. Perhaps when this war is over, you will be able to find solace from our little girl, and will be able to regard her as someone special in your life. I still think of Penny - we shared so much.*

Again there were the ambiguities. *'Someone special'*, *'We shared so much'*. Even *'Our little girl'* could have another meaning. But if these possible hidden meanings were ignored, it could simply mean that Dorothy had become a friend and counsellor to James, and that in love and respect for his dead wife, she had named her child after her. If there were other meanings, then Dorothy had not intended anyone but James to understand them. Addie looked on for more correspondence in Dorothy's handwriting, but could see nothing else.

She replaced the papers and closed the box. After all, there was no way of proving anything other than that she was the miserable Rodney's granddaughter, but at least her grandmother, Dorothy, was charming, much nicer than Addie had always envisaged. And if nothing else, for James, Adrienne was possibly a surrogate daughter - a replacement for the son he'd lost. Perhaps that at least would be revealed in some later correspondence. She was disappointed, nevertheless, and had no heart to continue. She sat pensively and tried to bring herself back to the present. For a moment, she remembered the bitter taste of the olive. It was better to know than not know, she reminded herself.

The telephone call that evening from Jonathan's sister came more quickly than expected. Nevertheless, when Sarah Amery asked where and when she would like to go, Addie was ready with her reply.

'Bath,' she said. 'Tomorrow.'

Addie's Russell's Family Tree:

26th June 1991

Dr Rodney Heron = Dorothy
(Schoolmaster, Marsh House)

|

Adrienne Penelope Heron b. May 1943 = ?
(died 7th February 1965)

|

Addie (Russell) b. 6th February 1965
(Adopted by Joan and Tony Russell)

_____

*Lieut. James Buckley = Penelope Grey
* *Could he be my*   (died with family in
real grandfather?   bombing raid, 1941)
                                      (sister of Peter Grey,
                                      pupil at Marsh House)

|

David b. 1940
(died in bombing raid with
family, 1941)

Chapter 7: Addie goes West

Addie liked Sarah immediately. She had arrived promptly at nine in the morning, running her fingers through rebelliously curly brown hair and yawning that this was not a time for students to be snatched from their beds. But when Addie apologised, Sarah just laughed. 'Just joking. It'll be fun, I'm sure - and you'll love Bath. It's a beautiful spot. And after that, we could try York and perhaps the Lake ...'

'I have a particular interest in Bath, Sarah. My grandfather taught at a school nearby - a place called Long Barton - and that's where my mother was born. Of course, I'd like to visit Bath itself, too.'

They went out to the car and climbed in. Sarah turned on the ignition and pulled away. 'What you said just before - you must be English, then.'

'It's a long story,' Addie said. 'I was born and raised in America. In fact that's why I'm grateful to have a driver - I can't get used to the idea of driving on the wrong side of the road.' She added, 'I'm embarrassed to be involving you. I feel I should be managing on my own.'

'Don't worry. I enjoy driving. The only thing is, Jonathan is worried that I have to be paid by the firm, or it'll have to come from the Estate. He was trying to work out how to sell the idea to Uncle Bruce. But I've got another idea. I want to go to America next year. If you can sort out some cheap accommodation with a family or something, we could call it quits. I certainly don't like the idea of being paid to run you around.'

'I know Mom would just love to put you up - she thrives on hospitality - and she's got relatives in other parts of the States. I'm sure we can arrange something. But you must let me pay for the gas.'

'The petrol. Yes. That would be a help. I'd be noble and say "no" if I could. But you know how it is, living on a student's income.'

They drove on to the motorway chatting about student life in England and post-student life in America. Sarah talked about her limited finances - limited because initially her parents thought it was character building to have to manage, rather than because of any hardships, and subsequently, because of her mother's natural caution when she was widowed.

Then she suddenly said, 'That's all the mundane stuff. Now tell me all about your inheritance. I'm absolutely eaten up with curiosity. Did you know this old man was your godfather?'

'My mother Adrienne's godfather. Not mine. But the will said that she or her dependants are the main beneficiaries and, as she's dead, here I am.'

'How long ago did she die?'

'She died when I was born. I'm adopted.'

'Goodness. I didn't think women died in childbirth these days - or even those days.'

'Well, actually she had some form of food poisoning, and she didn't realise. You know how excited everyone gets, now, about salmonella and listeria. Well, Mom - my adopted mother - that is, she said Adrienne just adored the delis, and she was always nipping in for a cream cheese on rye, or a turkey sandwich. Then she got very sick, and didn't realise how serious it was. I was pretty premature.'

A service station exit flashed past, and Sarah glanced out of the window. 'Do you need a coffee or anything?'

'No. I'd rather get on. Unless you want to stop.'

'No. Let's get there as quickly as possible. Carry on telling me - if you don't mind talking about it - how did your mother, what was her name? - Adrienne? - how did she know your adopted mother?'

'Adrienne had just graduated from an English college and was travelling through the States. She rented Mom and Pop's spare room - it was a bit of extra income, and company for Mom. She'd been in the States for a couple of months, already, and when she moved in, she told Mom she was pregnant and said she'd lost contact with her boyfriend in England. Mom tried to persuade her to write to him, but Adrienne said she didn't want him to know about it, and she wouldn't talk about it at all. So that's all I ever knew about my father. I guess he was one big mistake in her life.'

She was silent for a moment, thinking about her own big mistake, Lloyd Henderson. At least he'd never gotten her pregnant. Otherwise it would have been more difficult to put him behind her.

'I suppose if she'd known she was going to die, she'd have made more provision for you.'

Addie nodded. Joan Russell had always been reluctant to dwell on Adrienne's death. There was no doubt it had been painful for her. Once Addie had seen her reduced to tears as she described Adrienne's sudden deterioration in health, the hospital's battle to save her life and the realisation that Adrienne was not going to survive.

'It upsets Mom to talk about it. I think she blamed herself for not realising how ill Adrienne was.'

They fell silent again. The small car was vibrating as it sped along, and this and the noise of the motorway traffic was beginning to make talking an effort. And Addie herself became lost in a reverie, the eternal unanswered question revolving around her head. What were they like, her real parents? What would life have been like if Adrienne Heron had survived. Eventually Sarah, her thoughts perhaps focused on other questions, slowed down a little and turned to Addie with a puzzled frown on her face.

'So where does the old man, Adrienne's godfather, fit into things? How did you get in contact with him?'

'We never were in contact while he was alive. But my Aunt Katharine, Mom's sister, that is, came to England just a couple of weeks back, and sent Mom a clipping from an English newspaper. It said, 'Have you seen this girl?' and there was a photo underneath.

Addie smiled remembering how excited Joan had been on the telephone, reading out Katharine's note.

'I am just amazed at the likeness to your Addie. Could she be something to do with this British girl?'

'So if your aunt hadn't come to England, you wouldn't have known anything about it.'

'I guess that's right. Anyway, that was the start of it. Mom called me at my apartment, and told me to come over. She showed me this clipping, and told me this kid was my mother when she was a girl. It said she was the illegitimate daughter of Major James Buckley, who'd just died aged 79, and she'd be about 50 years old. And it said to contact Messrs. Palfrey, Willow and Amery - and the rest is history.'

'So he was your grandfather after all.'

'The newspaper hyped up the story a bit. When Mom called England, Mr Amery senior ...'

'Uncle Bruce,' Sarah put in.

'Your uncle. Yes, he told her they'd gotten it all wrong. And I knew my grandparents were called Heron; Mom had written to them when I was born, and they didn't want me. If they had, Mom and Pop might not have been able to adopt me.'

'So you knew a bit about your English background.'

'Yes, but I never expected to inherit a house and a few thousand pounds sterling. It's pretty exciting.'

'And *he* wasn't even related to you.'

'Well, it's probably dumb of me, but I kinda hope that old James might be my secret grandfather - I guess I'm hoping that the newspapers might have been right, all along – that Adrienne was illegitimate - or even that James could have been my father's father, and he'd found out about me - but so far, I haven't seen anything in his letters to show he had any surviving children.'

She told Sarah how James had lost his wife and baby in the Blitz.

'Well, I don't like to be too pessimistic, but it's looks like you're stuck with the one that didn't want you.'

'I thought maybe the telegram Dorothy Heron sent later was a coded message to James – telling him that Adrienne was really his daughter.'

'You're a born romantic, Addie. I hope you're right.'

They drove down the hill at the approach to Bath.

'I suppose they're holding your job open for you,' Sarah commented, slowing the car to join the queue of vehicles waiting to get into the town. 'You must be pretty high powered to be able to walk out at the drop of a hat.'

'I had some holidays owing. My boss more or less agreed. But in any case ...'

'Yes?'

'There was a bit of bad feeling between us, and if he'd said "no", I'd have walked out anyway.'

'That sounds pretty independent.'

'To be honest, we had a - a relationship. And it was over.'

'Have you got another boyfriend, now?'

'I'm not sure I'm ready. Although - your brother's kinda cute.'

Sarah looked at her sharply.

'Is that why Jonathan's giving you the special treatment?'

Addie was taken aback. 'I was just joking. I wouldn't say I was getting special treatment. He's behaving like a lawyer, isn't he?'

'You're sure he doesn't fancy you or something?'

'I doubt it. That's not the feedback I'm getting. To be honest, he doesn't seem very happy at all. I don't want to offend you, but apart from the first time I met him, I've barely gotten a smile out of him. He seems so tetchy.'

'You've got him wrong, Addie.' Sarah said, now rising to

her brother's defence. 'Underneath he's really good fun.'

Addie said, 'Oh,' rather non-committally. But she must have expressed some doubt in her monosyllabic comment, because Sarah said quickly, 'I suppose, he is a bit moody sometimes. He's got things on his mind. There's a couple of things worrying him. I shouldn't really say this, but he has problems working with Uncle Bruce.'

'What sort of problems?'

'I just get the feeling that Jonathan thinks Uncle Bruce is a bit careless about detail. And he gets worried about it. Don't say I said anything. Oh, look at this traffic - we're going to crawl all the rest of the way.'

'I hope they're sorting out my stuff okay,' Addie said frowning.

'I'm sure there's no problem with the important stuff. Jonathan's probably a perfectionist. I mean, it's nothing really. Sometimes bits of information don't get passed on to Jon and sometimes not to the clients.'

'That figures,' Addie said, remembering Mrs Grainger's unheralded arrival at the house. 'But is that it? It shouldn't turn him into a grouch. So what's the other reason?'

'Oh, damn, that's what I didn't want. The engine's heating up. It's always the same with this sort of stop-go.'

Sarah turned off the ignition and waited for the next traffic movement before switching it on again.

'You were saying?' Addie pursued.

'Was I?'

'Why Jonathan is so uptight.'

'Oh, yes. Well, a couple of days ago, he was full of the joys of spring because he thought he'd sold his flat. But when he rang me, yesterday, he said it had fallen through. The man wouldn't go up to his figure and he and Tibby are still stuck with it. So it was all doom and gloom.'

'Tibby?'

'Yes - his ex - Tabitha Plowright. I was at school with her, and Tibby was her nick-name then. Ghastly, isn't it? But once you get stuck with them, it's very difficult to shake off.'

Tabitha. Addie remembered the name from Jonathan's telephone conversation.

'So she's the girlfriend?'

'Well, she was. But not now. She was one of these mousy little creatures that no-one takes a blind bit of notice of. Then all of a sudden, she was tall and blonde and always swishing her hair back. And a right bitch.'

'How did she get together with Jonathan?'

'Well, through me, actually. A few of us had a party. She met him, and she made a play for him. And he fell, hook, line and sinker. They moved in together. Put some money into a flat when prices were at their top whack - only she made sure she didn't put too much in. Then about six months ago, he found she was having it off with some other poor sod. She wouldn't leave the flat, so he did and the other guy moved in.'

'And does he still love her?'

'Love her! He'd like to wring her neck. And so would I. It would solve a lot of his problems. Because, somehow or other, he's still paying the half the mortgage.'

Addie was silent.

'I suppose he does still love her a bit. Love, hate - it all fits together doesn't it? But aside from that, the financial side of things is so difficult - and every time she rings up, it upsets him or reminds him.'

The traffic was moving now and they soon reached one of the car-parks near Bath station.

'Let's get out and leave it here, Addie. We could go and get a Bath bun. Or shall we have a guided tour of Bath?'

'It's only just after twelve. Let's grab some coffee and have a look around. Then I'll treat us to lunch somewhere.'

The sun shone and they found a place to sit outside and watch the multitude of tourists being hustled from one place to another. Addie was enchanted by the town. But not by the tourists.

'I'd like to look around at my own pace. I don't want to join up with loads of other Americans.'

Refreshed by the coffee, they walked to the abbey and wandered in, gazing in wonderment at the intricacies of the building and the high ceilings.

'How in hell did they get up there to build it?' said Addie, her neck craned upwards. Then, as they looked at the memorials to the dead of past centuries, on the ground and on the walls, she mused wistfully, 'Imagine being able to trace your folks back to the twelfth century.'

'We can trace our family back to William the Conqueror,' boasted Sarah. 'Sorry, Addie. I didn't mean to rub salt into the wound. Look, I'd really like to help you find out about your family. I know quite a bit about this family tree stuff. We can spend a day at St. Catherine's House in London, where they keep all the old records. There'll be masses of information there.'

They walked back into the square, debating how Addie could establish with certainty her relationship with Rodney and with James.

'Ploughing back through old records isn't going to help with that, Addie. But at least you can find out about Dorothy. You do know she was - or is - your grandmother.'

'Yes - and I like her more now I've read those letters. But Rodney - well - I don't like him. I don't like him at all.'

'You're jumping to conclusions, aren't you?'

'I just get bad vibes from what I know about him. A bit like your Uncle Bruce.'

'What do you mean? You mustn't take what I said too seriously.'

'It's what you didn't say that's gotten me nervous. He is handling James's estate, after all.'

'I didn't mean to get you worried, Addie. Jonathan would kill me if he knew. I'm sure it's only trivial things that bother

Jon. It's their relationship that gets him ratty.'

'How do you mean?'

'Uncle Bruce is the senior partner. But he's a miserable skinflint and he keeps Jonathan on a string like a yo-yo. He's always promising a full partnership, then delaying things for some supposedly unprofessional behaviour. Every time he snaps, Jonathan toes the line for a bit - then things get back to normal.'

'So why does he stay?'

'Well, it was Dad's firm, until he died - and of course Dad hoped Jonathan would carry on. In fact Jon was with another firm - where he was articled - and he came back to help after Dad died. Jonathan doesn't want to see the firm go downhill. He's very conscientious. But Uncle Bruce takes advantage of that. He gets what he can out of Jonathan - he bleeds him.'

They were both pensive for a while, Addie's mind moving from the Amerys to her own male relatives.

Then Sarah returned to the present. 'Let's talk about this trip to - what was the name?'

'Long Barton. I'd really like to go there and see if we can found out anything about my grandparents, Rodney and Dorothy.'

'Well in that case, why don't we see if we can look at the parish records. With luck, we might be able to find details of Rodney and Dorothy's marriage and Adrienne's birth here, rather than in London. Do you want to do the tourist stuff as well?'

Addie said reflectively, 'I don't know how long I'm going to stay here, Sarah. The other day I thought - I'm home - this is it. I'm going to burn my boats and settle here. Now I don't know. It depends on what I find out about my folks. It depends on relationships, weather, atmosphere - all sorts of things. Do I want these people that didn't want me?'

'Yes, I understand. So?'

'What was the question?'

'Do you want a guided tour of Bath?'

They both laughed.

'The answer is that, just in case I go back to the States - next week, next month, whenever - I want to see Bath *and* I want to find out about the Herons.'

'One other thing?'

'Yeah?'

'Do you want to do that before or after lunch?'

They laughed again. The laughter of young women who shared the same sense of humour.

'Sarah.'

'Yes?'

'Is there any reason why you have to get back tonight?'

'No. Why, do you want to stay overnight?'

'Yes, if we can book in somewhere.'

'We could sleep in the car.'

'Sarah. I'm an heiress. We'll book into a fancy hotel.'

'If we can get in anywhere with all these tourists.'

'We'll get in.'

They walked through the streets, past Georgian buildings, their creamy white, cut stone fascias, so distinctive of Bath. There, in an airy square, which truly took Addie into the England of the various films and TV dramas she had seen, they found a hotel, where they booked lunch and a room for the night. They made straight for the restaurant.

'I'd like to see the Roman baths,' commented Sarah, when their lunch was placed in front of them. 'It's the sort of thing I'd never have thought of doing without a tourist to go with.'

'Let's do the tourist stuff today, and family tomorrow.'

'If Dorothy and Rodney lived just outside Bath, we could take the car to their local church tomorrow. That might sort out the records - the marriage, the christening - everything. And then we could go home after that.'

'No, there's one other thing. I'd like to go to the school where Rodney taught. I guess Adrienne would have spent part of her life there, even if she went off to school somewhere later. Hey, this steak is the best meal I've had in days. I've been living off pizza and eggs.'

'Me too,' commented Sarah. 'I think my diet recently could be described as minimalist. Apart from the last couple of days at home, it's practically the best meal I've had since the Christmas break.'

'Do you spend Christmas with your family?'

'With Mum. I told you my Dad's dead. He had a heart attack two years ago. I still miss him.'

'So it's just you, your mom and Jonathan.'

'Yes. Jonathan's home quite often too. We get on quite well, considering.'

'Considering?'

'Considering he's my brother. You're really quite interested in him, aren't you?'

'I told you, Sarah. I'm not ready to get serious with anyone yet.'

'I'm not talking about being serious. I'm talking about being casual - I mean picking him up and dropping him when you feel like it. I don't want to see him hurt again.'

'You don't know me. You shouldn't assume.'

'I'm sorry, Addie. Look, we're getting on well and I'm enjoying this trip. It's interesting and we're having a good laugh. But just be careful. Jonathan's had more than he can handle. Don't hurt him - or it's the end of a beautiful friendship.'

Addie fell silent for a moment. Then she said with a smile, 'It's a good thing we're in Jane Austen country.'

'Why's that?'

'Because you're getting to sound like Miss Bingley.'

Sarah grimaced.

'Are you saying I'm trying to organise his life?'

'He's a big boy, Sarah. I guess he can look after himself better than you imagine. Look, I told you. I've also had a relationship that went sour. Believe me, I just want a few good friends at the moment - of both sexes.'

They made straight for the Roman baths after lunch, saw the empty ruins in which the Romans had once enjoyed the most sophisticated of ablutions; trailed with other tourists round the steaming water, where visitors were warned not to dip in an inquisitive finger; admired the old coins and weaponry behind glass cases and examined the modern-day plans and models.

Addie stopped to buy the obligatory postcard of the tall white carved statues, which hovered over the baths, facing the square outside.

'I must send this to Mom.'

'Have you phoned home?'

'Yes, the first day I was here. But only to say I'd arrived safely. Then I tried her again and couldn't get through. I'll give her a call in another couple of days and fill her in with some more news.'

'Well,' said Sarah, as they emerged, 'Do we go on a walking tour now?'

But Addie had earlier taken note of the open-topped buses and they went in search of the starting point.

Afterwards, there was still time left in the day to squeeze in tea at Sally Lunn's and a look around the shops before returning exhausted to the hotel for a meal.

Other guests were still wandering in and out of the bar, when they retired to their room. Addie flung herself on her bed, looking at her watch.

'Ten o'clock. I'm never in bed at this time. Except yesterday,' she remembered.

Sarah commented, 'The end of term was pretty hectic. I'm quite glad of one or two early nights.'

Before they knew it, it was day. A second day without rain, in this area of the country where warm wet westerlies regularly deposit their burdens. The drive from the city centre to the outskirts was pleasant, and they soon arrived at their destination, the church at Long Barton.

The parish priest, initially, was a little reluctant to allow them to search the old records, explaining that he preferred people to make appointments, but he was persuaded by Addie's American accent and her story of searching for her lost relations. As they delved back through time, Addie felt her heart race faster. When she finally came to the entries for the baptism of her mother, and the marriage of Adrienne's parents, she could barely turn the pages for the shaking of her hands.

'You hoped you'd find something different, Addie, didn't you? Something wrong.'

'I guess so. It's all there in black and white. Even so, it's like they're more real. They really existed. And I did notice one thing.'

'What?'

'They waited a hell of a long time before Adrienne came on the scene. Look at the dates, Sarah - nearly ten years.'

'Yes, you're right. I wonder why. I'm sure people didn't muck about long, then.'

'And they didn't have the pill, either.'

'Adrienne was a war baby. Perhaps he came back from the wars in a grand passion that he hadn't managed before.'

'But he was there all the time. As far as I could tell from the letters, he never left. He probably invented some condition to get him out of the war.'

'I think you're being unfair to poor old Rodders, Addie. You've really got it in for him.'

'Perhaps. So they were married in 1934 and Adrienne was born in 1943. And Dorothy wrote to James for the first time in '41. Coincidence?'

'Romantic idea, Addie, but you're jumping to conclusions again. No evidence - and she'd have to do more than write.'

Addie laughed despite herself. Nevertheless, she spent a few minutes, carefully taking down details of dates, addresses and every scrap of information that might contribute to the jigsaw. The parish priest directed them to Marsh House and they drove off through the green countryside.

Chapter 8: The Schoolmaster

The school was a large pleasant-looking building with the character of an old country house. Though Sarah was already on vacation, schools had not yet broken up, and groups of boys and girls of various ages (for Marsh House was now coeducational) were talking in the grounds, as they trailed back from tennis or other sporting activity. They looked curiously at Sarah and Addie, as the two young women walked, a trifle self-consciously, towards the front entrance.

A secretary, brisk and protective, emerged from her room, possibly having spotted them from a window. She was one of those English roses, whose hair has changed uniformly to white, but whose pink and white complexion still blends, as if by design. Addie explained once again that she was a visiting American, that her grandfather (no need to go into the details) had been a teacher during the war and possibly afterwards, and that Addie's mother had been born there.

'I just wondered if anyone here knew my folks.'

The secretary listened patiently, made no promises and told them in her beautifully modulated voice that she would do what she could to help them. In due course, the headmaster arrived. He was dark-haired and surprisingly young, and had a thin, clever face. He shook them both by the hand.

'Please forgive me - there are so many duties to attend to. I can't do better, I feel, than pass you over to my deputy, who will be able to spend a little more time with you. Mrs Harrington will take you to his office.'

They walked in convoy down the corridor until the white-haired Mrs Harrington paused at a room marked 'Dr G. Tillotson'. The introductions were carried out a second time, and Dr Tillotson, also silver-haired, and resplendent in his gown that reminded Addie of someone from 'Goodbye Mr Chips', invited them to sit down, indicating to Mrs Harrington that coffee would be welcome.

He talked then in a perfunctory way of the dedication and knowledge that her grandfather had brought to the school in his long service. He expressed his regret that he himself had only just arrived at the school at the time when her grandfather left, so he did not ever get to know him very well.

'Perhaps, before you go, you would like to see the board where all the past heads and deputy heads are honoured for their service?' he queried, standing up, as they finished their coffee.

Addie and Sarah had no option but to take their cue from him. They stood, too, and followed him out of the room.

'Of course, he was acting headmaster during the war years,' Dr Tillotson elaborated.

Addie, feeling vaguely dissatisfied, gazed up at the plaque. There was his name embossed and looking important.

'Dr Rodney Heron,' she murmured. 'My grandfather.'

A small, elderly figure scurried past towards the entrance clutching his robes around him, and turned to look at her in some surprise, as he heard her words.

As she and Sarah reached the doorway, ushered in that direction by Dr Tillotson, she noticed the older man had slowed his pace and was still within sight of the entrance. And as they said their goodbyes, with much enthusiastic handshaking, she saw out of the corner of her eye that he was walking down the entrance drive towards the car park. By the time the young women had caught up with him, they were no longer within the field of vision of anyone at the school windows.

Addie coughed, and he turned, unsurprised at their appearance.

'Good afternoon.'

'Good afternoon, sir. I'm Addie Russell. I couldn't help noticing that you seemed to know my grandfather - Dr Rodney Heron. Did you happen to know my mother? I believe she grew up here.'

'How delightful to meet you, Miss Russell,' he said, bowing his head slightly. 'May I introduce myself. I am Dr Glossop. Yes, by a very fortunate coincidence, I do actually remember your mother, and your grandparents, because I have not only taught here for a lifetime, but was also educated here myself.'

'I'm so pleased to meet you, Dr Glossop,' Addie said excitedly. 'I'd love to talk to you about them. Would you mind very much? You see, I never knew my mother – she died when I was born.'

'My dear. I am so sorry.'

'What were they like? What was my mother like?'

'Your grandmother was a charming and gracious woman. As for your mother, well, Miss Russell, you must appreciate that although I'm nearing retirement now, I was only a ten year old boy when your mother - what was her name now? - yes of course - Adrienne - when Adrienne was born. However, it is obvious, my dear, that you are another in a long line of delightful women, and I am so very happy to have made your acquaintance.' He extended his hand again and made as if to walk on.

'Are we keeping you from an appointment, Dr Glossop?' asked Addie, racking her brains for some means of preventing him from slipping through her fingers.

'I was about to have lunch, my dear. And since the dreaded Sports Day is taking place this afternoon, I shall be taking a stroll to the local hostelry. The Somerset cider is exceptionally good, and some fresh bread and cheese fulfils an old man's needs.'

'Would you mind if we joined you, Dr Glossop. I should so much like to hear about my grandmother, and we haven't yet had lunch ourselves.'

'I should be privileged to have your company,' he replied gallantly, causing Sarah to titter quietly to herself.

Once in the public house, with Ploughman's lunches set

before them, Addie insisted on buying the old man a glass of the famed cider, sipping from a glass herself at his suggestion.

She waited impatiently for him to volunteer some more information, but when he did not, asked once again, 'Do tell me, sir, what you remember about my mother.'

'Well, as I told you, I was just a schoolboy - I came back years later to teach, as I said - but I remember the excitement and pleasure everyone felt at her birth.'

He had nearly drained the glass and his face flushed a little. He stopped talking for a moment and looked out into the distance, as if he was seeing another world. Addie felt he had almost forgotten they were there, and said nothing in case she broke the spell.

'Doctor and Mrs Heron had been married some time - the school itself was a gloomy place - all the young blood gone from it. But a baby - that's something of a novelty in any school - and Dr Heron was particularly transformed by the birth.'

In his reverie, he had let the last remark slip out; then he apologised profusely.

'I'm so sorry, Miss Russell. I didn't mean ... Naturally, the personalities of schoolmasters are seen through a distorted glass by their young charges. Why, the same, no doubt, applies to myself ... I believe I have heard myself referred to as Old Gossip Gl...'

Addie interrupted him, 'Dr Glossop, I didn't quite understand what you meant. Do speak frankly to me. I want to know the truth - warts and all.'

Sarah who had nearly finished her cola, interrupted with the offer of more drinks. Addie shook her head, but the schoolmaster gratefully accepted.

He briskly finished the first glass and bestowed a benevolent smile upon Addie.

'You were about to tell me about Dr Heron,' she prompted him.

'Well, Miss Russell, since you ask, as a pupil, I was rather in fear of him. He was known for being free with the cane - though I may say, I did not myself receive corporal punishment - and there were rumours - but one never knew what to believe. When the baby arrived, he seemed quite altered, he became quite genial, as I recall - but the effect only lasted a year or so. Then he changed again, quite suddenly, it seemed at the time. But the war ended, my father came home - we moved away.'

Sarah returned with two glasses and the old man smiled his gratitude. Addie, hardly noticing, ignoring her own drink and meal in front of her, continued her questions.

'But then you came back to teach. What was he like then? Had he improved?'

'It was not, of course, my first post,' he said, lifting the glass to his lips. 'By the time I came back, I had completed a doctorate in the Classics - I was nearing thirty. It gave me a shock to see him. He was at that time deputy headmaster, though he had been acting headmaster during the war years - and he was probably between fifty and sixty. Age had not mellowed him, I'm afraid.'

Dr Glossop's eyes glazed over again, and Addie noticed that his hands were shaking. 'My dear,' he said, 'this is all many years ago. Isn't it better to let it rest?'

Addie was still determined to know everything. 'I have the impression that my grandfather was not a kind man,' she said. 'He rejected me. You will not offend me by anything you have to say, so please, will you tell me about him?'

Dr Glossop looked down at his hands. 'He had his public face for the parents, of course, but to the staff and boys he was sarcastic, even abusive. Yes, to the boys he could be aggressive, not to say brutal.' He glanced towards Addie, then continued, still trying to mitigate some of his words. 'No, I am probably overstating the case; he had to discipline them.' His eyes wandered again, and it was as if he had forgotten she was there. 'But some, if not all of the boys were petrified of him. I tried to shield them when I could. I did my best.' An expression of pained remembrance passed over his face. 'But there are always boys whose parents have boarded them here of necessity. People abroad sometimes have no choice, and when they get letters of complaint from their sons, they hope that the stories are exaggerated.'

'But they weren't.'

He looked at her, reminded again of her presence.

'I do beg you, Miss Russell, not to dredge up these stories of the past.'

Addie hesitated for a moment, tempted to let things go. Could she bear to hear any more unpleasant revelations about Rodney Heron? Then, through gritted teeth, she almost commanded him, 'Carry on, Dr Glossop.'

'Very well, since you press me, I shall tell you. I believe there may have been events that took place in that study that I would rather not dwell on. Acts, shall I say, of cruelty, even sadism - no, that is probably too strong a word - I have no right to assume - but there were other things besides - I can really only guess at this because of the whispers that I heard when I, myself, was a boy. Boys do exaggerate for effect, of course, though some were greatly upset ... At any rate, it was only in the climate of the sixties that these stories started to emerge. Boys wouldn't tolerate this sort of thing - masters weren't all-powerful any longer. Something happened - it was all hushed up by the head at that time - he may have been turning a blind eye for years - and Heron went. The boy went too, and no-one mentioned it again.'

'Was he sacked?' asked Sarah.

'Oh no, early retirement, no doubt a generous pension - as I say, it was all hushed up. And I don't know where he went, but I saw his obituary in the Times just a year or so back, and it seemed that he'd died in London, in some sanatorium, I believe, and it was full of praise for his knowledge, his dedication - the rest, ad nauseam.'

Addie sat quite silent, her face pale.

'I'm sorry, Miss Russell. I'm afraid I did get carried away. Please don't let me stop you from eating your meal.'

Addie automatically put some bread to her lips and chewed a little. She felt sick at the thought of her relationship to this terrible man. She saw Sarah's eyes on her, looking at her worriedly.

'Do you want some coffee? You're not going to faint, are you?'

'I'll be all right. Low blood sugar. I'd better try and eat some of this.'

Sarah skilfully turned the subject to the schoolmaster's own discipline, asking him what he thought about modern day versions of mythological tales. Addie took a few deep breaths and recovered her composure whilst her companions discussed Orpheus and Eurydice. She managed to eat some of her meal, and sipped at some coffee.

Finally, Dr Glossop, now looking more alert, having eaten his own lunch, stood up to leave, and turned to Addie to apologise once again.

'I can only assure you that I feel sure that your own genetic inheritance must have come from your charming grandmother - and, of course, possibly Dr Heron's personality was a product of some dreadful traumas in his own life. Why in that very year ...' He stopped.

'What happened?' asked Addie.

'Addie,' said Sarah warningly.

'Well.' He hesitated.

'Yes ...?'

He sat down again, speaking in hushed tones.

'I'm afraid your grandmother, Dorothy, died from an accidental overdose of sleeping tablets.'

'Oh God, no,' muttered Sarah.

'Accidental?' echoed Addie through clenched teeth.

The schoolmaster looked down. 'That's what they said at the time. One can't be sure, I suppose. It was said she was in a lot of pain. She'd fallen down some stairs - or so I heard - and she was badly bruised. And there had been some bad news about her daughter - your mother. So she might well have had difficulty in sleeping. Dr Heron was mortified. I remember him on his knees, sobbing at the graveside ...'

Addie felt a single tear slide down her face that she struggled to control. She had no doubt that if Rodney Heron was as bad as Dr Glossop was implying, Dorothy, a charming and gracious woman according to him, must have found living with Rodney an ordeal. Heaven knows why she had stayed with him.

'Why?' she asked. 'Why did she put up with him?'

'I suppose there was no real escape for her. She had no training, as far as I know. She wasn't really qualified for anything. Married women were rather dependent then. Of course, after the war there was a lot of propaganda about women staying at home and looking after their children.'

'And Adrienne - what happened to her?'

'I believe she was away at school or university. I never saw her except as a baby. It's a pity Dr Charlton isn't around.'

'Dr Charlton. Is he another master?'

'No, he's the GP. He lives in the village. And I have a feeling that, since he took over the practice from his own father, he would remember the family. His father certainly knew Dorothy. But he's away on holiday - in America, if I'm not mistaken.'

'Perhaps we can contact him at some other time,' said Sarah.

The old man looked straight at Addie. 'Miss Russell, forgive me. I should not have started this conversation. I did not give sufficient thought for your feelings. Perhaps after all, you should now let things rest.'

Addie nodded, for the moment barely able to speak. She

might need a month to digest the information she'd received. She certainly did not need any more at this moment. Except for one thing.

'Where was Dorothy buried? I'd like to put some flowers on the grave.'

They walked silently through the churchyard, which they had visited only this morning. Addie had some fresh flowers in her arms. Any stranger seeing the young women would have imagined they had only just experienced a family death. They wandered around searching, until Sarah gave a low call.

'Here, Addie.'

There was the stone, obscured by grasses and simply marked:

Dorothy Ann Heron
Died 28th February 1965
Aged 49
Beloved wife of Dr Rodney Heron

'Sarah!'

'Yes?'

'That's only three weeks after my birth - and my mother's death. It must have been because of Adrienne.'

'It was the last straw - she couldn't take any more,' said Sarah.

Addie placed the flowers on the grave and the two girls turned and silently walked away.

Chapter 9: Researching the Tree

Addie was silent as they started the drive back to Surrey. Throughout most of her life she had had a mental picture of the Herons - an amalgam of all the elderly British people she had seen in films and read about in books. Somehow she had displaced them into the early part of the century, so that in her mind they had become more Victorian and at the same time more aristocratic than was likely to be accurate. They had become a single entity, snobbish and cold, rejecting her, and her wayward mother too, even in death. Dorothy's letters had immediately dispelled that illusion, and now this elderly, garrulous schoolmaster had drawn a new picture of Rodney Heron that she could never have imagined. To have been snobbish and cold alone would not after all, have been so bad. But to have been an abuser of the vulnerable, and from a position of power - the highest authority in the school during the war years - what could possibly be worse?

The quiet of the journey home was in marked contrast to the almost non-stop conversation of the outward journey. Sarah was obviously uncomfortable, fidgeting in her seat, adjusting her sunglasses and fiddling with the rear view mirror. After a while, she turned the radio on and then off again.

'It's okay,' Addie said, and Sarah switched the radio to a pop station, with the volume down. But as the countryside turned to interminable motorway, the unwavering cheerfulness of the music began to affect Addie's mood. When one of her particular favourites came on air, after humming to herself for a few minutes, she finally spoke.

'I don't know which was worse - finding out that he was such a shit - or feeling so desperately sorry for her. Could anyone be in any doubt that she killed herself?'

'I bet no-one let on, though - hushed it up, as he said - took too many sleeping tablets because she was in pain - a conspiracy of silence - all the establishment men. Even the old doctor, no doubt.'

In her anger at the men, Sarah put her foot on the accelerator and the car speeded up to eighty miles per hour, with Addie vibrating slightly in time to the inanimate objects in the car.

'There's just one - one single consolation.'

'What's that?' said Sarah, slowing again.

'Mom - Joan - has always been straight with me - so I always felt that Adrienne would have loved me - would have kept me if she could. She didn't try to abort, after all.'

'As far as we know,' said Sarah cagily.

'Oh, but I do know. Because she was lodging with Mom and Pop almost from the beginning, and she talked about her plans and how she would cope with me. They told me.'

She glanced out of the window, as the sign for Swindon flashed past. Clouds were moving in, blotting out the blue sky of the morning.

'So what were you going to say?' Sarah prompted.

'Well, they told me what Rodney wrote, and I thought it was awful that he - that they - my grandparents wouldn't want me - didn't want me. That I had to be taken in by strangers - even though of course I never thought of them as strangers. I mean they were my parents, weren't they? But when I got to be in my teens, then I started thinking about this family that didn't want me.'

'And now?'

'Well my entire feelings about Dorothy have changed. She was devastated about Adrienne's death - she must have been. And he wrote the letter - I guess she wouldn't have done that. But she wouldn't have had any choice. Maybe Dorothy was weak - maybe she was powerless - but she wasn't unloving.'

'There's another possibility, Addie.'

'Yes?'

'Well, it was the supreme sacrifice - she wouldn't have wanted him involved in the baby's upbringing.'

'My God, no,' said Addie reflectively. 'To think I could have been brought up by that bastard. Life wouldn't have been worth living.'

'And that's what Dorothy thought, no doubt.'

'Yes, but only when she'd lost everything - her only daughter - her only consolation.'

'And her granddaughter, to all intents and purposes,' reminded Sarah.

'Yes. Well, maybe I was wrong. Maybe she wasn't weak. Maybe she was a pretty tough cookie to put up with what she did.'

They drove on for a while, each lost in thought. Addie took in the unfamiliar names on the road signs. Reading, Bracknell. Getting from place to place seemed fairly simple, even though she was in a foreign land. She had no idea where these places were but, given a map, she could at least have followed the signs to get where she wanted to go. Tracing the route back through her family tree had also appeared simple at first. Now she didn't even know if she wanted to arrive anywhere. Why not just forget it? Why shouldn't she head back home to the States, and give up this unrewarding quest?

And what if she went back now? Stopped this excavation into the ugly relics of the lives of the Herons; the unlovely Dr Rodney and his unhappy wife. What memories would go with her? Yes, the trip would be memorable, certainly, but without any redeeming feature to lighten her disappointment. Surely, if she continued searching, something better would be revealed.

Sarah slowed the car a little and pulled into the left hand lane. A heavy lorry, overtaking, caused the little car to shudder in its wake.

'So are you going to call a halt there, Addie?' Sarah asked, her question echoing Addie's own thoughts.

'I admit it was a blow, hearing all that.'

'So?'

'You know what the answer is, don't you, Sarah.' As she said it, Addie knew the answer herself. 'Old James has given me the most unbelievable opportunity. He's offered me on a plate the one thing I've always wanted - to find out about my family - to know my family. Maybe he even had his reasons. I'm not going to let the opportunity slip.'

'Or let him down?'

'Or let him down. James was my mother's godfather, if nothing else. If I keep going, maybe I'll find out more about her - about Adrienne. As it is she's just a shadow - the lady of my dreams.

She told Sarah about her recurring dream - about the beautiful woman with the basket of roses.

'Hmm,' said Sarah. 'If she was in her twenties in the sixties, I'll bet she was no crinoline lady. You should see the photos of my mother then. Short skirts up to her thighs, nearly. You want the unvarnished truth about your dream mother, Addie? She was a sixties swinger, probably on cannabis or something, probably didn't even know ...'

She stopped.

'No, sorry. I'm letting my imagination run riot. She was probably a lady. Just like my mother.'

'Didn't even know who the father was?' ventured Addie, ignoring the last statement.

'I'm being unfair to her. Let's wait and find out. There is one thing, though.'

'Yes?'

'Why wasn't she on the pill?'

'Principles. Medical reasons. Who knows?' She pondered deeply. 'Where do we go from here, Sarah?'

'We come off at the next exit. Bracknell. And after that Surrey. Home ground.'

'That's not what I meant.'

Sarah grinned.

'And you knew it.'

They veered to the left as the car turned off and took the wide circle under the road they had just left. Addie was propelled against the window, as Sarah took the bend too fast. Her brow furrowed, as she concentrated on righting the car, and she did not speak until they had joined the new road.

'I think the next step is to go to St. Catherine's House. We could look for Dorothy's and Rodney's death certificates. And Adrienne's birth certificate. See who registered the births and deaths - it might provide a clue to some other bit of family.'

'And that's London?'

'Yep.'

'How do we get there? By car?'

'I think the car would be a pain in London. Let's go by train. I'll pick you up at about half nine tomorrow and we'll park at the station. That's if you want to carry on tomorrow.'

'That's fine by me.'

They left the motorway, and the faster roads narrowed into minor ones, cutting through the characteristic Surrey scenery, the massed rhododendrons, their flowers now faded. Addie looked out of the window, recognising some of the landmarks. They by-passed the town centre where early evening traffic was building up, and drove into the suburbs.

'We're nearly home, aren't we? Do you want a meal, chez Addie?'

'No, I think I'll go home, thanks. Mum gets a bit lonely sometimes, and she likes my company in the holiday. Would you like to come?'

'I think I'll take a rain check on that, Sarah.'

Sarah stopped in front of the house and Addie jumped out of the car, and ran down the path, turning to wave as the car pulled away. She opened the door and went straight to the kitchen to make some coffee. Glancing out, she saw that the lawn had been cut.

'I missed Mr Grainger,' she said aloud. 'Well that'll have to wait till next week. Unless I go to his house.' But the prospect of encountering the formidable Mrs Grainger was not inviting and there were plenty of other plans on the agenda now.

She was extraordinarily tired again, and not very hungry, though her lunchtime meal had hardly been substantial.

She knocked up a snack with the minimum of effort and then escaped to bed. All night she was haunted by schoolgirls in mini skirts pursued by schoolmasters in caps and gowns, swinging canes - dreams that would have been almost funny, but for their nightmarish quality. Finally, she herself was a schoolgirl with a tyrannical schoolmaster bearing down on her. She felt the sting of the cane on her legs, and looking into his eyes for some compassion, saw only evil in the blackness of his pupils. Some premonition of what might take place made her scream aloud, and she awoke to find herself sobbing and crying out, 'Mother! Mother! Help me.'

She got up, shaking all over, and looked out on the tranquil garden.

'Oh, James, James. I wish you were my grandfather.'

Chapter 10: The Paper Trail

With the prospect of her London trip, Addie felt ready to face the day, despite her disturbed night, and when Sarah arrived she had recovered her usual equilibrium.

Once on the train, she gazed avidly out of the window, taking in the green Surrey scenery enhanced by the morning sunshine, then the suburban gardens that backed on to the railway and finally the industrial outbuildings, some covered in graffiti, indicating their proximity to London. The train halted at Clapham Junction - the busiest station in England, Addie noted from the signboard - and she saw the tracks leading off in all directions.

As they covered the last few miles, Sarah pointed out the landmarks of interest, and Addie glimpsed in tantalising flashes, between the ugly modern buildings, the turrets of the Palace of Westminster and the pointed spire of Big Ben.

'We'll be at Waterloo shortly. Do you want to see the sights or what?' Sarah asked.

'Look, don't take this the wrong way, Sarah. I'm not rejecting London Town. I'd like to walk around a bit, but not all the tourist stuff. I guess I can come another time, and see the important places properly. But not today. I won't be able to relax, today. I want to see those records, see what we can find out about Adrienne and Dorothy - Rodney, too, I suppose.'

'It's your party, Addie. I'm just the guide.'

'But I would like to see Big Ben. Can we go there first? I have to send a card to Mom and Pop with Big Ben on it.'

'Sure. We can go that way.'

'It's like the Eiffel Tower, or the Statue of Liberty. You have to see Big Ben.'

'As long as you don't want to climb to the top,' Sarah said, laughing.

They took the tube to Westminster and walked all the way round Parliament Square, Addie gazing at the Gothic towers of Westminster Abbey and the Houses of Parliament, then at the white carved stones of the institutional buildings of Great George Street and Birdcage Walk. They heard Big Ben strike the hour, then, reluctant to leave the sunshine, they walked on down Whitehall, past the sealed off access to Downing Street, and the surly guard on duty outside Horse Guards Parade.

They had coffee in an Italian café near Trafalgar Square, and Addie was tempted into the square and bought nuts for the birds.

'Careful, Addie. You're in danger of behaving like a tourist,' commented Sarah, as she took a shot of Addie with a pigeon alighting on her hand.

In the Strand, they passed one or two groups of figures huddled in doorways along the route.

'Another typical London sight,' Sarah said dryly.

'I guess they're moochers? Freeloaders?'

'That's what this bloody government would say. I'm not so sure. I think people would rather work than spend their days and nights on the pavement. Don't you? Anyway, some of these people on the streets have been kicked out of asylums.'

'Oh, really?'

'Yes. There was this policy not to have the mentally ill locked up in institutions. I suppose the principle was okay. But I think it's backfired a bit. Some of them just don't know how to cope with life outside.'

'It's sad, isn't it. The same sort of thing has happened in my district.'

'My mother says London wasn't like this twenty, thirty years ago. But I suppose she sees her youth in a rosy glow.'

'How old is your mother?'

'About fifty something, I suppose.'

'Pretty much the same as my mother - Adrienne, I mean, not Joan - Joan's in her sixties. I guess that adds to problems.'

'What sort of problems?'

'Sometimes I used to feel that Mom and I came from two different planets. Not when I was little. But later. You know sometimes I'd get real mad with myself. I still do. I know what a good person Joan is - I don't need it spelt out. But I couldn't help noticing this barrier between us. She's not part of me and I'm not part of her. And sometimes, back home, the gap felt like the Grand Canyon.'

'I think you've got it all wrong, Addie. There's always a huge generation gap. It's nothing to do with being adopted.'

'Do you get on with your mother?'

'Well, yes, most of the time. But it's not just a case of getting on. There are still things you can't always share with your mother. And getting on doesn't mean we never argue, or that she never finds fault with the things I do. Sometimes I see her practically biting her lips, trying not to tell me not to do something or other. I suppose that's quite exceptional really.'

'What makes you say that?'

'Because some of my friends have fairly major rows with their parents - usually over money or unsuitable men or drink - the same old things. I mean parents think it's their duty to nag, don't they? Even Mick Jagger plays the heavy father these days. They're much happier if they don't know what's going on.'

Addie laughed. 'I guess things did improve when I got my own apartment.'

'Even *my* mum would have a fit if she knew some of the things I got up to in college, last year. Though it helps to have an older brother to carve out the territory.'

They turned into Kingsway and entered St. Catherine's House. Addie had expected the silence and dignity of a library. But instead there was quite a hubbub as people worked away, poring over huge bulky books, exclaiming at the weight as they took them from shelves, some excitedly consulting with friends, or murmuring to themselves as they uncovered information. They worked at high stands, without seats, sometimes moving along as they progressed through the years, sometimes hovering for a long time on one book, entering their findings on detailed sheets or making skimpy notes.

'Let's go for births first. Then we can confer,' suggested Sarah.

'You look up Dorothy and I'll look up Adrienne,' said Addie.

'Hey wait. We haven't got Dorothy's maiden name.'

'Yes we have. Seccombe. I took it down from the parish records.'

'Yes, of course. Well done, Cleverclogs. Funny her parents weren't mentioned on the gravestone.'

'I don't think that's unusual, is it? In any case, they were probably dead, themselves.'

'Perhaps. They wouldn't have been all that old, though. She was forty-nine when she died in '65. They might have been in their seventies.'

Though the books were divided up into the four quarters of the year, Addie, knowing her mother's birth date, only needed to take out one record book to search for the entry for Adrienne Penelope Heron in 1943. Sarah was not so lucky.

Lowering a heavy volume into the first desk space available, she was addressed by a thin, studious young man. 'Hey, do you mind? That's my place.'

'What do you mean, your place? You don't own it. We're all in the same boat here.'

Addie grinned, amused at Sarah's belligerence, and flicking through the pages, she started working her way through the aitches. Sarah, however, had to replace her book and take another, losing her space to her adversary in the process. It was not until she reached a third volume that she found the entry for Dorothy Ann Seccombe. She noted down the details to present to the bank of clerks that dealt with the various certificates.

'Good thing she had an unusual name,' she commented. 'There weren't all that many of them. And, fortunately, only one Dorothy Ann.'

'We're making the assumption that she was born in the Bath area.'

'Yes, let's hope she didn't come from Sheffield, or Cardiff or somewhere. I'm sure people didn't move around so much then. And she was only about eighteen when she married, wasn't she?'

After an hour or so, they had a lunch break at a small café in the Strand, and they returned there again in the afternoon, when they had gone as far as they could, to drink cappuccino and mull over their progress.

'My arms are aching, and I'm completely cross eyed,' commented Sarah.

'You're a real pal,' Addie said. She meant it quite genuinely. She had only known Sarah for a couple of days, and she was surprised herself at how much she had opened up to her. Back on home territory, she would never have criticised Joan. But perhaps that was because her friends all knew her.

'What I said before, Sarah. You must think I'm completely disloyal. But thanks for listening, anyway.'

'That's okay.' Sarah shrugged.

'I don't make a habit of talking about Joan. I haven't really talked about any of it to people before. Even at school - well they knew I was adopted, but you know how it is when you're in your teens, you don't want to be different. So I made out being adopted was no big deal, and that I felt exactly like everyone else. I didn't though. But there's this loyalty thing. You don't want to admit your interest in this other mother who hasn't made any sort of contribution to your life.'

'Not even to yourself, I suppose.'

'No not really, not until the dreams started telling me how

interested I was.'

'I don't think it's disloyal to want to know about your real mother. I'd be interested if I were you. I *am* interested.' She squared up the pieces of paper they'd been scribbling on. 'Let's see how far we've got.'

'They make good cappuccino. Do you want another cup?'

'I'll have a Danish, I think. I can't resist those custardy ones.'

Addie collected their refreshments, and they continued their post mortem.

'We've pinned down Rodney.' Addie said. 'Even though the old professor was wrong in his dates. He did say he saw Rodney's obituary a couple of years ago, didn't he?'

'Yes. It was a bit of a pain going back to 1986. I thought we weren't going to find him. People seem to lose all track of time as they get older.'

'And we've got Adrienne and Dorothy's birth records,' Addie continued. 'So we'll get all three of those certificates, and Dorothy and Rodney's marriage certificate. I guess it's all interesting. But I hope it's going to get us somewhere.'

'Particularly when you have to pay for each certificate.'

'I don't mind paying for them, but won't they have the same information as the records?'

Sarah carefully wiped the stickiness from her mouth and fingers with a serviette. 'Mmm. That was delicious. Satan, get thee behind me. Let's see; as far as I can remember from my course, the death certificate will have the name of the person who registered the death - that might be useful - and the dead person's age as well. So if you want to do a proper family tree, that helps to find the date of birth. And the birth certificate gives you the names of the parents.'

'I don't know that I care all that much about the family tree, Sarah. I just want to find out more about Dorothy and Adrienne. If the birth certificates give us their parents' names, perhaps James will be down as Adrienne's father. That would

88

be great, wouldn't it?'

'Yes, it would be. But, frankly, it's a bit unlikely, isn't it, because even if there was some hanky panky, I doubt if she would have told the truth to the registrar. Even so, I think we should check it out. Dorothy's more important really, because you know absolutely that she was your grandmother, so this will take you back to your great grandparents. Well, all will be revealed when the certificates arrive.'

Someone sat down at their table. The café was filling up.

'Let's go,' said Addie, collecting up their notes.

'You won't get them till next week. What are you doing over the weekend?' Sarah asked as they walked out into the street.

'I guess I'll get back to James's box of papers. Though I seem to have hit some business letters. They're not too exciting. I haven't dug down beyond them.'

'If you're getting bored, you could always kill some time with us. Come for the weekend. Mum would love to meet you.'

'I can't expect your mother to put up with me for a whole weekend, Sarah.'

'You needn't expect an English house party like in an Agatha Christie novel. We'd all be mucking in. Still perhaps you're right. Mum might get in one of her panics and start cleaning all the cupboards in anticipation.'

'Why would she do that?'

'She's a bit disorganised and she only seems to remember what she hasn't done when people are coming. Well, how about a spot of shopping on Saturday, and Sunday lunch at our house? That's nicely traditional.'

'I'll go along with that.'

Despite her earlier pronouncement, Addie did return to the deed box that evening. After the last letter from Dorothy, announcing the birth, there did not seem to be even the most formal of exchanges between her and James. But other formal letters, of little interest, followed James around the world. Addie almost felt like giving up when, starting on a new pile of letters, she noticed hidden underneath some wordy legal document, an envelope in Dorothy's now familiar handwriting. On opening it, however, she was startled to see the round-formed letters of a child.

Dear Uncle James and Aunt Lillian,
    She found she was short of breath, her hands shaking.
    Thank you very much for the musical box you sent me. I had a very nice birthday.
    Love, Adrienne

The initial disappointment engendered by the simple note to James, and possibly his new wife, was almost immediately erased by the confirmation of her earlier thoughts that there might have been contact between Adrienne and James, a contact that might be continued further along in the correspondence. She looked on, and there at regular intervals, at birthdays and Christmas, were similar formal little letters, addressed by the child's mother, with only the improvement in Adrienne's handwriting on the letter within marking the passing of the years.

Then Addie saw an envelope addressed in a youthful hand, and knew this one was different. She opened it up and, for the second time that evening, felt a shiver of excitement run down her spine.

The letter, dated May 1953 and signed with several flourishes, was on lined paper, the ink slightly smudged in places.

Dear Uncle James, it started. *Thank you for the lovely present you sent for my birthday. I really love the things you have sent me from abroad, but I would rather have a letter than a present. I have just been reading* Daddy Long Legs *about an orphan who writes to this*

*tall skinny man who's her guardian. I have just left home, because
my parents have sent me away to school, and I feel very lonely. I
would love to hear from you about the places you visit, and to have
someone thinking of me now that I am here, away from Mummy and
Dad. I wanted to write and ask you before, but Mummy said not to
bother you. She said she had written once or twice, but you didn't
seem to have much time to write back. I thought I would try anyway.
I would love to travel all over the world, like you.*

Love from your goddaughter,
Adrienne Penelope Heron.
P.S. Love to Aunt Lillian

Again Addie's hands shook as she rummaged through the
box, careful not to change the order of the letters. From here
on, there seemed to be quite a lot of Adrienne's letters, the
postmark clearly visible on some, and they stretched from the
early fifties to almost the mid-sixties. She replaced the letters
without reading them. Tears streamed down her face, and she
wiped them away with her hands, laughing and crying at the
same time. She's here, she thought. My mother. I can get to
know her. I can see her growing up. I can hear the stories she
might have told me, if she'd lived.

Pacing backwards and forwards in the room, unable to
contain her emotions, she thought, I'll ring Sarah. I'll cancel
tomorrow. She'll understand. She ran downstairs to the phone
and started to dial, then stopped. No, she told herself, I must
do it slowly. I must ration them. Just a few at a time. Maybe
they'll disappoint me. I must stay in the present. I must have a
foothold on reality.

She started reading, periodically stopping and day-
dreaming. She imagined young Adrienne at ten or eleven,
missing her mother, crying quietly in the dark dormitory,
hugging her teddy bear to her. Gradually, getting to know the
other girls, enjoying sports, enjoying midnight feasts.

One of the early letters was memorable for two reasons.

Dated 12th June 1953, it read:

Dear Uncle James,

Thank you for the postcard. I loved the animals. I have seen them at the Zoo.

Last week we all crowded into the main hall to see the Coronation on the television. It was raining all day. It was a bit boring some of the time but I thought the Queen looked so pretty. I felt sorry for her because I still remember last year when she was a Princess and they told her the King was dead. Also they showed a picture of the King waving to her when she was going away and he looked so kind and sad. I wish my Dad looked like him.

The next day, we had a photographer here, and we each had a photo taken. We had a picture of the Queen behind us, and it had CORONATION 1953 and ELIZABETH II written on it. We will get four copies and I will send you one.

Love to you and Aunt Lillian,
from
Adrienne Penelope Heron

And of course, she had, thought Addie, for it was the very picture that had been framed and placed on the hall table - the picture which had been instrumental in her coming here in the first place.

She walked downstairs to the hall to look again at the solemn schoolgirl, her braided hair pulled tightly back from her face. Addie guessed that life with Rodney and Dorothy at Long Barton must have been difficult for the little girl, even before she was sent away. Though she must have been at school, away from her parents for much of the day, there might well have been whispers in the community about her father, his sarcasm, his brutality and who knows what else; surely she would have been aware of this and of the way that the boys at her father's school kept their distance. What's more, she could hardly have failed to notice if her mother, too, was terrorised by her father. But then, even this must have paled into insignificance when she was first sent away from home so young. How odd the English were, with their boarding schools, their stiff upper lips, their rigid guard on their emotions. I guess in that way I'm as American as blueberry pie, Addie thought wryly and, with a moment of nostalgia, remembered Joan trying to teach her to make pastry at ten or eleven. She recalled the warmth of the kitchen and the warmth of the love that surrounded her. What a different life she had led from Adrienne and how lucky she was to have been adopted by Joan and Tony. She would call Joan in the morning, before she went off for lunch with Sarah and her mother.

She did not return again to Adrienne's letters that night. The sense of urgency had left her, and she felt soothed and contented. Her mother's young life was available to her; she could return to it whenever she wanted. She switched on Radio Three and made herself some coffee. As she sat there, with the daylight ebbing away outside and the quiet music in the background, she was filled with a sense of peace.

Addie Russell's Family Tree

29th June 1991

Dr Rodney Heron = Dorothy Ann Seccombe (1934)
(Schoolmaster, Marsh House)   (b. 1916, died 28th
(died 1986)   February 1965)

|

Adrienne Penelope Heron b. May 1943 = ?
                    (died 7th February 1965)

|

Addie (Russell) b. 6th February 1965
        (Adopted by Joan and Tony Russell)

Chapter 11: Unfair Dismissal

Despite her delight at having found the letters from Adrienne, the knowledge of what her real family was like hovered like a dark cloud above her, and Addie felt in need of the normality that Joan represented. She hadn't always given a lot of thought to the life that she had had with Joan and Tony. It took a jolt like this to remind her. Not only had Joan given her a loving home, which she had, until now, taken completely for granted, she had even been a mother figure to Adrienne, during Adrienne's few months' stay in the United States.

True Joan was a bit old fashioned in some ways - she was traditional; probably rather reactionary. Addie assumed it was because she originally came from the south, and had only moved to the liberal East Coast on her marriage. Addie had found her fairly strict when she was young. And, of course, she was older than Addie's natural mother. This probably accounted for the divide that had developed between them as Addie moved towards adulthood. But somehow, from this distance, all their differences seemed rather trivial.

At mid-morning, Addie glanced at the clock and went to the phone. She had waited long enough. Now she wanted very much to hear the warmth and kindness that was always present in Joan's voice.

She guessed that she would find Joan in the kitchen on Sunday morning when she telephoned, since Joan's homely attitudes extended to cooking, and she spurned the convenience food philosophy. Joan answered the phone almost immediately, her pleasure obvious when Addie greeted her.

'Honey! It's so good to hear you.'

'And you too, Mom.'

'I tried to call you a few times, but you were out.'

'I've been all over the place. It's been great.'

'The first time, a woman answered. She was a real grouch. And I couldn't understand a word she was saying.'

'You must mean Mrs Grainger. Did you give her a message?'

'Honey, it was too much like hard work. I said I'd call again.'

'What time is it in Newton?'

'It's only eight o'clock. Jason's just thrown the papers on the front porch, and I was making waffles. How's it all going there?'

'I've found out a lot about my folks. I guess some of them weren't much to write home about, Mom. Some of the English are kinda weird.'

'Sure, I know that.'

'I guess it made me think how lucky I was you took me on.'

'Addie. You don't have to think like that. We were the lucky ones. I've never had a day's regret.'

'How's Pop?'

'Missing his little girl, I guess. But he's okay.'

'I'm sorry if I've been a pain, sometimes.'

'I guess most families have their ups and downs. You were no different from the other kids.'

Joan was getting to sound a bit emotional. Addie brought the conversation down to earth.

'You said you tried to call me. Has something happened?'

'I had Lloyd on the phone last week. He wanted your number. He says he needs you back at the office. I said I'd get you to call him.'

'Why didn't you give him the number?' Addie said irritated, despite herself.

'I didn't know if you'd want to talk to that louse. It's bad enough you work for him.'

Addie knew Joan's feelings on that score. No wonder she'd delayed the phone call. She must have been torn, wanting Addie to have a reason to come home, but not wanting her to go back to Lloyd's firm. Addie herself had found it difficult to stay on, after what had happened. But her career was important to her, and the job was a good one with a salary that a lot of young women would have difficulty in achieving.

She'd have to ring him today. Even though it was Sunday.

Joan was still talking. There was trepidation in her voice, as she said, 'Just how long are you going to stay there, Addie?' It was too big a subject to discuss now. Instead Addie resorted to the trivia of the past few days.

'I don't know, Mom. There's a lot I like here. I have this friend, Sarah, and we went shopping yesterday and bought some clothes in the local town here. Guildford, it's called. They've kept the original cobbles, and I liked the atmosphere. There was a cute old clock hanging in the main street - from the 17th century, Sarah says. Oh and she's invited me for Sunday lunch today. She's coming to pick me up at twelve thirty.'

'You know I saw one of your friends last week. Marina. From Burntwood High. She was a cheer-leader with you, wasn't she?'

'Yes. She was.'

'She's having a baby shower next week. She lives quite near. I guess her folks are lucky she didn't move away.'

Addie ignored the heavy hint. 'I guess so, Mom. Look I'm gonna have to ring Lloyd before I go to lunch. I'll call you soon, when I see how things are shaping up. Kiss Pop for me.'

'Bye, Honey.' Joan said, with a sigh, and Addie could tell that she was a little sad and fearful - just in case what was on offer here in England was going to tempt Addie away from her birthplace.

The phone rang and rang. Addie hung on. It was still early for Lloyd - he wasn't the type to be out on the golf course. She knew where he'd be on a Sunday morning. In fact, if he had a woman with him, he'd switch off the bedroom phone. It wasn't an ideal situation - she'd much rather speak to him at the office - but she couldn't leave it till tomorrow. She didn't want this conversation with Lloyd hanging over her.

Eventually, a woman answered. She had a hint of a foreign accent, and more than a hint of irritation in her voice.

'Lloyd Henderson's apartment.'

'This is Addie Russell. Could I talk with Lloyd, please? He's been trying to get hold of me.'

'Oh, really,' came the reply, overlaid with sarcasm.

Another minute passed. Transatlantic call. Addie wondered how much it would cost her. She hadn't begrudged the call to Joan, but this was different. She could see Lloyd in her mind's eye, putting on his dark red silk dressing gown; combing his hair. He liked to be in total control of any situation. And it helped to wrong foot the other person, too. Finally he came to the phone.

'Addie. Why didn't you call me back earlier? I spoke to your mother nearly a week ago.'

'I only heard today, Lloyd. I've been travelling around.'

'I've got a really good project for you to work on. It's right up your street. You know you're my favourite copywriter.'

He couldn't resist the slight ambiguity - the sexual innuendo - even with another woman around.

'Cut the crap, Lloyd. Is that all you've got to say?'

'There's only one thing to say. How soon can you get back?'

'A few weeks, I guess.'

'This is serious, Addie. I'm talking days not weeks. Lorenzo Diaz want a completely new look for their autumn advertising campaign. I can give you till Wednesday.'

'No way. I've got four weeks' leave due. You know that.'

'Well, I've changed my mind, Addie. That's a man's prerogative, just as much as a woman's. I need someone now. And if it's not you, I'll have to use someone else. I can't put it more clearly than this. If you're not back at your desk in three days' time, you can kiss goodbye to your job.'

'You can't fire me just like that. I've done nothing wrong.'

'Well, you have a remedy. When you get back from your extended vacation, you can sue me. I'm sure we could spend many pleasant hours in court, with the entire judiciary speculating on whether you got into my bed to further your career. My, how accommodating you were in those days. I'm sure they'd be fascinated.'

'You son of a bitch, Lloyd. How can you blackmail me like this, after everything we were to each other? I loved you then. You took everything you could from me and you're still doing it.'

'You are still such a romantic, Addie. It's a hard world, you know. I thought I'd taught you that. Come back now, or you're out. This is business.'

Another voice very close to the phone, said, 'Darling, are you coming back to bed? I'm getting cold with only my teddy to keep me warm.'

Even now, it hurt to think of him with another woman.

'I'm not coming back,' Addie said. 'You can stick your job - up your ass.'

Chapter 12: Happy Families

Addie was reflective as she got into Sarah's car. Now with no job to go back to she was in a completely different ball game. She mentioned it briefly to Sarah, and she was still thinking about it, as they arrived.

'Don't come in the kitchen. I'm in a mess,' said Sarah's mother, as they walked into the house.

Addie glanced in. Chopped vegetables and fruit peelings covered much of the laminated worktop and there seemed to be a surfeit of saucepans and dishes on the central matching table. It was a far cry from Joan's beautifully organised kitchen.

'There was no need to go to any trouble,' she exclaimed involuntarily.

'I didn't. I always work like this,' the hostess replied, wiping her hands on a towel and flinging it on top of the cooker.

Sarah nodded and sighed. 'It's true. Mum, can I introduce you? This is Addie Russell.'

'And I'm Helen Amery. Please call me Helen.'

'You're privileged,' commented Sarah to Addie. 'I always regard it as grossly unfair that other people can call my mum anything they like and I can only call her "Mum".'

'Your privilege is to help in the kitchen,' replied her mother. 'And if you like you can call me "mother".'

'I'll help when World War III is over. In other words, later on when you're not in there. Mater.'

Addie smiled at the banter between mother and daughter. She had worried that Mrs Amery might be stuffy and typically English and it turned out she was informal and had a good sense of humour.

'Come and sit down in the lounge, Addie,' said Sarah, leading the way. 'Would you like a glass of something? Scotch, sherry?'

'Anything, as long as it's not cider. I shall never be able to drink apple juice in any form, without remembering that awful lunch.'

Sarah passed her a glass.

'Mm. That's nice. I guess I should make the most of this. Now I've lost my job, I might not be able to afford alcohol.'

'Seriously,' Sarah said. 'What will you do?'

'I haven't had time to think about it. But I know I'm not allowed to work without a permit. I'm all right for the moment, because of James's money. But I'll soon get through that.'

The sound of the key in the lock interrupted their conversation. Addie irritated, felt herself colouring as Jonathan Amery entered. She had not expected to see him there, though why it had not occurred to her that he would join his mother and sister for lunch she could not imagine.

Smiling, he shook hands with Addie, and commented on how nice it was to see her again. Then he kissed Sarah and ruffled her hair, bringing forth an outraged squeak, before wandering off back to the kitchen.

Addie, still at the lounge doorway, watched him greet his mother, and pondered on her own surprise at seeing him. Despite the facts of the situation, she had not pictured him as part of this household. His mother and sister were both so relaxed, so informal. And yet seeing him now, looking quite different in casual clothes, and observing how he hugged his mother affectionately and stole a slice of apple from the prepared fruit in the kitchen, it was as if he had shed his whole office persona with the shedding of his formal suit.

Aware of the sudden silence in the room, she turned back to Sarah, and more for the sake of saying something than for any other reason, asked 'What do you think of the skirt?'

'Is that the one you bought yesterday? It looks fine. I'm too short to wear a slit skirt, but you've got the legs for it. But you

101

didn't have to dress up for us, you know.'

Addie sat down and sipped her sherry. 'Well, I haven't been out of jeans the whole week and I was beginning to feel like a slob. I thought it would make a change.'

The sound of a raised voice came from the kitchen.

'Are you sure your mother doesn't need help?'

'I think it's just Jonathan pinching all the fruit salad. Mum will call when she needs me.'

'I thought you said we'd all join in.'

'Yes, but if we both descend on Mum now, she'll start dropping saucepans or burning the dinner. She has some kind of illogical method of doing things, and having a crowd in there will just distract her and spoil the creative process. She'll signal when she wants fetching and carrying done.'

In confirmation of Sarah's words, a call from her mother summoned her to collect the heated dinner plates. Then Jonathan came in with some table mats, and he and Sarah disappeared and reappeared alternately, carrying dishes, glasses and so on, and finally, roast lamb and vegetables. Helen herself sat down, her face flushed from the kitchen.

'Jonathan, will you deal with the wine, please, and Sarah, start dishing out.'

'I've seen you in action. I know you're a carnivore,' said Sarah, placing the sliced meat on Addie's plate. 'You can help yourself to the veg and roast potatoes.'

There was a brief silence, as they all started eating.

Jonathan poured wine into each of the glasses and then turned to Addie. 'How are you getting on with the search for your relatives?'

Addie gave a brief resume of their visit to St. Catherine's House, managing to omit the Bath trip completely from the conversation. She could not yet talk lightly about what she had learned of Rodney. She mentioned the pleasure she was getting from reading Adrienne's letters, and saw Helen's face register interest and sympathy.

Impulsively, Addie turned to her. 'I'm reading this stuff, and I have to keep saying to myself. "This is my mother." But as I'm reading it, I'm feeling, she's a teenage girl, just like me. Or just like I was.'

'There's more to being a mother than just having a baby,' Helen said.

'For goodness sake, don't get Mum on a hobby horse - she'll take all day.'

'I can only speak from my own experience, of course,' Helen continued, ignoring her daughter, 'but it doesn't necessarily happen overnight.' She added some mint sauce to her meal. 'It's a role that you learn. I'm still surprised sometimes to find myself talking like a mother. And of course, Adrienne never had the opportunity to take on that role.'

'Mum always sounds as if she's done a degree in Psychology,' commented Sarah.

Helen appeared unperturbed and Addie assumed that this was the way the conversations always went. 'I can tell you that when Jonathan was born, I had to keep reminding myself, I have the responsibility for this little creature.' She smiled to herself. 'I remember when he said "Mama" for the first time. I'm sure it was just a sound to him, as he wasn't yet a year old, but it had an effect on me. "That's me, I thought."'

Jonathan raised his eyes to the ceiling. 'Do I have to be the main event on the agenda?' he muttered.

'Of course, when Sarah came on the scene, it was quite different. I really felt like a mother.'

'I hope you don't mind my being personal, but I guess you are about the same age as Adrienne,' Addie ventured. 'Would you mind if I ask you something?'

'You can ask. I can't guarantee to reveal all the secrets of my youth.'

'Sarah and I were wondering how it was that she wasn't on the pill. We felt it might have been rather irresponsible of her.'

'Are you asking if I was on the pill?'

Addie felt herself blushing.

'I didn't mean to be that personal. I just wondered if girls did automatically. We tend to think there was a lot of - well - sleeping around then - in the sixties.'

'Don't believe everything you read in the papers. Apart from the Beatles and Carnaby Street, I don't remember the sixties as being exceptional. Except of course I got married.'

'Trust you to be conventional, Mum.'

'Well, a lot of us were still very conventional. If you were a teenager in the fifties, reading the Agony Aunties of that time.' She paused seeing Addie's puzzled expression. 'You know - the advice columns.'

Addie smiled her understanding - '"Agony Auntie" - oh, I love that - we'd call her a "Dear Abby".'

'Well in my teens, they were Evelyn Home and Mary Grant - I used to curl up with my mother's magazines - *Woman's Own* and *Woman* - just to read the problems. And some of them really left you guessing – "Jane, I cannot give you a detailed explanation on these pages. Please write again with a stamped addressed envelope."' She stopped talking and looked at her audience. 'Sorry, I've lost the thread.'

'Probably just as well,' said Jonathan. 'Is there any more lamb?'

'Yes, you'll have to carve it off the joint. Oh yes, I remember, I was saying, if you grew up with their advice - well, they were rather prim and proper ladies, not at all like Anna Raeburn and so on - they were always saying things like "Don't sleep with your boyfriend, or he won't respect you." You can't help being influenced by reading that over and over again. They put the fear of God into me.'

'Oh come on, Mum, I can't believe that everyone was so chaste.'

'Well no, they tended to start out with good intentions, but then they got caught out. You have to bear in mind that the pill only came in during the sixties - it was an unknown

104

quantity - and not suitable for everyone from a health point of view. A couple of my friends did become pregnant - well one of them, Mary Sylvester, you wouldn't know her, we lost touch - well, her wedding - morning dress, three bridesmaids, the works - and she could barely get into her wedding dress. But we all went through the pretence that everything was normal. And one of my old school friends, she thought she was pregnant and nearly went off to Denmark or somewhere for an abortion. Luckily, it was a false alarm.'

'Hang on, Mum, that doesn't tie in with what you're saying. If they got pregnant, they must have been sleeping around.'

Jonathan returned with a plate of meat and placed it in the centre of the table.

'No, on the contrary, it was usually the regular boyfriend. And as I say, they were full of good intentions - the path to Hell - they weren't going to sleep with their boyfriends - that's why they didn't take precautions.'

She offered the plate around the table, before taking another slice herself.

'It sounds like the dark ages, not the sixties,' said Sarah, shaking her head.

'Do you read, Addie?' Helen asked.

'I majored in Literature.'

'Well, read Kingsley Amis, *Take a Girl Like You*. That says it all. Mind you, that was the end of the fifties - a sort of watershed period. The whole book's about little Jenny Bunn trying to stay a virgin - and failing.'

'I think there's something rather refreshing about that,' commented Jonathan, who had said nothing during the discussion.

'Refreshing! Oh God, Jonathan. Get real.'

'I mean about the innocence. The idea of a young girl looking for her one true love. Women are so cynical now by comparison.'

Addie turned to look at him to see if he meant it, and thought she saw the suspicion of a wink.

'Your double standards just appal me,' Sarah exclaimed. 'It was all right I suppose for the men to have it off with all these innocent girls and leave them literally holding the baby.'

'I think you're the one who should "get real", Sarah. Despite the pill, despite legal abortion, there are still numerous young girls literally "holding the baby."'

'I must apologise for my children,' Helen said, turning to Addie, who noted with amusement how Jonathan winced at the word 'children'. 'They're not really angry with each other, but they do have a habit of arguing at the top of their voices, as if shouting at each other might right all the wrongs of the world.'

'Jonathan's trouble is that he's the innocent in this big wide wicked world,' commented Sarah tartly, 'as his dealings with Tibby Plowright demonstrate.'

Jonathan's face lost its half smile and he glared angrily at Sarah.

'Sarah,' chided their mother.

'Aren't I allowed to mention her?'

'Frankly, I'd rather keep her out of the conversation,' Jonathan said.

'I just wondered how things were going with the flat.'

'I don't know why you're so interested.'

'She was my friend once.'

'And then you dropped her. So can we do the same?'

'Yes, but what about paying for the flat?'

'For Heaven's sake, Sarah. Why are we having this inquisition?'

'I don't like to see her taking you for a ride.'

'Don't meddle in things you don't understand, Sarah. It just happens to be the most sensible thing for me to do, until the market picks up and we can sell the flat. Neither of us wants to make a loss on the property. Now can we please change the subject?'

'Don't tell me I don't understand. I ...'

'For Heaven's sake, Sarah, will you shut up?' Helen said, her expression becoming more irritated. 'You're being deliberately provocative. I don't want family meals spoiled by bickering. You know how your father always hated that.'

Sarah clamped her mouth shut tightly, and looked down at the table, obviously hurt by the mention of her father. Helen got up and said to Jonathan, 'I need some pudding plates down. They're at the top of the cupboard. Could you help me?'

He followed her into the kitchen, and Addie said tentatively to Sarah, 'This is very embarrassing for me. Look, I don't want to interfere, but aren't you coming on a bit strong? I mean, he's your brother, for goodness sake, not your child. First you warn me off. Now you're getting at him about the girlfriend.'

'I just don't like to see him hurt.'

'Sarah, you're the one doing the hurting. You're out-nagging your mother, not that your mother was nagging, I mean you're out-nagging any mother. You can't organise a grown man's life.'

Sarah carefully examined her fingernails without looking up. 'I know I'm being a cow,' she said. 'I can't help myself, sometimes. I do want him to be happy. I'm really fond of him and concerned for him too, since Dad died. Like, at the moment, he's the most important man in both our worlds - Mum and me, I mean. I suppose I feel a bit guilty about the fact he met Tabitha through me, and if he was finished with her, it would let me off the hook.'

'I'm sure he doesn't feel that way, Sarah. People have to take responsibility for their own actions. And if Jonathan's the main man in your life, why don't you go and find yourself another one? You can't be possessive about your own brother. You're going to get mad at any woman he gets involved with, whatever she's like.'

Jonathan returned with the plates, still scowling.

'Sorry, Jonny,' murmured Sarah, putting on a contrite baby voice. 'Got carried away.'

'The trouble with you is you just don't know when to stop.' His face did not lose its frown. 'And don't call me Jonny.'

'Oh, don't get all prickly with me. I've said I'm sorry.'

Helen came in carrying a large plate. 'I hope you like this.' she said to Addie. 'I've tried my hand at an American-style cheesecake in your honour. There's fruit salad as well, if Jonathan hasn't scoffed the lot.'

Addie took a large portion of cheesecake.

'This is great,' she commented. 'I could be sitting in the deli back home. I've tried the frozen ones a couple of times, but the picture on the outside of the pack is the best part.'

'How do you eat so much and stay so slim?' Sarah asked. 'That's completely unfair.'

'Well, back home, I used to work out at the gym. But mainly I went jogging two or three times a week, first thing in the morning. We've been rushing around so much, I've missed that, and I guess I'll start up again.'

'Oh what a terrible idea,' commented Sarah. 'Don't ask me to join you.'

'No-one would - the vibrations might crack the M25 again,' commented Jonathan, his good humour apparently restored.

'Better than being blinded by your iridescent cycling shorts,' Sarah retorted.

'Do you really cycle, Jonathan?' Addie asked, not sure how seriously to take the teasing exchanges.

'If I'm not going off somewhere, I sometimes cycle to the office. You can get very tense sitting there all day, dealing with legal niceties. It's a good way of unwinding.'

Addie remembered how irritably he had spoken to her on the telephone a few days previously. He was certainly more relaxed today, in spite of the verbal fencing with Sarah, which after all, didn't seem to amount to very much. She took a sly look at his grey eyes, which she had found attractive the first time they met, and thought of James, and Meera's description of his clear blue eyes and silver hair. There was something striking and attractive about some Englishmen, she thought.

'What's that smell?' Sarah said, wrinkling her nose, and putting a forkful of cheesecake back on her plate.

'Smells like ...' Jonathan stopped eating and sniffed the atmosphere.

'Something burning,' finished Sarah, leaping up and heading for the kitchen.

'Oh no, not the saucepan,' Helen wailed, closely following her.

'Aren't you going ...?' Addie asked Jonathan.

'Happens all the time,' Jonathan replied. 'Mum will leave the gas on under saucepans. I only go if it's chip pan fires and burnt tea towels. At least we've finished the vegetables. I do hate being served up with disguised, scorched Brussels sprouts.'

Addie laughed. 'I shouldn't laugh. I'm sorry. I've enjoyed coming here today. Your family's, well, so human. After what we heard in Bath, I began to think that all families were made up of dirty minded sadistic old men and neurotic women.'

Jonathan looked puzzled. 'I thought things were going well.'

'I didn't want to talk about Bath, but it seems that my grandfather - Rodney, I mean - battered his wife and screwed around with little boys. His wife committed suicide.'

She hadn't realised how just saying it would affect her; her mouth distorted and the last words came out in a sob.

'I'm so sorry,' he said, and put his hand briefly on her shoulder. 'What a terrible thing for you to find out.'

He's quite kind, she thought; the bad temper doesn't amount to all that much, after all. I don't think he's a bastard - not like Lloyd. He's just moody sometimes, like Sarah said.

The telephone rang in the hall. Sarah's voice could be heard, first neutrally stating the number, then in a very sarcastic voice, saying, *'Hallo*. How are *you*?' and finally coldly, 'Yes. He's here. I'll get him.'

She came back into the room. 'We saved the saucepan. It hadn't burned through. You're wanted on the phone, Jonathan. It's my dear ex-friend, and your ex - Tabitha.'

Chapter 13: Rodney's Wife

'We have all waited all day to find out what Princess Margaret decides,' read Addie. She had been reading the letters from Adrienne to James for the last half hour. She had come in breathless and sweaty from her morning jog, and having showered and breakfasted she had settled down for another session of reading.

She had spent a great part of the previous day seeing Adrienne turning from a gauche eleven year old to a rather romantic teenager. Now, in October 1955, Adrienne and most of her classmates were obsessed with whether Princess Margaret would choose her true love, Peter Townsend, or renounce him in favour of her royal duties. Adrienne was in no doubt which option she would choose.

A rap on the door startled Addie, and she ran down the stairs to answer it. Was it Mrs Grainger a day early to torment her? She'd managed to avoid her for a fortnight. She opened the door.

A young man in navy blue uniform, bag over his shoulder, stood in front of her, his red bicycle resting against the front porch. Behind him, the early morning sunshine had given way to dark clouds.

'Morning, miss. Just thought I'd check this is right. Are you Miss Russell?'

'Sure, that's me.'

He held out the letter. 'I didn't recognise the name. Thought I'd better check. Normally, there's only a few circulars for Mr Buckley. Since the old chap passed away.'

'I'll be staying for a while,' Addie told him.

'Okay. I'll keep an eye open.'

'Thanks a lot. That's great.'

The postman turned away, moving the bag of letters to a new position, as he wheeled the bike with his free arm.

'Have a nice day,' Addie called after him.

It would be the documents from St. Catherine's House, she thought, and wondered briefly whether to telephone Sarah to tell her to come over to see the results of their research.

But no. It was *her* family. She would have the first look. She opened up the letter, ripping the envelope in her enthusiasm, so that one of the sheets inside fell to the floor. It would be dumb to lose any of the papers, she thought, picking it up. Better to keep everything together.

Delaying the moment of truth, she ran up the stairs, placed them on the desk, and sat down.

'Rodney's death certificate,' she said aloud, picking up each one and laying it to one side as she identified it. 'Adrienne's birth; Dorothy's marriage; Dorothy's birth.'

Then she turned them face up again, like playing cards and looked in more detail.

Adrienne's certificate held no surprises, Rodney and Dorothy Heron having been registered as the parents by Dorothy. Nevertheless, Addie held the piece of paper in her hands for a moment, trying to imagine her mother's birth, in the turmoil of war.

Rodney's death certificate was interesting. Very interesting. And his marriage to Dorothy provided more information. Dorothy's father, Percy, was shown as deceased at the time of the marriage.

'Percy Henshaw,' she murmured to herself. 'My great-grandfather.'

There would be more information on Dorothy's birth certificate. She glanced down, and laughed a dry, rueful laugh.

'Well, what do you know? I guess it must run in the family.'

She ran downstairs, now eager to discuss her findings, and picked up the phone.

'Sarah.'

'Hi, Addie. How goes it?'

'The certificates have come.'

'Oh good. Is there anything interesting in them?'

'There are some major surprises.'

'What?'

'Rodney married again. His wife registered the death.'

'Oh, that's interesting. Anything else?'

'Dorothy's parents were dead when she married.'

'We thought they must have been old. Do you remember? We said.'

'Dorothy was illegitimate.'

'What? You're having me on.'

'Sorry?'

'You're joking, aren't you?'

'I'm telling you. There's no father on the birth certificate.'

'I thought you said Dorothy seemed such a lady.'

'She *was* a lady. It was her mother that wasn't.'

'Sorry, Addie. I didn't mean that - I mean I thought it was a very upright sort of family.'

'Well, it seems these upright English families had more skeletons in their cupboards than any other sort.'

'What did Dorothy's marriage certificate say?'

'Well, Dorothy's father's name was there - Percy Henshaw, deceased. But Dorothy's surname was down as Seccombe - her mother's name. I didn't notice at first. Not till I looked at the birth certificate.'

'Can I come over and have a look.'

'Fine. I'll get some coffee on ...'

Together they pored over the papers.

'There's no clue about what happened to Dorothy's mother. But the birth was registered by the grandmother. See, her name was Dorothy too. And it shows her address, Apple Tree Cottage, Orchard Farm Estate. Sounds idyllic, doesn't it? Too good to be true.'

'Perhaps Dorothy's mother died in childbirth,' suggested Sarah.

'That would be a weird coincidence,' said Addie. 'Though it wouldn't have been so strange at that time. But you would think that Dorothy would be named for her mother then, not her grandmother.'

'Ada Petitpierre Seccombe. What a mouthful. The French bit must date right back to William the Conqueror. Don't care much for Ada, though.'

'That's probably where Adrienne's name came from,' commented Addie.'

'It's a bit of a dead end, really.'

'Oh I don't know, Sarah. I'd really like to go back to Long Barton and dig around a bit more, some time.'

'Well don't leave it too long, Addie.'

'Why not?'

'Because I've been to an agency and put myself down for a summer job. Data entry, or something like that.'

'Oh, Sarah. You should have said if you were short of cash.'

'I couldn't take money from you, Addie. It wouldn't work. You know it wouldn't. Anyway, you're in the same boat.'

'Okay, we'll go soon. I'll leave reading the letters for now.'

'Is there anything important there?'

'No, Adrienne's quite discreet in what she writes to James. And some of the letters are quite trivial. You know what kids of thirteen or fourteen are like. Practical jokes in class. Dramas with the teacher. She seems very normal. She doesn't mention boys, though. But she likes sport. She doesn't talk about Dorothy and Rodney much either.'

'What about holidays?'

'She's mentioned staying with a friend one holiday. Otherwise nothing.'

'Well, you keep on with the letters, and let me know when you want to go back to Bath.'

'Actually, Sarah, there's something else I want to do.'

'What?'

'I want to visit the second Mrs Heron. I want to find out

what he was really like.'

Sarah whistled silently. 'Are you sure? I didn't like to suggest it.'

'That's unusually tactful of you, Sarah,' Addie said, with a grin, so that Sarah would not take offence. 'By the way, talking of your tactfulness, what happened about Jonathan?'

'Well, you know he rushed out the other day, after Tibby Plowright rang?'

'Yeah. Did he say what had bitten him?'

'Not when he went. You heard as much as I did. But he phoned up Mum later to thank her for dinner.'

'That was good. By the way, that was a lovely meal. I really enjoyed it.'

'Mum was really pleased that you sent those flowers the next day. You're in her good books.'

Addie smiled acknowledgement. 'What did Jonathan say when he called?'

'He apologised to Mum for rushing off. And apparently said that Tibby said he'd hit her.'

'Jonathan had hit her?' Addie echoed in disbelief.

'No, the other guy. The new man.'

'So what happened? Did they have a fight over her?'

'I don't know what happened. That was the only bit of information I got.'

'So Jonathan is still keen enough to be concerned?'

'Seems like it, Addie. It reminded me of that bit in *Private Benjamin* when the hero runs off to his previous girlfriend on the wedding day.'

'Hmm. I can't see the connection myself,' said Addie, looking down. 'Let's get back to Mrs Daphne Heron. If you're going to desert me soon, how about us going to visit tomorrow? Then I can miss out on meeting Mrs Grainger again.'

'You're paranoid about your horrendous housekeeper from hell, Addie! Where did you say Daphne lives? Is it another

London trip?'

'No. Rodney died in London. But Daphne comes from some place called Purley. Do you know it?'

'Yes. It's near Croydon. I think we'd best go by car. Are we just going to turn up? Without warning?'

'No, I guess it would be better if I give her a call. How do I get her number?'

'From Directory Enquiries, unless she's ex-directory. We can sort that out this afternoon. How about some lunch? What have you got in the freezer?'

Tuesday's dark clouds heralded drizzle on Wednesday. The windscreen wipers rhythmically swept from side to side throughout the journey. Sarah grumbled as the windows steamed up, obscuring the roads outside, whilst Addie hoped that the summer rain would not lead to storms, which she hated. But despite the bad weather, and even though they had left well after breakfast, they arrived not long after eleven.

The properties in Purley were quite a mixture. They ranged from spacious detached houses to unassuming semis. Daphne Heron had been non-committal on the telephone, but had made no objection to the girls' visit, and both were curious as to the sort of person who would have married Rodney.

Daphne Heron's home was in a street of semi-detached houses, certainly not at the bottom end of the market. There were some orderly rose bushes in front of the windows, on either side of the short path which bisected a small paved area. Addie knocked on the door and Sarah hovered a discreet yard behind.

A woman of no nonsense answered the door. In her early seventies, Addie guessed, with waved hair, very blonde, and red lipstick. She was shortish and buxom, without being obese, rather well put together, in fact, giving an impression of compactness. But Addie detected a nervousness about her and smelt alcohol on her breath.

'Miss Russell.'

'Yes, hi. Please call me Addie.'

'You'd better come in. Is this your friend?'

'Yes, my friend, Sarah Amery. I guess you're Mrs Heron.'

'Yes. Pleased to meet you. Come in.'

She turned and led them through the hall to a room on the left. A vase of artificial flowers adorned the hall table, and Addie could see the kitchen straight ahead, small and tidy.

A man in his mid or late forties stood with his back to the imitation fire. His hair was thick though greying at the temples, and he looked somehow too tall, and slightly too distinguished for the small room.

'My son, Julian,' said Daphne Heron, still in the same abrupt way.

The man smiled at Addie and his smile was both welcoming and interested. His whole demeanour was of someone completely relaxed wherever he found himself.

'What a pleasure to meet you, Miss Russell. My mother explained you're the granddaughter of my late step-father. It's quite a bolt from the blue. We weren't aware he had any living relations.' He cleared his throat, and just for the moment Addie was aware of a slightly tense expression on his face. 'Mother wanted me to be here, in case there were any legal matters to sort out.'

'I hoped this would just be an informal chat,' Addie said, suddenly aware that she was being called upon for reassurance of some kind. Searching for the right words, she said, 'I have no claim on Dr Heron's estate. I am only interested in understanding him and his relationship with my grandmother.'

She saw immediately that both mother and son relaxed.

'Mother, we're forgetting ourselves. I'm sure Miss Russell and her friend would like some coffee.'

'I certainly would; I'm sure Sarah would –' Sarah nodded in agreement. ' - and please call me Addie.'

'Won't you sit down, Addie, and Sarah, was it? I hope

you'll both call me Julian, since we're practically relatives.' He laughed again, and once again, the laugh was relaxed.

Daphne brought in the cups of coffee on a wheeled trolley, which she left standing in the middle of the room, while she passed round digestive biscuits.

'What part of the States do you come from?' Julian asked, as they drank their coffee.

Addie briefly described her suburban home town in Newton, and politely listened to Julian's experiences on his own recent trip to America, wondering how quickly she could decently divert the conversation back to her English family. Daphne said little, and Addie noticed that the woman's hands were shaking slightly. But Julian, obviously polished in the art of small talk, moved seamlessly on to Addie's inheritance, and the value of property generally, in the south of England. The introduction into the conversation of James and his goddaughter Adriennne enabled Addie to get finally to the topic of interest to her.

'Did you know about my mother?' she asked, addressing her question directly to Daphne.

Daphne nodded, still unsmiling. 'He told me about the daughter, said she died in America. Then his wife did herself in.' She nodded again. 'Yes. He used to get very emotional about it. I didn't want him to sit there crying his eyes out. I used to tell him to snap out of it.'

'How long were you married, Mrs Heron?' Sarah asked.

'Nearly thirteen years in all,' said Daphne, shaking her head in disbelief, presumably at her own staying power. 'And I knew him before that. I used to let out a room in my house for paying guests - after my first husband died. To get in a bit of cash, you know. Life's not easy for a widow. He came along, saw my notice in the window, and I took him in. Seemed respectable enough. Course, I didn't know all his funny ways, then.' She hesitated, as if she hadn't meant to let that comment slip, but with no reaction from Addie or Sarah, she continued.

'Since he retired, he'd been going from pillar to post. Couldn't settle, he told me. He was with me about a year, and he says to me. "I've got a bit of money. If you marry me, we could buy a bigger house. Better area, with a nice little garden. It'd be a bit of security for both of us," he says.'

She took a sip of her coffee, and looked at Julian, who nodded reassuringly, adding, 'I'm sure that Addie realises that this house represents, to a great extent, your personal investment.'

'Yes I gave up my house when I married him. But a widow of my age doesn't turn a man down in a hurry. As I say, I didn't know what he was like then. I might have thought better of it.'

'How do you mean?' enquired Sarah.

Mrs Heron looked dubiously from one to the other.

'Mother, I don't think ...' Julian started to say.

'Have you seen my fags, Julian?' his mother said, getting up and rummaging through the top drawer of the sideboard.

Addie turned to Sarah quizzically.

'Cigarettes,' Sarah translated in a stage whisper.

Addie laughed in relief, and Julian laughed too, obviously understanding American slang.

'I think you finished them, Mother.'

'Run out and get me some from the machine, Julian.'

'I thought you were cutting down.'

'I've only had a couple today.'

He looked reluctant but went anyway.

Waiting till she heard the door slam, she went to the sideboard and took out a bottle of gin.

'Do you girls want to join me in a tipple?'

They both shook their heads.

'He makes a fuss about it. A woman of my age has to have some pleasures.' She poured a tot into her empty coffee cup and drank it down quickly, before refilling it and putting

119

away the bottle.

'You were saying that things didn't go too well with Rodney,' Addie prompted.

'It's not very nice to mention in front of you young ladies,' Daphne said, taking her seat once again.

'We do have some idea of some of my grandfather's habits, Mrs Heron,' Addie said.

Daphne seemed reassured, and perhaps even relieved to be able to talk of her marital problems. It was obvious from the way she kept glancing at the door that her son had not been privy to all the details.

She leaned forward towards Addie and Sarah and, despite the absence of her son, she spoke in a low voice.

'It upsets me sometimes to think of him. He was a dirty old man, all right. I've never talked about it to anyone. People just wouldn't believe the half of it.'

'I guess there's nothing you can say that will surprise us, Mrs Heron,' Addie said gravely.

'Well, when we got married I didn't imagine a man of his age would be very interested in, well, you know. He was over seventy, after all. Turns out I was wrong. He was very interested. But he was impotent. Used to get very frustrated and start sobbing like a baby. Then he'd talk about his wonderful Dorothy, the mother of his child. It was very difficult, I can tell you.'

She sipped the gin from her coffee cup and looked down at it.

'One day I lost my temper at him. Not that I cared about the sex. Could well do without that. But hearing him droning on about her. It got on my wick. I shouted at him and told him where to go. Then he hit me. Right across the face. Made my nose bleed, the old sod. Then he gets excited and the next thing you know, he's ripping my clothes off. I won't go into the rest of it. But it seems like - him beating someone up - it's the only way to get him going.'

Addie sat quietly listening to the confirmation of Rodney's character, imagining the refined Dorothy suffering this man for thirty years.

'The next thing he's on the floor on his knees, *on his knees*, sobbing again, telling me I'm wonderful, begging me forgiveness.' She shook her head.

'I says to him, "How have you been managing before I came on the scene - before we were married?" Turns out he's been going up to London, going to pros. He's getting a bit tired of that. It's an effort for the old bugger. And it's not just women. I got it all out of him. He nearly got caught in a toilet with a young boy. The boy started yelling and he just got out quick, just before the Old Bill comes on the scene.' She stopped abruptly, as the sound of the key in the lock heralded Julian's return.

He walked in. 'Here you are, mother. Filter tipped. That was what you wanted, wasn't it?'

'Thanks, Julian,' Daphne said, pulling off the cellophane and extracting a cigarette. She pushed her cup to one side, so that the contents were not in evidence.

'If you don't mind my asking,' Addie said, taking care how she phrased the question, now that Julian was back. 'I know my grandfather was not the most pleasant of men. How could you put up with him?'

Daphne lit her cigarette and took another sip of her drink. 'Most marriages are about putting up with. It's only when you're young, you think it's all going to be a bed of roses.'

The telephone rang in the hall. 'I'll take that,' Julian said. 'I'm expecting a call.'

As he left the room, she finished the gin and leaned forward, 'I wouldn't have said in front of the boy. I put on an act - that's what I did. He wanted to beat me - what could a frail old man do to me? I screamed and shouted - made a fuss. He was satisfied. It didn't happen too often. He was an old man.'

She looked directly at the girls. 'I can see you're shocked. But I was stuck with him. There was a nice little pension, and I'd given up my house. I put up with him for eight years.'

The conversation in the hall ceased and Julian returned. Daphne puffed at her cigarette in silence and Sarah commented, 'Didn't you say you were married for thirteen years, Mrs Heron?'

Daphne nodded and picked up her coffee cup again. 'He was a nut case. I made up my mind to get him in a home, and after eight years, I did. He was losing his marbles, anyway, and I wasn't putting up with his nonsense any longer. He spent the rest of his life in this geriatric home. Serve him right. What he did to me. And what he did to her.'

'Mother. Aren't you forgetting ...?' Julian said.

Daphne put her cup down and spoke directly to Addie.

'You seem a nice sort of girl. I'm sorry to speak ill of the dead, and I'm sorry he's your grandfather. But he was a wicked old man. *I* could put up with it. I've always looked after myself all right. But your grandmother - he drove that poor woman to her death.'

'You can't be sure what went on, Mother,' Julian intervened.

'Julian. You don't know the half of it. You don't know what that old bastard told me.'

Julian subsided and Addie and Sarah waited expectantly.

'She had a boyfriend - somewhere abroad. She wrote to him. She wanted to get away with her baby. Who can blame her, poor cow? The old man told one of his little boys to collect all her letters - he had to say he'd post them for her - then he'd bring them straight to Rodney. Otherwise he'd be in for a thrashing - and the other goings on.' she added in an undertone. 'He'd steam open the letters and keep back any he didn't want to go. So her soldier never gets the letters, see, and she thinks he isn't interested in helping her.'

'He told you this?'

122

'Sometimes after ... He used to get very upset sometimes – like, want to be forgiven for what he'd done.' She looked meaningfully at Addie. 'Then he starts pouring it all out. I listened. I listened to it all.'

'Did he ever say that Adrienne wasn't his child?' Addie asked tentatively.

'Oh no. He was proud of the daughter. Called her wilful and stubborn. But he was proud, all right. Kept on about his nights of passion with Dorothy, when he was a young man. More of a lucky accident, I thought.'

Addie stood up. 'Thank you, Mrs Heron, for being so frank with me. I'll leave you my number, in case you think of anything else. I'm only sorry we don't know what happened to Dorothy's letters.

'Oh, I found those.'

Addie stopped in her tracks.

'You did? You have them?'

'No I gave them to the solicitor, when the old man died. 1986 it was. I went through his things, and I found this box. Letters and a diary. The solicitor looks at the letters, and says, "James Buckley - my father knows him. He got an OBE recently. Travelled all over with the army, and the diplomatic service." "That'd be him," I says. "Well give them to him. Better late than never," I says. "I don't need any of this stuff around."'

Addie turned to the door again, her hopes once more receding, and Sarah followed suit. They exchanged goodbyes and Julian followed them to the door.

'Don't be too upset about anything my mother said. People do forget and exaggerate events as they get older.'

Addie smiled politely, but she didn't believe that he was right. He shook hands with both of them, and stood at the door as they walked down the path in silence, past the pair of matching rose bushes.

'What a character!' exclaimed Sarah, as soon as Julian had

123

closed the door. She fished around in her bag for the car keys. 'A bit different from Dorothy, wasn't she? I mean fancy someone like her getting together with Rodney. He must have really come down in the world. I can't see *her* at that posh school.' She unlocked the passenger door for Addie and went round to let herself in. 'Mind you, you couldn't help admiring her. She was a survivor, wasn't she?'

'Unlike Dorothy,' Addie said through gritted teeth.

Glancing at Addie's set face, Sarah said, 'I'm sorry. I wasn't thinking.'

'Every time we hear about my illustrious grandfather, I want to take a shower,' Addie said. 'Do you understand that, Sarah? I feel like walking through the streets shouting, "Unclean, unclean."'

Sarah nodded. 'I'm surprised you can bear to put yourself through it.'

'If you knew how much I wanted her to say that Adrienne wasn't his daughter,' Addie said, aware of her lips trembling.

'I can guess. Is that why you wanted to come?'

'I sure as Hell didn't want to hear a confirmation of everything that Dr Glossop told us. Only spelled out more graphically.' She wiped her eyes. 'And I just hoped that Rodney might have said something to Daphne that cast some doubt ... Dumb of me, I guess.'

'But she did say about James being Dorothy's boyfriend. That's good news, isn't it?'

'Rodney could have said anything to justify how he behaved. We don't know what was true. Dorothy wanted out, and maybe James was a last resort.'

She sighed. Unusually for her, she could not recover her spirit of optimism.

'Let's have a break, Addie. Let's park the car in Croydon and look at the shops. There's a big store there. We could have some lunch.'

Addie nodded, saying nothing, her eyes fixed on the

windscreen and the greyness outside.

The rain, which had barely ceased all day, started up heavily now, the sound drumming on the roof of the car.

'You know, Sarah. I may put the house on the market. Why am I being sentimental about this place? It's brought me nothing but sadness. Maybe I could go crawling to Lloyd and persuade him to give me back my job. '

Sarah touched her arm. 'This is not like you, Addie. Don't think about going back home, yet. What about Dorothy's letters to James? There's still hope, isn't there?'

'There's no sign of them in the box. There's nothing else in her handwriting. I'd have noticed. They're probably lost. And as for Adrienne's letters to James, she's not giving anything away. I might as well read *Jane Eyre*.'

Sarah looked downcast. 'You're just feeling low, Addie.'

Addie smiled ruefully. 'I know what you're thinking. And it's not PMT. Perhaps I just need meat. Let's go and have a really big steak and then look at some expensive clothes.' With an effort, she tried to jolly herself along. 'Chauffeur, lead the way.'

Sarah pulled away from the house, and the pair drove off through the rain.

Chapter 14: Act of Faith

It was sunny again as Addie jogged down the road. Waking up early that morning, the memory of everything Daphne Heron had said the previous day had come back to her, weighing down on her and filling her with depression, despite the sunshine streaming in through the patterned curtains.

I will run before breakfast, she had decided. Then I will come home and walk around the garden. That will make me feel good. I will not make any decision about going home until later.

Yesterday's puddles had dried away. She ran until she was short of breath, enjoying the feel of her muscles obeying her instructions, her limbs moving rhythmically in accord with each other.

She slowed to a stop outside the Indian grocery shop, her attention caught by the newly painted shop sign, 'MEERA'S DELI'. There were tables and chairs on the wide pavement, and in the window a notice in large letters read: 'Meera's Special Brunch today - fresh rolls and bagels'. She went in.

'Hi, Meera. Your shop's had a personality change.'

'Since my uncle bought this shop, I have been trying to convince him that we had to provide something that the supermarket does not. I have been thinking about doing sandwiches or something like that, for some time. You gave me the idea to get in bagels as well. Then when we had some good weather a little while ago, it came to me - why don't we have a couple of bar stools, and chairs and tables outside - at least in the summer? We can offer a snack in pleasant surroundings.'

'And has it worked?'

'It has been very successful. I was surprised how quickly the permission came through. We have had quite a few businessmen stopping for coffee on their way through, and other people who are interested in the delicatessen that we have inside the shop. Uncle has been several times to Brick Lane in London - we know people there - and stocked up on bagels, and they have been very popular too.'

'And you have lox, too?'

'We have smoked salmon and cream cheese - whichever you wish.'

Addie took her breakfast and coffee out into the sunshine, and stretched lazily.

'Good morning, Addie. Can I join you?'

'Hi, Jonathan. What a super morning. Are you having breakfast?'

'I was just going home to change. I have an appointment in London later on. But I might as well have something here before I go.'

He had wheeled his bicycle off the road when he saw her, and now propped it up against the wall. As he walked into the shop, she noticed he was wearing the rather garish shorts, which Sarah had joked about. She couldn't help thinking that the shorts did nothing to detract from his quite muscular legs. She looked at them for a moment too long, noticing that they were covered in dark hairs, and just managed to turn her gaze to her coffee cup, as he walked back towards her. Why the hell was she getting the hots for someone who was only politely interested in her?

He brought his tray to the table and sat down. 'What do you think of Meera's changes?'

Ah, small talk. What a useful function it performed.

'I think it's a great idea. She's very enterprising.'

'Yes, I've been trying to persuade her uncle to let her join a law firm - not ours necessarily - I don't have that much clout with *my* uncle.'

'Has she studied law, then?'

'Yes, she has all the qualifications. But her uncle thinks she's more use here, for the time being, and I think he wants her to get an insight into the difficulties of running a business.

Still, they're a close family. I think he'll give in the end.'

'She makes a good cup of coffee,' Addie commented sipping from her cup. She smiled with pleasure. 'At this moment, I could almost be back home.'

'You miss it.' Jonathan said in a way that was more statement than question.

'You know, I don't normally miss places. I miss the people I love; places no. But now, I miss the feeling of knowing who I am. You know, all the time I was growing up, I felt comfortable with people. I never had problems making friends and I guess I thought "I'm an okay person."'

'I'm sure that's absolutely right,' Jonathan said.

'And part of that was feeling that my real folks - well they were okay guys too. Even if I didn't know them. Now I'm finding out the truth about my grandfather - we heard more yesterday. And it seems I have this terrible man's blood running through my veins. What does that make me?'

Jonathan put down his cup. 'It's the old nature/nurture debate, isn't it? I don't know anything about biology, but talking to barristers, you get people from the best families going off the tracks and, at the same time, you get kids struggling to rise above appalling families.'

'I guess so.'

'If you look at my own family. Sarah and I could hardly be more different. A shake of the dice - a twist of the kaleidoscope - has made us different people from potentially the same genes.'

'But, despite your differences, you're still honourable people, aren't you? That's stayed the same.'

'Well, I hope that's true. But if you take my uncle, he couldn't be less like my father. As a matter of fact - and of course, I'm speaking off the record - I don't think he's been entirely fair to me - holding back on a partnership. In other words, I'm not totally sure that he's honourable, though my father was the most honest man I know.'

'I'm surprised you'd say that to me. A client,' Addie said.

'Well that shows that I've very quickly summed you up as trustworthy, doesn't it?' he said, smiling at her.

She looked down, embarrassed. Since that time when she'd tried flirting with him, and she'd met with a polite rebuff, she'd been careful to keep her distance. Now he was opening up. Maybe he'd gotten used to her. Maybe he just unwound in sunny weather. But she certainly shouldn't read anything into it. Better to keep her guard up.

Seeking to change the subject, she said, 'I forgot to ask you. Was your friend all right?'

'My friend?'

'Tabitha?'

His smile faded. 'She makes a drama sometimes, out of nothing. I should have remembered.'

'But you went anyway.'

He looked at her again, 'As a matter of fact it was something you said.'

'Me?'

'You said your grandfather beat your grandmother and she eventually committed suicide. Tabitha got very upset on the phone. She said Alex had hit her. I felt she needed support.'

'That was nice of you.'

'But it turned out it wasn't quite as it seemed. I should have known.'

His relaxed mood seemed to have left him and he downed the last of his coffee quickly. 'I'd better get going. I've got a train to catch. I'll see you around, no doubt.'

'Goodbye Jonathan,' she said. She watched him as he wheeled the bike back on to the road and watched him cycle away. When he was out of sight, she too got up and now, her breakfast over, strolled home.

She noticed the bicycle propped against the wall of the house as soon as she arrived, and for a moment she felt an unexpected frisson of anticipation - that Jonathan was waiting for her for some more intimate exchange. She walked towards the house, seeing, as she got closer, that the bike was much older, and that a figure in worn blue dungarees and check shirt was bent over the shrubs.

She put aside the brief fantasy, and approached the man. A dog sprawled in the passageway, lifted his head up to glance at her and then flopped down again in the sunshine.

'Hi. I'm Addie Russell. You must be Mr Grainger.'

He stood erect. She took in the thinning grey hair; pale blue eyes set in a weather-beaten, brown face met hers.

He offered a hand, withdrew it to wipe it on the back of his dungarees, then extended it again.

'Pleased to meet you, Miss Russell. Very pleased to meet you.'

'Addie. My name's Addie.'

He smiled an open, warm smile and took a pipe from his pocket, lighting it and puffing. 'I was beginning to think you didn't exist,' he said jovially. 'Only the wife said you weren't sure you wanted me to come. I thought I'd just carry on and wait to hear from you. Hope that was all right.'

'Oh, absolutely, Mr Grainger.'

'And the dog? I always bring him. He used to live here.'

'He's lovely.'

'I didn't know if there was anything special you wanted doing, but I thought I'd just carry on like I always have. Hope that was okay.'

'Yes, that's fine, Mr Grainger.'

'Only if you let things go, it all gets out of hand. You get weeds creeping through, shrubs getting overgrown. You don't mind my saying?'

'I agree with you entirely,' Addie said, running out of new ways to agree.

'I wanted to say, I'm sorry if the wife was a bit shirty with you. She loses her rag sometimes.'

'Really?' said Addie, trying to follow the vernacular, and

130

guessing at the meaning from Mr Grainger's facial expressions.

'Did Mrs Grainger think you'd get the house?'

Mr Grainger looked down and wriggled uncomfortably. 'Well now you mention it, that was in her mind. I said to her, "You leave things be. He's always played fair with me." I'd have trusted that man with my life.'

'Even so, Mr Grainger, I really feel bad that the major part of his estate has come to me. And so must you. You don't have to be polite about it.'

'Miss er Addie. Money's never meant a lot to me. Mr James - he made sure we was secure. He was always a good boss, but after his illness, he arranged for our rent to be paid, as part of our wages, and now the estate pays it. We never have to worry about that again.'

Addie nodded without comment, drowsy now in the warmth of the sun. She noted that Bill Grainger wasn't quite comfortable with her first name, and he was obviously going to call her "Miss er" for a while, until he was used to the idea. But other than that, he seemed a pretty relaxed sort of guy - the antithesis, in fact, of his buttoned up wife. You only had to give him one prompt, and he was off; it was like turning on the ignition of a car. Now he was continuing, 'But that wasn't the only thing. You see, I come out of the army twenty years ago, and the wife and me, we had nothing. I couldn't get a job and I started to get very depressed, drinking a bit. He spotted me one day, and he remembered me from the army days. He'd only just come back to England, and straight away, he offered me a job - and Nora too. He arranged everything. He got us straight, and we've had a good life.'

'Do you have any children, Mr Grainger?' Addie asked, realising as she said it, that she was triggering off another narrative.

'Yes, I've got a daughter. Carol. She works in a bank. And my son, Terry - he's an engineer. They're doing very well.

Course, there's something special about your own flesh and blood. Nora's always saying about my boy, "He's a chip off the old block." And Mr James, he used to say, "Bill, you know I really envy you. Lillian and I - we weren't so lucky."'

'Lillian was his second wife, wasn't she? What happened to her?' Addie asked.

'They were together near enough twenty years, if I'm not mistaken, from the late forties on. Then she died of cancer before Mr James came back to England.'

'Was he happy with her, Mr Grainger?'

'Yes, I think they had quite a good life.'

'I'm really glad about that. But you say no children.'

'No. And he used to make a real fuss of our kids when he saw them. That's why I'm glad you're here, Miss Addie. I know what it would mean to him. He'd set his heart on leaving *Tamar* to his granddaughter. He used to say to me, "She'll turn up - one of these days, Bill."'

'You mean goddaughter,' Addie said automatically.

'Oh no, Miss Addie,' Bill Grainger replied emphatically. 'He knew by then she was his granddaughter. You were, I mean. It was in them letters.'

'What letters? I've got all the letters Jonathan Amery had.'

'No. These letters he gave to me. "Look after them, Bill," he said. "I don't want them getting filed away and lost in some lawyer's office. And I don't want them getting into any other hands. I want you to give them to her and no-one else." He was very particular about it.'

Addie felt the sun burning on the back of her neck. The scent of the roses was suddenly cloyingly sweet. For a moment, she thought she was going to faint. It was impossible. It was everything that she had hoped for. Surely, it was too good to be true. She took a deep breath.

'Mr Grainger -.'

'Are you all right, Miss?'

'It's just a bit hot out here. I just need - Look, I want to go through this carefully. Give me five minutes, and we'll have a cup of coffee and talk it through. Is that okay?"

He nodded his head up and down slowly, his face concerned. 'I'll just carry on with the summer pruning, then, in the meantime.'

'Yes, you do that.'

Once inside, she tried to calm down. She was aware that her heart was beating very fast and that she was shaking. The possibility that Bill Grainger's casually dropped information was accurate was overwhelming. But the idea that he had somehow gotten it wrong was unbearable. She needed to be prepared for the worst option. She went upstairs, pulling off her shorts and tee-shirt, sweaty from her early morning run, and got into the shower, turning the control to tepid. As she dried herself off and found clean clothes, she took several deep breaths, and became calmer. After all, she told herself, if he is wrong, I am no worse off than yesterday.

She went downstairs, put on the kettle and called to him from the kitchen door.

'I'm making coffee, Mr Grainger. Perhaps you'll join me?'

'The wife doesn't like me coming in the kitchen with my boots on.'

'I'd really like to talk to you in the cool, here. I won't tell Mrs Grainger, if you won't.'

He managed to wriggle out of his boots and deposit them at the door and, brushing down the dungarees, finally sat down.

'Mr Grainger, can we talk about these letters you mentioned?'

'I didn't mean to shake you up, Miss Addie. I thought by now you knew everything there was to know.'

'Unfortunately, I haven't come across any proof at all that James Buckley was my grandfather.' She passed him a cup of coffee and the sugar bowl. 'I guess he had a good relationship with my mother because of the letters she wrote to him, and -

well - a special and perhaps very intimate relationship with my grandmother, Dorothy. But other than that, there's nothing to suggest anything different. Now you say there are some other letters, Mr Grainger. Do they really throw a different light on it?'

'Miss Addie, I can only tell you what happened a few years ago. I never read the letters.' He added several spoonfuls of sugar to his coffee and stirred it slowly. 'An old friend come to visit and he brought with him this box of papers and letters. I suppose it would be about four or five years ago. The wife was in that day, cleaning and getting Mr James a bit of lunch. She rang me up and said, "Bill, the Major has had a nasty turn." She always called him the Major - "You'd better come over." He was as white as a sheet when I got over here. And the dog was sitting at his feet, quiet, like he knew something was up. I said "Do you want us to get you up to bed?" and he said, "It's all right, Bill. I've had a shock. Get me a drop of brandy and I'll be all right." I got him a drink and he said, "Sit down a minute, Bill." I sat with him, and his colour came back. I told Nora to get on with his lunch, and I just sat there quietly with him. Then he put down the glass and said, "I've loved three women, and they're all dead. I lost my son. And now I know I that Adrienne Heron was my daughter and she's dead too," and I saw the tears come to his eyes. I never saw that in my life before.'

Addie saw that Bill Grainger too had tears in his eyes. Impulsively she reached across and touched his hand.

'He said, "Penny and David. Lillian. Dorothy and Adrienne. All lost. And my poor Dorothy - what she suffered. If only I'd known."'

'That was all he said?' Addie asked.

'He rambled a bit. Something like "The swine kept the letters from me. If I'd known I'd have got her away from him." I didn't like to ask too much. He had another brandy. It wasn't like him. Then he just sat there and stared into space.'

'But is that all? Didn't he say anything else?' Addie said desperately.

'The next day, he was very shaky. Didn't eat and the wife called the doctor. I've never seen anything like it in my life. It was like he lost the will to live. He got pneumonia. The doctor said that would be it. But Nora wasn't having it. She nursed him like a baby. She fed him broth from a spoon. She wouldn't come home. She stayed here three nights.'

Glancing at the surprised look on Addie's face, he said, 'She's a good woman, you know. She doesn't always give a good impression. But her heart's in the right place.' He paused for a moment, and scratched his chin. Addie could almost see his mind going back through the memories. 'Anyway, he rallied. Course the drugs helped. These modern antibiotics do wonders, don't they? And Nora put her foot down. She told that doctor. "He's not going to die now," she said, "He wasn't ready and he wasn't at peace. So you give him what's necessary."'

'So he recovered,' said Addie, 'And you say he lived for another four or five years.'

'That's right,' said Mr Grainger, 'And when he was feeling a bit better, he was sitting out in the garden, one day, with the dog, and he called me over. He says, "Bill. I want to tell you about my will. It's only fair you should know, because you and Nora, you've been like family. And I'll see you're all right." He may not have used them very words, Miss Addie. But that's what he meant. Then he said - and I can remember it like it was yesterday - "You know I always intended to leave the house to Adrienne. I always had the suspicion that I might be her father, but she never knew. Of course, I was disappointed we lost touch, but I was abroad and so was she. Well, she's gone, but I know from those letters that I've got a granddaughter. Born premature in 1965 - very frail - but I know in my guts she's survived. And this house belongs to her." I knew it was important to him, Miss Addie. I'd never

135

fight against that. Then he told me he'd asked Amery's to look for her; said they'd written to America, and advertised in the papers too. Then he says, "But if she turns up after I've gone, Bill, you keep an eye on her." And that's when he went inside and got the papers and told me to put them away safe, until you came.'

'But why didn't he get in touch with the Russells? My parents? I could have come over. I could have met him.'

'The solicitor wrote to them for him, but the letters came back marked "Not known". You're forgetting - these papers he got - they was more than twenty years old.'

'But if he knew Adrienne was dead, why didn't he change the will? And why did he leave it saying "whether or not she is my blood relation" or whatever it said? What was the point of all that?'

'I don't know what he did about the will, Miss Addie. But maybe he didn't have the heart to change it. Sometimes, I think he only survived those few years, living in the past and day-dreaming; reading the letters from Adrienne, imagining how she might have been, what his little granddaughter might be like - and talking to us about the old times with Lillian, out in the Middle East and India.'

'Mr Grainger - would you mind if I call you Bill?'

'I'd be pleased if you would, Miss Addie.'

'Bill, what you've told me today is so important to me. I'm adopted, and I have no blood relations at all. Do you really think I could be James's granddaughter?'

'Well, in looks, I can't say you're much like him. Your eyes are a different colour, and your hair, Miss Addie. And as for the rest, well when I've known you a bit longer, I'll be able to make a judgement.'

'I hope I measure up,' said Addie, standing up, and taking her cup to the sink. 'Bill, I hope you can find those letters pretty quickly. I really want to be sure you've got it right.'

Bill Grainger pushed back his chair and padded to the

kitchen door. 'I'd like to finish the roses, if you don't mind, Miss Addie.' Balancing on one foot, he started struggling into his boots. 'If I don't spray them today, we'll have them covered with greenfly, before you can say "knife". I'll go home for my dinner, and I'll bring them back with me later. If that's all right with you.'

'That will be fine, Bill,' said Addie, resigned to wait a little longer for the truth.

And when she sat down later at James Buckley's desk, with the sunbeams from the window making patterns on the deep mahogany, she was quite calm. There were, in fact, just three letters from Dorothy, one of them minus its envelope, and a locked diary with no key. Addie, automatically put the letters in date order, noticing that neither of the two remaining envelopes had been postmarked, and turned to the first.

14th July 1944

My dearest, she read.

I have written this letter over and over again in my mind. And now on paper. Will it get to you? Are you alive or dead? I have no way of knowing, and no-one to blame but myself. In my last letter, I dismissed you. After all we had meant to each other, I sent you away to war without a loving word. But there was so much love in my heart.

You must have guessed why I did it. When I wrote and told you of the birth of my daughter, Adrienne, you must have wondered if she could be your child. Now I want to tell you what I couldn't bring myself to say before. Yes. Adrienne is your daughter. You knew, from what I had told you, how humiliated I was by my own illegitimacy. And you must believe me when I say that I only wanted to protect her from that stigma.

Our baby is now over a year old. She is lively and intelligent with beautiful blue eyes - your eyes. At first, I told Rodney that most babies are blue-eyed at birth, though he thought it strange, since both he and I are brown-eyed.

I had to lie about the date she was expected, and I begged Dr Charlton to back me up. He - dear, good man - knowing something of my previous troubles, he agreed. There were occasions - you will remember… that allowed Rodney to believe he was her father. In his mind, those assaults became moments of passion, and he was very proud of himself and of Adrienne. For a while he became almost genial. I thought I could live with him.

Suddenly the situation changed, and this is why I am writing now. He became suspicious. Then, he became once more the tyrant I had come to know in the first years of my marriage - alternately bullying and tormenting me and ludicrously begging my forgiveness, when his appetite was sated. During one of these nightmares, he beat the truth out of me.

You can imagine how I feel. If you can send me any word that we can eventually be together, I will leave him. I have no money, no means. I am desperate. For Adrienne's sake and for the sake of the love we shared, please, my darling, send me some word, or means of escape.

Your loving Dorothy

Addie folded up the letter, and looked straight ahead. I should be feeling triumphant, she thought, knowing the truth at last, but all I can feel is anger and pain. She re-read Dorothy's plea for help.

'Desperate,' she repeated aloud, 'and how much more desperate, when he didn't reply. What must she have felt then?'

She took a deep breath and started the second letter.

Dated January 1946, the restrained excitement in the words was obvious.

Oh my darling,

I hardly dared to hope that I would hear from you. When I heard the news of the end of the war, first in Europe then in Japan, I can't tell you how many times I prayed that you were safe. But your

138

Christmas present to Adrienne gives no indication that you received my last letter, or that you know the truth - that she is your daughter.

She is over two now, my little one, and she loved the toy you sent. We have so few things in the shops for children. Life is still as austere as it was during the worst part of the war.

I can't remember what I said in that letter. All I can say is that my life is not happy, and when I think of the brief period of happiness I shared with you, living with Rodney seems even more of a prison.

If I don't hear from you, I will, of course, carry on living with him. I have no choice. He knows that she is not his child and he makes me pay for it. He humiliates me in every way he knows how, both physically and mentally. But he has made me a promise. That no-one will know, including Adrienne herself, that she is illegitimate.

When I made up my mind to stay with him, I did it for her sake, I promise you. My darling, forgive me, but I couldn't be sure you would survive. He could give us security, and Adrienne would not be subjected to the shame that I experienced.

But now you are safe, I long to be with you. Please say you want me too.

My hopes and dreams for the future go with this letter.

Your ever-loving Dorothy

Addie sat, sombre, picturing the situation. James, still caring for Dorothy after all this time, sending presents to his godchild, wondering as he did so, if she was really his daughter. Longing for some confirmation of Dorothy's love, but receiving only formal thank you notes, first from Dorothy then from Adrienne herself. And all the while, Rodney was opening the notes and extracting anything personal from them, before sending them off. Whilst Dorothy waited for the intimate reply that never came. How many more of these letters could there be? Perhaps no more. Dorothy had her pride. She surely would not have begged a third time for James to rescue her. She would have accepted the presents unaccompanied by any intimate note, as a sign that James was himself not prepared to be involved in the scandal of a divorce case; that he perhaps did not want to jeopardise his career in the army. How painful it must have been for Dorothy to receive the gifts on Adrienne's behalf, with no accompanying message for her alone.

Addie sighed deeply and picked up the third letter.

28th February 1965

My dearest James,

I have to tell you that our daughter, Adrienne, is dead. You have never indicated that you wanted to accept Adrienne as your daughter, but I feel you would want to know, just the same, that she died in America, having prematurely given birth to an illegitimate child, your granddaughter. I have enclosed the address of the kind people who are at present looking after her.

In the circumstances in which I live, there is no possibility of my taking on this child, who may or may not survive. I cannot bring the child to this household, and I have no will or strength to do anything else. I have only recently heard terrible rumours about my husband. He has frequently demonstrated his sadistic nature to me, but if I had known earlier of the way he has treated some young boys of the school, I could not have stayed with him. As it is, I have no will to carry on. The prospect of life with him, and without the joy which Adrienne brought me is unbearable. There is nothing to live for. Perhaps in some other place, I will find my daughter again.

I want you to know, I don't condemn you. The war changes people, and you were always very kind to Adrienne. She often talked of you and your wife Lillian, and I was glad that you, at least, found happiness. Rodney kept his promise and treated Adrienne as a daughter. She went to good schools, enjoyed life, and was vivacious and spirited. She was a permanent reminder of you, as if I needed one. Nothing could take away my memories; they were my means of escape.

Dorothy Heron

Addie felt the tears run freely down her cheeks. What a waste of a life. Dorothy could have been so happy with James. She sat silently at the desk, her hands over her eyes, sharing with her dead grandfather all the emotions of bitterness and regret that he must have felt when the truth was eventually revealed to him.

Finally, when the sun had faded from the sky, and the room was beginning to darken, she wiped her eyes, and went to the telephone.

'Sarah. James Buckley *was* my grandfather.'

<u>Addie Russell's Family Tree:</u>

Thursday, 4th July 1991

Ada Petitpierre Seccombe by Percy Henshaw

|

Dr Rodney Heron = Dorothy Seccombe (1934) by James Buckley
(died 1986)   (b. 1916, died Feb 1965)   (died March 1991)

(Second wife = Daphne Gilpin)

Julian Gilpin
(from first marriage)

Adrienne Penelope Heron b. May 1943 = ?
(died 7th February 1965)

Addie (Russell) b. 6th February 1965
(Adopted by Joan and Tony Russell)

Part 2

Chapter 15: New Friends
4th July 1991

'You should have come over last night, Addie,' Sarah said. 'Why be on your own and miserable? Don't you think so, Mum?'

Helen turned from the worktop, where she had been arranging a plate of biscuits. 'I can understand that Addie might have wanted to be alone for a bit,' she said.

She put the plate on the kitchen table and sat down.

Addie took a biscuit, and munched as she talked. 'I know we knew all about Dorothy, but seeing it confirmed in her own hand - I guess I felt really sad - for both of them - Dorothy and James. I couldn't feel cheerful. I needed to mourn for them.'

'And how do you feel now, Addie?' Helen asked, picking up her mug of coffee. 'After all, nothing has changed. It's only a matter of how you yourself adjust to it.'

'I'm always going to feel sad for them. But I went through all the "if onlys" last night. If Rodney's little helpers - and I guess there must have been more than one between 1943 and 1966 - if they'd been brave enough to post the letters without him seeing them; if Dorothy had gone away with James in the first place; if she hadn't married Rodney. The list is endless, and what I come back to is this. If things had been different, Dorothy and James might not ever have met, and my mother - Adrienne - might not have existed. Or her life might have been completely different, and I might not have been born.'

She stopped talking and sipped her coffee, looking out of the window, as she did so. It was another hot, cloudless day, just like the previous one. This time yesterday, she had only just met Bill Grainger. She had not yet learned the truth about her grandparents.

Sarah interrupted her reverie. 'So no regrets, then.'

'Well of course I have regrets for Dorothy and James, but I don't regret my own life.'

'Have you learned anything else from Dorothy's diary?' Sarah asked.

'Oh, it wasn't Dorothy's. It was Adrienne's,' replied Addie. 'I guess it won't add anything much to the letters she sent to James, but I won't know till I get a key for it.'

'Why don't you break it open?'

'It was probably very precious to Adrienne and I don't want to feel I've desecrated it. Even Rodney didn't do that. But perhaps he didn't care about a teenage girl's diary. What strange standards he had, though, didn't he? You'd have thought he'd have thrown everything away. It was like he was paying homage to their memories in keeping those letters and the diary.'

Sarah finished her second biscuit and, with the side of her hand, carefully brushed the crumbs into a neat pile.

'Addie, you said he kept back the letter in which Dorothy talks about suicide. That amounts to murder, doesn't it?'

'I don't think so, Sarah. Saying she'd lost the will to live didn't necessarily make it obvious that she would kill herself there and then. But in any case, it doesn't tie in with his character. I guess he would have stopped her taking an overdose if he could, but he may not have seen the letter until it was too late. You remember, Sarah, what Dr Glossop said.'

'What - about him being in tears at the funeral?'

'Yes. I guess he needed her - even loved her in a funny kind of way.'

'From what you said about him weeping and begging forgiveness,' Helen said, standing up and collecting up the mugs, 'it sounds as if he was racked with guilt for what he did. He may have been a very sick man.'

'Huh,' grunted Sarah.

'Well, sick or not, I can never forgive Rodney, but I am just so thankful that I'm not related to him. I feel as if a weight has been lifted from my shoulders. In fact I almost called home, this morning, to tell Mom, but then I realised it was too early. I'll try her before lunch, so I won't stay much later, if you don't mind dropping me off, Sarah.'

'I can go that way round to the agency.' Sarah said, standing up. 'They told me to call in sometime today. They may have a job for me next week.'

'That's great. Sounds as if I should find out about my driver's licence, if I'm losing my chauffeur.'

'You could ring the AA and find out.'

Addie was puzzled. 'Alcoholics Anonymous?'

'Automobile Association. I've got the number in the car.'

Addie too got up from the kitchen table, and said goodbye to Helen, before following Sarah to the front door.

Outside the house, Sarah bent to retie the shoelaces on her trainers. Straightening up, she said, 'You are staying longer then? After what you said about putting the house on the market ...'

'That was when I was Rodney's granddaughter. Now I'm James's granddaughter. I'm in my grandfather's house. I feel so proud I want to shout it from the rooftops.'

'Okay, okay, I get the general idea. Anyway, now that you know you come from such good stock, you're going to be brave and have a go at driving.'

She unlocked her car on the passenger side, and Addie slid in.

'I'm sure with all the driving we've been doing together, I'll remember which side of the road to drive on,' Addie said optimistically, as Sarah settled herself in the driving seat.

'Are you going to buy yourself a little car? If so, can I come and drool with envy?' Sarah said, pulling away.

'I have a car back home - and I have to watch the finances. I thought I'd hire something while I'm here.'

'There's a place that Jonathan sometimes uses. Rydale's. Do you want me to drop you there?'

'Well if you could come by when you've finished at the agency. I could call them this morning, and arrange it for this afternoon.'

'If you have time, Addie. It's nearly midday now.'

'I have to ring Mom first. If I don't catch her at breakfast time, she'll be off somewhere.'

'Right. I'll ring you later, to see if there are any snags.'

Addie walked into the house that now felt even more a part of her life - something shared with James, her real grandfather. She felt enormously satisfied, and yet, despite this, vaguely unsettled. It was as if the successful outcome of her quest, which had occupied so much of her mind in the past few weeks, had left a vacuum which needed to be filled with something else. Somewhere at the edge of her mind, intrusive thoughts were making themselves felt. She was used to Lloyd being there, as he had been for months - a wound, at first unbearably painful, now gradually healing; she was used to the sudden surge of physical longing for him which continued to occur, but which she managed to control. Now though, this same feeling was creeping into her mind and her body and, of all people, Jonathan Amery was the cause.

But Jonathan had made it abundantly clear that their relationship should be polite and professional. Somehow, she would have to expunge him from her thoughts. If she were back home, she would throw herself into something completely different - maybe even a new man. Here, where did she go? What did she do?

The phone started ringing, breaking into her thoughts.

'Addie Russell,' she answered.

'Hello, Addie. This is Julian Gilpin.'

'Who?'

'Julian - Daphne Heron's son.'

146

'Oh, Julian. Of course. I'm sorry. How are you?'

'Yes, fine. It was so nice to meet you the other day.'

'It was very kind of you and your mother to talk to us,' Addie said.

'I did get the impression you were looking for confirmation that Rodney Heron was your grandfather.'

'Well, actually ...'

'I know my mother had a little chat with you. I hope you didn't get the impression that she was anything other than the best of wives to him.'

'I'm sure she ...'

'And I wouldn't want you to think that his mental state prevented him from making the right judgement as far as his will ...'

'Julian,' Addie finally interrupted, 'I told you. I'm not interested in Rodney's will. I never was. What kind of a person do you think I am? I don't want to rob an old lady of her house and her pension. But in any case, you're behind the times. I've now found out that Rodney was absolutely, definitely not my grandfather.'

'I see,' said Julian obviously surprised. Then, recovering his equilibrium, he said swiftly, 'Addie, I never meant to imply ... I'm so sorry. You must think me most unpleasant. Will you accept my apologies?'

'Of course.'

'Do I gather that you are happy with this new situation? Has it made any difference to you?'

'Well, you know that James Buckley had left me this house anyway. My mother was his goddaughter. I have to say he seemed a kind and good man, and I'm very happy to find that she was really his daughter.'

'Addie, I do feel very badly about what I said to you. Will you let me make it up to you? I was going to ask you this, anyway. There are some very good shows on in London at the moment, and as a tourist, you really ought to see them. I happen to have tickets for *Miss Saigon*, and I'd very much like to take you.'

His statement was unexpected and Addie was taken aback.

'Why I ...'

'Please say yes, Addie. It would give me great pleasure.'

She still hesitated.

'I'm sorry - I know I must have offended you with what I said. I hope I haven't compounded the offence by my choice of show - it's all about America's involvement in Vietnam.'

Addie laughed, 'No - it's not that at all - it's just that ...'

How could she say that she was reluctant to go out with a man she hardly knew? The relationship via the Herons was so tenuous as to be non-existent, and yet somehow a relationship had been established between them. And he was being extremely kind. In fact, maybe this was what was needed. Something and someone completely different. She pushed any lingering doubts to one side.

'When are the tickets for?'

'Tomorrow.'

'Oh. I hadn't realised you meant quite so ...'

'Perhaps I could meet you in London. Is that all right?'

'Well, yes, I guess so.'

Addie was still pondering over the speedily made arrangements when she spoke to Joan.

'Hi, Mom. How are you both?'

'Honey. We're just fine. How are you?'

'I'm fine too, Mom. I've loads to tell you.'

'Addie, you just caught me. I've just had breakfast, and I'm on my way out in ten minutes.'

Addie relayed all the news in a brief précis to be enlarged upon in her next letter home. Now that she was more relaxed, she could feel an enormous warmth and pleasure as she spoke of James Buckley.

'I feel really proud that he was my grandfather, not Rodney,' she told Joan. 'Everyone that knew him seemed to

148

respect him. He was in the diplomatic service after the war, and he got an OBE from Queen Elizabeth. I feel so good about that.'

'That's wonderful, Addie.'

Joan was less enthusiastic about Addie's date.

'How old did you say? Forty something? Why honey, he's nearly old enough to be your father. Your real father, I mean.'

Addie laughed.

'You're right. I'd better be careful about dating anyone over forty-five, while I'm here. Anyway, he seems a nice enough guy.'

'It's not the Lloyd thing all over again, is it, hon?'

'It's okay, Mom. There's nothing serious about it and he's not another Lloyd. He's just a friend. Anyway, I read the review of *Miss Saigon* in Time Magazine when it came out on Broadway in April. I really fancied going to see it.'

'Well, you have a good time then, hon. I have to go. Write soon. We miss you.'

'I miss you too, Mom. And Pop. Send my love.'

As she put the phone down, she realised she had not asked Joan if she could look out the key to Adrienne's diary. Too late now. Joan would be on her way out.

It was nearly lunch time and she still had to find out about driving in the UK. A quick phone call to the AA reassured her that she could use her current licence in England for the next twelve months - that was well beyond the life of her visa. Her conversation with the local car hire company was fruitful too, when Addie had managed to get past the introductions.

'Rydale's reliable and roadworthy vehicles for hire. Trevor speaking. How can I help you?'

Addie explained her situation and was thankful that Trevor got down to the business without further preamble, though he had a tendency to sound as if he was reading from a pre-arranged script. She arranged to call in later, with her US licence and fix up the insurance.

'If you take one of our automatics, you'll have less to worry about, and you can concentrate on the road,' Trevor suggested.

'Thanks a lot, Trevor,' she said. 'I guess I'll see you later.'

She noted with relief that he didn't say, 'Have a nice day.'

Sarah picked her up shortly after lunch. She had changed into a floral skirt and drawstring blouse for her interview, and looked less tomboyish than usual.

'Well, I've got a job. I start on Monday. So that means any trips we make together will have to be at weekends. When do you want to go back to Bath? Tomorrow?'

'Sorry, no dice. I have a date.'

'You have a date,' Sarah said incredulously. 'But I only saw you two hours ago. Who with?'

'Julian.'

'Julian. You're kidding.'

They got into the car, and Sarah said nothing for a moment. Then, as she pulled away, she said, 'How on earth can you go out with Julian? He's a complete phoney.'

'How do you mean?'

'I mean - well his mother's pretty common, and he puts on this pseudo posh accent.'

'I didn't know you were such a snob, Sarah. In the States we approve of people aiming to move up market.'

But, he's old enough to be ...'

'I know. I know. My father. Listen I'm not planning on marrying the guy.'

'I doubt if he's got marriage on his mind.'

Addie began to feel irritated.

'Sarah. I've got two mothers to worry about. I don't need a third. Let's go look at autos.'

They pulled up at Rydale's, and wandered around, examining the cars.

'It has to be a red one,' said Sarah, whose own car was red.

'I don't want to send out the wrong signals,' Addie

commented.

'You already are,' Sarah said, half under her breath.

Trevor, a smartly dressed young man in his twenties, who looked better than he sounded, soon joined them and gave them a guided tour round the various models. Addie finally decided in favour of a natty little Peugeot automatic, and left Trevor talking to Sarah, as she went into the office to fill out all the forms.

She could see Sarah from the window, and noticed that she was laughing a lot, looking up at Trevor and tossing her brown curls.

Oh no, Sarah, she mentally warned. He's not your type.

She walked out with the keys. Sarah was leaning back against the Peugeot, her hands on the bonnet, one of her bare legs extended forward, so that it appeared to be almost touching Trevor's trouser-clad one. She could hear fragments of the conversation.

'I get the feeling you've been staring at me.'

'When you're thinking what I'm thinking, looking is safer.'

'Who needs safety?''

Usual chat-up stuff, Addie thought. As she approached, they each shuffled into new positions, further apart.

'I'll follow you home, Addie,' Sarah said, blushing slightly. 'Do you know the way?'

'It's just down the main road and turn left, isn't it?'

'That's right. But I'll be with you shortly - just to make sure you're all right,' Sarah said.

'See you back at my place, then.'

'See you,' said Trevor, turning towards the office.

Addie pulled away, and drove carefully out on to the road. She checked her mirror, but Sarah was not immediately behind her.

Driving the three or four miles to her house fairly slowly, she soon caught sight of Sarah's red car, and they pulled into the driveway at the front of her house almost together.

Addie opened the door and went straight to the kitchen, putting the kettle on. Sarah joined her, a smug grin on her face.

'Snap,' she said.

'Come again,' Addie said, pretending ignorance.

'Now we've both got a date, tomorrow night.'

'You're not going out with that smoothie?'

'I think he's rather gorgeous.'

'Gorgeous! I know his sort. He's just like Lloyd.'

'Well why did you go out with Lloyd, Addie? To improve your mind?'

Addie coloured. 'I guess every time I looked at him, I got the hots for him. Just be careful, will you?'

'Now it's your turn to be mother, eh, Addie? You grumbled at me for going on about Julian.'

'That's different.'

'Give me one good reason why, Addie.'

'Because it's completely platonic, that's why.'

'Addie, I don't believe I'm hearing this. How can you be so naive?'

* * *

Addie decided against taking the car to London. Julian had suggested that they met at Charing Cross, and she parked the car at the local station and took the train.

It was the first time she had travelled to London on her own, but it was a warm summer evening, and there were quite a few people on the train to Waterloo. From there, she went on to Charing Cross, and met Julian without difficulty outside Tie Rack.

They wandered through to Leicester Square for a cocktail at Chiquita's, before cutting through Covent Garden to the theatre. Addie, who had imagined it would still have all the fruit and vegetable stalls she had seen in *My Fair Lady*, was surprised to find it buzzing with activity, people taking drinks and coffees outside, in the late sunshine.

It was a good evening. An enjoyable musical, seats in the

middle stalls and drinks in the interval. Julian, though probably around the same age as Lloyd, seemed older, and she felt as if she was with a distinguished and rather attractive uncle. But she found it quite relaxing to spend an evening with a man on a completely platonic basis. In fact, Julian was articulate and intelligent and Addie enjoyed discussing the show with him.

'When the troops left Vietnam - I found that very moving, didn't you? I remember how upset my dad was, at the time,' Addie said, as they had a last drink before returning home. 'It really took me back to how it must have been. And the helicopter taking off was fantastic.'

'I enjoyed the noise and colour - it felt as if we were right there in South East Asia.'

'Yes, and the girls were certainly lovely,' agreed Addie.

'Of course, this theme runs through so many plays and musicals,' Julian said. 'The attraction between the oriental girl and the white man. Madam Butterfly, South Pacific, the World of Suzie Wong. Not that western girls aren't extremely attractive,' he added, smiling at her. 'In fact, it's like choosing the right flavour from a box of chocolates, and finding that a different variety is even nicer.'

Addie made no comment at this. She thought how easily an apparently innocent statement could be picked up and extended into a preamble to something more romantic. It was an interesting sort of opening gambit. It could either be followed by, 'What sort of chocolates do you like?' or 'What sort of women do you like?' But she wasn't ready for this. He was attractive, it was true. But there was still the dull ache left from the loss of Lloyd - and Jonathan - no, she could not even consider Jonathan. Even so, she was not ready for games with Julian. Instinct told her that men of forty-eight who were unattached were not looking for serious relationships. So somehow the conversation was turned to her job - or lack of it - her family in Boston, and she even, probably unwisely, found herself talking about Lloyd. She ended the evening, however, not knowing a great deal more about Julian.

He took her back to Waterloo in a black cab, and they sat with a good six inches of space between them. It seemed that he was aware of her lack of response and it probably didn't bother him. Of course, he might be gay but, somehow, she doubted that.

'I feel very badly about letting you go home on the train alone, Addie,' he said, as they walked into the station. 'Next time you must let me pick you up.'

'Next time?'

'Yes, I do hope you'll come out with me again. I enjoy having a companion at the theatre. I often book tickets months in advance and then find a friend to go with.'

She hesitated for a moment. It had been a pleasant evening and as long as Julian wasn't rushing her into anything more than that, it would be fine. But the way he had spoken of 'a companion' did not suggest that he was necessarily looking for romance.

'Well, I certainly enjoyed the evening. Thank you very much for the invitation, Julian.'

Sarah's evening, too, had been a success. Sarah phoned briefly on Sunday morning to say she was going with Trevor on a car rally. And with work starting on Monday, she wouldn't see much of Addie for the next few days.

Addie didn't mind too much. She was no longer lonely in her grandfather's house. During the next couple of weeks, she jogged every morning, called in sometimes for breakfast or lunch at Meera's Deli, wrote a few letters, including a long one to Joan, explaining in detail how she had come about her new knowledge of the family history, and read systematically through Adrienne's letters to James. Somehow her restlessness abated and thoughts of Jonathan fortunately receded into the background.

Dear James,

Thank goodness, it's holidays, and I'm staying with my friend, Charlie and her family.

Addie noted with amusement that nicknames were in vogue then too.

They're very nice, particularly her father and brother, though he's a bit superior.

The end of term was quite fun. Addie skimmed through the details of the end of term high jinks.

Charlie's brother went off on a march to somewhere called Aldermaston on Good Friday. He tried to persuade Charlie and me to go with him. He also asked me to go with him to a Labour party meeting, but I said no. Charlie said he gets very excited about politics and the bomb, and has lots of arguments with her father about it. I think my father would be the same, because I've heard him say that Britain would be mad to give it up. Do you think that Britain should ban the bomb?

Charlie and I have been for lots of walks, and we went into a public house one evening, when we knew her parents weren't coming back till late. We each had a glass of cider, and got talking to some boys. Actually, you're not supposed to go into a public house until you are eighteen. But I suppose you know that.

Love to Lillian.
And Love from me,
Adrienne

Many of the letters were full of trivia - the sort of thing one might expect of a girl in a single sex boarding school. April Fool Jokes, midnight feasts, occasional mentions of crushes on film stars and male teachers, with the likelihood of romance on either front equally remote. On the whole though, Adrienne didn't sound traumatised, Addie thought. It would be interesting to see if the diary gave a different impression. She had remembered to mention the key in her letter to Joan but, if all else failed, she would have to break the lock. She could not leave an important slice of her mother's life unread.

Long Barton High School
15th January 1959

Dear James,

The last few weeks have been so boring, and now we are in the throes of the Mocks. I'm supposed to be revising, but I couldn't stand it, so I thought I'd write to you instead. Don't grumble at me when you write, will you. I've got to the stage where I know it's too late for the revision, so I'm just going to see how I get on without any - well, very little. Then I'll work in June, when it's the Real Thing!

Of course, when I go home, my father will look at me over his glasses, and say, 'Adrienne, we expected better things from you.'

Today was the Biology exam. Fortunately, I gave that up last year, but we sat in on the exam and revised while others were taking it. Every now and then I looked out of the window. It's a cold day, but quite bright and sunny, and I thought how nice it would be to go for a nice brisk walk, instead of being stuck in facing these horrible exams.

Must return to revision now. Best regards to Lillian.
Love from Adrienne

Adrienne was now more pre-occupied by her exams, and her letters were increasingly skimpy. She mentioned them again later in 1959, when once again she spent Easter with her friend's family.

I've got to know Charlie's brother Richard much better this year. He stopped treating me as if I was completely stupid, and helped me with some revision. The three of us went to see 'On the Beach'. It was rather horrifying - all about nuclear war. Even so, I've really enjoyed this holiday. But school starts soon and I am not looking forward to going back to the O-Levels proper. I may not have much time to write in the next few months.

P.S. Your last letter was so interesting. I would so love to travel to all the places you've been. What O-Levels do you need for the diplomatic service?

Love to you and to Lillian
from Adrienne

From her desk, Addie heard the sound of the key in the lock, downstairs. She had had a cool truce with Nora Grainger, since her meeting with Bill. She had to accept at face value that the woman had good qualities. Her recognition of this did not change the fact that Mrs Grainger's resentment of her was demonstrated by her prickly and difficult manner. No amount of courtesy from Addie appeared to be able to change that situation, and she had planned her morning accordingly. Having run, showered and breakfasted already that morning, Addie had allowed for a slow walk down to the deli and a leisurely lunch in the sunshine, by which time, Nora would have departed.

The sound of the vacuum came from below. Then Addie thought that she heard the phone ringing, and started towards the door, but the vacuuming ceased and Nora's voice could be heard even before she got to the landing.

I wish she wouldn't answer the phone, Addie thought irritated. But it would only cause more bad feeling if she said anything to Mrs Grainger. As she ran down the stairs, she made a mental note to arrange to have an extension phone fitted as soon as possible.

'It's for you,' Nora said, handing her the phone, disapprovingly. 'A man.'

'Hallo, Addie. It's Julian. Who was that dragon?'

'Hi, Julian. How are you?' Addie said, ignoring the question, since Nora showed no sign of attempting to leave the room, but instead started dusting the ornaments.

'Addie, I have tickets for the musical *Blood Brothers* on Saturday. I wondered if you'd care to join me. It's supposed to be very good.'

Addie hesitated. She still had reservations about Julian, despite the enjoyable evening she had spent with him. He was such an unknown quantity, that was the trouble. Still, what harm could there be in a pleasant evening at the theatre?

'That sounds great, Julian. Shall I meet you at the same place?'

'Yes. Right. But I feel very uncomfortable about your going back by train, and I wonder if you'd consider staying over.'

'Staying over?' Addie echoed. What was he getting at? A hotel room? This was really not on her agenda.

'Yes, a friend of mine from the office is a member of a ladies' club in London. It's a very good idea. She can use it as a meeting place when she comes to London and eat at the restaurant, and sometimes, as I say, she stays overnight. I could arrange it for you and you could take the train back on Sunday morning.'

Addie agreed that, in principle, it was an excellent idea. 'But I really think you're worrying quite unnecessarily, Julian. The train was packed when I came back last time. The station was bright and my car was waiting for me. So, please stop worrying about me. I shall be fine.'

The outing was just as enjoyable as the previous occasion. Addie found herself very moved by the show. The plight of twins, born of the same parents but brought up in totally different environments seemed so relevant to her own life.

'You're very thoughtful, Addie,' Julian said, as they came out of the theatre into the crowded streets. He skilfully moved to the pavement side of her, putting a protective arm lightly on her shoulder to steer her through the crush.

'Just wondering what makes us what we are,' she said. 'What sort of a person would I have been if I'd grown up, Addie Heron, in a public school in the English countryside, with a terrible, wicked grandfather?'

'I'm sure you'd have the strength of character to make something of your life. You're a very optimistic person. Your adoptive parents would have been the ones to miss out.'

They reached Waterloo and Addie thanked him once again for a delightful evening. She offered to pay for the theatre tickets, but Julian was adamant in his refusal. She felt she had discovered the perfect English gentleman and was genuinely grateful for the undemanding friendship.

'Then you must let me cook you a meal to repay you for your kindness,' she said. 'Perhaps you'd come over next Saturday. I could ask Sarah and her friend if she'll join us.'

He accepted with alacrity, and thanked her again warmly for the invitation when they parted at Waterloo. As she sat on the train, her mind wandered back to the show she had just seen and forwards to the dinner party next week. She felt quite pleased at having spent an interesting evening, and also at the prospect of entertaining for the first time at James's house. The warmth and movement of the train lulled her into a doze, and she nearly missed the stop, her head jerking her awake as the train pulled into the station. But her car sat reassuringly at the car-park and the night air woke her up a little. She drove home carefully, concentrating hard, still wary of the eccentric roundabouts of all shapes and sizes, which the Brits seemed to love so much. It was not until she was in bed that her mind returned to the forthcoming dinner and she was suddenly aware of an unexpected feeling of apprehension.

Chapter 16: Summer Storms

'Morning, Addie. You're looking a bit down.'

Jonathan sat down beside her on one of the seats outside the deli, coffee cup in his hand.

'Hi, Jonathan. I haven't seen you in a while. How are you?'

'I'm fine. I've been involved in a court case. Sarah told me about your grandmother's letters. She mentioned you were very upset by them. Are you all right now?'

Addie smiled and nodded. 'I am all right, Jonathan. Thank you for asking. It was terrible what she went through, but I can't mourn indefinitely for something that happened before I was born.'

'Has something else happened to upset you?'

'I didn't feel too good this morning. I dreamed I was running through a storm, and I woke up at half five, and it was still banging and crashing outside. I couldn't get back to sleep, and now I have a headache.'

'Yes, I heard it too. I got up and watched from the window. You're not scared of thunder, are you?'

'Storms do make me kinda jumpy. It's pretty dumb, I know.'

'I've always found it fascinating to watch lightning.'

Addie shivered, 'I guess I'd rather be under the bedclothes. Are you having breakfast?'

'I've just got time for coffee before my first appointment. Have you been running this morning?'

'No, I just had a slow walk down here. I'll wander back and chew the fat with Bill Grainger. He'll be pleased it's rained. He's been saying the garden needs it. Then I have to go to the supermarket to get in stuff for the weekend.'

'Are you entertaining?'

'I'm hoping to do a little dinner party. Sarah and Trevor, and Julian, who we met in London. Perhaps you'd like to come?'

'It sounds as if you have the right numbers already,' Jonathan commented, a little stiffly.

'Julian's been so kind. We've had some great times,' Addie said, wondering, as she said it, if 'great' was an overstatement and 'good' would have been better.

'Things are going well for you then. You're enjoying your social life, you're running a car, and of course, you've finally found out that James Buckley was your grandfather. You've got everything sorted out.'

'Yes, of course, though it does mean that Adrienne was illegitimate. So I'm a bastard from a long line of bastards. Let's hope it's not catching.' She said it with a little laugh, trying to lighten the atmosphere, aware that Jonathan had returned to his formal, solicitous solicitor manner.

'Well, just be careful who you sleep with,' he said, unexpectedly, his face unsmiling.

Addie stared at him, taken aback at the implication.

'I'm not ...'

What the hell, she thought, angrily, I don't have to justify myself to him.

He looked contrite. 'I'm sorry. I shouldn't have said that.'

'You're damn right you shouldn't. When I start telling you how to organise your life with Tabitha Plowright, or whatever her name is, then you can start telling me how to run mine.'

'I'm sorry. It was just something Sarah said. Please forget I said anything.'

'What did she say?'

'Look, please, let's drop it. You ask her when you see her. I have to go anyway. I'm sorry. I didn't mean to upset you.'

She was angry. She wanted to know what Sarah had said, and he obviously wasn't going to tell her. But his sudden contrite smile diffused her anger, and she relented.

'Okay, Jonathan,' she said, resignedly. 'See you soon.'

'Yes,' he said. 'Perhaps we could ...' He hesitated.

'Could what?'

'Could ... Oh, it's not important. It was just something I wanted to sort out about the will. There's no rush.'

'Okay. Bye then.'

That wasn't what he was going to say. She could tell he'd changed his mind. Had he wanted to date her? And if so, why didn't he? Professional ethics? Julian? Damn.

She finished her breakfast and strolled back home. The atmosphere was only slightly cooler now, despite the storm, though the deep puddles at the side of the road revealed the extent of it, and clouds still hung low overhead.

What was it about Jonathan, she thought. The eyes, the reserved manner, the sudden changes of mood. They were beginning to get to her again. Yet he was nothing like Lloyd. Nothing at all. Lloyd had been a callous and manipulative bastard of the first order. She had been unprepared for him, being a sporty girl who had had lots of boyfriends, many of them platonic, many of them pals. And she hadn't been terribly interested in sex with any of them, so those that got fresh, she had easily put them in order, with a bit of a laugh and no hard feelings on either side.

But Lloyd was different. He was much older than her college boyfriends, and as her first employer after graduation, she initially thought of him only in that light. As a newcomer, she was, in the beginning, almost as lowly as the clerical staff, for Lloyd believed in his staff starting at the bottom of the advertising tree, but she was soon moved to copy writing. Then he let her work on an important account, and she was thrilled to have that ambition fulfilled. So, to start with, all she felt was gratitude at the chance he had given her.

She had said that Trevor was just like Lloyd, but in fact he was nothing like him at all, she now realised. Trevor was a good looking guy of the type that women immediately noticed and regarded as sexy.

Thinking back, she remembered that she had not thought Lloyd sexy at all when she first met him. He wasn't tall or powerful looking, or athletic. He was quietly spoken, and distant in his manner to her. She found this irritating. She liked to establish proper relationships with people, irrespective of their position, and she disliked the feeling of being kept at bay. Automatically, she was extra bright, extra friendly, trying to obtain some reaction from him.

One day, a few weeks after she had started the job, when she was discussing some work, he leaned across the desk, looked her in the eyes and lightly ran his finger across her cheek.

He said without smiling, 'Miss Russell, you're a very attractive girl. Will you stop trying to turn me on? If you're not careful you might succeed.'

The remark was so unexpected it made her blush. After that, she couldn't look at him without seeing that mocking look in his eyes, the half smile on his face. In her mind, she kept feeling the light touch of his finger, more arousing than the exuberant and enthusiastic kisses of her former boyfriends. She became aware of each casual touch of his hand - when he passed her documents, when she gave him a cup of coffee.

The kiss, when it came, was equally subtle, yet evocative. Their clients had accepted an advertising package for which she was the main copywriter.

He came into her room with the news, and walked up to her. 'You've done well,' he said, and placing his hands on her shoulders, kissed her lightly on the lips. She found that she was shaking and sat down quickly, trying to hide the effect he had on her, at the same time knowing that he knew.

'Now that we can relax a bit,' he said, 'We'll have a celebration meal. How about tonight?'

'I'm not dressed for ...'

'You're fine as you are,' he said, and walked out.

He had assumed that she would go with him, and she knew that if she did, she would sleep with him, probably that night. Her mind told her, don't go, you'll get hurt. She went anyway.

'Bit cooler now, Miss Addie.'

Bill Grainger's voice broke into her thoughts and brought her back to an English garden, very far removed from an office in a high rise block in Boston.

'Sorry, I didn't mean to make you jump.'

'I was just day dreaming, Bill. I walked home on autopilot.'

'I do that myself, sometimes, Miss Addie. I'm driving along and I get home, and I don't know how I got there. Funny sort of feeling that. I thought I'd start on the lawn today. If that's all right with you.'

'That's fine, Bill,' Addie said. 'Do you want a cup of coffee?'

'That would be very nice. But I'll just keep going for the moment. Quite a few weeds growing up through the shrubs, now. The rain's brought them all on. Just leave it on the window sill.'

She made the coffee and took her own up to the study. The atmosphere was heavy, and the scent of the privet - more exotic than the small white flowers warranted - drifted disturbingly through the window. She picked up Adrienne's next letter and read it, then realised that she was unaware of anything on the page. Irritated with herself, she stirred her coffee and tried to return to the fifties, banishing Lloyd from her thoughts, together with the eighties and nineties - and Jonathan too.

29th August 1959

Dear James,

It has been the most wonderful summer. Mummy seemed delighted when I said I wanted to go on a school journey and my father didn't seem too bothered. It seemed selfish of me, because I thought Mummy might want my company, but she was quite insistent that I should go. Charlie was going too, and at least half a dozen from my year. We were away for fifteen days, travelling by train across France right to the Pyrenees to a lycee in Perpignan. There were several other schools taking part too. It took twenty five hours to get there - train to Dover, ferry across the Channel, train to Paris - we had croissants and coffee there - then train to Perpignan. We went to sleep on the journey of course, and Charlie woke me up at some unearthly hour and said we were in Switzerland, though I was sure we didn't go that way round. When we got to Toulouse, we saw fruit stalls on the platform, and suddenly, it really felt like being abroad.

Addie read on through Adrienne's description of the holiday - the beach at Perpignan; Spanish style folk dancing in the French border town; a trip to the monastery at Montserrat, shopping in Barcelona. Adrienne ended her letter with a postscript about the exams she had taken in the summer, and though Addie had no knowledge of the English examination system, she saw that Adrienne was satisfied with her own efforts.

I got all my O Level results, just before I went. I really did quite well, and passed in all eight subjects. I will probably do English next year, as I got distinctions in both English Language and Literature.
Love to you both,
Adrienne

There's no indication of what she thinks of Rodney, Addie thought, except the way she says 'my father' and not 'Dad', but perhaps through loyalty she doesn't set out to reveal too much to James.

Dear James,

Thank you so much for your congratulations and the gift. The holiday's nearly over now; back to school to the sixth form next week. Then come two years of work, work, work. You and Mummy have both convinced me that I should think about University, but I'm not looking forward to the A-Levels. It was such a relief in the summer not to have to worry about exams. I enjoyed our trip to France so much, and also staying with Charlie, which I did for a further two weeks in the summer. Charlie's parents were very kind, as they always are, particularly her father, and her brother too.

I have thought a lot about what I want to do. Of course, I am taking English Literature, but I do so want to travel. I have thought for some time that perhaps I might be able to become a journalist. I mentioned this to my form tutor, when we discussed my future. I told her I wanted to be a foreign correspondent. She was very off-putting and told me I would probably have to start on some local paper reporting weddings and funerals. I could see that she had no intention of encouraging me, because she thought I should go into something boring like teaching.

Why don't they understand that I have been in the same place for such a long time - for as long as I can remember - and will be for another two whole years - a lifetime? I want to see the world out there. I know you can understand.

Love to you and Lillian
Adrienne

Addie put down the letters with a wry smile. It was fascinating to see Adrienne's character develop. She recognised in her mother a love of the English language, and also of travel and adventure. She was enjoying making these discoveries, empathising with traits that were part of herself. Even so, today was not the right day. Her eyes were tired after waking too early, and her head was still aching in the heavy, stormy weather. In fact, she was probably best doing something else, like shopping for her dinner party. She hadn't even decided what to make.

She wandered downstairs again, and found Bill drinking the last of his coffee.

'I have a problem, Bill,' she said. 'I'm having a dinner party here on Saturday night, and I don't know what to make.'

'Now I'm no cook, Miss Addie. It's Nora you want to speak to.'

'No, I won't bother her,' said Addie hastily. 'I just want to bounce some ideas off someone. If you were going visiting, what would you fancy?'

'A nice bit of hotpot, or steak and kidney.'

'Something a bit more summery.'

'Well now,' said Bill thoughtfully. 'If I was going to make dinner for a young lady from another country, I'd give her an English dinner, like I said, steak and kidney or something like that. So why don't you do like an American dinner. What do you think to that?'

'You mean like a steak with French fries?'

'Well now, now I think of it, my son and daughter, they took us out on our anniversary to a restaurant where they do a meal from all different countries. I had Chicken Maryland. That was very nice. Bit like having your dinner and your pudding all in one go. Nora thought that was very peculiar, but as I said, it all ends up in your stomach, in the end.'

'It's not very typical of where I come from, Bill,' said Addie doubtfully.

'Miss er Addie, I don't think it matters what people eat, when they're together with their friends. As long as they have a good old chat, they don't really notice the food too much. It's when people get bored, they get fussy. I always noticed that with our kids. Noticed it too with Mr James. Hope you don't mind me saying.'

'Not at all,' laughed Addie, 'Though I guess your Nora was - is a far better cook than I am.'

'You get in something fancy to drink and it'll all go down a treat. You see if I'm not right.'

The American theme was quite a good idea, Addie decided on balance. She spent Thursday afternoon at the supermarket, and Friday making a cheesecake and some chocolate brownies, which, since Joan had first taught her to make them, had been a Russell speciality.

She bought the wine, not at the supermarket, but at the wine merchant near the deli, where the manager told her about a visit to his American second cousin, and sold her a couple of bottles of Chablis from the 'bin end', which he said were remarkably good value.

By Saturday afternoon, she had battered the chicken portions, the banana fritters and corn fritters ready to go in the pan, dug out some attractive china from the antique sideboard and laid it out on the table with silver cutlery, undoubtedly regularly polished by Nora Grainger, and some delicate long stemmed wine glasses. She enjoyed the unaccustomed industry. She had become sated by leisure.

Her pleasurable anticipation was marred by a sudden clap of thunder overhead, so close she nearly dropped the precious wine glasses. She looked out to see a dark ceiling of black and grey thunderclouds hanging ominously in the sky. The stormy weather had been circling round the south of England. After a break of a few days, it had returned, to Addie's dismay.

The phone rang at just after four-thirty.

'Addie Russell.'

'It's me. Sarah. Addie, I'm awfully sorry, but ...'

'What is it?'

'We can't come.'

'What? You can't desert me. What's wrong?'

'Mum fell over. We've just got back from Casualty.'

'Oh Sarah, no. Is she okay? Has she broken something?'

'She hasn't broken anything. But she's twisted her ankle very badly. She can't even walk to the loo without help. I'm really sorry, Addie. I just can't leave her today. If you could postpone your do till tomorrow - the swelling might be down.'

'Let me try to get hold of Julian. I'll call you back.'

The telephone rang and rang. Either he'd left or he'd called in somewhere else first. She tried again twenty minutes later, but with no success.

She rang back to report to Sarah.

'I can't tell you how sorry I am, Addie. I know you were looking forward to entertaining at home for the first time. Do you want me to send Trevor on his own?'

The thought of Trevor with his special brand of salesman-speak was not inviting. No, without Sarah's exuberance and quick tongue to act as a counterbalance, Trevor would be quite unpalatable.

'Sarah, why don't you bring Helen? There's enough for five.'

But Sarah responded without even checking. 'She's really in pain, Addie. She's only just taken pain killers and they've had no effect so far. I think we've got to forget it for tonight. Will you be all right?'

'How d'you mean?'

'I mean with Julian.'

'I told you, Sarah. He's the perfect gentleman.'

Addie put the phone down having tried to hide her disappointment. In fact it was more than just disappointment; actually, she was aware of feeling slightly ill at ease. Despite her protestations to Sarah and with no logical feeling to back it up, she did not want to entertain Julian Gilpin at home alone.

He arrived promptly at seven-thirty and she produced cocktails. She had stored the cooked chicken and the fritters in the oven whilst they ate Waldorf salad, and when she dished out the main course, still piping hot, Julian was full of appreciation. The conversation, as ever, was most civilised, and as they talked of theatre, books and music, Addie began to relax. New rumblings of thunder overhead made her jumpy again during the dessert, and she took a little too much of the wine, aware of Julian's eyes on her, as she did so. Julian had brought an additional bottle, but the wine, which was more than enough for the original four, disappeared rapidly as he, too, drank several glassfuls, and Addie herself became concerned.

'I don't want to be a killjoy, Julian, but do you want to slow down on the wine if you're driving?'

'What makes you think I'm driving, Addie? Tomorrow's Sunday. I don't have to rush off.'

The uncomfortable feeling, which had remained with her as a backcloth to the evening, surged within her. Julian placed his hand on hers. She was aware, as she tried to remove her own, that his hand felt clammy.

'Addie, let's not go on with this pretence. I'm flattered that you should have fabricated a story so that we could be alone. It wasn't necessary. I've found you most attractive ever since I met you.'

Despite her earlier premonition that things were not going to go well, she felt sure that he would understand as soon as she explained it to him.

'You've gotten it wrong, Julian,' she said, jumping with nervousness at a loud crash of thunder, and irritated that the storm was distracting her. 'I didn't invent the reason why Sarah and Trevor couldn't make it.'

'Well, even if your friends were going to come, it's our good fortune that they're not here after all. I can't tell you how much I've been looking forward to being with you. And I feel instinctively that you're attracted to me too.'

This needed damping down right now. Addie didn't like the way the conversation was going.

'Julian, I really appreciate your taking me out, and I've enjoyed our trips tremendously. But I'd rather we just stayed friends. I don't think I can handle any more than that right now.'

'Addie, I'm sure you don't really mean that. You're a lovely girl, and I've seen from the expression on your face that you need someone to make love to you. It must have been months since … You can't waste that wonderful figure.'

His eyes moved slowly down from her face to her legs.

Why hadn't she changed when she realised she would be alone with him? She had kept on the slit skirt and now realised that he was staring at a flash of leg, which the skirt had revealed.

'No, Julian. No. I thought you understood - about getting over Lloyd and everything - I'm just not ready for this.'

It was as if she hadn't spoken.

'And you have no need to worry - as you see, I've thought of everything.' He withdrew a pack of condoms from his pocket.

In alarm, Addie interrupted him, 'Julian, I'd no idea you felt like this. I'm really sorry if I gave you the wrong impression.'

His face lost its smile for a moment and then recovered.

'Your body's crying out for it - and so is mine,' he said, his voice raised. 'I've been waiting impatiently for the moment when I could take hold of you; fondle your breasts …find all your secret places …'

Addie saw that he was panting now with anticipation. Though she had found him quite attractive earlier, she was now filled with revulsion.

'Julian. I don't feel the same way and I can't make love to you.'

'Come on, Addie. We're two experienced people. Why don't you stop being coy, and let yourself go? I know a thing or two, and I dare say you've got some little tricks.'

Addie stared at him in disbelief. Why wasn't he getting the message?

'Let's not play-act, Addie. You're no innocent virgin. I got the impression there was a pretty passionate affair with your friend Lloyd - and I dare say he wasn't the first.'

'Now just a minute,' Addie started indignantly, but he ignored her.

'Not that I would expect anything else. With your looks and figure.'

There was no way that politeness was going to get through to him.

'I'd like you to go, Julian. You've had too much to drink. Nothing's going to happen between us.'

A subtle change came over his face. His mouth set and grew harder. His voice suddenly became terse.

'Addie, I can't believe you're so naive as to think that any man's interest in you is likely to be platonic. I certainly would not have spent time and money on someone who was not going to provide a return, and you must have realised that. But I'm quite happy to play games with you, if that's the way you want to play. It'll make it even more interesting.' He caught hold of her hand again and, pulling her towards him, he said, 'Now we'll have some fun.'

Wrenching her hand away, Addie tried to stop her voice from shaking. 'We've both been mistaken. Would you please leave.'

Ignoring her plea completely, he reached for her thigh.

'Your skirt is very fetching, Addie, but I prefer what's underneath.'

She pushed him away, and he caught her hands once again and imprisoned them. As she struggled, she remembered a report in last week's paper with a banner headline, '**DATE RAPE**'. The potency of the word 'rape' only now hit her, so muted was it by the word 'date'.

His pale face was flushed now - with excitement or alcohol, she couldn't tell which - and beads of sweat were forming on his forehead.

She struggled to free herself and screamed at him, 'Let me go, you bastard.' Not that the outburst helped - the words only

172

excited Julian more.

'What dirty talk, Addie. How about some action as well?'

His face twisted in a smile, as he continued, 'What a delightful little tease you are. I'm going to give you a good sorting out. I'm going to fuck you well and truly.'

A chill ran through her. She was quite suddenly both terrified and enraged. This man in front of her was a threat. He was tall and quite well built. He would not easily be fought off, and he had stated what he wanted quite clearly. He wanted sex. He wanted variety. And he liked the idea of a fight. Wrenching her hands away from him, she picked up a fruit knife from the table. Her voice came out in an angry shriek. 'Don't come near me.'

'Don't be silly,' he said, his eyes glistening. 'You won't use that,' and she knew too that she could not plunge it into him.

Her half full wine glass was on the table. Still holding the knife, she threw the contents of the glass in his face. He wiped his eyes and laughed. Catching hold of her wrist, he forced the knife out of her hand and as it fell to the floor, she lifted her knee and aimed for his groin. His face lost its smile and he yelped in pain.

Suddenly the room was lit up by a brilliant flash of lightning. For a moment, as a clap of thunder shook the house, she was distracted, and stepping backwards, caught the heel of her shoe in her long skirt and fell, her arms flailing wildly as she tried to get her balance. The lights in the room dimmed, recovered and then went out. Her senses intensified, she heard the tearing of her skirt, the sound of her own scream and the barking of a dog somewhere outside. She felt a sharp pain as she hit her head against the mahogany sideboard, and then she blacked out.

Chapter 17: Visitors for Addie

Addie felt something wet on her face, like an animal's tongue. She opened her eyes: faces above her, slightly blurred; one of them - thank goodness - a dog - a dog she recognised. How long had she been unconscious? Long enough for Julian ...? She glanced downwards. Her clothes were tidy - too tidy. Even so, she felt instinctively that despite her brief loss of consciousness, she had not been touched.

The figures cleared - Bill Grainger, kneeling, one hand on the collar of his labrador, Winston, the other holding a torch; behind him, Julian, his face pale now, looking concerned - was that genuine? But otherwise inscrutable, betraying nothing.

'Addie, my dear, are you all right?'

She started to sit up but, overcome by dizziness, groaned and lay down again.

'I'm afraid she panicked at that last clap of thunder. She's very nervous about thunder, aren't you, Addie?'

'Is that right, Addie?' growled Bill protectively. She noticed he had dropped the 'Miss'.

'I guess so, Bill,' she replied. She stared into Julian's eyes. *I will deny everything*, they said. Incoherent thoughts came into her mind. For a moment she wasn't sure if he'd said the words aloud. *She panicked. She had too much to drink. She's inventing stories.*

I think we should take you to Casualty, Addie,' he now said, sounding perfectly composed and solicitous. 'I'm very happy to take you and stay with you, rather than go back tonight, as I planned.'

'There's no need, Julian,' she said. 'Bill will look after me. You go on home.'

'Very well. I'll ring tomorrow and see how you are.'

After that, the next few hours merged into a blur. Bill, on the telephone calling an ambulance. Nora, surprisingly, at her side, first in the Casualty Department, then the X-ray Department; a doctor telling Nora that there was no sign of fracture, just mild concussion. She remembered him saying that if there was any sign of nausea, he was to be contacted. She felt very tired and kept dozing off, missing bits of what was happening. Then there was the journey home after what seemed like a long wait, and finally the sheer bliss of her own bed. But once asleep, Julian pursued her through her dreams, masquerading first as Lloyd, then as Jonathan, his own face only revealed as she opened up her body to him. Then, as she recoiled in horror and disgust, he became Rodney to her Dorothy or Daphne - she was not sure which - still with Julian's face, hitting her so that her head hurt, beating her about the face and body, before the inevitable rape.

'It's all right, my pet.'

It was her mother with a basket of roses.

'It's all right, pet.'

She opened her eyes. There were the roses, their scent filling the room, not in a basket, but in a vase, half a dozen plucked fresh from the garden, still moist from the previous day's storms.

'I've brought you some breakfast.'

She shook her head, her mouth too dry to speak.

'Just a lightly boiled egg and a little toast. And some coffee.'

'Coffee,' she echoed in a croak.

'Let me help you up then.'

And Nora Grainger, her arch enemy, helped her into a sitting position, plumped up the pillow behind her and held the coffee for her, until she was ready to take it.

'Nora - you and Bill. You are so kind. Unbelievably kind.'

'Just behaving like decent human beings, I hope.'

'More than that, Nora. Particularly when I know you should have had this house - and I've ...'

'Shush, it's not your fault - you're his grandchild after all. We was just helpers.'

'Much more than that, Nora. I'm sure he meant to do something more for you. Maybe he just got confused.'

'We'll find out when the time is right. Don't you worry your head about it.'

'Did you come in this morning specially?'

'No, I stayed in the little bedroom. Like I used to sometimes when the Major, may he rest in peace, was alive.'

Addie opened her eyes incredulously.

'Nora, you did that for me?'

'Well the doctor, he said we must be sure and contact him if you was sick. So I thought I'd better stay - and when I heard you screaming your head off, just now, I thought it was time to wake you up. I expect you had a nightmare, didn't you?'

Addie said nothing more than 'Thank you.' But to herself she said, if the will doesn't give them something extra in December, I'll arrange it myself.

She didn't get up right away. She lay there thinking about the events of the previous day, her head still hurting a bit. The unpleasant dream stayed with her, merging with yesterday's reality. She thought about Lloyd and wondered why it was that every touch of his fingers had seemed like an electric charge surging through her, and why Julian's advances had been so totally abhorrent. Then unbid, the question of whether, given the chance, he would have - whether he could have raped her while she was still unconscious, entered her mind, and she felt nausea sweep over her, so that for a moment she thought she was going to be physically sick. I'd better not tell Nora, she resolved, or she'll have the doctor back again.

The feeling passed and she lay back against the pillows, and thought of Dorothy, sharing her bed with a man she

176

loathed, often raped and beaten by him, and she understood how Dorothy could want - could long to - end this cycle of abasement and humiliation.

Nora put her head round the door. 'It's him. On the phone. Do you want me to get rid of him?'

The spectre of the Julian in the nightmare loomed in Addie's mind. She took a deep calming breath. 'No. I'll speak to him. I'll come down.'

She took the navy blue robe that Nora offered - ironically it was James's robe - the one she had put on when she first met Nora. It was comforting, as if her grandfather had his arm round her shoulders. But her legs felt a little shaky, and she wished once again she'd organised an extension phone in the bedroom.

Nora preceded her down the stairs and proprietarily took the phone to say, 'She's just coming,' before passing it to Addie, glaring at the receiver, as she did so. Addie recognised the expression on her face. She herself until yesterday had been on the receiving end of that cold dislike, but now it was Julian who was the enemy. She wondered exactly what Bill had said to his wife about the previous evening to inspire such feelings in Nora. Did they both know something she did not?

The voice at the end of the phone was terse. But he sounded pretty much like the old Julian, except somewhat less friendly than usual. 'Is that you, Addie?'

She half whispered 'Yes', almost wondering if the whole episode had been a dream. Fleetingly, she speculated on why he was telephoning. Was it an act of concern, or perhaps a fairly cynical desire to check what action, if any, she was going to take?

'Are you all right?' he asked stiffly.

'I guess so.'

'Well I'm glad to hear it. I have to say I think you're an extremely foolish girl. You should be wary of putting yourself in such a dangerous situation.'

So there was to be no apology forthcoming. She was not all that surprised. How pompous and patronising he sounded. She had certainly misjudged him.

'Fortunately for you, I am a gentleman. I would not force my attentions on someone where they were unwanted. But you should be careful of giving the wrong signals to men; otherwise you might not always be so lucky.'

She got the impression he was already covering himself; it was both an attack and a defence. She could not be bothered to respond in kind. She just wanted to get rid of him.

'Thanks for phoning, Julian.'

'Needless to say, Addie, I doubt if we'll see each other again.'

Involuntarily she said, 'No, Julian. I'm sorry.'

She could hardly believe her own ears. *She* had said sorry to him. But that was to the old Julian. The nice guy Dr Jekyll. Regaining her spirit, she addressed herself to Mr Hyde: 'I guess that'll suit us both very well.'

Sarah arrived mid-morning. Addie was still sitting downstairs in James's bathrobe.

'Addie, I'm so sorry. If only we'd been there.'

Addie sighed, 'It would have happened sooner or later. No point in your feeling guilty. I've been feeling guilty enough.'

Sarah sat herself down on the other armchair.

'Well that's stupid. Why should you feel guilty? I mean what happened for heaven's sake? That is if you want to tell me ...'

Addie described the evening to her. She felt better for talking about it, though Sarah was outraged.

'He's an absolute bastard. I always knew it. Did you think of contacting the police, Addie? I mean, he might have ...'

Addie pondered for a moment. Sunshine was streaming through the windows and gradually both Julian and the dream were becoming more distant. After all, nothing much had actually happened, had it? A bad headache was the only legacy of the previous night.

'Briefly, last night, as I opened my eyes, I wondered if he'd - he'd done anything when I blacked out.' She shuddered with distaste at the idea. 'But now, no. I would have known if he'd touched me.'

Sarah looked doubtful. 'You're sure, Addie?'

'I'm pretty sure. As a matter of fact, Sarah, I think knocking myself out saved me. I have a nasty feeling that if I'd been awake and fighting, things might have been quite different. Because up to then, he was enjoying every minute of it. And the awful thing is, he convinced himself I was too.'

She chewed the end of her fingernail reflectively.

'I guess if I hadn't been so tense about the storm last night, I'd have handled him a lot better. I'd have had my wits about me.'

She looked out of the window again. The night's storm had left only a calm, sunny day in its wake.

'That was something else I meant to ask you,' Sarah said, following her gaze. 'Did you once say you had a bit of a hang-up about thunderstorms?'

Addie nodded. 'Yeah. Stupid I guess.'

'Why do storms upset you so much?'

'Oh, when I was a kid, one of my pals - her dad was struck by lightning out on the golf course. She went on and on about it. About the zipper on his jacket turning to molten metal - about his blackened face. She sure got it out of her system - and into mine.'

She forced her mind away from the subject. 'Let's forget it all, shall we? Tell me, how is Helen?'

'She's much better today. We sent Trev out for a Chinese take-away last night and she just kept her feet up. And today, she's hobbling about with a stick. In fact she started to feel better last night when the painkillers took effect, and then she was really angry with us for letting you down, particularly when I said you were on your own with Julian. She hadn't realised earlier.'

'That's sweet of her.'

'And Jonathan was so angry when I told him on the phone.'

'Sarah, ' Addie said, 'You said something to Jonathan about Julian last week. What was it you said?'

Sarah flushed, 'I'm sorry, Addie. I did rather put my foot in it. I said I was surprised you'd agreed to go out with Julian because he had "bedroom" written all over his face the first time he saw you. But Jonathan got totally the wrong end of the stick and lost his temper and walked out in a huff.'

'I see, that explains that,' Addie said. Then her mind returning to the present, she carried on. 'I guess you must be thinking I'm pretty dumb. If Julian says I was asking for trouble and you could see I was heading for trouble, why didn't I realise it?'

'Addie, I think you're open and jokey and pleasant with everyone. I just think some men might take it as a "come-on".'

'So you're saying Julian was right.'

'No, I'm not saying that. And frankly, I'd be the last person to say women should have to change the way they behave because there's some aggressive men around.'

'Well that's good - because I was beginning to think I had to behave like a nun here. You know, in the States, I have several men friends who I don't sleep with.'

'All I'm saying is - well just be more careful. I always knew Julian was a wolf in sheep's clothing.'

'I thought Julian was a polite mature Englishman. I'd have been far more wary of Trevor.'

'Well Trevor is just transparent. In fact, he's really quite a lamb. Anyway, he doesn't spring any surprises on me, and I can handle him. He's a WYSIWIG type. You know the jargon?'

'What You See Is What You Get?'

'Yes. Anyway, all I'm saying is, keep an eye on the quiet ones.'

Without being asked, Nora, who had been upstairs tidying the two bedrooms, came in with coffee for the two girls.

'Thank you so much, Nora. And when you see Bill, will you tell him how grateful I am to him?'

Nora shot a look at Sarah. 'He'll be over here on Thursday, as usual. He'll want to talk to you about it, I expect.'

'That's good. I'd really like to talk with him.'

Even after a dramatic event, Nora remained her usual reticent self, Addie thought. To satisfy her own curiosity, she would try to get a fuller account from Bill.

'She's not an easy person,' she told Sarah, when Nora had left the room. 'You should have seen her face yesterday. She came in here holding Julian's pack of condoms with the tips of her fingers, as if they were something with a nasty smell, and put them down on the dressing table - as if I might be expecting a stream of lovers to call. It was the best laugh I had all day.'

'How embarrassing. What did you say?'

'I just followed her lead. She didn't say a word, so I had to pretend not to notice them. As soon as she'd left the room, I got up and hid them away.'

'God, it's as bad as having your mother breathing down your neck. Oh sorry, Addie. I'm always putting my foot in it, aren't I?'

'It's okay. And Nora's okay too. She's actually quite different now she seems to think I need looking after. I can see now why James told Meera she was really kind. She is, and I've really appreciated how she's treated me this last couple of days. But I still find her difficult to get to know. She doesn't open up.' She picked up her coffee cup and took a mouthful. 'Even so, I owe Bill and Nora so much, I've got to make sure that they don't get left high and dry. I just can't believe James didn't make more provision for them.'

'Have another word with Jonathan,' Sarah said. 'Or make an appointment to see Uncle Bruce. Perhaps he'd be able to clarify things.'

'Yes, and there's another thing I want to do now. I want to find out more about Dorothy.'

'I thought you knew all there was to know.'

'I want to know how she came to marry Rodney.' Addie said after a moment's thought. 'I was very lucky, Sarah. I was in Dorothy's shoes there for a few minutes. But you know - it's taught me something. You know how we all fear being attacked by a stranger - on the street.'

Sarah nodded.

'People underrate what it feels like to be faced with someone you know. What do they call it - a domestic? I mean I thought he was an inoffensive sort of guy. Stupid of me, but I got him wrong. Even so, I'd gotten to know him a bit.' Remembering the nightmare she'd had earlier, she gripped the arm of her chair. 'But when he was there in front of me and he started to say what he had on his mind - he wasn't the same man - he was a stranger.' Involuntarily, she wrapped the navy robe more tightly around herself. 'I thought I was tough. Suddenly, I was feeling like a victim.'

Sarah interrupted. 'But you're very far from that, Addie.'

'You see, I keep thinking of Dorothy. Her husband's a professional man. He's respected. Then when they're on their own, he's a stranger; he's an animal. Poor Dorothy, she never escaped from being a victim. And she went through that over and over again. I want to know how she got herself into that situation?'

'How do you plan to find out, Addie?'

'I'm going back to Bath, to Long Barton - and I'm going to ask around some more. And I think maybe Ada Petitpierre Seccombe is going to provide a clue.'

'Dorothy's sinful single mother.'

'Yeah. I'll bet she had a story to tell.'

'Perhaps you should look her up in the records at St. Catherine's. She might have married later, and Dorothy might

182

have been pushed out.'

'Just what I was thinking, Sarah. Maybe I'll go in the week.'

'Make sure you're okay, Addie.'

In fact she did not feel quite back to normal until the middle of the week. And since she was stuck at home, she finally remembered to get an extension phone fitted. She was tired of having to go down the stairs at inconvenient moments.

Nora came in and insisted on cooking and tidying each day for the next few days. No longer was Addie 'Miss Russell'; she was 'Addie' or 'my pet', scolded and bossed by Nora and generally treated as an errant child.

Jonathan popped over to see her, in the middle of the week, after work, bringing a tub of ice-cream - the sort she had seen advertised by a pair of half clothed lovers.

'Ice-cream's always comforting when you're feeling low, and indulgent when you're not,' he said, and since she was actually feeling much better, she made them an omelette and found some fresh bread in the larder, and they sat outside and ate it with a glass of white wine. Unusually, Jonathan discarded his suit jacket over the back of the garden chair, and loosened his tie, and Addie relaxed in the warm sunshine, enjoying his presence.

She dished out the ice-cream, and they spooned it into their mouths in appreciative silence, until Addie noticed that Jonathan had a blob of the creamy mixture on the tip of his nose. She leaned forward impulsively and wiped it away with a finger, which she involuntarily licked. Then inwardly she groaned at herself, 'Addie, will you never learn?' Thank goodness she hadn't been tempted to lick the ice-cream off his nose. They could have made that into one of the Häagen Dazs ads.

He stared at her surprised, then they both smiled like children at a shared joke. She looked into his eyes and stopped smiling.

'Addie,' he said to her, suddenly serious, 'You've got to be more careful - I mean with people like Julian.'

She flared up suddenly, 'Are you saying that I led him on? It's typical of you men, isn't it? It's always the woman's fault.'

He looked upset. 'Of course I'm not saying you led him on. And I'm sorry about what I said to you the other day. It's just - you always imagine that Americans will be 'streetwise' and perhaps that's not always the case. And *you* may get the wrong impression about the English. Just because they're sometimes reserved, or they don't always say exactly what's on their minds, it doesn't mean that the idea's not lurking there underneath.'

'You're giving me the same lecture that I got from Sarah,' she said, her anger subsiding. 'I know. I'll be careful.'

'I - we wouldn't want any harm to come to you, Addie,' he said. 'We're all very fond of you. But you're a very attractive girl in - believe it or not - a different culture. Just remember that inside every Englishman with a copy of *The Times* is an Italian just waiting to pinch your bottom.'

It was such an unexpected comment that she put down her spoon and laughed and laughed, and before she could restrain herself said, 'Do you read *The Times*, Jonathan?' and laughed again. And then the laughter just wouldn't stop, as the tension of the last few days ebbed away, and she knew she was bordering on hysteria.

She could see Jonathan looking at her, his face serious again, wondering perhaps if the laughter was going to turn to tears, and she turned away from him and tried to recover herself. There was an expression on his face - concern, sympathy, affection, even - she was not sure what - it made her want to say 'I'm all right - I just need a hug', but she didn't. She didn't know if the concern was brotherly, professional or if she was completely misjudging yet another man, though she couldn't help feeling that even a brotherly hug would be quite nice. As her laughter subsided, she looked at him again, and half thought he had read her mind and was going to take hold of her, when the garden door opened and Sarah and Helen came in, Helen limping and supporting herself with a stick. Jonathan jumped up to help his mother to a chair and, in that moment, Addie recovered herself. She welcomed them with genuine pleasure, then she and Sarah fetched more things from the kitchen and they spent the rest of the sunny evening drinking wine and eating ice-cream, until a plague of midges broke up the party.

In the end, she did not go to London on Thursday. She would have missed seeing Bill Grainger and she wanted particularly to hear his version of what had happened.

For the first time since the accident, she took a jog before breakfast and had coffee at the deli. Sitting there, she saw a cyclist in turquoise lycra shorts in the distance and felt a schoolgirl's flutter in her stomach, and then a pang of disappointment as the cyclist, his hair, in any case, the wrong colour, rode on by.

She returned home to find Bill spraying weed killer over the patio.

'You have to clear these weeds once or twice a year,' he commented, 'otherwise it gets untidy.'

'Bill, would you mind if we talked for a few minutes - about last Saturday?'

'I'll just finish off this patio and wash my hands, if that's all right with you, Addie.'

She put the kettle on, and waited for a minute or so, before sticking her head out of the door. 'You can wash your hands in the kitchen, Bill,' she called. But she could see he had been running the garden tap, and now took a small frayed towel from the shed and carefully wiped his hands before approaching.

Taking off his boots and placing them outside the door, he walked in stockinged feet to the kitchen table.

'Would you mind just telling me what happened on Saturday night, Bill?' Addie said, passing him the coffee.

Still he would not be hurried, first picking up his cup, tasting the coffee, replacing it and reaching for the sugar bowl, before he spoke.

'Well, as far as I remember, we'd had our tea, and Nora was watching one of them game-show things. It started to pour again, and I thought I'd wait a bit before I took old Winston out.' He spooned sugar into his cup and stirred it reflectively. 'One of those crime stories was on - I don't watch the telly much, but I like a nice detective story - Agatha Christie, or that Ruth Rendell, you know what I mean.'

Addie nodded and passed him a plate of digestive biscuits.

'Well it finished off and Nora gets up to make a cup of tea. She says, "Listen to that thunder again. You want to unplug the telly if you're not watching it." I said, "I'll just see the news," when Winston started scratching at the door, and whining. I reckoned it was the thunder upsetting him.

'The way he was carrying on I reckoned he wouldn't take "no" for an answer. I got my waterproof jacket out and said, "Come on then, Winston."'

Addie wished he would get to the point of the story, but she nodded.

'As we got out, I heard a big crack of thunder and the lights went out all the way down the road. Lucky I had my torch. I reckoned you'd be worried with no electricity, and we headed down here. I could see it was pitch black. I banged on the kitchen door, and Winston starts scratching and whining again, like he knows something - maybe he did. Then that chap Julian comes and unlocks the door.

'Just then the lights went back on again and I could see he's looking all worried. I said, "Where's Miss Addie," and he says, "She's had an accident," and I said, "What d'you mean?" and I pushed him out of the way, and there you were on the floor in the dining room.'

'Bill,' said Addie, knowing that this would be as embarrassing to him as it was to her. 'Did I look as if I'd just fallen - or as if anything else had happened? I mean, did my clothes look mussed up at all?'

'Well now, Miss Addie,' his face reddening a little. 'I reckon you'd just fallen. Your skirt - it was half pulled off - but it was caught in your shoe and there was bit of a tear. That's all. He was as white as a sheet, and I reckon he was scared out of his wits that you'd really hurt yourself. I says to him, "What's she doing in that state?" and he says, "You can see for yourself - she just fell. I haven't touched her - she might have broke something." Well, I just bent down and put your skirt straight - like it should be. Not that you don't see just as much - and a whole lot more - on the telly these days. A lot more than I like to see, sometimes. At any rate, it didn't seem right to me. I hope that was all right with you, Addie.'

'I appreciate it, Bill. Very much.'

'And then old Winston, he starts to get worried and lick your face. And then, if I'm not mistaken, you opens your eyes.'

'Yes, that's right.'

'Miss Addie, if I'd of thought that he'd touched you while you was lying there - I'd of - well, I can tell you Winston would have had him for dinner. But he was too edgy - I reckon he was scared stiff that you'd cracked your head open.'

The flush died away from his cheeks now, and Addie saw his mind was shifting back to other matters.

'That was a fair old storm that night. It did the garden a bit of good. Poor old Winston, when he comes back in the kitchen at home, he shakes off a good few pints of water. Just as well Nora had gone off with you by then. She'd have had a bit of a go at the state of the kitchen floor.'

Addie laughed and, half rising in his seat, Bill said, 'You're all right now, Addie? You're over it all right?'

She nodded and smiled her answer.

'I'll be in the garden if you want anything else. If that's all right with you.'

187

She was all right, she was sure. All right enough to take the train to London to visit St. Catherine's once again, reassured by the landmarks, now familiar, confident on the subway system, and soothed by the strangely unemotional task of sifting through old records at St. Catherine's House.

Though she had said her intention was to find out more about Dorothy, she had only the vaguest of ideas how she was going to go about this. Somehow it seemed important to set Dorothy in the context of a family, so the logical thing would be to get details of Dorothy's parents - her own great-grandparents. At the back of her mind was an impression she had gained from Dorothy's marriage certificate, that her parents were deceased, so she made for the section devoted to deaths. Unaccompanied by another person to feel guilty about - had they been there too long? - was it time to go for coffee? - she worked without a break through all the record books from 1934, the year of Dorothy Ann Seccombe's marriage, backwards to 1916, the year of Dorothy's birth, in her search for Dorothy's parents. In vain, she scoured the pages for a mention of Ada Petitpierre Seccombe and Percy Henshaw. She found two other Seccombes of note, Dorothy Victoria Seccombe, and George Arthur Petitpierre Seccombe, both of whom died in the same district in the thirties. The distinctive Petitpierre name marked George out as a relation of Ada, almost certainly her father. But in book after book, she failed to find Dorothy's parents. As her eyes grew more and more tired, she became convinced that she must have missed them, until suddenly, there was Percy - his name standing out as if written in bright red ink, and she knew that she could not have missed Ada's ungainly mix of French invader and English plebeian. It simply was not there.

But Percy was there, his death in 1916, only two months after the birth of his daughter, suggesting that he was one of the many young men lost in a war that left behind a vast army of weeping widows and empty-armed girls. Addie looked on, made sure that Ada had not herself died of infection following the birth, or in childbirth itself, and then closed the books and left.

As she walked away, her brows furrowed in thought, her eyes aching a little and her head reminding her of the blow she had sustained, a bent figure lurched out of a doorway, saluted smartly and said, 'God save the King.' And for a moment she saw how it could be Percy Henshaw or one of his comrades, lost in a war of past times, and she stared in pity at the hollowed eyes and the unshaven face, and flipped a coin from her pocket into his cap, which lay in a doorway. And the old man saluted again, and said, 'God bless you, Ma'am. God save King George,' and she walked reflectively on to a lunch of pizza with garlic bread and English butter, a Viennese gateau and cappuccino - Europe now united, here at her table.

It was the nearest café to St. Catherine's House, often frequented by researchers, and a couple were discussing their own findings at another table. As she sat there, Addie thought about the morning's efforts. Why couldn't she find Ada? If Ada had produced a child in 1916 and was dead in 1936, why wasn't her death on record? She pondered on the possible reasons. Had Ada's name been changed at some stage? Possibly; she could have wanted to leave the stigma of her illegitimate daughter behind her - yes, she could even have married and died, legitimately bearing a new name. She could have married and had other children, who were Dorothy's half brothers and sisters - additional relatives for Addie. It was possible too that Dorothy and her mother had been estranged - that something had happened to cause Dorothy to lie when she married - and describe her as dead. No, that did not fit in with Dorothy's loyal nature.

Addie chewed a fingernail reflectively, took a sip of her coffee and then exploded aloud, 'Who said she was dead?'

The other diners looked round at her in surprise, and then, as she laughed in embarrassment, a woman said, 'It gets to you - this family tree stuff, doesn't it? - we've done the lot - the records at Kew, the Census records. I've got a notebook; I put it all down and then set out everything we know when we get home.'

Addie agreed. 'I guess I didn't think it through.'

That was it, of course. She hadn't referred to the notes that she and Sarah had already made. She'd just assumed that Dorothy had lost *both* her parents at the time of her marriage. The marriage certificate had certainly said that Percy was dead, but now she suddenly remembered that it was only the fathers of the bride and bridegroom whose names were included on the marriage certificate. So the mother, Ada, was not mentioned at all. Addie had simply assumed that she was dead - why? Because Dorothy seemed so alone, so lacking in support of any kind - isolated with Rodney till Penny Buckley befriended her - no-one to turn to for protection from her husband or indeed to escape to with her child. So what had happened to Ada?

'The thing is,' the woman continued, 'You have to pause sometimes, and consolidate. Sometimes when you're getting in a muddle or you're frustrated, the best thing is to go home, wait for the next lot of certificates. Get it all down on paper and sort it out in your mind. Then you go off and get the new information you need.'

Addie knew she was right. She had only three options - to go forwards up to fifty years to find Ada's death, or backwards from between eighteen to forty years to find Ada's birth, or to go home - and she was tired after the morning's endeavours. It would be sensible to go home. She got up and left the café and, completely ignoring good sense, she made her way back towards St. Catherine's House.

190

Chapter 18: Addie goes back

'Are you sure you got it right?' said Sarah, dishing roast potatoes onto the four waiting plates. 'Six, Jonathan - how can you put away so many?'

'I'll cycle it off,' said Jonathan, passing the plate of chicken portions to Addie. 'White or dark meat, Addie?'

'I'll take the white, thank you, Jonathan.'

'Jonathan's a leg man, aren't you, Jonathan?' Sarah giggled.

Jonathan glared at her, though he couldn't stop a small grin appearing at the corners of his mouth.

A week after Julian's bungled assault on her, Addie felt relaxed enough to wear her repaired slit skirt again. Checking now, to make sure that not too much of her own leg was showing, she noticed Jonathan's involuntary glance in the same direction.

'And a reader of the Times,' she murmured leaning forward to direct the comment at him.

Sarah stared at them blankly, as they both laughed at the shared joke.

Helen, sitting at the table, abdicating her normal role and allowing her children to cook and serve this Sunday lunch, interrupted the banter.

'Go on telling us what you found out, Addie.'

'Well, first I thought I was wrong all along about Ada. She could have been alive at the time of Dorothy's wedding. But there's no proof about that, because the mother's never shown on the marriage certificate. So, I went back to St. Catherine's and looked for her death after the wedding. She wasn't there either. Not unless she changed her name. I'd already found Dorothy's grandfather. He died in 1939. Oh I forgot to say - the grandmother - she was Dorothy too, Dorothy Victoria - she died in 1934, before Dorothy's marriage. So then I looked back through the books to see when Ada was born. I started at twenty years before Dorothy's birth, and then went backwards another ten. Pretty tedious stuff, I can tell you. No sign of Ada. Then I thought - Percy was almost certainly a young soldier, so Ada would have to be young herself - certainly not in her thirties. So I came forward year by year, until I got to 1902 - and there she was. I could hardly believe it at first. Just a kid. A fourteen-year-old schoolgirl.

'Well, no wonder she did a bunk,' commented Sarah.

'If she did,' Addie said. 'But yes, I do have this gut feeling that she wasn't around for Dorothy. Anyhow, I ordered the birth certificate, and also Percy's birth and death certificate - I found them too. Poor Percy was just a kid too - only eighteen himself when he died in 1916. I suppose he was killed in the First World War.'

'"Gone for soldiers, everyone,"' quoted Helen. 'Tragic waste of young lives.'

'But as for what happened to Ada after that, well, we just don't know.'

'I'm telling you, she got out and left the baby to the doting grandparents,' said Sarah.

'But it wouldn't be that easy. Where would a young girl like that go? Mind you, it wouldn't be unusual for parents to bring up their daughter's child. Even make the pretence that it was their own,' Helen remarked.

'Young Ada was a bit of tearaway, wasn't she? Having it off at fourteen - my goodness, you can imagine the rumpus when they found out - bringing disgrace on the family and all that,' said Sarah.

'Yes, and no chance of her marrying, because Percy had probably already enlisted.'

'Poor little Ada, waiting for her soldier to return and make an honest woman of her,' said Jonathan, 'and of course he never does.'

'What did you do for dessert, Sarah?'

'Oh I just bought some of that delicious passionfruit and

mango ice-cream. I read all the nutrition info and it says fifty grams of aphrodisiac per pack - and I'm seeing Trevor later.'

Helen frowned and shook her head as Sarah left the room. 'I don't know what's wrong with that girl - two years of university education and all she's got on her mind is Trevor with his twenty-two-carat sex appeal.'

'She's only teasing, Mum, to annoy you.'

'I hope so. I sometimes feel she's afraid of making serious relationships.'

'She'll be all right.'

Sarah brought in the ice-cream in on a china plate and dished out. Jonathan took a spoonful from his glass fruit bowl and turned to Addie. 'Fifty grams eh? Do I have any on my nose, Addie?'

Their eyes met in an intimate silent joke for the second time. Addie felt an overwhelming desire to reach out and touch his face, a desire she swiftly conquered. For what seemed a long moment, surely blindingly obvious to the rest of the family, she stared into his eyes, feeling her face grow pink and yet unable to look away.

'Is that the phone, Sarah?'

'Oh, that'll be Trev now.'

Sarah skipped away.

The conversation resumed at the table. Amazingly, nothing seemed to have changed. Helen was continuing to talk and Jonathan to respond as though the world had not stood still for a moment.

'Frozen peas?'

'Yes, frozen peas. That's what they said. "Go home and put a pack of frozen peas on it and that will help the swelling go down." I nearly asked them whether they should be mint flavoured.'

'To get you back into mint condition?' quipped Jonathan.

Sarah returned.

'It's for you, Jonathan. I can't help wondering if she's

psychic, the way she manages to interrupt your life.'

'Tabitha?' said Jonathan.

'Is there anyone else?' said Sarah.

So they were left, the three women, once again, with Jonathan speedily disappearing after his phone conversation, leaving the rest of his ice-cream, and going without coffee. He'd picked up his keys from the sideboard, dropped a quick kiss on the cheeks of his mother and sister, and, after a second's hesitation on Addie's cheek too.

'I'll explain later,' he said as he rushed out and a moment later they heard the car start up outside.

'That bloody Tabitha,' commented Sarah to no-one in particular.

The afternoon had lost some piquancy for all of them - the two women for whom Jonathan was their closest male relation - and Addie, still recovering from the look in Jonathan's eyes. And the kiss - did it mean anything? She shouldn't read too much into it. He was surely just including her in the family.

'I think I'll move to a more comfortable position,' Helen said, interrupting her thoughts as she rose from the table.

'What I can't understand is why you're so obsessed with Dorothy and her side,' said Sarah, as they lounged in armchairs, 'Why not go back and look at James?'

'Well, you suggested that we start with Dorothy. And now I just can't stop.'

'I suppose James's life would have been more conventionally structured - perhaps a little less interesting from that point of view,' Helen commented.

'Maybe. But in any case, I don't feel the same need to get to know James. He's all around me - in the house, in the garden. The regard that people had for him - the Graingers - the way they respected and cared for him; Meera - at the deli.' She turned to Sarah, 'Why even your Uncle Bruce called him a fine old gentleman.'

'I should take anything he says with a large pinch of salt.'

'Well, anyhow, I guess a list of names and dates wouldn't add anything to what I know about James already. A good man - a kind man. Three loves - two children. Tragedies - and contentment too.'

'Another cup of coffee, Addie,' Helen offered.

'Thanks, I'll pour it myself. Can I get one for you, Helen?'

'Thank you, but no more spoiling today. I shall be back to normal by tomorrow. So what do you hope to find out about Dorothy?'

'Looking into Dorothy's life is like peeling the skins off an onion - her being illegitimate like me - being brought up by elderly parents - having a teenage mother - I'm just fascinated by each layer of the story.'

'Are you going back to London to look at more records?'

'Not yet. I've decided to take another trip to Long Barton. I'm going to ask around some more - maybe at the school, Marsh House - see if people remember the family.'

'Can you wait till next weekend, so I can come too?'

'I'm sorry, Sarah. I'm going in the week. I'm beginning to feel that time's moving on. I can't stay here indefinitely using up James's money. I've got to make a decision about staying or going home. If I stay, I've got to find out my rights here - whether I can work or not. The estate isn't a bottomless pit - and neither are my savings back home.'

'I suppose your flat is a drain on your money too,' Helen commented.

'I had a bit of luck there. Mom met a friend who was looking for an apartment - I said I'd be prepared to sublet for six months, so she's gone ahead and arranged it. I can always move back with Mom and Pop if I have to.'

'But isn't that less convenient for your job?'

'There's no job any more. Lloyd's gotten himself a new copywriter. He called Mom and told her. He said he would treat my holiday as notice - no hard feelings on either side,' Addie said with a shrug.

'Do you mind?'

'Mind about the job? No, I was head-hunted a while back, but I wouldn't leave Lloyd then. Mind about Lloyd? No - that's over too. I guess it was hard, working through the pain at the time. You think it's going to last a lifetime, but it didn't.'

She saw Helen's eyes glaze over, and regretted the comment. Helen made an excuse to leave the room and Addie turned to Sarah.

'That was tactless of me - really dumb.'

Sarah shrugged, not unfeelingly. 'Don't worry, Addie. It isn't words that cause the pain - Dad's not coming back. We know it, but it doesn't make it easier. There are so many things I want to tell him and he's not there. And Mum - well, I heard her crying in the night, no so long ago - but she wouldn't want anyone to see.'

Helen returned with fresh lipstick on, and brushed aside Addie's apology.

'You mustn't feel you have to watch what you say, Addie. Some things catch you in the raw. That can't be helped. Now look, you two. You see I'm not limping at all now. So I'm going to clear up and you two can have a chat before Trevor comes and whisks Sarah away on his dashing white turbo-charger.'

* * *

It was strange, Addie thought, how someone like Lloyd kept flitting back into your mind. She was sitting on the train going west to Bath, and reading the book that Helen had loaned her, *Take a Girl like You*. At the end of Jenny Bunn's seduction, she thought of Lloyd and that first night. At least she did not end up drunk and sick, when she made that transition from her virgin state. It could so easily have happened with one of her college boyfriends, if she hadn't kept a firm rein on them, but instead she was with a master, so to speak, not a student, and though she may have lost her innocence, she did not do it in ignorance.

196

Staring out of the train window, she felt herself go hot at the memory, how after dinner that night he had taken her back to his flat. Served coffee and brandy. How the carefully chosen dinner wine and the spirit had warmed her, dulled her nervousness and tension, without dulling her senses. The hands of the clock on the wall had stopped moving, and he had simply stroked her hair and face for hours or minutes, before kissing her - and then - no undignified struggle - each piece of clothing loosed and removed the moment she was ready, longing for the touch of his hand. Somewhere in those moments or hours, her cerebral self had been lost and only primeval instincts remained.

At work, in the days that followed, the air was electric, and the sparks that flew in the office brought out the best in her work - wit, humour, sensitivity, sensuality.

There was of course the payment to be made. Joan, immediately suspicious of the truth, still herself bearing the more puritanical or religious morals of her southern upbringing, observed her adopted daughter, cynically held in thrall by a man in his late thirties; watched that previously happy-go-lucky girl grow thin and edgy, hypnotised by a magnetic but unscrupulous personality. The air rang with the arguments, always returning to Joan's plaintive, 'Honey, I just don't want you to get hurt.' She did not suggest, as she might have been tempted to, that Addie would end up like her real mother, with an unwanted bundle. Never in Addie's entire life had Joan spoken with anything but affection about Adrienne, and that did not change. As it happened, Lloyd was meticulous about protection, but after a decent interval, Addie chose to go on the pill.

But Joan was right of course. There was never any doubt that Addie would get hurt. Lloyd, so sophisticated in arousing her, so animal, once he had succeeded, needed variety - a harem, a herd. By the time she was aware of the other women in his life, some casual, others like herself, occupying a regular place, she was already addicted to him.

For a while she put up with the humiliation of knowing she was not the only one, able to put the others out of her mind as long as she did not have to face their physical presence. But when, at the office, she saw their newly acquired seventeen-year-old secretary looking at him in that transparent revealing way, he now nearly forty, she knew it was all over. That was only a few months before her flight to England.

The train pulled into Bath Station. A man in the seat opposite lifted down her small suitcase, and she peered out to see that it was raining again. She did not this time intend to enter the city, though it was a place she would like to visit again. Instead, she asked at the ticket office how she could get to Long Barton. There was, it appeared, no train, only an hourly bus, and no hotel, but the ticket inspector thought there was a pub - The Stonemason's Arms - and almost certainly, a B & B. So there was more waiting, and another journey, more time for chewing over the past and the present before she arrived at Long Barton.

In the end, she had to go for the B & B accommodation, though there was only the one room available and that was tiny. Mrs Simpson, the landlady, offered her a lunch, but Addie rather liked the look of The Stonemason's Arms, and in any case, she wanted to sit and think on her own.

The public house was quiet, with two or three men in conversation at the bar, and a few people sitting at the tables in the dining area. She ordered a chicken salad and walked to one of the empty tables, only vaguely aware that the men had turned to look at her. Her mind was focused on what she might find out about her family this time. Her meal was placed in front of her and, as she ate, she made a plan of campaign. She would not, she felt sure, get any more help from the school; as it was, Dr Glossop had let slip far more than she would have expected - far more than he could have intended. But he had said something about the doctor - the young doctor, the son of the old doctor - and the old doctor had been specifically mentioned in Dorothy's letter to James. What had she said now? Something like 'I begged him to say the baby was premature, and he, dear man ...' So what information, if any, would he have passed down to his son?

'Do you know if a Dr Charlton's surgery is round here?' she asked the barman, as she ordered a glass of white wine at the bar.

'Right opposite the green on the other side of the road,' he said, leaving his post for a moment to point across the village centre to some dignified nineteenth century houses. 'If you go over now, you might find they've got one of the afternoon clinics on.'

Crossing the green, glad to have remembered her umbrella to protect her from the damp drizzling shower, Addie found herself in the midst of a melee of push chairs and baby carriages, many parked within the entrance area of the surgery. She carefully picked her way through the mothers and babies to Reception.

'Could I get to see Dr Charlton?' she asked.

'Have you had the pregnancy confirmed?' said the receptionist, glancing up from her notes.

'No, I'm not pregnant,' Addie replied.

The woman looked again. 'Are you one of Dr Charlton's patients or are you a visitor?' she asked, obviously taking in the accent.

'I'm just visiting, but I was hoping to have a private word with the doctor,' Addie said, wondering if it was ethical to gloss over the lack of any medical problem.

'I could make an appointment for tomorrow. This afternoon's just the M & B's - the mothers and babies, that is - and Prenatals. Could you fill out a visitor's form?'

Addie decided to come clean.

'Look, I don't want to give you the wrong impression - there's nothing wrong with me. I'm trying to get some

199

information about my - she was about to say 'grandmother', but changed it on an impulse to 'great-aunt' - 'She was treated by Dr Charlton senior in the sixties. Her name was Dorothy Heron.'

The woman's face was unchanged. 'Before my time, I'm afraid. I've only been here ten years.'

Addie tried to break through the barrier of lack of interest.

'I've come over specially from the States to find out about my family,' she smiled, 'and I was hoping that Dr Charlton might be able to help me.'

A bell sounded from within the doctor's office and the receptionist looked at her notes.

'Mrs Boorman, could you take Katie in, now please. Look, I'll tell you what,' she said, turning to Addie, 'I'll put your name down after the evening surgery. If there's an emergency, he might have to rush off, but things are quiet at the moment, what with holidays and so on. It'll probably be all right. Say about ten to seven.'

'Well, look, if the doctor has any difficulty, some time tomorrow would be fine. Or I'd be very pleased to meet him for lunch or coffee at the 'Stonemason's Arms'. Perhaps you could tell him that. I'll leave my name with you anyway.'

She scribbled down her name and the B & B telephone number and handed it to the Receptionist, and then walked out, feeling satisfied at her efforts. An elderly woman entered the surgery, smiled fleetingly at Addie, and walked up to Reception. As Addie stood at the entrance opening her umbrella, she heard the woman say, 'Good afternoon, Angela, would you tell the doctor to pop in and see me tonight.'

As she glanced back, Addie saw the Receptionist point in her direction and the older woman's face grow stern and cold. It was impossible to interpret the meaning of the angry glare.

Turning her attention away, she called in at the local grocery store. Admiring the old style bubbled glass windows, she managed to get into conversation with the proprietor about village life.

'Did you know the people at the school - I'm trying to trace Dr Rodney Heron or his wife?'

The man looked blank. No, the school people kept away from the village. 'A bit like the old universities - town and gown,' he said.

On an impulse, she introduced the Henshaws and the Seccombes into the conversation.

'Seccombe - that name's familiar,' the man said, scratching his head, 'But if you want to know about the old-timers, you want Wynne Pullen in the post office. I've been here fifteen years, but she's been here at least forty.'

However, the woman in the post office was in her mid-thirties - Mrs Pullen was not in till tomorrow.

Arriving back too early at her accommodation, Addie was somehow unsurprised to be met by Mrs Simpson clutching a message.

'It's the surgery, m'dear. They asked if you'd ring.'

'Can I call from here?'

'There's a payphone in the hall, m'dear. And I've got the number here.'

'Oh, Miss Russell,' said the receptionist, when Addie had identified herself, 'I'm sorry, but Dr Charlton won't be able to see you after all.'

'Oh, that's a shame,' said Addie. 'Tomorrow then.'

'No, I'm sorry,' said the woman again, sounding embarrassed. 'He won't be able to see you at all.'

'Did you tell him I'd see him privately?'

'Er, yes. Well, no.'

Addie felt herself growing angry, knowing instinctively it was not the woman's fault. 'You mean you took it upon yourself not to pass on my message? Will you give me his telephone number, so I can speak to him myself?'

'No, I'm afraid that's not possible.'

'Look, Angela,' Addie said, remembering the woman's

201

name in a brief flash, 'I was straight with you. Will you please be straight with me? What happened? It was that woman that came in, wasn't it?'

'That was Mrs Charlton - senior,' said Angela. 'And she didn't want the doctor bothered. She was quite dogmatic.'

Addie thought quickly. 'Angela, if you'll give me Mrs Charlton's number, I'll be a good girl - but otherwise, I'm going to make a nuisance of myself at the surgery. And I'll be staying here quite a few days.'

'Miss Russell,' Angela said, 'I'm not being difficult, but I'd rather not give you her number. Just a hint: it is in the phone book and you could look it up yourself. It's Elizabeth R.'

'Elizabeth Regina?' said Addie raising one eyebrow.

Angela laughed weakly, 'Rose, I think. She's not usually quite so bloody- minded. I can't think what's got into her.'

'Well thanks anyway, Angela. Sorry you were caught in the crossfire.'

'Miss Russell, if you could manage to keep me out of it ...'

'Sure, Angela, don't give it another thought.'

With that aim in mind, Addie approached her landlady. 'Mrs Simpson, does the doctor have any family locally?'

'Oh yes, m'dear. His mother. She's about my age - I see her at the WI - the Women's Institute, that is. And his sister, too. She lives out at ...'

'No, I think the mother is the person I need. Do you happen to know where I could find her number?'

'Well of course, m'dear. She's the Chairman at the moment.' Mrs Simpson rummaged around in her bag and found a note from the WI, with Elizabeth Charlton's name and number clearly shown on it. Gratefully, Addie went to the payphone, armed with several coins.

'Mrs Charlton, I'm sorry to bother you. I'm Addie Russell. Mrs Simpson, who I'm lodging with has given me your name. I'm a visitor from the States, trying to find out about a relation of mine, who would have been a patient of your husband. I wonder if you could spare the time to talk to me.'

The reply was frosty. 'I'm sorry Miss er Russell, did you say? Naturally my husband's records of patients would have been confidential.'

'I got the impression that your husband was very kind to my - to Dorothy Heron.'

'Really, well, I wish *I* could be so helpful. But I'm afraid I'm really too busy for discussions that would be unlikely to lead ...'

'Maybe your son, the doctor, could look through his records,' interrupted Addie, aware that the conversation was about to come to an end.

'My son is a busy man. I'd rather you didn't bother him.'

'Surely your son can decide for himself.'

'Miss Russell,' said the voice at the end of the phone. 'My husband was very upset by Dorothy's Heron's death. We all were. However, my husband blamed himself. He suffered a nervous breakdown, and not long after, a major coronary. It was a very traumatic time for our whole family and I would rather my son was not drawn into your research.'

Her voice was cold and final, and Addie could only say weakly, 'I'm sorry. I'd no idea.'

A click at the other end of the phone pronounced the end of the conversation.

As Addie stood, for the moment deflated and unsure of her next move, Mrs Simpson approached.

'Did you manage to find out what you wanted, m'dear?'

'Well no, actually, Mrs Simpson. The information I wanted seemed to be tied up with the old doctor's death. And Mrs Charlton didn't want to discuss it.'

'Oh yes, now I come to think of it, there was some gossip when the old doctor was taken bad. In the sixties it would be, I suppose, because the son and the daughter were quite young then.'

Mrs Simpson seemed to be one of those people who didn't

stop once she had started, but Addie was all for encouraging this particular anecdote.

'They said it was to do with a suicide, but there was a lot of talk, because the son - Dr Charlton, the present Dr Charlton, that is, he nearly gave up his studies - and the daughter, Pat, she took a year off college and came to help her mother. Some people said there was something going on between the woman that died, and the old doctor, and that's why they all got so upset. But no-one ever really knew for certain.'

Addie nearly interrupted then to say she was positive there was nothing going on, but managed to keep her thoughts to herself.

'We thought at first they might have to move out of the surgery an' all - because we had another doctor in from Hassocks Town. Still, they came out all right in the end. Pillar of the community, Mrs Charlton. Drove an ambulance in the war. Involved in the church.'

'Hmm,' said Addie, unconvinced that Mrs Charlton was anything other than an old battleaxe. Even so, she could see Mrs Charlton's point. What right had she, Addie, to stir up another family's grief for her own ends? She wondered if the trip was going to be abortive after all. There was only Mrs Pullen tomorrow morning to provide any information.

Mrs Simpson, a motherly soul, insisted on cooking her a Cornish pasty for her evening meal, and, full of pastry, meat and vegetables and everything else that had gone into the traditional pasty, Addie thought she might have an early night. Still disappointed, she felt quite inclined to see Mrs Pullen as early as possible on the following day, and then return home. But after the meal, Mrs Simpson cheered her with stories of the area and on an impulse, she went to her room and started work on an article - calling it, tongue in cheek, *A Yank in the Wild West*. She had been thinking of some freelance work for the past few weeks, and the idea of a series of articles about England had come to her. Publication in the

States, or in England if it was possible, could bring in a useful income.

By the time she had produced a rough hand-written manuscript, she was quite tired and went off to sleep almost satisfied with the day's endeavours.

* * *

Mrs Pullen in the post office was ripping off a sheet of stamps, as Addie waited smiling at the other counter. She came round and took Addie's money for the chocolate bar she'd picked up. Like Mrs Simpson, she 'm'deared' Addie, and all the more once she heard the accent.

'I wonder if you could give me some help,' said Addie. 'I'm trying to find out about my folks - I understand that I had some relations called Henshaw and Seccombe, and I wonder if you know of anyone by that name living locally.'

'Henshaw, Henshaw, can't say that I remember that. And what was the other one - Seccombe - there's old Miss Seccombe? She used to come in for her pension regular, up till about two years ago. Now she's in a nursing home, but Sister comes in to collect all the pensions. We're the nearest post office, you see. It's terrible the way they're closing down.'

'How old would this lady be?' Addie said, her mind turning over. A pensioner and much older than Mrs Pullen, obviously, so well over sixty. Could Ada have had another daughter? Not another illegitimate daughter, still bearing her single name, surely. Perhaps it was some distant cousin? That was more likely.

'Oh, she'd be eighty, if she was a day, m'dear.'

A contemporary of Ada. She would surely remember something about her. She must meet this other Miss Seccombe.

'Do you know her - do you remember her?'

'Always very quiet, as I recall. Kept herself to herself. She lived in a little house just out of the village, with another lady. Came here about thirty years ago or more - I remember, because my little one - course he's a married man now - he started at the nursery school and I worked here at the post office two mornings - that's how I got to know everyone. But no-one knew much about her, or the other lady - people said they'd been in a sanatorium and now they was better. I reckoned it was the TB.'

She paused to enter Addie's purchase in the cash till.

'Anyway, they used to walk into the village together and buy liquorice allsorts and peppermints and cat food. Not from here, of course, the cat food, I mean. We're lucky we've still got the grocery store here, *and* the post office. But for how long I don't know. So many shops have closed down. It's a tragedy what the supermarkets have done to villages like ours.'

'Could you tell me where to find this nursing home?' interrupted Addie, sensing that Mrs Pullen was touching on a subject dear to her heart.

'Certainly, my dear, but you'd need a taxi to get there. I'll give you the telephone number, if you like. Taxi driver's married to my daughter's best friend. School friends they were - nice girl, and he makes a good living from the taxis.'

Ten minutes later, Addie was on her way.

Chapter 19: Lost and Lonely Years

'You say you think you're a relation of Miss Seccombe,' said Matron, putting her coffee cup down on her desk, as she spoke.

'Well, I don't know for sure, Miss - Daborn - did you say?' Addie said. 'I only know it was my grandmother's maiden name and I guess I should check on any possible connections.'

Veronica Daborn nodded not unsympathetically. 'Well, most of our residents like having visitors, Miss Russell. Obviously, their lives are fairly humdrum, though we have entertainments and outings. So I've no objection to your meeting Miss Seccombe, though obviously I don't want her upset in any way.'

'Naturally, I'll be as tactful as I can,' Addie said, hoping that the lecture wasn't going to go on for too long.

'Now Miss Seccombe has some short term memory problems, though in the main she's quite on the ball. Occasionally, I hear stories from my ladies - and gentlemen, of course - which sound most plausible, but are not quite based in reality. They tend to lose fragments of memory and piece them together in a way that is not quite accurate.'

Is she trying to tell me something, Addie wondered? If the old lady was suffering from dementia, she was not going to find out very much. She voiced her concern.

'Is she here because she's mentally or physically frail?'

'Well, to all intents and purposes - physically. She, unfortunately, last year, lost most of her sight, and has been waiting for quite a few months for a cataract operation. But that's now in hand. Also, she has difficulty in walking. We understand that until a couple of years ago, she lived with another elderly lady near Long Barton, and they looked after each other until the other lady died. Then there was no-one to help, so her GP, Dr Morgan, had her admitted here.'

She seemed about to embark on another part of her set text, when a uniformed nurse knocked on the half open door, then came scurrying in.

'It's Mr Wilcox. He's upsetting everyone. He's shouting again.'

Veronica Daborn got up quickly. 'I'll see to him. Would you take Miss Russell to see …'

A deep masculine voice interrupted her, bellowing, 'Help me. Help me. Somebody help me,' and she left the room hurriedly.

'Who did you want to see?' said the nurse.

'Miss Seccombe.'

'Okay. I'll take you along. Would you like some tea?'

'That would be nice.'

They walked along the corridor past several other rooms, some with their doors open and elderly people, mainly women, peering out. A few were in bed, but others were sitting in chairs, knitting or talking to other residents. One door was closed, with the words, *Margaret Holbrook, do not disturb*, inscribed on a card on the door. Addie assumed she was an important staff member. Eventually, after another corridor, they arrived at a modest little room. Addie found her heart was thumping.

The nurse ushered Addie in. 'There's a young lady come to see you, dear.' Turning back to Addie, she said, 'I'll get the tea.'

The woman was seated in an armchair. She was looking at the television, though Veronica Daborn had said she could see very little. It was difficult to gauge her age, for she had a ruddy, healthy complexion, hardly lined at all, and her hair, though thinning a little, was a mix of light and dark grey. Addie saw that her brown eyes were misty. Even so, she turned her head towards them at the sound of voices.

'Hallo. Who are you? Come a little closer, dear.'

Addie walked over and took the thin, veined hand in hers.

208

'Are you from the social?'

'No,' Addie responded, trying to keep her voice calm and measured. 'No. My name's Addie and I'm from the States.'

'The state. Is it to do with the benefit?'

Addie tried again. 'I'm from America, and I've just come to say hallo.'

'That's nice. Your hand's very cold. Are you all right, dear?'

'Yes. I'm fine,' said Addie, withdrawing her hand. 'I always have cold hands.'

'You sound like a nice girl,' Ada said. 'What are you wearing?'

'I'm wearing jeans - blue jeans - and a white shirt and a coloured waistcoat.'

'Yes. I can see the shirt. And you've got dark hair, haven't you?'

'Yes I have.'

'What did you say your name was?'

'It's Addie.'

'That's a funny name,' said the woman. 'I don't know that name.'

'I was named after my mother, Adrienne,' Addie said, sitting down on a footstool by the old lady's chair.

'Adrienne. That's like my name.'

'And my grandmother's name was Dorothy.'

She wondered if she sounded patronising. She was feeling her way, unsure how to proceed.

'Dorothy?'

There was no mistaking the change in the elderly woman's manner.

'Do you know someone of that name, Miss Seccombe?'

'Call me Ada, dear. Everyone does. Yes, Dorothy was my mother's name. That was a long time ago.'

Addie was silenced, aware of a sudden pounding in her ears. Like an echo in her head, the words repeated themselves. *Dorothy was my mother's name. Call me Ada. Call me Ada.* The

Family Tree she had so laboriously drawn out flashed through her mind. Dorothy Victoria who begat Ada Petitpierre Seccombe, who begat Dorothy Ann Seccombe.

'And it was my baby's name.'

Addie's heart started racing again.

'Your baby?'

Was it really possible that Ada, fourteen year old mother of Dorothy, had outlived Dorothy and Adrienne, that Ada Seccombe was here in the flesh, and could be reached, touched and spoken to by Addie, her great-granddaughter?

'Dorothy was your child?' she said shakily.

'I haven't got no children. Not now. But I had a little baby. Poor little thing. They took her away from me. And she died.'

The woman paused and lifted a frail hand to wipe the glazed eyes, which had now become watery and sad.

Addie, confused again, waited for a moment, then asked, 'Would you mind telling me about your baby, Ada?'

'My baby? That was a long time ago. What did you say your name was, dear?'

'My name's Addie.'

'That's a nice name, dear.'

'Ada, would you tell me about your baby, about Dorothy.'

'My little Dorothy. He said they'd call her after my mother, Dorothy. "After a respectable Christian woman," he said. That's what me dad said. And me ma put down Ann on the certificate, too. He was angry about that. It was his mother's name. But me ma did it anyway.'

'Why was he angry about that, Ada?'

'He said he didn't want any bastard brat carrying his mother's name. That's what he said. That's what he said after he thrashed the living daylights out of me.'

'He beat you?' Addie said, shocked.

'I had the baby in the privy, at the back of the house. I didn't know I was going to have a baby. No-one told me nothing about it. But me ma found me on the floor with the baby. She come to see why I was such a long time.'

'And your father beat you?'

'Are you from the social?'

'No,' said Addie patiently, though she wanted to urge Ada to go on with the story. 'I've come to visit you. I'm from America. You were telling me about your baby.'

'I held her in my arms. My little Dorothy. Her little hands. Her little feet. She was so warm. My ma showed me how to feed her.' Another tear ran down her face. 'Then I went to that place, and I never held her again. I never held a baby again.'

'What place was that?'

''What d'you say dear? Is she bringing us some tea? I thought she was bringing some tea and biscuits.'

'Ada,' Addie said, guiltily wondering for a moment if it was fair to take the old lady back to this sad time in her life. 'What happened to your baby?'

'My dad took me to that place. I wouldn't tell him who did it to me. I wouldn't tell on my Perce. I was a pretty thing then.' she laughed suddenly, like a shy young girl. 'I had 'em all flocking around. But my Perce was the only one for me. Me dad kept asking me over and over, and the baby kept crying. I wanted him to leave me alone. Then he got the strap out. He used to beat me regular, when he saw the lads come courting. But that was the worst time. I didn't tell him at first, even then. He just went on and on. I was black and blue afterwards. Said he hadn't beat me enough to keep me respectable. Then I told him, and he said Perce had gone and I'd never see him again. I cried and cried. I couldn't stop. He was so handsome, my Perce.'

'What happened to Perce?' asked Addie, though she knew.

'We was going to get married, so he said it was all right, what we did. But then he went off to the war. He said he'd come back and marry me. But then me ma told me he got killed. They put his name up on the monument in the village green. But that didn't help me. I wouldn't have got taken to

211

that place, if he'd been around.'

'What place do you mean?'

'I thought it was a hospital, but it was a mental home. My dad took me and he left me there. He never told me he was going to leave me. I thought he was coming back later.'

Addie was aghast. 'He didn't tell you? He just left you?'

'He left me there with these mad people, and I couldn't get out. And he and my ma kept the baby and it died.'

'How do you know that?' Addie asked.

'Me dad came and told me God had punished me by taking away the baby. He said I was wicked and didn't deserve any babies.'

'Didn't your mother visit?' Addie asked.

'She came once. She came after I been there a few weeks. I thought she'd come to take me home. She was all frightened like, and she wanted to tell me my Perce was dead.'

'Then when I started screaming, they sent her out. I called out, "Come back Ma. Come back and take me home. I'll be good." She turned round towards me, and she starts crying. But they just pushed her out. Then my dad come after, when he told me about the baby.'

Addie, shaken by the story, was silent for a moment. She could hardly keep back her own tears. Then she asked, 'How long were you there?'

'Years and years. I can't tell you how long. Me and Lily Horrocks, we came out together, and we went to live in her house. Her daughter used to come in and look after us. But mostly we looked after ourselves - like we used to in the hospital. We did a lot of things at the hospital. We helped in the kitchen, and we did sewing. It was all right really.'

'How old was Lily?'

'She was the same as me. We was both about fifty.'

Addie felt a shiver of horror run down her spine. 'You were there till you were fifty?' she said incredulously.

'I can't remember exactly. It's a long time ago. We always

212

looked after each other in that place, and we just carried on like we used to. It was nice being in that little house. It was lovely. Me and Lily used to have a good laugh together.

'Sometimes we'd have a little drink of that Liebermulch, or some sherry.' Her face contorted. 'I ain't got no-one now.'

The nurse came in with a pot of tea and two cups. It gave Addie a moment to think. She could not just blurt out their relationship. Instead, she said in a low voice, 'I'm so sorry,' and she took hold of both of Ada's thin, veined hands and held them tightly in her own.

Chapter 20: The Power of the Press

Addie did not return to Long Barton right away, but took a cab to the nearest small town. She had the sudden claustrophobic feeling that everyone in Long Barton knew her entire family business.

In Hampton Leigh, where the taxi driver dropped her, Addie found an Italian restaurant and ordered a pizza. Waiting for her order, she looked out into the street of the small market town. There were the usual ubiquitous department stores, chemists' shops, electronics displays. Across the road, with a window display of photographs, were the offices of the local paper, the *Hampton & Barton Gazette*. As she took in the surroundings, the waitress brought her a pizza on a large dish, the multi colours of peppers and pineapple spilling over the edge of the dough.

'That looks delicious,' she said, smiling at the waitress. But her thoughts were not really on the meal before her. Instead, Ada's weather-beaten face came into her mind, and the story that had unfolded at the nursing home. She imagined the fourteen-year-old child with her unexpected baby, and her grief at the supposed death of that baby. The terrible father who lied to the teenager, stole her child, Dorothy, and incarcerated her, nearly seventy years ago. Poor woman, she had been denied almost every solace that life ought to offer.

But despite her sympathy for the woman, Addie was guiltily aware of a sense of detachment. Try as she would, she could feel no sense of kinship with Ada. She could not think of her as family.

Fortunately, at the moment, Ada was quite unaware of their connection. Addie had revealed her new knowledge to Veronica Daborn, who had promised to try to prepare Ada. I could have done with some preparation time myself, Addie thought.

Her plate was empty; she had eaten her meal automatically, hardly noticing it. The waitress removed her plate and took her order for coffee, and Addie looked out of the window again, turning her mind away from the morning's events. She glanced once more at the photographic display outside the *Hampton & Barton Gazette.* Perhaps the local paper would be interested in the article she had written the previous night. Why not?

The English are at their best in non-intimate situations, Addie thought, as she sat in *The Gazette's* somewhat cramped offices. Everyone from the taxi driver to the post-mistress and now the chief reporter here had been unfailingly courteous and helpful. As soon as they heard her accent, they practically fell over themselves to assist her. Not only had this reporter, Chris Templeman, said he would be interested in seeing her article but, over a cup of tea, he had asked her the reason for her stay, and was both fascinated and aghast at her great-grandmother's story.

'She's an old lady.' Addie said, 'And perhaps she rambles a bit - according to the matron, Veronica Daborn, some of them get a bit forgetful and invent things. And she says obviously Ada didn't have much of an education. But she certainly isn't mentally ill - heck, a lot of the people I've worked with back home seem crazier than her.'

'It's a very interesting story,' said Chris Templeman, 'and at the back of my mind, I think I remember reading something about the Barton Bridge mental hospital when it closed a few years ago. There was a big article about the sort of people put away at the beginning of the century - and they weren't what we would describe now as insane. I'll see if I can find it in the archives. Perhaps I could give you a ring. Where are you staying?'

'Well actually, I was thinking of going back to Surrey tomorrow.' Addie said, idly picking up a pencil from Chris Templeman's desk. 'I'll see Ada again, and I'll probably tell

215

her I'm her great-granddaughter. Then I think I'll come back and see her again in a few weeks. Of course, I'm interested in my grandmother's life too - that's Ada's daughter. That's one reason I came here - and I'd like to find out about her childhood and schooling. In fact there's a lot of things I want to find out, but the people involved haven't been too helpful.'

'Anything I could help with?' Chris asked.

'I ... no I don't think so,' said Addie, tempted for a moment, then remembering that she didn't know this young man too well. The last thing she wanted was for anyone to read the entire Heron scandal, plastered all over the local paper. It would certainly put paid once and for all to any help she might get from the doctor's family.

'Well, leave me your number at your place here and at home, and if I find anything out about Barton Bridge, I'll get back to you.'

She scribbled down the two phone numbers on a memo pad on his desk and passed them to him as he spoke.

'In the meantime, get your article typed and send it on to me. If I can use it, I'll pay the normal rates. And if you want to use it in the States, go ahead. There won't be any conflict between First British Serial Rights and any American rights. We're not so important that anyone would give a damn, anyway,' he said smiling ruefully.

'So why are you here, Chris?' asked Addie.

'It's a step on the ladder, I hope. London papers eventually. Hopefully, not too long in the future. My girlfriend and I both graduated from Bath, and we liked the area and stayed around. Now we've broken up, but I'm still here, for the time being.'

It seemed she was to be surrounded by men with the spectres of ex-girlfriends leaning over their shoulders, Addie thought, though she was not really interested in Chris as a potential boyfriend. He was a pleasant enough guy, but it was still Jonathan's face that kept appearing unsummoned before her. Yes, it seemed that even when she was thinking back to her affair with Lloyd, as she had the previous day, Jonathan was now able to push him from her mind.

She followed Chris's directions to the bus station and, as she wandered along, she wondered why Jonathan could not shake off Tabitha Plowright, who seemed to haunt all social occasions, like Banquo's ghost. Was he just a coward? Perhaps her presence protected him from getting involved with anyone else. And yet, the way he had looked at her - surely he was not just flirting with her. He was not a womaniser, like Lloyd.

She arrived back at Long Barton, and took time to walk to the war memorial in the centre of the village. Amongst the inscribed names of long dead soldiers from the first and second world wars, she found Percy Henshaw's name carved into the stone. As she stood there, she thought silently and sadly about the teenage lovers, Percy and Ada, torn apart by war, neither knowing of the fate of their tiny daughter, nor of the further tragedies that would occur as a result of their immature fumbling love affair.

I must be very careful what I say to Ada, she thought. It would be very unfair to tell her how Dorothy suffered.

She returned to the B & B and spent some time making notes about her various trips. With some of the personal details edited out, she felt she could come up with several travel articles describing parts of England of interest to Americans, and at the same time, give an American's eye view, which might go down well with the Brits. It would be a start. If, as now seemed likely, she was going to stay for the full six months, certainly until the additional provisions of the will were read, she must have some occupation and income, and not fritter away the few thousand pounds that James had left.

She was completely engrossed, when Mrs Wilson called up the stairs, 'It's the phone for you, m'dear.'

She was surprised to hear from Chris Templeman so soon.

'Hallo, Addie. You don't mind me calling you Addie, do you? Well, I haven't got a lot of time just now, but I have picked up some interesting bits of info for you. Would you like to have a quick bite with me this evening, and I can fill you in?'

Addie hesitated, wondering if she was falling into the same trap as before.

For God's sake, she thought, we'll have a meal in a public place. Anyway, he was not like Julian, she was sure of that. He was normal - an ex-girlfriend was something she could relate to. Julian was different. She could recognise it now. What she had mistaken for lack of interest was actually a kind of coldness - an ability to enjoy sex in a clinical, uninvolved way, an emotionless, unloving way - probably much as Rodney must have behaved. She felt convinced that Chris was not like that. He reminded her, in fact, of one of her old college boyfriends - good fun to be with and not too intense.

'Sure, that'd be great, Chris,' she replied. 'I can't wait to hear what you've found out.'

They met at The Stonemason's Arms. It was easier for Chris to drive into Long Barton than for Addie to take another taxi, and when she walked into the bar in the early evening, Chris was already sitting there wearing a hand-knitted jumper.

'Can I get you a drink?' he asked her.

'Let me get them,' she protested. 'You're here because of me.'

'I've already got a pint,' he said. 'Really, it's all right.'

'Okay, but please let's go halves on the meal. Otherwise I'll feel really bad.'

'All right,' he said, not putting up too much of a fight; she imagined that journalists on provincial newspapers weren't too highly paid.

'The first thing is,' he said, as Addie sipped a glass of white wine, 'I've found some interesting stuff in our archives. Until a couple of years ago, we had an old boy working for the paper,

218

who was meticulous about records. He wasn't much of a newspaper man. But he was an obsessive filer. You know the sort - if it moves, salute it; if it stays still, file it.'

'Lucky for me,' said Addie.

'Absolutely. Well he kept all the copies of the paper - every copy - in various boxes and he labelled them and noted them down in a record book and - would you believe - cross referenced them as well. If he ever started talking about the system, you couldn't get him to stop. He was a real barrel of laughs, I can tell you.'

They finished their drinks and got up from the bar stools. Chris stooped slightly as they walked through an arch to the dining room, and his curly hair brushed the top of the entrance. Addie followed him to a seat, noticing that his shoulders remained hunched until he sat down. She hadn't realised before how tall he was.

A waitress took their order. Addie went for steak and salad, before realising that Chris was a vegetarian, but he waved away her apology. He started telling her how he'd become a vegetarian when he was an impoverished student, and Addie didn't interrupt him, but once the waitress returned with the meal, she was eager for him to get back to the original story.

'You were telling me before, what you found in the archives, Chris.'

'Oh yes. Well, first of all, I looked up Barton Bridge Hospital to see if my memory was correct. There was an article in the paper a few years ago, telling some of the history of the mental hospital, and some of it was unbelievable. What you wouldn't credit is how easy it was to get someone committed as mentally ill. In fact - it's pretty irrelevant, of course - but I think I read somewhere that T.S. Eliot had his poor wife shoved into a mental hospital. Anyway that's nothing to do with your great-grandmother.'

Addie now waited patiently for him to come to the point,

219

enjoying her steak, which was rare and tasty.

'Anyhow, there were various Acts brought out in the late nineteenth and early twentieth century, The Lunacy Act, the Mental Defectives Act - I can get you more details if you're interested - and some aspects of these acts, well, it seems to me it was nothing more than Victorian fuddy-duddies imposing their own particular morality on society. Mental health didn't come into it. Puritan values with a capital 'P' - that was the name of the game. Now I can't quote it verbatim - should have got a photocopy really - but basically, a girl could be committed for having sex under 16 - morally defective, you see - or for having an illegitimate baby. Now if she had post natal depression into the bargain - as well she might have in those circumstances - they had all the ammunition they needed.'

He rested down his knife and fork for a moment to open both palms in the gesture of a conjuror. 'QED.'

'Ada certainly fell into the first two categories, and possibly the third,' said Addie. 'It's pretty much as Veronica Daborn implied - that there was no other reason. It's quite horrific. I didn't want to believe it. I thought she must have been ill or something - but you're saying she could have been put in a mental hospital for life for no other reason than having sex when she shouldn't, and possibly being tearful after the baby was born.'

'Well it was another time, Addie.'

'The beginning of this century - this is our time.'

'I don't want to make excuses for this country, Addie, but look what's happened during this century. I mean even if we put aside the Holocaust as some appalling aberration, look at the way women were treated in China for example - I don't just mean footbinding - I mean being beheaded for unfaithfulness - look at the Russians in our time - incarcerating enemies of the state in lunatic asylums. And as for the "Land of the Free" - you've also done things you don't have to be too

220

proud of.'

'I take your point, Chris, and at an intellectual level, I agree with you. But this was just an innocent schoolgirl. She probably didn't know what she was doing - her Perce said it's okay - and she did it. But the worst thing is ...'

'Yes?'

'No, it's not the worst thing. The worst thing is that she was there at all - a whole life wasted. But I can't get over the fact that her father did it to her. Am I being unrealistic? Because Pop - my adopted father - is a really great guy, and if I had to choose my dad, I'd choose him *again*, and the idea that he would take my child away from me - put me in a mental home, lie to me - it doesn't bear thinking about.'

'There is something else, Addie.'

'Yes.'

'I looked up Mental Health in the index, and I did actually find a report that some women were released in the fifties, after lifetimes in these mental homes. I must say that I agree with you that that's the worst part - that these women spent the best years of their lives banged up in Barton Bridge Hospital and others like it. Those that came out were often completely institutionalised, and had to be trained to understand money, and how to run their lives and take some responsibility for themselves.'

Addie sighed. 'It's all so unbelievable - and to be honest - so entirely detached from my life - I feel guilty that I can't feel more pain for her - but above all, I feel relief that I'm me and living in the 1990s. I wonder how Ada will feel about me being her great-granddaughter.'

'She doesn't know?'

'No - and I wonder is she going to feel better or worse knowing that her daughter survived into middle age without her. And if she does know - is it going to benefit her - it's not as if I'm going to stick around for ever?'

'You mean here in Long Barton.'

'Well no, certainly not here - I meant here in England. I have to re-apply to immigration to stay on beyond December - so all sorts of decisions have to be made.'

She felt again the need to hold back on some of her story, and chose not to go into the details of James, Dorothy and the house.

'You say Ada's in her late eighties. If you don't mind my saying, she may not have all that long to live, so wouldn't she like to know she was leaving part of herself behind.'

Addie shrugged helplessly.

'I just don't know. I guess I'll just have to see how the cookie crumbles.'

They ate in silence for a moment.

'Did you find out anything else, Chris?'

'Well the other thing you mentioned was wanting to find out a bit about your grandmother as a young girl. Now that was more difficult, but I looked up "Education" and what I did spot in one of the back numbers was a report on the retirement of the headmistress of the local girls' school, Mrs Furneaux - that was about four years ago, so she would be about mid-sixties now - and she said she was going to stay in the neighbourhood and grow roses. She'd been teaching at the school all her life. I wonder if she might be able to help.'

Addie swiftly thought back and counted on her fingers. 'If she was sixty-five now, she'd be younger than Dorothy. Much younger. Dorothy would be - let's see - she'd be mid-seventies; I can't see how that would be of any use. Thanks for trying though, Chris.'

'Yes, of course - sorry, I'm a writer - I'm not numerate too. But there was something else I thought you might like.'

He pulled a photocopy out of his wallet and handed it to her. It was a clipping from the Gazette.

'February 1934: The engagement is announced of Dorothy Ann, granddaughter of Mr George Arthur Petitpierre Seccombe, and Mrs Dorothy Victoria Seccombe, to Dr Rodney Heron, Housemaster at

Marsh House School.

It didn't really add anything to what she already knew, but she thanked Chris just the same and put it away in her purse.

'I'll keep my eyes open,' he said, 'In case I spot anything more.'

He smiled at her as they stood up to go, and cracked his head on a beam almost directly above. But he must have been quite used to the experience because he just carried on talking. 'And of course, it's up to you whether you try to get hold of Mrs Furneaux. She may know of previous teachers at the school. Certainly, she would know who her predecessor was.'

She made the decision in the end to explore every possibility. She was, after all, going to stay another day and see Ada once again. She would call Mrs Furneaux, ask to see her in the morning, see Ada in the afternoon, and go home the following day. She would take with her some of the sights she had seen and commit them to paper.

As it happened, the thatched cottage in which Mrs Furneaux lived was worth looking at. The garden was a kaleidoscope of reds and pinks and purple flowers; roses trailing down the wall, busy lizzies spilling out of hanging baskets in profusion and beds packed full of begonias and petunias.

Addie arrived on foot, following the directions Mrs Furneaux had given her on the phone, and found her sitting at a garden table with a coffee pot and bone china cups at the ready.

'I don't quite understand the purpose of your visit, my dear,' she said, 'but I'm always delighted to show off my little garden. My one regret is that my husband didn't live long enough for us to share our retirement. We both had demanding lives in the teaching profession. But how typical it is that sometimes when a man stops working he doesn't live long enough to enjoy the leisure time which he has been looking forward to.' She glanced away from Addie to pour the coffee. 'Now tell me again what you wanted to know about the school.'

Addie explained that she hoped to find out about the period from the late nineteen twenties to the mid nineteen thirties, and told her a little about the progress she had made.

Mrs Furneaux sipped her coffee thoughtfully.

'I always prefer ground coffee, my dear, don't you? Well now, let me see. I came to the school as head in the mid sixties. I hadn't taught there before. My predecessor was a Miss Ashendon, and she died within, say, ten years of my taking the job.'

Addie let out a small 'Oh' of disappointment - not that she had expected anything other than this.

'Yes, I'm sorry to disappoint you, my dear. I don't think you'll find any teacher from that era who would have survived to tell you anything about it.'

She glanced sympathetically at Addie's expression. ' I hope that doesn't put a complete full stop on your research.'

'I guess I don't know quite where to go from here, but thank you for your time, Mrs Furneaux.'

'Would you like another cup of coffee, my dear, before you go? Or perhaps you would allow me to show you my roses.'

Addie, determined not to allow her disappointment to get in the way of common courtesy towards this kindly woman who had so willingly welcomed a stranger into her home, requested a walk round the garden.

'May I take your arm, my dear. I'm not as agile as I used to be. Arthritis in the knee joint, unfortunately.'

Mrs Furneaux, walking with a stick in her right hand, her left arm lightly resting on Addie's, led Addie through an arbour into her rose garden.

As she walked, she said, 'There is one thing, which you may find helpful. Nowadays, records are kept of every girl in the school - their personal file - and at the end of their stay, the records are often stored. Now I don't think that would have

224

been the way of things in the thirties and forties, but there may well have been a log book kept, which would have had limited information on the girls' examination successes and so on. However, whether records from the period you are interested in are still intact remains to be seen, of course.'

'Thank you,' Addie replied. 'I will find out about that.'

'Now what do you think of this?' Mrs Furneaux said, with not a little pride. 'There are so many wonderful varieties now and I have tried to achieve a blend of new and old roses, and to find some appeal for all the senses.'

'It's very successful,' said Addie, inhaling the delicate scent.

'Naturally, the visual element is the primary consideration, but I like to feel that if I should lose my sight, heaven forbid, the fragrance of this little sanctuary would give some consolation.'

Addie nodded in agreement. 'My grandfather put some marvellous scented roses in his garden.'

'Gardens are the most wonderful places of creation. I always found, when I was teaching, that pottering among the plants was the most soothing of activities after some very frustrating days. In a way dealing with plants is like dealing with children, except that they don't answer back.' She stooped to break off a dead flower head.

'But as I said before, though one cannot actually listen to roses, any more than, shall we say, the sound of air moving through the branches of trees, or the wind rustling the foliage, one can enjoy the *feel* of velvety petals.'

Addie began to enjoy listening to the woman's beautifully modulated and erudite words. They walked back through the arbour, and sat at the small table once again. On impulse, Addie asked if she could put some questions and take down the answers. She was aware, at the end of her discussion, that she had all the ingredients for an article on roses for the uninitiated.

As she put her notebook away and prepared to leave, the other woman said suddenly, 'I've just remembered that there was a very elderly lady who taught the choir. I think her name was Margaret Holroyd. A friend suggested we might have things in common to talk about, but it was never followed up. But how you would go about finding her, I just do not know.'

She cut Addie short in her expressions of thanks. 'Wait and see, my dear, if you find out anything, before you thank me. I know you are not intending to stay too long here, but if you come back again, do call in. I have enjoyed meeting you.'

Addie decided she still had time to visit Ada that afternoon. She had, after all, made a commitment to Veronica Daborn, and though no-one would be affected if she broke her promise, she was beginning to feel some sense of obligation.

Returning by taxi to the nursing home, she was greeted by Veronica Daborn herself, her office door wide open. 'Hallo there, Miss Russell. Glad that you managed to get back.' She beckoned Addie inside and motioned to her to close the door behind her. 'I've had a little chat with Ada. I've taken the liberty of suggesting that it's possible that a long lost relative has been found. She was very excited at first. Then she seemed to get a bit worried about it. I didn't go into any detail. How you tell her about your relationship, I'm going to leave up to you. But I would suggest you simplify the story if you can.'

Addie nodded, analysing the story to herself, and wondering how she could abridge it. Could she tell Ada that her daughter, Dorothy, had committed suicide, that her granddaughter, Adrienne, had died in childbirth, that the stain of illegitimacy had run through the lives of each generation of women. It was, in truth, a terrible story to tell to the old lady.

The lies, as it happened, came out easily. She had one moment when she remembered a comment by Jonathan - '... an honourable person ...' She was still honourable - the dishonest story she was to tell to Ada was to spare an old woman's pain - for no other reason.

She sat close to Ada on the footstool. There was a subtle change since the previous day.

'You're the young lady that came yesterday, aren't you? Is it you that's supposed to be related to me?' The old woman's brow was furrowed.

'That's right, Ada.'

'I thought you was from the social.'

'No, I've come specially to see you. I'm from America.'

'You're after the house, aren't you. You don't catch me that easy.'

'The house?' said Addie, gaping.

'My little house, where I lived with Lily. The social tried to get it off me, but I sorted them out. I'm not stupid. I know I haven't got no relations. My little baby died and my mum and dad, they died. And I got the house. No-one else is going to get my house.'

'I'm not after your house, Ada,' said Addie gently. 'I've come to tell you something important.'

'Important?' Her face still showed her suspicion. 'Is it about Lily Horrocks? Are you related to Lily? You're not Lily's daughter.'

'It's not about Lily. It's about your baby, Dorothy.' She waited for Ada to take in the name.

'Dorothy?'

'Yes, I have a shock for you, Ada,' Addie said hesitantly. 'Your baby, Dorothy Ann, she didn't die then, not till much later. She was ill, but she got better and then your parents looked after her, while you were ill.'

'Didn't die?' echoed Ada, her voice puzzled, as if trying to take in the information. 'He come and said she was dead.'

'She didn't die,' Addie repeated firmly. 'She grew up and had her own daughter.'

Quite suddenly, comprehension dawned and Ada reacted. Her unseeing eyes opened wide and her lips shook. Her words came out in an anguished shriek. 'She didn't die? He kept her

227

from me. My baby.' She rocked backwards and forwards, clasping herself as she did so, moaning rhythmically in time with the rocking movement. Words tumbled out. 'That wicked old man. God strike him dead. May he rot in hell.' She carried on moaning and rocking and Addie, horrified, searched for a way to continue. This was only the beginning. How could she make the rest of the story more palatable?

'Dorothy grew up and married an army officer, James Buckley,' she lied. 'They loved each other very much and they had a daughter, Adrienne. Dorothy didn't know you were still alive.' That, at least, was true.

Ada stopped rocking, and Addie saw that she was listening now. 'She's alive. My Dorothy Ann? My baby?'

'No, I'm sorry. Dorothy died suddenly.' Once again Ada moaned in sorrow, a low animal sound which cut Addie to the quick. Again she used her powers of invention. 'She had a heart attack.'

She saw tears running down the lined cheeks.

'Poor Dorothy, poor little Dorothy.'

'But by then her daughter, Adrienne, was grown up.' Addie said, trying to add the new information in single sentences so that Ada could grasp it.

'Adrienne. Are you Adrienne?' said the old woman, her eyes suddenly excited behind the opaque screen of the cataract.

'I'm Adrienne's daughter,' Addie said, taking her hand. 'You're my great-grandmother.'

'The woman looked down at the hand and held it.

'What was your name again?'

'Addie - Addie Russell.'

'You're not Adrienne.'

'No.'

'What happened to Adrienne?'

'My mother went out to the States and got married. She's still out there. My dad is called Tony Russell.'

It was all nearly true.

'You're my granddaughter.'

'Great-granddaughter.'

Once again, tears streamed down the old lady's face.

'You'll come back and see me when they've done me eyes. I want to see what my little girl would have turned out like.'

Chapter 21: A Door to the Past

It was Friday. Addie went through her plans for the day. She would contact the local girls' school, Long Barton First & Middle, and see if they would let her see the school reports and personal files in their archives. If they agreed, she'd go there in the afternoon. Then what?

In fact, after another night in Long Barton, she was hankering for home. She was feeling too enclosed in the small bed and breakfast accommodation, missing her belongings, James's house and garden, and her friends. The people she had left behind, the Graingers, the Amerys, even Meera, they were like a second family now - people whose reactions she could anticipate to a certain extent, no longer people whom she had to address with caution and tact. She was tired of the effort of being amongst strangers. And Jonathan - though he was not in the forefront of her mind all the time, he often came into her thoughts - his face, frequently serious, but of late, more often lightened by a smile, the grey eyes, penetrating, trying, it seemed, to read her feelings, or to tell her something. Was *she* herself reading more into it than there was? She wanted to get back and find out. It was crazy, but once or twice, she found herself getting those 'first date butterflies' when she thought of him.

She turned her mind back to the work in hand. She would regret it if she did not make good use of her trip.

Telephoning the school first, she found she was talking to the headmistress herself. She was disconcerted to hear that the school was now a private school.

'We used to be a girls' grammar school,' the head commented, when Addie had explained her interest. 'But my predecessor decided not to join the comprehensive system, at the time when schools were changing over. As far as I understand, she wanted to keep it single sex. But you don't have to worry. We are, in effect, the same school, we've retained our old records and in fact we've recently appointed an archivist, Mrs Hawthorne, to get them in order - that's the good news - but it might take a while before she can sort them out for you.'

'Not today or tomorrow, then?' Addie asked tentatively.

'Oh, good gracious, no. I'm sorry, I obviously didn't explain properly. This is the school holiday. It just happens that a few members of staff are around, because our GCSE exam results are in. I only came in, myself, to see how some of our pupils had done.'

'So when do you think …?' Addie started.

'I couldn't commit Mrs Hawthorne to anything without checking with her. But allow a couple of weeks so that school has restarted, and then you could ring up and make an appointment with her. That's assuming, of course, that we have the right records.'

'Are some missing?' Addie asked anxiously.

'To be realistic, Miss Russell, we're talking here about documents dating back fifty years - before the war. There are almost bound to be files missing. Anyway, we should have a better idea in a week's time.'

'I am coming back in a couple of weeks to see a relative,' Addie said resignedly. 'Would you mind if I could call you then and check when it would be convenient?'

'Yes, that seems sensible,' the woman replied. 'Perhaps in return you could give a talk on your research to our genealogy group. They could use it as part of a project.'

Addie managed to give a non-committal reply, thinking she might make a small donation to the school instead, and put down the phone.

She had now no further reason to stay, and she packed and paid her bill. She managed to catch Chris Templeman on the phone to thank him for his efforts and to say that she would be returning. She could tell he was quite disappointed that she was leaving now, and she kept the tone of her conversation bright and chatty and avoided anything leading to greater intimacy. Putting the phone down, she told herself she could well do without any more involvements.

She remembered suddenly that she had meant to ask if he knew of the choir mistress, Margaret Holroyd, when some words floated into her consciousness - Margaret Holbrook - Do Not Disturb. Where had she seen those words? Holbrook; Holroyd; was it possible that Mrs Furneaux had made a mistake?

She arrived panting in Veronica Daborn's office, her small suitcase in one hand. 'Hallo,' the matron said. 'I didn't expect you here today.'

'Can you tell me something about Margaret Holbrook?' she asked. 'Is she a member of your staff?'

Miss Daborn looked surprised. 'She's one of our residents. A very old lady, almost completely blind and fairly disabled.'

'Why does she have that card on the door?'

'She is a very intelligent woman who can't bear to be patronised. She has a dread of do-gooders coming in and treating her like an "old dear".'

'Could she have been a teacher?'

'Yes, she taught at a local school here, I believe.'

'Do you think there's any possibility she'd talk to me? I believe she may have taught my grandmother.'

Veronica Daborn looked doubtful. 'I could ask her. Perhaps she'll find the idea interesting.'

'Do you think you could ask her now? I'm going home today.'

Margaret Holbrook sat in a small armchair, her body shrunk down to the size of a twelve or thirteen year old. Her hair was thin and white and the face small and doll-like too. But her voice, when she spoke, had retained its strength.

'Well?'

'How do you do, Miss Holbrook? I'm Addie Russell - from the States.'

'*Mrs* Holbrook. What do you want?'

'I'm trying to find out as much as I can about my English family,' said Addie, recognising the importance of coming straight to the point before she was evicted for procrastination. 'I believe my grandmother, Dorothy, was taught by you. Dorothy Heron - no, Seccombe, then. She was in the choir.'

'Dorothy Seccombe,' the woman said, and from the change in her voice, Addie knew she had caught her attention. So her hunch about the name had been right.

'You remember her then.'

'Yes, of course I remember her. Do you think there's something wrong with my brain?'

'I'm sorry. I just thought it was a pretty long time ago.'

'It is a long time ago. Nevertheless, I remember all my girls in the choir. I remember them as clearly today as if they were in front of me. And I remember Dorothy particularly. So what idle curiosity brings you here to talk about little girls of fifty years ago?'

'Really, Mrs Holbrook, it's not idle curiosity. I'm desperate to find out about my family.'

'Desperate. The young are always desperate. It is hardly ever justified.'

Addie took a deep breath. 'I've come from the States.'

'So you said.'

'I've been researching my family tree.'

'If you want to put names on bits of paper, I've no patience with it. This obsession with recording names is no better than collecting cigarette cards. What do names and dates reveal of history and personality?'

This woman was going out of her way to be awkward, Addie thought, trying to keep her temper. Still she was obviously bored and perhaps this was one way of entertaining herself.

'It's true that I am recording details of my family. But when you are adopted, as I am, names and dates do mean something. Until two months ago, I knew nothing of my real family at all. I've been building up a picture since I came to England.'

'And so you have persuaded yourself that Dorothy Seccombe was your grandmother.'

'I *know* she was my grandmother. I still have the letter in which she says she wants nothing to do with her bastard granddaughter,' Addie said, now deliberately aiming to provoke the other woman. 'I just wondered what kind of person it is that rejects their flesh and blood, like that.'

She saw the woman's distorted hands clench together in a sudden movement.

'This does not sound like Dorothy. A gentle girl. Without malice. Not as you describe.'

'I was brought up by strangers when my mother died, so why should I believe what you say?'

The woman turned her unseeing gaze towards Addie. 'Believe it or not, as you like. Either you have the wrong person, or you have the wrong information. Whatever traumas Dorothy was exposed to would not have changed her into a vicious person.'

Veronica Daborn's head appeared in the doorway.

'I am tired,' the woman said, turning her face towards the sound of the opening door. 'Perhaps this young woman would be kind enough to leave.'

Addie left the room, unsmiling, angry with herself. She should have kept her patience. Her strategy seemed to have failed, and she knew better than to argue. She would have to try again, when she returned to the area.

She spent an hour with Ada, and then she left Long Barton, took the coach back to Bath station, and from there the train home.

The undulating slopes of fields and pastures rushed by the train window, the lowing cattle and the sheep inaudible through the train's double glazed windows. She reminded herself to take in the scenery, in case, after all, she was left with only memories of the home of her original family. Would she stay in this country, or would she be back in the States by Christmas?

The train dipped into a shrub-covered valley, before rising up high again, the tree-clumped ground far below. Then a patchwork of fields lay beneath her, dotted with the minute shapes of cattle and edged with farm buildings. Isolated trees marked the landscape, the grass, pale green, stretching out towards the horizon.

She thought of Ada, who had never left this county in her whole life, imprisoned not only geographically, but literally, in an asylum with people in straitjackets, people banging their heads against walls, people crying but not knowing why. Once Ada was in love, once she felt passion. Somewhere, perhaps in the long grasses of the local fields, Ada and Percy had experimented in making love. On some occasion, these innocent teenagers had unwittingly carried out their act of procreation. And as a result, their baby Dorothy had started her life on the privy floor. But then in the prime of her life, Ada had been removed from all prospect of love, had had her wicked sexuality quashed and had spent the rest of her fertile years imprisoned for her sins. At fourteen, she must have been quite a girl, thought Addie. But what a punishment. How unfair life could be.

The hills levelled out and the sun glinted down on neatly arranged haystacks. Black and white cattle stood out against the verdant background. Telegraph poles linked by wires appeared at predictable intervals at the edge of the track. In the distance, an occasional elegant church spire rose up in contrast to the more mundane cottages and houses. Patterns, Addie thought, do we just repeat the same inevitable pattern?

Ada, thrashed by her father, Dorothy, abused by her husband. What about Adrienne? For a moment, Addie felt a weariness sweep over her. Her mother was a mystery; but then optimism rose up again. Instinctively she felt that Adrienne had been a free spirit, unquenched by her bullying so-called father. Dorothy had ensured that her daughter was out of his reach and, with Adrienne's death, the line in any case was broken. Addie herself was the product of liberal and loving parents, not the recipient of the troubled emotions of her maternal forebears.

The train now moved through small urban developments interrupting the countryside. Signs of industry signalled the approach to Reading. Addie took down her suitcase, folded her unread magazine and, clutching her purse, prepared to make the next connection.

Managing to navigate her way round Reading Station, she was pleased to find a seat on the small conductor train for Guildford, and sat daydreaming again. What she had learned about Ada and Dorothy had put her own life into a new perspective. Compared with her grandmother and great-grandmother, she had led a privileged life. To think she had once been quite resentful of Joan's attempts to protect her from pain. All that business with Lloyd had hurt Joan almost as much as it hurt her. And Addie had thought at the time that her real mother would have understood her passionate obsession with Lloyd and not interfered. It was pretty unfair to idealise Adrienne, she thought now, because Joan was a kind good woman who deserved to reap happiness from her adopted daughter.

The train made its way through Berkshire and Surrey. As hazy sun shone through the window, she smiled at familiar landmarks. A new thought came into her mind. What if she stayed here in England? How would Joan feel? How hurt would she be at that?

She took a taxi home and, when she walked down the path

to the house, she felt its welcome reach out to her in an almost physical way.

As she pushed open the door, she saw a blue envelope on the carpet. As she picked up the letter with its airmail sticker, she noticed a slight bulge. Putting down her suitcase to open it, she saw Joan's handwriting and, as she unfolded the flimsy sheets, a small gold key fell to the floor. The key to Adrienne's diary. A welcome back indeed.

Chapter 22: Adrienne's Diary

She was welcomed back in more ways than one. Now that Nora Grainger was an ally instead of an enemy, the freezer was full and the fridge well stocked. Addie took a steak and defrosted it, found some frozen hash browns and put them in the oven, and preheated the grill for her steak. Then she read Joan's letter, filled with family gossip. The diary was a treat that could be saved until after she had eaten. When the meal was ready, she turned on the radio and listened to the lunchtime news, as she ate, finishing off with the remains of a tub of ice-cream. Unsolicited thoughts of Jonathan came into her mind. She remembered him laughing as he asked her if he had any ice-cream on his nose, and she remembered her legs going weak as she looked into his eyes. Then he had rushed off, without explanation, to Tabitha. It was obvious where his affections really lay. How stupid to allow herself to get interested in someone who was so entwined with another girl. Of course, he was getting more friendly now that he knew her better; treating her like another friend of younger sister, Sarah, no doubt. She sighed to herself. If he knew the effect that his little joke had had on her, he would probably be appalled.

Philosophically, she picked up the key from the sideboard where she had placed it and took it upstairs, where Adrienne's diary lay, with the other papers, on James's mahogany desk.

She read without interruption for two hours. Initially, Adrienne's personality, as revealed by the diary, did not differ greatly from that shown in her letters to James. The diary, which started in 1958 when Adrienne was about fifteen, contained much of the trivia that she had already seen in the correspondence. Only when Adrienne had occasion to go home did she turn to the diary in sombre mood. Addie recalled how a letter to James had described spending part of a holiday with friends. A new aspect of this visit was revealed in the diary.

When I told Mummy that I wanted to spend two weeks of the summer holiday with Charlie's family, she looked sad for a moment. I said 'You don't mind me going, do you? I thought you preferred me being away from home.' I didn't mean to say it like that, but it slipped out. I just remembered how I begged her and begged her not to send me away to school, and she kept saying 'It's best for you darling.' Anyway, she said to me very seriously 'I do miss you terribly. Don't ever think that I wanted to part with you. But when you write and tell me about your life, and you sound happy and enthusiastic, I feel it was worth it. Some day you'll understand.' Something like that. I said 'But why? Why did you think it was for the best?' and she said 'Circumstances, darling. I'll explain when you're older.' I said 'Do you mean because of home being a boys' school?. Do you think I shouldn't be with boys all the time?' She just smiled a bit. I said 'I know about all that stuff, you know. I wouldn't do anything like that. It's horrible.' Because I remember when we were talking about it one evening, and everyone in the form agreed it was disgusting. Then Mummy laughed. She doesn't laugh very often, and she always looks so lovely when she does. She said 'I know you're very trustworthy. But it's other people, not you.' Then she looked sad again, and she said 'I'm sure you'll have a lovely time with your friend. Just write and tell me all about it.' I never realised till then that she had missed me as much as I missed her, and I made up my mind to write much more often than before.

Adrienne entered another revealing passage in her diary when she arrived home early in 1959, with information about the school journey to Perpignan in the summer.

Mummy's lying down, and my father's out and I had to write this. I came home last night and my father picked me up from the station. I told him about the school journey and gave him the letter

239

about the trip. He didn't say much. Just 'Well I suppose it will improve your conversational French.' So it seemed as if there wouldn't be many problems.

Mummy was pleased to see me, and we had a nice meal and we all talked about France. But in the night I woke up. I didn't know what had woken me, but it sounded like a gasp or a scream, but muffled. And in the morning, Mummy was terribly white and said she had a headache. I thought it was The Curse. I don't think she's too old for that. No-one said very much at breakfast, and then the phone rang and someone wanted my father so he went out. Then Mummy got up to go and get dressed, and she sort of slid to the floor. I ran over to help, and her dressing gown had slipped to one side, and she had the most terrible bruises, I mean blue and black - and all colours - like some were new and some were old. 'I said 'What happened?', and she said 'I fell down.' But I knew it wasn't true. I made her a cup of tea and gave her an aspirin. Then I said 'It was him, wasn't it?' She said, 'It's not always like this. He can't help it. He's a sick man.' I said 'How can I leave you and go away?' and she said, 'Don't be silly. It's been going on all your life.' I said 'Why don't you go away?' She said 'I wouldn't know where to go or what to do. I know that sounds stupid.' Then she sort of bit her lip and tears came into her eyes, and she said 'I'm trapped, Adrienne. I have nothing. No-one. I can't leave him. But you must live life to the full. That makes it worthwhile. You must go away. Go to France. Go everywhere. Do everything. And don't ever be dependent on anyone. Don't get trapped.'

I shall never bring my diary home again. Because I have something to say that I don't want anyone to see. I hate him. I absolutely hate him. And though it was all so awful today, it was like a kind of relief. I always knew he was strange, and I didn't want to be in the same room as him. I felt bad about not liking my own father. And now I know it's OK. I remember he once hit me with a ruler on the knuckles really hard, for being cheeky. That didn't bother me, though it hurt for days. But I thought he smiled when I cried out, like he really enjoyed that. Then he gave me five pounds

240

and told me not to tell my mother, because she didn't approve of corporal punishment. I was glad to have the five pounds, and never said a word. But I always kept out of his way, if I could.

Later

He came back, and he gave her some flowers. I couldn't believe it. He said 'You're looking a little peaky. So this is just to cheer you up, my dear.' Then he turned to me and said 'Your mother is a wonderful woman.' And she looked as if she was going to be sick. But then she smiled a little, and took the flowers, but her eyes looked terrible. Like a ghost. Poor Mummy. I never, never realised. She is wonderful. I love her so much. But I'm so thankful to be getting out of the house, and going back to school, tomorrow. She says when it's just the two of them, she can cope with him better. I don't think he likes me very much. I asked if she wanted me to contact anyone. She said it wasn't necessary, but she promised to go to the doctor to make sure everything was all right.

Afterwards I wondered why she didn't ask James for help. I know he's a long way away, but surely he would send money or something. They must have been close at one time. When I mentioned him to her, she said quite angrily, 'He's the last person I would go to. I know he's been a good friend to you, but it's really quite inappropriate.' I didn't really understand why, but I thought there must be something I didn't know about, so I never said any more about it.

Addie read on, with ambivalent feelings. Glad in some ways, that Adrienne knew what her mother was enduring. Sadness for that poor tortured woman. No matter how many times she read or heard a new version of Dorothy's life, it never failed to upset and anger her. But there was a new feeling too. Was Adrienne right to leave her mother? She had said something in one of her letters to James about being selfish. Perhaps she was. But then, should one expect a fifteen-year-old girl to take responsibility for an adult situation? And Adrienne could imagine how insistent Dorothy would have been. Whether Dorothy was afraid of Rodney carrying out some physical attack on Adrienne or whether she was fearful of some sort of sexual abuse was not clear, since Rodney's sexual preferences were in any case ambivalent. But what was certain was that he had reason to hate Adrienne simply for not being his real daughter, and that, since she was not his daughter, he would not be deterred by the taboo of incest. In any case, it seemed his pleasures were always gained in a sadistic enjoyment of another's humiliation and pain.

Addie herself suspected that he would not take the risk of disclosure by attacking Adrienne. He was dependent on Dorothy giving him the appearance of being a respectably married man, just as Dorothy depended on him for financial security for herself and Adrienne. He would not rock the boat and give Dorothy a final reason to escape from her unhappiness. But Dorothy's torment would only be increased by her fears for her daughter. So perhaps Adrienne was right to go and to live her life in the way her mother wished her to do.

Addie read on, anxious to see if Adrienne said any more about her parents, but it seemed that she had settled back in school, and did not mention the conflict again for a while. Perhaps it was too painful for her to think about. Shortly afterwards, there was another visit to her friend Charlie, and a new side of her life was revealed.

24th March 1959

Last night, Charlie and Richard and I talked about the Bomb. You remember Richard tried to persuade me to go on the March last year. Well, they are doing it again this year, and he's going. He said 'This is our future we're talking about, and they're going to ruin it. Do you want to have a life, or do you want to see us going up in a mushroom cloud like Hiroshima?'

Charlie said 'Yawn. Yawn. I've heard it all before. I'm going to bed. Are you coming?' I thought she didn't have to be quite so nasty,

242

so I said I'd stay up a bit longer. He got out a 78 and put it on the record player and said 'This is Tom Lehrer. Have you heard him?' I said I hadn't and he played it. It was really horrible - all about the Bomb, something like 'Well, we'll all go together when we go.'

Then he said, 'Why don't you come with me this year? It's a challenge, and it's wonderful being part of a group all doing something together. There's such a terrific spirit. All sorts of people.' He looked at me very seriously and I felt really strange. I mean, I never thought he was good looking. I told Charlie once I shall marry someone very handsome with jet black hair and ice blue eyes, and she said 'Don't look at my brother then.' Then when I saw him the first time, I saw what she meant. He's got ginger hair and freckles, same sort of colouring as Charlie, and sort of green eyes. Also, he's got a sort of thin, bony face. But last time, when he was talking, he sounded so, well so intense, and when our eyes met, well, it was quite, well - romantic, I suppose - and for a minute I thought he was going to kiss me. Anyway, he didn't, and I found myself saying I'd go with him. Then I went upstairs and Charlie got quite shirty. She said she absolutely wasn't going to ruin the holiday by going off with a lot of nut-cases, and I could jolly well go with him on my own, if I wanted. Then she calmed down and said she was sorry, but she really didn't want to row with her parents over it, and there was a terrific row last year about it. I knew Richard wasn't going to change his mind, and I was remembering what Mummy said. About experiencing everything. I made up my mind I was definitely going.

Addie rested the diary down, a little smile on her face. She was touched by Adrienne's first romance. Green eyes, she ruminated. She got up and went to the mirror in the hall. Her own green eyes met those of her reflection. Was it possible? Or just a coincidence? After all, there was nothing else in her appearance to suggest that she might have had a red-haired freckle-faced father.

She hadn't really thought a great deal about her father. Her mother had always been her obsession. Knowing from Joan that Adrienne had made up her mind to keep her baby, and had not, from Day One, contemplated either abortion or adoption had given Addie a feeling of security; she had none of the feelings of low esteem or rejection that adopted children might sometimes have. On the contrary, from an early age, she knew that not only had Joan and Tony chosen to adopt her, but Adrienne had loved her unborn child too. But, somewhere at the back of her mind was the shadowy figure of her father. A man whom Adrienne had not spoken about, except to say to Joan, 'He's English. It happened before I came away. He doesn't know, and I don't want him to.' And that was it.

Addie had had some vague feelings that he was a nasty piece of work - that somehow she and Adrienne were a team and he was on the other side - an enemy. Later, her affair with Lloyd suggested to her that her father had been that kind of man - attractive, sexually experienced and amoral in his dealings with women; perhaps even married. She did not condemn Adrienne for this shared experience. She was even reasonably comfortable with the idea of such a man being her natural father. He was not wickedness personified - he was actually typical of many men that she knew in the advertising field. Of late, and since she had been investigating the life of her antecedents, the horrifying and unspoken idea had entered her head - that Rodney might have succeeded in abusing Adrienne, despite Dorothy's efforts to keep her away from home. The thought that she could be Rodney's daughter had come into her mind once or twice, and had entered into her dreams and nightmares. She had managed to convince herself that it was unlikely, his apparent sterility being one logical reason for doubt. Adrienne's diary had, in fact, been remarkably reassuring. The one occasion of physical violence that she had mentioned was quite trivial, and Adrienne's expressed hatred of Rodney would have been a good reason for her to stay away from him. Now faced with the possibility of Adrienne's first romance, she wondered if she might view

244

her real father in a new light.

This is the first opportunity I've had to write about Aldermaston.

We decided to hitch there, join the March on Easter Sunday evening, and march with it to London on Monday.

It was amazing that so many people were accommodated so easily. There were thousands of men, women and children, but the organisers found places for all of us. On Sunday night, we slept on a cold marble floor and on Monday, we had soup and sausages for breakfast.

It was very embarrassing when Charlie's mother heard that Richard and I were going. She cornered me and said to me in a very cold voice that she thought the idea of my being there was as company for Charlie. She said something like 'Aren't you behaving rather ungraciously?' (Or was it ungratefully? I'm not sure.) I couldn't think what to say, anyway, but Charlie came up behind me, and said, 'It's OK. I'm going too.' Then Mrs C. looked even more angry and cold, but before she could say anything, Charlie said. 'Don't treat us like children. We're sixteen, and Richard's eighteen. There's lots of people our age going.'

I said to her afterwards, 'What changed your mind?', and she went red, and said that Richard had told her he was hitching with one of his friends, who she's quite keen on.

Charlie's parents were pretty irritated by the whole thing. Charlie had told me about the row last year, and they couldn't understand why Richard would want to get involved with 'The Bolshie Brigade' as they put it. They're very Conservative. Well, of course, I can understand that, because my family are exactly the same. Then there was the hitching, and they didn't like that either. And even though it was Richard's idea, I got the feeling they felt that I was leading Charlie into bad ways. I thought if they'd known that we'd paired up, so that Charlie and Alan hitched together, and Richard (or Ricky, as Alan calls him) was with me, they would have been even less happy, although, in fact we were all together a lot of the time, because we got into a lorry on the A4, which took us all the way to Reading. Also you feel a lot safer with a boy, and it makes it easier for them to get picked up.

On the way there, I felt a bit of a fraud. I hadn't thought at all about the Bomb, and I knew that Richard felt very strongly about it. But when we were on the march, singing and waving banners, it was absolutely marvellous, even though it was pouring with rain. I hardly noticed that my feet were hurting, but once I got cramp as we were walking along. I nearly fell over, and Richard caught hold of me, and pulled me to the side of the road. Then we sat on the grass and he massaged my leg. After that, he helped me up and he didn't let go my hand, and I thought that it was all worth it just for that. And when we eventually got to Trafalgar Square, the speeches were so stirring and I felt very emotional. Standing beside Richard in the rain - it felt like the most important moment of my life.

But once we got back, he didn't talk to me much at all, and it was just torture. Nearly the whole holiday, just Charlie and me, playing Monopoly, going for rides on the ponies - nice things, but all the time, I was thinking, doesn't he care about me? Isn't he going to say anything?

The night before we went back to school, Charlie's parents went out to a dinner party, and Charlie said she had telephoned Alan and asked him to come over. He'd told her all about this new record he had, called 'West Side Story', so she asked him if he'd bring it. Richard wasn't too pleased, because she'd phoned Alan behind his back, but in the end they both persuaded him to come and listen.

We sat on the floor with cushions and played some other music first. Alan had some Ella Fitzgerald and Frank Sinatra. Richard said it was bourgeois, but I thought it was lovely. Alan told us the Romeo and Juliet background to 'West Side Story' and as it had started to get dark, Alan put it on. The music was harsh and exciting and also beautiful and melodic. Then Richard suddenly seemed to relax, and I could see in the darkness that he was looking at me, and suddenly he stretched out his fingers and touched my hair. I wasn't aware of moving, but as we listened, first I found that our hands were *touching and then we had our arms round one another.*

When the record came to an end, it was quite late. Charlie got up and said she'd see Alan to the door because her parents would soon be in. She looked at me very meaningfully, and I knew she was giving me an opportunity to be alone for a minute with Richard. And then he kissed me, and we stayed holding each other for what seemed like a long time, before Charlie came back.

The next day, before Charlie and I went back, he came up to help me carry my case downstairs. I could feel my heart beating really fast, and I said to him 'Am I ever going to see you again?' He said, 'Of course, if you spend another holiday with us, I expect I'll see you.' He was so offhand, I nearly burst into tears, then he said 'Look, I don't want to hurt you, but I don't want to get involved with a girl now. I've got some important things to do.' I knew he was involved with CND and the Young Socialists, but even so, I was really upset, though I managed not to show it too much. I didn't say anything to Charlie, but when I got back to school, I found a quiet spot and had a good cry. I shall never forget him and I don't know why. He's almost ugly, but he makes me feel ... I just can't describe it.

So Adrienne was rejected. I suppose that means he wasn't my father after all, thought Addie ruefully. But then, at sixteen, Adrienne was a bit young to have settled on the man of her dreams.

Adrienne, it seemed, had turned her attention conscientiously to her work during the term, and there were only a few skimpy entries in her diary. Similarly, her letters to James were sparse, until the exams were over. But the diary provided a detailed report of a school dance, in which her school was joined by a boys' school in the area.

25th July 1959
It was a wonderful relief to have finished the exams, and the dance at the school was supposed to be the high spot of the term. In fact, some of the boys are so unbelievably gauche (good word, isn't it)

247

that I feel like Mata Hari. I danced a few dances with Tim Waverley, who I've met on and off on previous occasions. He's got a pale face, which shows off his acne; flappy, fair hair which droops down over his face, and he held me limply in his arms, as if he was afraid of touching me. Then I saw Alistair Hobbs trying to catch my eye. Well, he's quite good looking with dark hair, so I was pleased when he asked me. But his dancing, well, he told me he's a member of some cadet force, so I suppose that's why he treated dancing like it was a parade-ground exercise. Each time we were forced to start afresh, he said 'One, two three, now let's go.' They were playing Paul Anka's record - 'Put your head on my shoulder', but he was acting like he was terrified of getting too close to me, too; he held me about ten inches away from him, so stiffly that I thought he might break my wrist. Charlie had told me that Alan was coming, and I saw her on the dance floor with her arms tightly round him. I suddenly thought of Richard and wished he was there too. I remembered walking along with him, on the March to Aldermaston, holding hands, knowing that it was something special. But Charlie had already told me he wouldn't come to the school dance. He couldn't be bothered with anything like that.

Adrienne's disappointment was evident, but Addie could not find another mention of Richard, and the event that followed next was Adrienne's first holiday abroad.

Addie had already read Adrienne's description of the holiday in her letter to James and Lillian, and she now looked with interest to see if the diary contained more detail.

Initially the reports were rather similar. Addie recognised the description of the two-day trip into Spain and the overnight stay in the monastery. But Adrienne had omitted some innocent meetings with the local French boys, for the group of English schoolgirls proved to be quite an attraction. There was also a more romantic occasion with a Spanish boy.

The night before our last full day, some Spanish boys had arrived

248

at the lycee, and were standing together in a little group playing some music. Most of them had guitars or mandolins, one of them was a singer and one had a tambourine, and the music was lovely. Barbara Preskitt, a girl from the sixth form, who had taken a fancy to one of the boys said to me, 'Tell him to play his tambourine,' because she was too shy to try out her French. I was rather interested myself, so I tried out a mixture of French and sign language and succeeded in making him understand. After that I took it from him and had a go at shaking the thing myself. He introduced himself as Jose and said he would like to meet me tomorrow. When I told him we had to stay in twos, he said his friend Pepe would come, and I should bring a friend. In the end, Barbara agreed to come, as friend Pepe was quite nice too. We arranged to meet at the beach.

Of course, once we met up with the boys the next day, we did split up. I went in the water with Jose and we swam together. Once I got water in my eyes, and couldn't see. He took my hand and led me out of the water to the beach. We sat on the sand, getting closer and closer, and then he pulled me down and kissed me. It was the most romantic moment. Then I felt his hand on my breast. He was very gentle and I wasn't sure if I ought to be shocked. We were surrounded by other people on the beach and I didn't know what to do. So I got up and told him we would be late back for dinner at the lycee, and I must find Barbara.

I thought we might have gone out with them in the evening, and I was wondering how I would behave with Jose, but instead we found they were giving a performance of their music at the Spanish Consulate. So we (girls) went out dancing and the next day, we left Perpignan. I thought a lot about Jose on the long train journey across France; wondered what would have happened if we hadn't been leaving so soon after meeting the Spanish boys; thought a lot about being kissed by a passionate Spaniard; tried to picture his face - dark hair, olive skin, brown eyes and suddenly, instead of his face, another face came into my mind - with green eyes and ginger hair, and I felt really sad and wished that it had been Richard who had been there at that moment.

Chapter 23: Adrienne at University

It had almost become a ritual to have Sunday lunch with the Amerys. Jonathan was away for a few days, but Sarah and Helen were very interested to hear about Addie's trip to Long Barton. It was the first opportunity she had had to tell them about finding her great-grandmother, Ada, and the story horrified them.

'So Dorothy was brought up by her grandparents, as we thought,' Sarah said. 'And maybe her grandfather ill-treated her too. Judging by the way he treated Ada. Sounds like he was another Rodney.'

Addie disagreed. 'Don't think I'm exonerating him in any way, but I think the old man was more like some of our right wing religious zealots. You know the sort - patriarchal, anti-love, anti-abortion, pro-corporal punishment, puritanical. Rodney was different. He was just plain kinky.'

Addie described her visit further to Helen and Sarah as they ate the meal. When she told them that she was writing some articles for Chris Templeman, the journalist on the West Country paper, she noticed Sarah raise her eyebrows.

'Oh, how old was *he*?' she asked, as Helen went to the kitchen to check up on the dessert.

'About late twenties, I guess. Why?'

'Oh, that's better.'

'How do you mean?'

'Well, to be honest, Addie, after Julian, and your ex - Lloyd Thingy - I thought you were looking for a father figure.'

'Sarah. My dad is the main father figure in my life. I'm not looking for a replacement. I've never had any hang ups about him. He is just a lovely man.'

'Then why ...?'

'I don't know why you keep getting the wrong end of the stick. There's no connection between Lloyd and Julian. Lloyd was just plain sexy. It wouldn't have mattered what age he was. He was just one of those people that's got it. I didn't find Julian remotely sexy. I was just a bit bored and felt like a few outings. I was stupid enough to think I could go to the theatre and have an interesting conversation with a man without ending up in bed. As for Chris Templeman, why should you think there's anything between us? He was just helping me for God's sake.'

'You're always the last to know, Addie.'

'And when did you decide to become a "Dear Abby"? Data entry not good enough for you, huh?'

'A dear what? Oh, I remember - you mean an Agony Auntie.'

'By the way, Sarah,' Addie said, privately congratulating herself on diverting Sarah away from thoughts on men friends. 'I have to get hold of a word processor. Have you any idea where I could get one?'

'You could look up ads in the local paper and see if there's one nearby,' Sarah said. 'You're taking this writing seriously then?'

'I have a contact in the States who works on a paper and I'm sending Chris Templeman a couple of articles.'

'I see,' said Sarah, with a smug expression on her face.

'Read my lips. This is about money, not men.'

Helen brought in the dessert with a peeved expression on her face.

'Sorry, I thought the apple crumble looked a bit anaemic and could do with another couple of minutes - turned my back for a minute and the top was turning black.'

'Mum uses up smoke alarm batteries twice as fast as the rest of the world,' Sarah commented.

'Well, I thought the roast lamb was delicious, and I'm sure I'll enjoy the crumble,' Addie said smiling and feeling at home.

She was lucky enough to get hold of a word processor that

251

afternoon because, with Sarah going off with Trevor, the evening would have been quiet. As it was, Addie was able to install it on the dining room table, and start work on her articles that evening.

There was no point in going back to Long Barton for a fortnight – not till September. Ada would have had her eye operation by then, and the school would be open too, so she could look for any information about Dorothy. Until then, she would send off articles to the States and to Chris Templeman, and continue with Adrienne's diary. She felt vaguely empty and dissatisfied, and disappointed not to have seen Jonathan that day. In addition, dreadful though it was to admit it to herself, she quite missed her outings with Julian, but that was a completely different sort of feeling.

She worked methodically throughout the evening, on the articles. The word processor wasn't a bad model at all for the price. She copied out and tidied up the article on roses and the piece she had called *A Yank in the Wild West*, added in a few more ideas, typed a letter to a contact in Boston and a second one to Chris Templeman and printed the lot out ready to post the next day.

It wasn't yet nine o'clock. Turning on Radio Three, she went upstairs to the study, the background music drifting up the stairs. By rights she should have brought the word processor up here, but there was always a feeling of stepping back into the past at James's desk, and somehow new technology seemed out of place.

She unlocked Adrienne's diary, and found her way back to the last entry she had read.

Adrienne was growing up. Of that there was no doubt. Sometime during the two years of working for her A-level examinations and applying for universities, she became less innocent. There was more freedom at the school during that time, and she had several boyfriends, though Addie got the impression that the boys she met were rather correct.

252

Sometimes she talked of frustration, and sometimes of being deliberately provocative to the boys she met on dates. But Addie doubted that she had had any real sexual experience. Something apparently held her back from that, though Addie was unsure whether it was fear of pregnancy, lack of opportunity, or a desire to meet someone particularly special.

Nevertheless, there was now, in the way that Adrienne wrote, a kind of desperation and intensity to her, as if she was determined to fulfil Dorothy's entreaty to 'experience everything ...' Addie worried for her, as if she were hearing about a younger sister, whose life she could influence in some way. Dumb, completely dumb, she told herself, because she knew full well what happened to Adrienne. Perhaps Adrienne had some premonition that her life would be so terribly curtailed, and had to squeeze in more than others whose lives would stretch on for an additional fifty years. Her personality, as revealed by the diary, was so full of life and vitality that Addie felt angry and powerless. It was like reading a novel, or watching a movie, whose end you knew, and you wanted to shout a warning at the crucial time. She remembered how she had wept on the death of Bonnie in *Gone with the Wind*, and every time she had seen the film wanted to call out, 'Don't let her ride over the jumps.'

But what dangers would she have pointed out to Adrienne, had she had the power? Would she have said, 'Don't sleep with anyone, because you'll get pregnant and then you'll die?' Or would she have said more pragmatically, 'Be careful what you eat. Don't eat the cold turkey from the local deli'? If Adrienne had taken one different step, maybe her whole life would have been altered - and Addie's too. On the other hand, wasn't there a British play - *Dear Brutus* - in which all the characters got a second chance and still ended up with the same fate?

At one point in the diary, Adrienne described how she had pre-exam nerves and was violently sick, but she recovered when she got into the exam room. She seemed quite philosophical about it and said she often got sick when she was tense. It seemed to answer one of the puzzles that Joan had mentioned - that when Adrienne was sick with salmonella poisoning, she did nothing about it initially.

'The doctor said that she must have been ill for days, and if only she or I had realised, she might have been saved. I blame myself for not noticing that it was anything unusual, but she carried on working, so I thought it wasn't too serious. She had been pretty sick at the beginning of the pregnancy, and some women do seem to suffer from nausea all the way through.'

'It wasn't your fault, Mom. You weren't her mother.'

'No, that was it,' Joan had replied. 'I never had been a mother. I didn't know how ill pregnant women were supposed to be.'

An entry in Adrienne's diary in 1961 was echoed in one of her letters to James and Lillian.

I've waited for today with bated breath, and finally have my results. I passed English with a distinction, and with my French and Latin results, my place at Bristol University is guaranteed. I'm reading English, and hope when I leave to become a journalist. I haven't forgotten what I said to you about travelling, James. You know how I've always envied your roving life. I hope my pen will take me to places that I could not otherwise hope to go to. I know I'm no diplomat - ask any of my friends - they'll tell you I'm too headstrong - but words on the page - that I think I can work with. Sorry not to have written for so long. The revision has been tedious, and I have to admit to having a busy social life, which has led me astray - and away from my desk.

Much love,
Adrienne

Following Adrienne's fairly conventional late teens, it was easy to forget about Dorothy's troubles, but suddenly there was a jarring reminder.

8th September 1961

Managed to get a temp. job, filing, and am paying money into a bank account. It should help me when I'm at Bristol. I wish I didn't have to be dependent on my father. I don't know if I'll get a grant, though that would help. I haven't spent much time at home, but last night came home after spending a few days with Charlie. Mummy was sitting in an armchair alone, looking white and strained again. I said 'He's beaten you again, hasn't he?' and she just drew in her breath and sighed. I said to her, 'You're not staying with him because of me, are you? Because I can manage. A lot of people work their way through college. I can't bear it if you're putting up with him because of me.' (I've been worrying about this.) She said, 'It's not because of you, though he's done a lot for you. I suppose all marriages reach some strange sort of accommodation.'

I said, 'You mean you're happy with him, treating you like this,' and she smiled a little, and said, 'We survive.'

She's so dignified and brave - I'm so proud I'm part of her. I just wish he *wasn't my father. I feel so powerless to help her. Afraid that anything I say or do may make matters worse.*

20th September 1961

I have had the most terrible row with my father. The way he treated Mummy has nagged and nagged away at me since I've been home. I found it almost impossible to be even civil to him. I knew things were building up between us. Earlier today, I was standing in front of my mirror, putting on some makeup. The door was open behind me, and I saw his reflection. He walked into my room, but I ignored him.

He said 'You're going to have an unpleasant shock at university - you're going to have to start paying respect to people in positions of authority.'

I didn't bother to turn round. I just looked at him in the mirror, and I said, 'I give respect where it's deserved. In your case, I find it quite unwarranted.'

I saw his face go red with anger, and he suddenly picked up my hair brush which was lying next to my makeup, and hit me hard across my backside. I was furious. I turned and seized the brush from his hands, and broke it into two pieces and flung it in his face. Then I shouted at him. 'Don't you ever dare touch me again. Nor my mother. If I hear that you've been beating her, I'll call the police. What's more, I'll spread your name over the papers. Mr Respectable Schoolmaster, who beats his wife black and blue.'

His face by now had turned white, and he was shaking, as I was myself. I saw that Mummy had heard me screaming at him, had come up the stairs, and was standing behind him. He hissed at me, 'You little bitch. Bastard. After everything I've …'

Then Mummy came forward, and put her arm on his shoulder. Her lips were trembling, but she said, 'The child's just overwrought. University is a big step for her.'

I saw him take a breath, and he seemed to calm down a bit. I said very quietly, 'I'm not overwrought, Father. Just remember what I said.' He just turned and walked away.

Mummy didn't follow him. She sat down on my bed, and patted the place next to her. I sat down, and she put her arm round me. Then she took my hand and turned it over and I saw that my fingers were spotted with blood from the bristles of the brush. I hadn't noticed. She said, 'Adrienne, you have such spirit. Thank God you're not like me.' And I said, 'Please, can't you leave him, Mummy. I can't bear to think of you with him.'

She smiled her little sad smile, and said, 'I just wouldn't know where to begin. I'm forty-five. How could I start my life again?' Then she said, 'Once I thought of leaving him, but it came to nothing. It was before you were born. I would have gone then. Strange, he almost seemed to know what I was thinking. He said to me, 'You wouldn't ever leave me would you?' After he's beaten me, he's almost pathetic, like a child who knows he's done wrong. Something builds up in him, some rage that he has to let out. When he's - satisfied, he calms down, and he's very contrite.' She said it all sadly and quietly, with tears running down her face. I cried too. I

256

feel so guilty about leaving her again, but at the same time, longing to get away.

Even so, I felt I had to say what was on my mind. So I said, 'Do you really want me to go to Bristol?' She said, 'You know you've got to go. I've told you I want you to make the most of your life. There would be no point to my life if you weren't fulfilled.' So Bristol and Life awaits me.

The horribly prophetic statement that Dorothy's life would be pointless without Adrienne seemed to scream out from the page. But the whole conversation was significant. If Dorothy was ever going to tell Adrienne that Rodney was not her natural father, this was the time. After all, Rodney had got very near to blurting it out himself. But Dorothy had said nothing. Her knowledge of her own illegitimacy had, it seemed, made her determined not to allow Adrienne to experience that same humiliation. Dorothy had not come from the generation of women who proclaimed their single-parenthood without shame. She lived in a different era, a different climate of opinion. So Adrienne went, free of that particular burden, into her new life.

Some time in the next three years, Addie reasoned, Adrienne was going to meet Addie's father. The question was would she recognise him, and in fact, would Adrienne even mention him. Addie was tempted to go to the end of the diary, and work backwards to find her own conception. But if she found the act; if she found a name - the name of her father - what would it mean to her? Very little, without an earlier knowledge of the person, so just as the diary enabled her to know Adrienne - better than she ever had before - so if her father were to be found in these pages so she would get to know him too. But Addie reserved the right to skip any passages that seemed really uninteresting or irrelevant to her own life.

Once at Bristol University, Adrienne showed no signs of

difficulty in settling down, though periodically she mentioned her concerns for her mother. But there was no reason for her to be uncomfortable away from home; after all she'd been away from her parents since she was twelve. In any case, soon a familiar name cropped up. It appeared that an old friend from school had also gone to Bristol.

5th October 1961

Went for a drink in Manor bar tonight, and to my surprise saw Barbara Preskitt. Don't know why I was surprised, but it's always a shock seeing someone in the wrong place. Because she was a year ahead of me, I'd forgotten she'd come to Bristol. I was pleased to see a real old friend, though I've made quite a few new ones. I miss Charlie, though perhaps we can get together in the hols. Barbara and I talked about our holiday two years ago, and the two Spanish boys. We were a pair of innocents then, and we've both moved on a bit since Jose and Pepe, though frankly, from what Barbara said, university is light years away from Long Barton High. I remember when we sat and giggled and discussed what it would be like to see a naked man. Somehow I feel that she's gone beyond that sort of speculation. We discussed who she'd met here, and she's involved with quite a lot of people, and not just from the university. She said she'd invite me over when she has a party. Can't wait!!

So Adrienne was turning into a 'wild child', thought Addie, and again felt concerned, and yet amused at herself at the role reversal. She was like a mother clucking in horror at her daughter's sexuality. It was a punishment, she thought ruefully, for what she herself had put Joan through. She wondered what had happened to Charlie, who seemed to have her feet more on the ground. Maybe she was not bright enough to get into college, or perhaps she would pop up again later.

Meanwhile, Adrienne described one of her lectures with enthusiastic enjoyment.

Went into my first lecture with Dr Piggot. Haven't asked around but I wouldn't mind betting there's a nickname which is regularly applied to him. We discussed the way that language is put together, which was quite interesting. It was obvious from the way people spoke that an awful lot of them come from very similar schools to mine. Of course, the subject being English, there were loads of girls in the lecture. I'd got lost and had to sit myself at the back, next to one of the few males in the class. He was dressed in a suit and had a smart brief case on the floor beside him, with the initials J.H. on the side. Quite nice looking - dark hair and rather stern expression. Suddenly this Piggot fires a question at him: 'Well, Mr Harkness, can you enlighten us as to the derivation of esoteric?' He turned very red and muttered something totally wrong - spoke with some northern accent, too. 'Are you sure, Mr Harkness' says Piggot 'that you are quite comfortable in this gathering? Perhaps you should have considered joining a technical college?' There was really nothing funny about it. It was just that he looked like a dummy from the window of Burtons, and then when he spoke, it was a complete transformation. So at least half the girls in the room tittered. He sat there and fidgeted and got even redder, and I felt really sorry for him. I could just imagine this balding plump fifty year old looking at this good looking bloke in a sea of women and sort of locking horns with him, like an old stag. (May have my animals wrong.)

Anyway, at the end of the lecture, I walked out with him, and said, 'Don't let him get you down,' and then he asked me to go and have a drink with him. I saw one or two of the girls eyeing me. Not good enough for them, obviously. But this is the first red-blooded male I've seen in a long time, and since the hall of residence is an all-female affair, I wasn't going to turn it down. We went to a student pub, and I had a shandy and he had a beer. He offered me a cigarette, and I said I don't smoke. Then, would you believe, he took out one of these little boxes with strong tobacco and half a dozen thin papers, and started rolling up his own home made cigarette. I could just

259

imagine my father's face if I started doing something like that at home, so I asked if I could try one, after all. When I tried to smoke it I really choked, and I accidentally inhaled too. My head started spinning, and then he just laughed his head off. 'I think you're more the filter tip type, Miss Heron,' he said, mimicking the Pig. 'Or better still - how about a cigarette holder.' 'What about you?' I said to pay him back. 'Don't you think you'd be more comfortable in a set of overalls or dungarees, instead of the suit and brief case. I thought you were masquerading as an insurance salesman.' Then he said something like the way he felt this morning, he wished he were. 'Which?' I said, and he said 'Either would do.' Apparently, his parents had bought him the brief case as a going away present, and they all thought the suit was the right thing for a student. No-one in his family had been to university before. I could imagine how his family would be working class and warm hearted and I told him about my father being a cold fish, and that he was jolly lucky that they were so proud and pleased with him. But he said he'd never imagined he'd be stuck with a load of posh-talking Mary Quant clones from the south.

Later

As I walked into hall this evening, I heard a girl say loudly, 'Miss Heron's come back from her fishing trip.' Then another one came up to me and said 'How did you get on with Mellors?' She'd separated herself from some girls, who were standing in a little group giggling, and I got the general idea that they were having a laugh at both me and this John Harkness. Of course, I understood. I doubt if there was anyone who hadn't got hold of 'Lady Chatterley's Lover' after the famous Trial.

I said 'Fine, thanks. If I'm supposed to be Connie, I'm working on the next stage.' Put that in your pipe and smoke it, you cat, I thought.

Adrienne obviously didn't mind one or two sneers. She had lived in a girls-only world for many years. She had the odd few drinks with John Harkness, who had rapidly adapted his clothing to suit the surroundings. The name was vaguely familiar to Addie, but she couldn't remember where she had heard it before. Soon Barbara Preskitt re-emerged and the party that she had promised was described.

8th November
1961

Barbara and some friends had a bottle party a few nights ago. I took a bottle of red wine, and sampled several others. As a matter of fact, I lost track of how many glasses I had. Barbara had put out some crisps and some cheese, and I had a few nibbles, but like most student dos, it was awash with cheap wine, and short on the food. I was necking with a med. student called Colin, when I began to feel rather queasy. A great pity, because Colin was quite attractive - dark hair and very blue eyes - and sexy too. Made the boys I've been out with before seem like schoolboys - which of course they were. (In fact I was feeling quite weak at the knees, until I started feeling weak in the stomach.) I felt so ill I had to excuse myself from the party, but Colin took me home, though I was quite incapable by then of being any sort of companion. He rang up the next day to see how I was, and I couldn't even talk to him. My room mate gave my apologies, and in fact, my head was spinning for the next twenty-four hours. Never mix cheap wines. Next time, maybe I'll stick to whisky.

15th November 1961

Haven't had time to write before, but I must get this down. Colin rang up and asked me over for a meal last week. He told me he could turn out quite good Indian food. I'm quite a good cook myself, but everything I make, I learned at school - real traditional English stuff. Colin's interested in mysticism, and when I arrived at his door, I could smell joss sticks burning. I walked in, and the place was in semi darkness and he had Indian music on. We sat on cushions on the floor to eat, and the meal was really good - and just a couple of glasses of wine with it. When we'd finished, he said to me, 'You ought to learn how to enjoy yourself. Don't get drunk and sick. I've got something that's much better than that.' He started rolling a

261

cigarette, and I said, 'I don't smoke.' thinking back to the roll-your-own John Harkness had given me. He said, this isn't an ordinary cigarette - it'll make you feel quite different. Just take a puff.'

'I didn't really need much persuading. You could say he'd already seduced me with the music and the food and everything. I wasn't going to miss out on anything. I took a puff, and at first nothing much happened. I took another drag and the room started swimming a bit, and then I just had this great feeling. I felt wonderful, relaxed and ready for anything. He smiled and said, 'Feel good?' and then, 'Life is about letting your hair down.' I had my hair up in a pleat, and when he said that, I pulled the grips out of the pleat and let it fall down. He just looked at me, and said, 'Wow.' Then he bent forward and started to undo my blouse.

Addie stopped reading, embarrassed. She'd felt the same way when she'd read Adrienne's account of the kiss on the beach in Perpignan, but then nothing much had happened. Now, she felt a little like someone voyeuristically observing a couple through a spyhole. A Peeping Tom. Do I go on, she thought? This is my mother I'm reading about. Her private life. She thought of Joan, solid and reassuring. Had she ever let her hair down? She smiled. They had all had that conversation at school, the one where everyone compared notes about sex and discussed in shocked whispers the fact that their parents must have done IT - at least once. Being adopted, Addie had had to admit at the time that Joan might never have done IT at all. Now Joan's voice came into her mind, reassuring and full of practical wisdom. 'When I read what that old goat Samuel Pepys got up to, I was amazed. What would he think if he knew that millions of people had read his antics? Then I thought, I guess he'd be pleased as punch. All writers want an audience - even diarists are wondering what their kids will say when they're dead.'

Adrienne would never have told me about this, Addie thought. All mothers - not just adoptive mothers - keep a distance between their youthful selves and their mother role, but Addie had been denied the normal memories that mothers are allowed to share with daughters, and this would have to be the substitute. She read on.

I thought - this is it. I'm going to lose my virginity now. I'm going to find out what it's all about. I dropped my blouse and bra, and he took off his shirt and pulled me down on to the floor. I could feel his hands on me, and I thought - this has nothing to do with love, but the way I feel at this moment, love doesn't matter.

You just won't believe what happened next. I couldn't believe it myself. Someone knocked on the door. I heard a girl's voice call 'Colin, let me in.' I thought he would ignore it - I was so sure he would just carry on, but instead he looked quite shocked. He muttered something under his breath - Linda or Lydia and he swore. Then he pushed me away and said, 'Get into the other room. Take your clothes.' I just stared at him, and he said 'Go on, go.' I went and tried to listen to what was going on and I heard him say something about taking a bath in a minute - that's why he only had his jeans on - and making other excuses why the girl shouldn't come in. Then he started talking softly to her - like he'd talked to me before. Then there was a long silence. I got chilly, and I slipped my blouse back on. Finally he came back and he was relaxed again. He walked up to me, and said, 'Let's carry on where we left off.' I said to him, 'You make me feel very sexy. Why don't you take your jeans off.' He didn't need a second invitation. He laughed and peeled off his jeans and pants. I just stood there looking at him. Then I grabbed my coat and put my bra in my pocket. He said, 'What are you doing?' and I said, 'Now you're in the mood, why don't you ring Lydia.' And I walked out.

Addie almost cheered. She had steeled herself to be confronted with all the intimate details of the first sexual encounter between her mother and Colin. Obviously it would not have been her own conception - it was too early for that, but perhaps the precursor to a long-term relationship. She was delighted that Colin, who sounded decidedly untrustworthy and unpleasant, had been so ignominiously squashed. She was also glad that Adrienne was not allowing herself to be pushed around. She's broken the mould, she thought.

18th November 1961

It seems I'm famous. Barbara rang me and apparently it's all round her gang that I walked out on Colin. He's been going around saying I'm a bitch and other not very nice things. Half the people that know him say he's been asking for it. The other half (the ones that have slept with him, I suppose) say I didn't know what I was missing. Have arranged to meet her for coffee after lectures tomorrow - she wanted to hear more about it.

20th November 1961

I went for coffee with Barbara and we had a good old chat. She said I was probably sensible not to get involved with him. Then she owned up that she had slept with him when she first came to Bristol. He always goes for 'little innocents' as she put it. She said they'd often smoked pot - he always brought it. At first she wouldn't have it and she wouldn't sleep with him, and he kept persuading her. She said once she'd slept with him, he just treated her like dirt. Never took her out, just called in when he felt like sex, and expected her to be waiting for him. And she usually was - until it all got too painful and she told him she didn't want to see him again. Then she started going out with a friend of his, Dave - a really nice boy. But it meant that Colin often got invited to parties and things. I asked her if she'd ever worried about getting pregnant, and she said Colin had taken care of that, and Dave as well. I asked her how, and she said 'Withdrawal.' I didn't know what she was talking about, and felt an absolute fool, and she had to explain to me. Still better than showing my ignorance when I'm with the opposite sex.

21st November 1961

Lectures today - John grabbed my arm at the end and said, 'Hey you, come and have a drink.' We went to our usual pub. He practically marched me there, still holding my arm. He got the drinks this time, and before I had a chance to speak said - 'You're daft getting mixed up with the likes of Colin Whittington.' I said 'What the hell's it to do with you? Am I supposed to behave like a nun or something?' 'You don't want to start taking pot and all that stuff,' he said. 'And you deserve better than someone like him, anyway.' 'Well like who?' I said. 'Like me,' he said. Well I was really taken aback - I mean I hadn't meant all that stuff about Mellors and Connie. Not that there's anything wrong with him. I just thought we were drinking pals. Anyway, I didn't say no. I looked at him and he could see I was surprised. Then he just leaned forward and took my face in his hands and kissed me. And he said, 'You don't need pot to make things work, lass.'

25th November 1961

John and I went out together a couple of nights ago. One of the girls asked me how's my bit of 'rough'? That's the last thing I'd call him. I'd no idea I'd find him so sexy. When we went to the films, he only had to touch me to send shivers down my spine. My god he feels different from the boys I met when I was at Long Barton. Quite a match for Colin. In the back seat of the cinema, he undid my shirt and slid his hand onto my breast. All sorts of bits of me were screaming out for him to go further. But not there. I mean, it's so bloody public, isn't it. Next day, I could barely concentrate on lectures, particularly when he was sitting next to me. But nothing's going to happen is it. I mean with both of us in halls, when can we ever move on?

I said to him, 'Can't you get hold of a car, so we can have some privacy?' He just laughed. 'Chance'd be a fine thing. Why are you in such a hurry, lass? Do you want to make an honest man of me?'

'I've got lots to do before all that,' I said to him, even though I knew he was joking, and he said, 'You're not like the girls where I come from. You put a hand on their knee and they'll be ordering the bridesmaid's dresses.' Then he said 'But if you really want sorting, we could always go on the downs.' I didn't take any notice of that. He'd already said I was a softie, when I complained of being cold in

265

halls, never mind about being starkers on the downs in November. At least the Odeon was nice and warm.

28th November 1961

We had a long chat at the pub, last night. (We don't spend our entire time together necking, and I really like talking to John.) He was telling me a bit about his family, and I just realised how miles and miles apart our lives have been. When he started talking about his mother baking, and the kitchen always being warm, even when they were short of money, I asked him if his father ever hit his mother. He looked quite shocked, and said 'Of course not.' I couldn't tell him then - not about my father. I was ashamed of him. Then he said 'Just because we haven't got brass, doesn't mean we're savages.' 'You've got the wrong idea,' I said. Then I made up a story about a posh friend of mine and her father hitting her mother. He just shook his head. 'We all respected our Mam,' he said. 'She held our family together.'

15th December 1961

Incredible to think that a whole term has gone. My father is collecting me tomorrow. Christmas will be ghastly, no doubt. Spending time with my family always is, but this time it will be worse. I shall miss John a lot. I like him more and more, even though we're sometimes like people from two different planets.

12th January 1962

1962 - I wonder what it's got in store for me. Starting a new year in my diary always has that effect on me. Thank goodness I'm back here anyway. I feel so much as if I belong here but perhaps that's partly to do with never belonging at home. My dreadful father. He was his usual icy self when he met John at the end of last term. John was helping me carry my stuff down the stairs, and my father positively dismissed him, with the type of superior comments he uses for his own students - no - even worse than that - more like he was treating him like he was a porter here, or something. Poor John has had quite enough of that here already.

16th January 1962

We had a long chat once my father had dropped me here last week. John was excited and pleased with himself. He told me that when he was back home, he wrote an article for the Manchester Guardian - a sort of bitter satirical commentary on University life here in the south of England. It started out with John feeling genuinely bitter and resentful about the way that Piggot in particular has treated him. He told me once that when he was at school, he was treated as if he was something special. They thought he would write a novel or something. One particular teacher encouraged him to come to university. His parents wanted him to go into a bank. They knew he was bright, but that was the extent of their ambitions for him. Anything clerical really, so he didn't have to work in the mine at Brighouse. His older brother had a terrible accident down the mine and is disabled. Anyway, this teacher came to see them personally, and said that it would be an awful waste if John missed out on university, and they gave in. Now he's having to convince them that it was all worth it, even though he gets so demoralised.

When they saw his piece in the paper, they were really puzzled. Why did he want to stick it, if it upset him so much? I don't think he had an answer for them, but on the other hand, they were all rather pleased that he'd actually earned some money from writing.

Here Addie realised why John Harkness's name was familiar to her. If it was the same John Harkness, then he was one of a group of playwrights whose work she had studied when she was writing an essay on British playwrights of the late fifties and sixties. She felt a shiver of excitement run through her, partly out of sheer pleasure that he had succeeded in confounding the unpleasant Dr Piggot and also at the possibility that she might be the daughter of a well-known writer.

10th March 1962

John has been so pre-occupied recently that I started to wonder if he was interested in someone else. I had a tutorial yesterday afternoon, and when I got back to my room, there was a note on the door from him, saying he wanted to see me. You can't keep anything private here. He might at least have stuck it under the door. Anyway, I took it to mean that we should meet at the coffee bar (pubs being closed in the afternoon) and I went straight there. He was sitting in a corner, drinking a coke.

I went and sat down, and he said, 'I've got something to tell you.'

I said, 'It's over between us, isn't it?'

He said, 'What makes you say that?'

I said he hadn't been himself recently, and I thought he'd lost interest in me, and he said 'It's not that. Not that exactly. You're a great girl, Adrienne.'

'Are you letting me off lightly?' I said. 'Is it because I haven't slept with you? Because I will. You know I want to.' (I was thinking that now the weather's warmer, we could find a field, or a wood, or something.)

'You're very self centred,' he said. 'It's nowt to do with us. It's to do with me - and this place.'

I was a bit taken aback because I thought he'd say yes, straight away.

Then he said, 'I'm not going to sleep with you. I know why you want to - for the same reason you'd have slept with Colin Whittington. You just want to find out what it's all about, don't you? And that's not a good enough reason.'

I got quite angry with him, and said, 'Why do you have to be so noble? You're like the Savage in "A Brave New World."'

He laughed and said, 'Aye, that's me. The Noble Savage. "Oh brave new world that has such people in it." And that's why I'm taking myself away from all you so-called civilised people. I'm going back to my own kind.'

My heart sank, because that chat we had at the beginning of term did stay at the back of my mind and worry me from time to time.

I said, 'You can't go. Piggot will have won then. Why are you letting him drive you away?'

And he said, 'He hasn't won. Because I've been offered a good job *on the Manchester Guardian on the strength of the articles I've sent them. And that's just the beginning. I'm not staying here, picking away at the dry bones of literature. I'm going to create my own literature, with red meat in it, with feelings and emotions. This place is suffocating me.'*

I couldn't argue, because I knew he was right. I said, 'Oh John. I'm going to miss you.'

Then he said, 'Look there's another thing. I'm not quite so noble as you think - there's a girl back home. I thought it was all over between us, with me coming down here and all. But now - if I'm going back up North, things might have changed.'

I said, 'So I was right, wasn't I? I was just a stop-gap. And it is all over between us,' and he said, 'Be honest. You don't really love me, do you?' and I said, 'I don't know.' I mean at that moment I didn't really know what I felt. I'd somehow always known that we wouldn't end up together - I just knew it wasn't going to last forever. But I really enjoyed his company, and I knew I was going to feel sad without him.

Then he said, 'You'll get over me fast enough, Adrienne. I'm just a novelty.' And I said, 'That's not true. I really will miss you.'

He said to me, 'Well, I'll miss you too, lass. If things had been different... But they're not. Promise me one thing. Just don't throw yourself at Colin Whittington when I've gone.'

I said, 'I'm not interested in phoneys like him. I prefer real people. Honest people - like you. And don't you ever forget it. You've been special to me, and I won't forget you.'

He said, 'OK, Connie,' and laughed as my face went bright red. Fancy him knowing about that.

12th March 1962

Well John's well and truly gone. I didn't realise at first that he meant he was going straight away. I saw him to the train, and after he'd gone, had a good cry. Emily, a dimwit with money who comes from Kensington, couldn't resist saying to me when I came in to Manor from seeing off John, 'I hope you said goodbye to John Thomas.' 'Still flogging the same old dead horse,' I said. I shan't be

269

sad to see the back of her.

We'd had a long chat the previous night and I said to him, 'You think you know it all, don't you - about people down here in the south. You've got this big chip on your shoulder and you think you've cornered the market in suffering and poverty. I think you're really lucky and you don't always realise it. You've got this wonderful warm family who think the world of you. I've got this cold fish of a father, and my mother constantly watching her words, in case she upsets or offends him.' Then I told him about how I'd seen her sometimes, after he'd beaten her. How she always tried to hide it from me. I said 'Just remember when you're the new Angry Young Man of the sixties, writing about LIFE, that things aren't always what they seem.' He said, 'I'm sorry, Adrienne. I wish I'd known before' and gave me a great big hug.

The end of another era for Adrienne. It seemed an appropriate place to finish reading. Addie closed the book on her mother's life, to return again another time.

Chapter 24: Adrienne in Love

25th April 1962

Well, back here at last. The relief at the end of another holiday. Managed to keep away from the house as much as possible, helping out at a local riding stables. I've always rather liked horses and have never had one of my own. They have a scheme for helping disabled children to ride and they asked me if I'd be one of the helpers. I thought of John's brother and said yes. I'm glad I did.

John. Well, the days feel quite empty without him. He was such good company. It just seems that the place is dreary, and there's nothing much to look forward to.

The only bright light on the horizon is that during the last couple of months, I've linked up with a girl called Valerie Sayers, and we've agreed to share a flat. I became friends with her when she let me come in through her window (ground floor) one night when I knew I was going to be late. She's one of the only decent girls here. And I can't face another year in Manor Hall. It's too claustrophobic particularly with some of the bitches here.

I'm going home for a couple of weeks in the summer, seeing Charlie in Cardiff, then moving into the flat and taking a temporary clerical job for the rest of the holiday. Before that, of course, there's first year exams, so it's nose to the grindstone for the next few weeks.

29th July 1962

Valerie and I are finally in our own flat. It's three floors up in a Victorian terraced house, with ill-fitting windows and (apparently) a leaky roof but it's home to us. Oh if only I'd been here when John was around. I've heard from him. He's getting on well. And that old flame is back in his life again. Well good luck to him. He deserves it.

There are not too many students around at the moment, and Valerie and I have both got temporary jobs to help pay the rent. Val has a grant, but unfortunately, my father's income is too high for me to qualify, and he *wouldn't give me anything extra. But I'm enjoying going to work - enjoying the independence. Val and I get on well, and I'm really pleased we made this decision. We are going to have a flat warming party once everyone's back. I've also volunteered to help with the horses at the local stables. Life is improving.*

13th August 1962

Val and I are getting a little bored with each other's company. Hardly any of our friends are around, and though we are quite busy, things are a bit flat. Still it's nice to be putting money in my bank account. On Saturday, we went for a picnic, and we've also met one or two other friends at the pub. I have to keep reminding myself how much better it is than being at home. I've written to my parents. I'd prefer to write to my mother, but I can never be sure that he doesn't read her letters. Also been catching up with my reading. I've read 'On the Road' and was envious of the feeling of total abdication of responsibility. How exciting to drop everything - live from hand to mouth - go anywhere, see everything. Of course, you need a big, big country like America. Maybe, one day, I'll trek across that country myself.

In the meantime, although Bristol is freedom compared with home, I can't help realising how narrow my life has always been. Life in a little corner of the West of England. Yes, I have to say at the moment, that even here, I do feel a bit hemmed in.

28th September 1962

Had a call from Barbara. She is coming back before term starts. She's also moving into a new flat. By rights, she should go back into Halls of Residence, as this is her final year, but she and Dave are so serious now, and she says she's getting too old for climbing in and out of windows at midnight. It's nice to feel that people are gradually returning. It's a measure of the good relationship that Valerie and I have that we are not tearing each other's hair out by now. Valerie has started preparing a list for the party we're having. She wants to invite a couple of students she met at the Bristol Labour Group. I think she's taken a fancy to one of them, so she's making sure that both he and his friend get an invitation well in advance. She's being a bit coy about it – doesn't want to jinx it, I suppose. Of course, at the last minute, I know we'll be issuing invitations to all and sundry, with a bottle of something being the only entry ticket required.

16th October 1962

We decided to hold our party at the end of October, and yesterday evening, Valerie took a couple of invitations, beautifully inscribed by our own fair hands, to her political meeting. When she came back I said, 'Did you see your friends, Alan and Rick?' She said, 'Yes, they're both coming. It's funny; they knew you.' I tried to remember an Alan and a Rick, and she said, 'When I gave them the card, Rick said you knew his sister - I can't remember her name. He said you were great friends and stayed a lot at his house when you were at school together.' It suddenly clicked, and I said, 'Rick. Do you mean Richard?'

I was so amazed, I could hardly speak. At first, I just couldn't believe it was my Richard. He was my first love, I suppose, but so much has happened, I've hardly thought of him, since that summer. I asked if he gave her any message, and she said he'd try and look in, in a day or so, so she'd told him when I had lectures. I was worried suddenly, and said to Valerie - 'You never told me. Which one did you fancy?' and she said, 'Alan, of course. He's much better looking.' Which is quite true. Charlie always thought he was the cat's whiskers. Anyway, I was very relieved. Today, I got back from a lecture as Valerie was leaving to go to a tutorial. Just after she left, there was a knock on the door, and it was Richard. I opened the door, and he looked exactly the same - face, thinner, if anything, and hair, just as ginger. For a second I felt shy. Then I just wrapped my arms round him and hugged him. It was so lovely to see him. We started exchanging news and gossip, and I happened to let it out that I'd met up with Colin Whittington at the beginning of last year. Then he started lecturing me. It seems he knows Colin and couldn't believe I'd get involved with someone like him. I got slightly irritated, because after all, I soon realised what Colin was like and ditched him. But I said, 'It's no good your talking to me like a Dutch uncle. I'm having some fun while I'm here. I know you're too busy doing good

273

works to have time for me, so don't try to organise my life.' Then he smiled, and took my face in his hands and said, 'Don't hold that against me. We're both three years older now. You're not a little girl any more. And I'm not quite so idealistic.' Then he kissed me. Properly. Magic. Can't write any more now. Will report as soon as poss.

In spite of this statement, there were no entries for a few months, and in the next entry, Adrienne's life had undergone a dramatic change.

8th February 1963

The last few months have been wonderful. To meet Richard over again has been like a dream come true. Apart from John Harkness, the boys I've met during the last couple of years were completely inadequate. I always knew that. Stuffy and unimaginative - rigid public school backgrounds - just like my father. And completely sexless. To find again someone so challenging - idealistic (despite what he says) thoughtful - thought provoking - we have such wonderful discussions - and at the same time, so attractive to me. Nothing to do with looks. He's not handsome like James Dean or Paul Newman or any other film star. I only know I want to reach out and touch him, every second I'm with him. And of course, I want to be with him all the time! He's very sensible - not like me - and insists we put in time on our studies. So I don't see him every day. In fact if either of us gets behind, we sometimes have to be apart for a week. Which is agony!! It is much more important for him of course.

I had to survive Christmas at home, but fortunately, my father had invited some colleagues to join us, so was on his best behaviour. I missed Richard terribly. One thing that concerns me is that I haven't told Charlie yet. Didn't get to see her in the hols. I know she will be happy for me - she was always aware about how I felt about Richard - I didn't have to spell it out. But at the moment, it's something only we know about - no that's stupid - all his friends here know and so do mine. But not back home! I've always had this feeling that his mother disapproves of me - all the years I've been friends with Charlie, she's always had a special 'cold' look - specially reserved for me, I mean. I never told Charlie - never wanted to hurt her feelings, because, frankly, the feeling was mutual. So I'm just not ready for the family to be involved. As for my family, I've just kept it as vague as possible. My father's never been interested in personal relationships and, as for Mummy, does she know what it's like to be in love? Was she ever in love with my father? If so, he must have totally destroyed her feelings over the years, for her to speak to me the way she once did - I mean about being trapped.

But anyway, back to Richard, and the big question is have I slept with him - the answer's 'no.' As a matter of fact, it's him holding back - not the other way around. I know he thinks I rush into things for the wrong reasons, and I admit I was quite prepared to sleep with Colin for all the wrong reasons - and John too, though not for the same wrong reasons. But with Richard, it's quite different. I love him. He's special.

10th June 1963

Why do diaries become less important when you have someone special in your life? Can't believe it's four months since I last wrote. But confiding to an unknown audience seems inadequate when you can talk to the person you love - a warm responsive human being.

I have finally been to the FPA and got fitted with a cap. It had become very difficult. At first Richard refused to sleep with me until we made arrangements about birth control. When I said to him what Barbara had said to me about withdrawal, he didn't look happy, and said 'You can never be absolutely sure. The last thing either of us needs is for you to get pregnant.' But then one day, it just happened. Neither of us meant it to - we just couldn't hold ourselves back. It's been so many months, and we were both getting so desperate - I mean every time we kissed it was like switching on the ignition and not being able to stop. Of course, it had to be withdrawal, and actually it was rather unsatisfactory. You think of that first time as a sort of honeymoon, and it didn't really feel like that. But afterwards, once we got used to each other, things were different. To try to describe how we both feel would take away the magic. This overwhelming physical feeling has nothing to do with words. Words would only debase it. So I'm not even going to try.

But back to more mundane matters, i.e. birth control, well, after that first time, Richard got some Durex; that side of things is so difficult though. That decided us to do something more permanent. But I'm not really sure about this either. It's not exactly spontaneous (though the way we feel about each other, we don't have to debate whether it's going to happen.). Even so, I may go back to the FPA for more advice.

Can't really talk about it to Valerie; she's seems a bit embarrassed about it, though she's the most tactful of flatmates and obviously knows what's going on. She never did make it with Alan, and there hasn't been anyone else serious. As for Barbara; she's so engrossed with Dave to the exclusion of everyone else, I hardly see her.

Had exams. They seemed to go reasonably well. It's unfair really that whereas people seem to have to study so hard to understand things like physics and chemistry - reading, looking critically at what you're reading and finally writing about it can be such a pleasure.

10th October 1963

I've been so busy during the summer. I decided to stay in Bristol and got a job here, taking just a couple of weeks off first to go home, and then to stay with Charlie's family. They all know now, of course, about Richard and me, though we tried not to make it too obvious. Separate beds, of course, and no creeping around after midnight. As it was, his mother gave me the usual cold shoulder, though his dad is really kind. Rich got a job in Bristol too, hospital portering. I thought the summer was going to be so good. Then his father had a mild heart attack and he had to rush off home. Things were worrying for a while, and he wanted to relieve his family of as much pressure as he could. Instead of getting an office job, as I'd intended, I worked as a tour guide - my languages are quite good – and I travelled around a great deal.

Richard didn't come back till the beginning of term. It was wonderful to see him again. I've missed him so much. I went to the FPA and got fitted with a coil. But after a few days I felt dreadful, started bleeding heavily and had to have it removed. So it's been back to the old routine.

I was worried about Richard when he came back. He had got so thin, and was very tense and tetchy. Unfortunately, the problems with the coil made him even more tense. I said to him, 'We managed before and we'll manage again. Don't worry, nothing will happen.' That's the trouble with Richard; he's always taking the world's problems on his shoulders. Big problems and little problems. It took him a month before he seemed more relaxed. Of course by then, the news from home was better, and I was quite well again.

I've been writing for the university newspaper, and may well take on the job of editor.

22nd November 1963

Tonight something unbelievable happened. Val and I were at the local bar, and the television was on behind the counter. We were talking and drinking, when we saw President Kennedy's face come up on the screen. Someone who was fairly near could hear what they were saying, and shouted, 'Be quiet, everyone. Something's happened.' The bar started quietening down, and then we heard the announcer saying something about the last rites of the Catholic Church. It was President Kennedy. He'd been shot. A little while later they said he was dead. There was a terrible hush over the place. Quite a few people started crying. Then they showed the motorcade in Dallas, and John and Jackie Kennedy smiling and waving. And then the shot. Most of us started drifting off, talking about it. Someone said she didn't remember anything as terrible as this happening in the whole of her life. I suppose in a way that's how we all felt.

Despite her desire to come to the end of her mother's story, Addie did not skip this part. As an American, she was surprised at the impact the death of President Kennedy had made on British people, even the young, and the next few pages continued to demonstrate how people had been affected. And then there was a break, and Adrienne wrote nothing for nearly three months.

6th February 1964
Must tell someone. I've missed two periods. Have booked to go to the doctor.

Addie read the words with a shock. Was Adrienne pregnant? Surely it must be a false alarm, because it was too early to have led to her own birth. But only one year before her birth. Would Adrienne still be with Richard in late June 1964? Addie was stiff and cold from reading without a break, but she couldn't stop now. She read on.

12th February 1964
I heard from the doctor today. I'm pregnant. He doesn't seem to be in any doubt. I don't know what else I thought he was going to say. I haven't told Richard yet. Haven't told anyone. I don't know what I'm going to do.

22nd March 1964
I'm not pregnant any more. I haemorrhaged a few days ago, and went into hospital. They gave me a D & C. I came out today. The last few weeks have been so dreadful. I feel so terribly depressed that I had to write. I can't talk about it to Richard, because he got so worried and upset himself. It was my fault. One of my friends who is a lapsed Catholic told me all about the rhythm method of birth control, and I decided to try that. Richard didn't realise, because in between this so-called 'safe period', I was using the cap. Then suddenly I missed a period. Waited a bit and then went to the doctor. He said I probably was.

When I told Richard, he went white, and started pacing up and down the room. He looked so awful. Then he sat down on the chair and put his hands over his face. I said to him, 'I suppose we'd better try and find out about an abortion.' He said, 'You're not going to some filthy back street abortionist.' I told him I'd heard some people say that you can get it done in some Scandinavian countries. Legally, I mean. And they're very clean there, so it wouldn't be a problem. He said to me, 'Look, I could probably find out about the abortion situation, but I don't want you to do it. We can manage. We will manage. We're not children. We can get married, we can get a flat here and carry on with the studies. You graduate this year anyway.'

I didn't want to tell him that I hated the idea of this thing invading my body like a parasite. I didn't want to be tied down for ever with a child. Trapped like my mother. I just wanted it to be the two of us. But I couldn't tell him that. He said something like this child being part of both of us, and we couldn't kill it. He even said I should give up smoking, because it would be better for It, though I didn't. I needed the fags more than ever.

I don't know how I carried on going to lectures and so on. Trying to pretend everything was normal. I couldn't bear to tell my parents. I even thought of Colin. Barbara told me once that he had all sorts of contacts. So I telephoned him, and he told me to get lost. Then suddenly out of the blue, I woke up and had this terrible pain. It kept coming and going, and then I started to bleed. I called Valerie and she rang for an ambulance. The stupid thing was, that when they saw me in the hospital, they asked if I'd done anything to myself. I told them I hadn't but I didn't think they believed me. They said I had to have this D & C - under an anaesthetic, and I signed the consent form. When I woke up it was all over, and I just had a bit of a stomach ache. Then Richard came, and as soon as he walked through the door, I just burst into tears. He said 'Don't ever frighten me like that again, will you.' We sat and held hands, and I told him I was sorry. It seems so stupid after what I said, but, I told him I was sorry we weren't going to have a baby, and when I said it, it was true. And then, I just kept on crying and thinking of this little person who would have been part of us.

That's not the only thing. The second night after the D & C, Richard didn't visit, and I lay there on my own thinking all sorts of

279

things. When all the husbands came in the evening, with chocs and flowers, I felt really alone and deserted. I lay down and pretended to be asleep, but actually I was crying. I wondered if he thought I'd let him down, because I lost the baby - and maybe that's why he didn't come. They told me I'd be able to go the next day - that was yesterday - and, of course, I couldn't contact him. Then Valerie rang, and said that Richard had had to go home because his father was ill. He'd tried to ring me, but someone else was using the hospital trolley phone. Valerie said either she or Barbara would bring in some clothes for me.

Barbara and Dave collected me in the end, in his car, and when I walked out, I felt as if everyone was looking at me, thinking 'That's the girl who had an abortion.' Dave went off and Barbara made a big fuss of me, made me some scrambled eggs on toast and told me to go to bed for the rest of the day.

23rd March 1964

Felt very angry with Richard - kept thinking that everything he'd said to Valerie was just an excuse - so I rang his digs tonight, and his flatmate told me he was still at home. Valerie told me not be a fool, but I rang his home and his mother came to the phone. I asked to speak to him and she said, 'Haven't you done enough damage? Why can't you learn some responsibility? As it happens, he's with his father. I expect you know he has a serious heart condition, and he was extremely upset by the whole situation.' I was so taken aback at her knowing, I couldn't say a word. She wouldn't put me through to Richard. She just refused and said, 'You're going to sabotage Richard's future, if you're not more careful.'

24th March 1964

Richard got home yesterday, and he came straight round. Of course, it had all blown up in my mind, and I thought he was going to say it was all over between us, because he looked absolutely grim.

I felt all tearful, and said, 'How could you desert me like that? It's because I've let you down, isn't it?' and he said, 'Don't be silly. You know it was you I was worried about - but then there was my father, too.'

280

I felt a bit guilty then, and asked how he was. Richard said, 'Look. I really thought my father had had another heart attack. My mother made it sound very serious. And when I got home, I found it was angina. But just the same, my father was very, very upset. I really needed to spend time with him, and convince him that we were responsible people; that we would not have aborted the baby, and that I would never have let you down. I wouldn't. Not in a million years. Even though it wasn't the right time for a baby.'

I said, 'All right. But why did you tell them. And he said 'I didn't. They found out.'

He told me that one of his father's friends, one of the big guns in the hospital saw him in the waiting room outside 'Gyny'. He'd recognised him and asked one of the hospital staff what he was doing there. It wasn't a case of Rich talking. This so-called friend had told them. I mean for heaven's sake, Richard might have been quite innocently visiting a friend. Anyway, he wouldn't lie to them (not his nature), so he didn't deny it - his mother particularly went on about him being irresponsible - (unfair, because, of course, I was the irresponsible one.)The worst bit for him was upsetting his father. After the heart attack last year, the last thing he'd want to do is upset him. They are so alike and do take things so terribly to heart - literally it seems. It somehow made me feel that just as Rich feels protective towards his father, so I have to protect Richard and not offload all my worries on to him. Somehow the worries about having let Richard down by not being able to stay pregnant - not being a proper full-blooded woman - seemed to ebb away. It suddenly seems more important to look after Richard.

20th April 1964

Things are pretty much back to normal. Richard is anxious about his course, but at least he's not worrying about anything else at the moment. Most important, he doesn't have to worry about me any more. Because I am on the pill. This wonderful, phenomenal invention that means no more nasty greasy cap, no more nasty coil to tear up my insides, and best of all no nasty rubber balloons. It is a joy for us both to feel so free. In some ways we are like an old married

281

couple, we have been together so long. But in other ways, it's just like a honeymoon - like the beginning all over again.

I would make love to him day and night, if I could, and sometimes when he's sitting reading, I get up and stroke his hair, or sit at his feet and rest my head on his knees.

Sometimes things happen when we really didn't mean them to - when we're about to have a plate of spaghetti, or go to a party. But sometimes, his face gets tense and he says to me, 'Please go away, Adrienne. I need to read this - and you've got work to do too - your finals are coming up.' I don't know why it hurts me when he says this. I know I'm being illogical. I know he loves me. I shouldn't need reassurance. But he is the only person in my life who has loved me like this. My father has never loved me at all, I feel sure. And my mother - she has always been so restrained - and still is. Sometimes I wonder if she's afraid to hold me in case she can't let me go. So I have to get all my hugs, all my cuddles, everything from Richard. Sometimes I know it's too much to ask of him - to be my mother, father, lover - and baby too, I suppose. Other times I can't bear him to reject me in favour of studying and tickle him or torment him until he gives in.

4th May 1964

Everything has gone terribly wrong. I don't know how to write this. But I have to get everything down. I have to sort everything out on paper so I know what to do. Richard's mother telephoned me today. She was very short and said she wanted to meet me. I was completely taken aback - had no idea she was in Bristol. Neither apparently did Rich. She said she hadn't told him, and she suggested we meet well away from Clifton. I had no lectures or tutorials, only revision, so we arranged to meet at midday. She offered me lunch, and though I was tense as can be, and didn't really want anything at all, I asked for an omelette. First we talked about Charlie and how she was getting on at Cardiff. Then she asked if I was all right now. As expected, we moved on to the pregnancy. I told her I didn't abort the baby, but she'd stopped worrying about that. She said she was far more worried about Rich. Important exams were looming and his work was erratic - he was tense all the time. Finally she said, 'He has years of study ahead of him. He's not going to cope with it while you're occupying so much time and space in his life. He talks about marriage. He'll have no income while he's studying. It's a ridiculous thing to contemplate. You'll both be restricted - and trapped, and you'll both regret it.' I felt a shudder go through me, when she said that - not for myself but for Richard. Maybe making the wrong decision and being stuck with me for the rest of his life, resenting me - and maybe resenting that he hadn't done as well in his career as he should. If you love someone you want to be fair to them. My finals are virtually upon me. I will have to decide what to do when I graduate. Maybe I shouldn't stay in Bristol at all. Maybe we should just see each other occasionally - no that wouldn't work. It would tear us apart. But perhaps that applies only to me. Richard has been more distant recently - I know he's worried about the amount of work he's got to do, but is it more significant than that?

The next entry was in June. Addie had reached the crucial month of her own conception; she had been born one month prematurely the following February - and Adrienne had told Joan that the father was English. If they were still together, there could be no doubt that Richard was her father. Strangely fearful, she read on.

25th June 1964

I wrote to James to tell him of my 2.2 result. A couple of days later, I got a telegram saying 'Have wired you £1,000. Congratulations - since you have no job lined up, why not use it for a year's travel, before you settle yourself down.' I told Richard. 'What do I do Rich, buzz off and leave you to some other girl?' He looked me very seriously and said, 'You'd be mad if you didn't take advantage of an offer like that. I'll cope without you.' Did he mean 'I'll be glad to see you go?' I wasn't sure.

Later

I've made up my mind. I'm going on a trip to the USA. I can't bear to think of Richard slowly cooling off and not wanting to tell me. Next week is the Ball. I'm going to make it a special night. It's going to be memorable - I'm going to go with a bang not with a whimper.

30th June 1964

We went to the ball. Danced all night. I had too much to drink. Kept singing 'Tonight' and thinking I was Anita about to lose her love. Richard kept fussing - what's wrong with you Adrienne, etc. Went back to my flat at 3.00 in the morning. Threw up over my ball dress. Richard made me change and tried to feed me coffee. Started to do a dance of the seven veils - throwing jeans and jumpers around the room. Richard (not drunk at all) saying - calm down for God's sake. But couldn't resist me when I ended up singing The Stripper at the top of my voice with just the last veil. (His college scarf).

The next day I was as sick as a dog. Reminded me of the party when I met Colin. I couldn't even think straight.

Valerie is away till tomorrow - she's hoping to get a job, before she starts at teacher training college. Rich didn't know how sick I was - he'd also gone off for a holiday job interview. Didn't tell him - don't want him to feel guilty about everything. We can't think about marriage. He's only 23. One of us will end up trapped - him not really loving me. Me, like my mother. I've got to go - got to give him a chance to do everything he needs to do. Saw him next day when I was OK. We made love in the afternoon. Very quiet and restrained. What's wrong he said. It's all coming to an end, I said and I couldn't help crying. Don't be silly he said. I'll be here when you get back. Don't I said. I don't want to think about the future. I only told him at the last minute that I'm off tomorrow. He was very upset that I hadn't told him earlier. I wish I wasn't going. I must have been mad. How can I manage without him?

There were no entries after that. Addie turned over the leaves of the diary to be sure. Nothing more. The empty, unfingered pages held no clues, no answers to the remaining questions. But there was no doubt now. Richard was her father. And far from Adrienne being cynically betrayed by him, he was quite innocent of his child's conception.

Addie picked up the book again, and turned over the blank pages. In a pathetic mirror of her mother's life, the smooth unused sheets contrasted with the earlier pages crowded with words and vitality. She felt tears start in her eyes. More than anything before, the abrupt end to her mother's diary now brought home to her the unfairness of Adrienne's premature end; a life brought suddenly to a close before its rightful time. The diary slipped to the floor, and, finally, Addie wept uncontrollably for the mother she had never known.

Part 3

Chapter 25: Son et Lumiere

27th August 1991

The night had been unbearably humid. Lurid dreams disturbed Addie, until early in the morning, she awoke sweating and uncomfortable and got up and, with James's robe around her, walked outside.

The garden offered no sanctuary. The clouds overhead seemed so close as to press down on her head, the garden flowers wilting in the oppressive heat.

Restless still, even after a glass of fruit juice, fresh from the fridge, she put on a tee-shirt and shorts, attached the house key to her waistband and went out for a run. She took her normal route, along the main road up the hill where the town opened up into country roads. The sky was matt white and impenetrable, and the atmosphere still and muggy. She could feel the perspiration dripping from her as she ran, and there was no relief from the heavy weather. After twenty minutes or so, she turned and started descending the hill. Ahead of her she saw that the sky had darkened to the colour of charcoal. Commuters heading for work started switching on their headlights, and odd streetlights came on too, in response to the blackening sky. Heavy clouds scudded through the heavens. A rumble of thunder, like an injured beast, sounded from beyond the hills. Addie shivered, and hoped she could get home before the weather broke. She ran on down the hill, her heart beating faster.

Suddenly, without warning, the sky lit up and, with no pause, a crash of thunder followed. In front of her a white zigzagging line etched a path from the sky to the horizon.

Addie stopped still, her heart pumping in fear. Another silver line streaked through the sky and cut like a knife through a tree a few hundred yards from her. The tree shuddered and then, as if in slow motion, she saw it split in two, its branches arcing majestically downwards to topple on to the road. A car came to a screeching halt, swerving to miss the tree, another ploughed into the first car's rear side, ripping off its bumper, and others stopped to the accompaniment of squealing brakes and noisy hooters, in an untidy line.

Addie froze. Her legs felt weak and her brain seemed unable to give instructions. She noticed objectively that her whole body was shaking. As if on a given signal, huge drops of rain started to fall from the black sky. Then the sky lit up again, as flash followed flash, and the scene ahead was illuminated like an old-fashioned black and white picture show. Addie stood, still paralysed, with the cold hard rain falling mercilessly on her skin, panic churning up her stomach, her limbs incapable of movement. Another minute, she thought, and I would have been under that tree. If I stay or if I go, I could still get struck by lightning.

She heard Joan's voice in her ears, 'It's all right, honey. Don't cry. It's just the gods having an argument. They're not angry with us.'

The hooting from the line of cars continued, one car sounding a long insistent note.

A voice called from behind. 'Addie. Addie. Get in the car.'

She did not turn. A car door opened and slammed. She felt a hand on her arm, pulling her insistently. 'Addie, get in the car.'

She obeyed like a child. He opened the door and pushed her in, running round his own side and jumping in and expertly pulling out of the queue, turning and driving back along the main road, before eventually turning off into side roads she did not know. With one hand, he pressed the buttons of his mobile, calling the emergency services and reporting the accident. From a long way away, she heard him talk to his own office, telling them too of the incident and saying that he would have to come in from a different route. All the while, she sat, still shaking, her eyes fixed on the windscreen wipers, crazily swivelling backwards and forwards like demented metronomes, the rain dripping off her hair and arms, forming a puddle at her feet.

They arrived at her house. The rain was still drumming on the roof and he parked as near as he could to the door.

'Come on,' he said. 'We'll make a run for it.'

But when she sat, unmoving, he got out and came round to her side once again, taking her hand and pulling her from the car. 'Where's the key?' he asked, but saw it almost immediately and, with no response from her, unpinned it himself from the waistband of her shorts, unlocked the door and pushed her into the house.

She shivered as he touched her. For a moment, as she stood there, she thought of Julian and the night of that other thunderstorm. She stood shaking at the foot of the stairs.

'Go and get those wet things off and get into something warm,' he said.

She did not move.

His face concerned, he found a towel in the kitchen and started to wipe her face and shoulders. His hands were warm and comforting and smelt of fresh soap. They felt familiar, as if they were hands she had known for a lifetime. She felt some of her shock and panic ebb away. She stared at him, in silence. So kind, so gentle, so completely different from Julian, so different from Lloyd.

He looked down at her again, wiping the rain from her face.

'Do you want a doctor, Addie?'

Now that she was safe, the storm was suddenly unimportant, irrelevant. Except that it had brought them together in this moment of shared intimacy. No flirting, no pretence, no little quips to hide behind. There would never be another moment like this. She knew what she felt for him. Had she misinterpreted the way he had looked at her recently?

She shook her head and found her voice at last. 'No, Jonathan. I want you.'

The look in his eyes turned from concern to surprise to recognition in a few seconds. Then he hesitated.

'Addie? We can't - you don't ...'

The towel dropped to the floor but his hands still rested lightly on her shoulders. His eyes met hers, silently questioning. One finger traced the path of a raindrop down the side of her face.

They were strangers still, she thought. He needed to know that there was no ambiguity in what she had said. That she knew what she was doing and what she was saying.

'I want you, Jonathan,' she repeated.

Throwing off his own wet jacket, he walked back to her, picked her up easily and carried her upstairs to her bedroom. Pulling her drenched tee-shirt over her head, he wrapped her carefully in James's robe. Then he kissed her.

She was trembling, but she was no longer cold. She could feel his warmth through the material of the robe. A pulse was beating fast in her ears. There are few moments in life like this, she thought. When you fantasise about someone, when your heart misses a beat at the thought of them, and suddenly you have their physical presence. The reality. The tasting of the unknown fruit. The robe slipped from her shoulders and she reached out to unbutton his shirt. He slipped his arms round her. His fingers were smooth on her skin. A thunderbolt rattled through the sky, but she was no longer afraid. The sound seemed to come from far away, as though someone had turned down the volume control. The fury of the storm faded into insignificance, the flashing lightning merely a backcloth to reality. There was only one reality - the insistent demand of her body, of his body, of their one body. She was light headed.

There was no longer any sense or reason. She was intoxicated; lost in a soundless garden of unnamed scents and sensations. Moments of unbearable sweetness. Then, briefly, sadness and bereavement. She lay quietly in his arms under James's robe. The storm had ceased.

Outside, she heard a bird sing.

'I shall never mind thunder again,' she said.

She stared out of the window in wonderment, long after Jonathan had gone. Steam drifted upwards from the shrubs as the warmth evaporated the rain. Soon little white clouds floated across the sky and pockets of blue appeared.

'Jonathan, I think I'm in love with you,' she whispered to herself.

He came back again that evening. She heard the car draw up and ran to the door. His face was unsmiling, apprehensive almost, and she wondered fearfully if he thought he had made a terrible mistake.

As he walked towards her, she held out her arms to him. She saw him relax, his shoulders unstiffen and he took her hands in his, held them tightly, then dropped them and took her in his arms.

'Oh, Addie. Are you all right?'

'Of course. I couldn't be more all right.'

'I was afraid, worried. Taking advantage of you when you were at your most vulnerable … of our professional ...'

'You didn't. You didn't. I knew what I was doing.'

'I haven't stopped thinking about you all day.'

'Me too.'

They went to bed again. Made love, drifted off to sleep, and woke hungry in the middle evening. Then they showered, dressed and went out to a Chinese restaurant. It was their first date.

'What did you say at the office?' Addie enquired, as the waitress walked off with their order.

'I told them I called in at a client, and I booked down an

hour and a half to your account.'

'I always knew it. Gigolo. You didn't really.'

'Well I might have,' Jonathan replied unrepentantly, 'but as it happened, everyone was in late. On the other side of town, an electric cable was struck by lightning. No-one hurt, thank goodness, but all the traffic lights were out. There was a five-mile traffic queue around Middleton Road and all roads leading in to the centre. And flooding near the river, so that created havoc too.'

'Well thank heaven for that. I wouldn't want to cause you any embarrassment.'

'It's not my normal sort of activity at 8.45 in the morning. I know you said you liked to be under the bedclothes in a thunderstorm, but you didn't mention you wanted company.'

Their first course arrived. Addie picked up her chopsticks and asked, 'How did you know it was me standing there? From behind.'

'I'm an expert on behinds. I thought I mentioned it.'

'Oh yes. I remember. Something to do with your Italian ancestry.'

'Actually, I remembered the slogan on your tee-shirt - what was it - "my other tee-shirt's a Gucci."'

'How do you remember so much about me, Jonathan? What I wear. What I say.'

'Ever since I met you, I've been looking at you, liking you, wanting you and wondering - would you be interested? Is it ethical? Would it be sensible? Isn't my life complicated enough already?'

'Thank God, you didn't bother to ask all those questions this morning.'

'You didn't give me much chance.'

'So *you* were the reluctant victim.'

'Actually, Addie, after Tabitha, I wasn't sure I wanted to get involved - with anyone.'

'While we're on the subject,' Addie said, aware that her

voice suddenly sounded cold and irritated, 'I would like to know how Tabitha fits into your life? I'm not trying to dictate to you, but I'm not that keen on your rushing off to another woman, every time she gives a little whimper. I just want to get the picture straight. Am I a substitute for the real thing? Haven't you gotten her out of your system?'

Jonathan started to interrupt her a couple of times, but she managed to finish what she wanted to say first.

'I don't know how you can ask that, Addie. Don't you know, after today?' She felt contrite and reached out and took his hand. 'There's nothing between Tabitha and me now,' he said. 'I don't love her. I realise we never had a lot in common. But we do jointly own a flat. That's a bit like having a child. We have to talk to each other about it, discuss its future, its prospects. We also have to spend money on the damn thing. The good thing about it is that we'll eventually get rid of it, and then we can each get on with our lives. In fact, of course, Tabitha has already got the new man installed.

'Sarah mentioned that.'

'As far as Sarah is concerned, I don't know why she thinks that she can discuss my life like it's the latest episode in a soap. Or why she's even angrier with Tabitha than I am. What happened between Tabitha and me happened. She was very attractive and fun, at first. Then things just didn't work. She was only interested in having fun. She said I was too serious. And it all started to go wrong. The only thing I regret is buying the bloody flat.' He was getting that tense look that seemed to happen at any mention of Tabitha. Addie squeezed his hand and smiled at him.

'I'm sorry,' she said. It occurred to her then that she did not actually know where he lived. 'If Tabitha's in the flat and you're not, where are you? Are you living with your Mom and Sarah?'

'I couldn't go back to that, Addie. No believe it or not, I'm living in a rented house with three other guys. In fact, it's quite like being a student, again.'

'You didn't mind going back to that, then.'

'Being a student is your first taste of independence. I don't mind living with other people, even sharing a kitchen with people who don't always wash up. But I couldn't go back to telling my mother I might be in late.'

She looked down at the hand she held. Long fingers, neatly trimmed nails. She thought of him wiping the rain from her face, this morning. Was it really only this morning? It felt a lifetime away.

'Will you stay with me tonight, Jonathan?'

'You're a very forward woman.'

She smiled, 'Sex has been the downfall of all my ancestors - just blame it on the genes.'

For the sake of appearances, Jonathan did not stay at *Tamar* every night. Addie was concerned that, in view of the complications of the Buckley estate and the way that the Graingers' lives were inextricably woven into it, they should not form an incorrect impression. If they knew that she and Jonathan were an 'item', they might think that their inheritance was at risk - that the terms of the will, with its additional instructions, most of which they found completely incomprehensible, could be distorted to provide Addie with more benefits. Addie was sure they knew her well enough now to be confident that this would not be the case, but it seemed wrong that Jonathan's reputation should be damaged. She was still determined to provide some extras from the estate for Nora and Bill, this being one of the reasons why she had decided not to use up the capital but to continue to try to bring in an income.

So on Tuesday and Wednesday of that week, Jonathan left at midnight to return to 'the guys' and, as Addie watched him from the window, she felt very much like Adrienne, wanting to haul him back to her side by any means, so she could reach out and touch him whenever he was near. True, she had felt the same magnetic attraction to Lloyd, but with Lloyd came a lot of other baggage - insecurity, pain, even the feeling of exploitation - baggage that had no appeal for the sane feet-on-the-ground Addie with expectations of equality and fair deals in the world of men, but which nevertheless added an extra dimension to the love life of the Addie that lay under the sheets, or (more likely) on the rug in front of the fire with Lloyd.

Lloyd didn't even disguise his infidelity; he used it. She recalled how she had prepared a candlelit dinner on one occasion, foolishly hoping to cement the already fractured relationship, and he arrived three hours late. She turned off the chicken in the oven, left it to go cold and ate the smoked salmon starter with half a bottle of wine on her own. When he came in, she accused him furiously, 'You've been with another woman.'

He had picked up the salmon with a fork and eaten it in a few mouthfuls. 'Just an appetizer, my dear Addie - to give me all the more time and patience for the main course - and - like all the best starters - to whet the appetite.' And in spite of herself, she had given in, been seduced all over again, as she so often was then. But that was before she knew that the hors d'oevres was the seventeen-year-old secretary.

She was older and wiser now and Jonathan had come to her without that baggage. Well, almost without - there was always Tabitha. And the subject of Tabitha had come up again on Thursday evening.

'Why did you have to rush off to see Tabitha that time, when we were all having lunch?'

He looked irritated. 'I told you. She was in tears and said that her new man had thumped her. Goodness knows why that should have involved me. Except she might have needed a lawyer. But she didn't.'

'Did you bill her?' Addie enquired, straight faced. But he

didn't smile.

'What had happened?' Addie asked.

'She'd nagged and he'd been sarcastic. That had annoyed her. So she'd slapped him and he'd slapped her back and gone off to the pub. Perhaps he wasn't a new man after all.'

'So what did you do?'

'I told her she always was an irritating bitch and, thank God, it wasn't my problem any more. Then I made her a cup of tea and reminded her that she'd always found me boring and now she was having an exciting life with him. Then he came back and, before you knew it, they were like two pieces of Velcro, and I was saying good night to the air.'

'But then there was another time,' Addie pursued, after she had laughed at the scenario.

Jonathan looked at her carefully. 'We've only been together three days, Addie. How long have you been harbouring these concerns about my private life?'

Addie said slowly, 'I'm sorry if I seem a bit paranoid, Jonathan. I just want to make things quite clear between us. I don't want to share you. I've had that experience before, and I didn't like it one bit.'

Jonathan didn't smile. He just said. 'I don't want to be nagged and I don't want a drama queen, Addie. I've had *that* experience and I don't want a repeat of *that*.'

They looked at each other coldly for a moment. Then Addie said, 'How do you feel about getting together with a piece of Velcro?'

He unbent.

'I think I could hack it.' Then he growled in an appalling phoney American accent, 'Stick to me baby and you'll be okay.'

It was Friday before Addie thought about telling Sarah. She's bound to ring about lunch on Sunday, she thought. She could hardly sit there through a full roast dinner, pretending nothing had happened between her and Jonathan. She had half a mind to ring on Friday evening, but then Jonathan appeared with tickets for a show at the local theatre and, by the time they'd had a pizza afterwards, it was much too late. So it was not until Saturday morning that Sarah found out.

Addie was dreaming at the time. It started out like her usual dream, with her mother, long dress sweeping the ground, coming across the lawn towards her, a basket of roses on her arm. But then she set down the basket and disappeared. Addie became aware that she was lying next to a man with ginger hair; she was nestled in the crook of his arm. 'I have to go,' she said, and tried to struggle up. The arm caught hold of her and held her more tightly. 'Don't leave me,' the man said. From the basket, there came the sound of a baby crying. She tried to pull away from the arm. It was not fair to burden him with the child. She must go to the baby, which now was screaming in a regular rhythmic fashion, pausing only for breath. She tried again to get up to deal with the penetrating sound. She opened her eyes. Jonathan's arm, not that of a red haired stranger, was round her shoulders, and his eye lashes were flickering, struggling to open. The shrill sound was no baby but the extension telephone. Jonathan's free hand reached out, before Addie could stop him.

'Palfrey, Willow, Amery,' he croaked into the speaker.

'Jonathan, is that you?' came a startled voice at the end of the phone.

He was awake now. 'Sarah?'

There was no answer. Sarah had slammed down the receiver at the other end.

In some ways, it was just as well that Sarah had given them an alarm call. Jonathan had completely forgotten about a four-day conference he'd booked to attend. He didn't even stay for breakfast, but downed some coffee and went straight back to his flat for the appropriate clothes and overnight gear. It gave Addie a chance to ring Sarah later.

'Do you want to get together for a coffee?'

'If you like,' said Sarah coldly.

Sarah wasn't going to put herself out, Addie could tell. So she drove to the house.

Sarah opened the door without speaking. She walked into the kitchen without speaking and she switched on the kettle with an abrupt click.

Addie spoke. 'Where's Helen?'

'She's gone shopping in town. How long have you and Jonathan been screwing?'

'Sarah, you don't have to be so uptight. I was going to tell you.'

'I don't care about your telling me. I just wish it hadn't happened.'

'I thought we were friends. Don't you approve of me?'

'You'll go back to the States. We'll have to pick up the pieces.'

'Jonathan's not a wimp. You can't protect people from pain. You can't live your life without pain.'

'We've had pain in this family. I don't want it again.'

'You're being ridiculous, Sarah. And anyway, Jonathan's not a child. It's not your job or business to protect him. He's a perfectly able, red-blooded man.'

She couldn't resist a little smile at her mental image of him, which Sarah caught.

She banged the cup down on the table, the coffee spilling as she did so. 'If you're planning to come to lunch tomorrow, don't expect to find me here.'

Leaving her cup on the table, she marched out into the garden, slamming the kitchen door behind her. Addie drank her own cup of coffee – waited for a few moments, in case Sarah had a change of heart, and then went home.

It was a difficult day. Addie did not enjoy conflict of this sort and, if she was not careful, she would waste the day pacing and musing on it. Instead, she went deliberately to sit in the garden with a notepad and put random thoughts down, in preparation for another article. She skimmed sporadically through Adrienne's diary, in part to recapture her mother's life once again, and partly to spot anything she'd missed. She looked for clues, too, that might help her to find out more about Richard, her father. But through the day, the Amerys kept re-entering her mind. Brother and sister. Jonathan, good looking; sense of humour; nice eyes; shy, but only at first sight; very sexy; lover. Sarah; friend; enemy; jealous; immature. Addie hadn't set out to divide brother from sister. She hadn't wanted to alienate herself from Sarah. It simply wasn't an issue. Why in heaven's name, should she have to choose between them? Richard's sister had been pleased for her brother and friend to be together.

The phone rang in the evening. It was Helen.

'How would you like to go out for a Chinese meal with a middle-aged widow?'

'I'd love to go out for a meal, Helen, but I only know a young widow.'

'Thanks for the compliment. They're few and far between, these days. So I'll pick you up in say half an hour.'

'Unless you want to come over here. You never did get that meal I promised.'

'Another time, Addie. This time I just want to talk - I don't want to peel potatoes or watch you peeling potatoes, and all the rest of it. Let someone else do it.'

'Okay,' Addie said, 'but my treat this time.'

'If you say so,' Helen said.

They went to The Red Pagoda, where Jonathan had previously taken Addie, and ordered half a crispy duck to start.

'Sarah is being infantile,' Helen stated, covering her pancake with sauce and wrapping it round a portion of duck with spring onions. 'She thinks she's King Canute and can stop the tide from coming in. I could see you and Jonathan getting together, a mile off. Both giving each other surreptitious looks.'

'Do you mind?' Addie asked.

'I can imagine worse things happening to him. Of course he'll be hurt if you go away. And no mother wants to see her children hurt. It tears you apart when your baby falls over for the first time.' She munched reflectively on her pancake. 'But as they grow up, you learn to distance yourself. You have to, because no reasonable mother wants to restrict her children so much that they're afraid of taking any steps at all. Anyway, I know you wouldn't set out to hurt Jonathan. It's Sarah I'm really worried about.'

'Do you think that we're responsible for Sarah being in a state?'

'Of course I don't. No, this is much more long term than you and Jon. It's a great deal to do with her father's death, and it's also partly to do with Tabitha. I just wish she'd get it all out of her system.'

'Go on,' Addie said, helping herself to some more duck.

'Well, Sarah was really rather possessive about Jonathan when she was younger. She was bit short and dumpy and bad at sport and she used to boast about him in a rather proprietary way. Take in photos of him to show off, to detract from her own shortcomings. I should have put a stop to it then. I didn't see it as very important at the time. And then he met Tabitha who she was friendly with.'

'Was she a good friend?'

'Not really, well, in fact, almost a rival. Tabitha was particularly good at sport, and by the time she got to that age, very tall and slim with a good figure.'

The Chinese waiter brought their second course, and Helen took a sip of white wine before continuing.

'So then she was lording it over Sarah. Particularly if she came over, as she did sometimes - you know the sort of thing - "Oh, Jonathan doesn't like Kate Bush any more, he prefers Spandau Ballet." - can't remember the details - I may have the names wrong. Or "Johnny and I cycled half way to Brighton yesterday," knowing how Sarah hates any sort of physical activity. Yes, Tabitha was pretty immature too.'

Addie nodded, smiling, remembering 'Johnny'.

'But she grew up and she wasn't a bad sort of girl. They both grew up and grew apart. I didn't see it lasting forever. But it certainly wasn't all as traumatic as Sarah implies.'

'Was she his first girlfriend?'

'Oh good gracious, no - but the first one that Sarah knew personally - that was what rankled. As a matter of fact, he was far more hurt when the first one broke up - he was seventeen or eighteen and she was about three years older. I shouldn't be surprised if she taught him a thing or two. But it's not the sort of thing a mother enquires about - however curious we are. I think she was playing games with him and he was very hurt at the time. If I could have done anything to help then I would - but of course, I couldn't, and in the end he got through it. I shouldn't be saying all this to you, of course. It's giving you an unfair advantage.'

'You needn't worry. I don't treat love as a game of chess,' said Addie solemnly.

'I'm sure you don't, Addie. Do you love him?'

'That's an unfair question, Helen. Even though I asked for it. But I don't think I'm going to answer it.' She knew that the older woman wouldn't be offended. Just as she hadn't been by the question. 'Perhaps we'd better get back to Sarah. You were going to tell me how your husband's death affected her.'

'What worries me now about Sarah is that it seems she can't let go of the people she loves - she wants to possess them - and she can't form new loves.'

'But she's with Trevor, isn't she?' Addie said.

'I'm not talking about sex, Addie,' Helen said, topping up her plate with more rice and sizzling beef from the serving dish. 'I love fried rice, don't you? Of course, rice would hardly be fattening at all if it weren't fried and it weren't for the egg, would it? She's not coming home tonight - I expect she's sleeping with him. I haven't enquired.'

'You're the perfect mother,' Addie said without irony.

'I wish. I just know there's no emotional commitment there - not her side anyway. It's like she's afraid that someone she loves will be snatched away, and she won't take the chance. So she deliberately picks out a sort of male bimbo, an airhead, sorry Trevor, so she won't fall in love with him.'

'And all this started when your husband died?'

'She was at the funeral, dry eyed, stiff lipped. She's never really let it out. Not to me, at any rate. She'll say to people, "My father's dead," of course. But she won't talk about how she feels. The pain. Jonathan and I talked about it a great deal. Such a shock to all of us. A man in his prime. Mid-fifties. Good looking, a bit like Jonathan.' She paused and wiped her eyes. 'Sorry. I miss him so much still.'

She put down her cutlery and rested her hands on the table.

'I've never talked about it to anyone before, but I had an affair with his brother - Bruce. Afterwards, I mean. About six months after. I was so desperate - desperate to replace him and desperately frustrated. Does that shock you? Some people think that your nether regions grind to a halt at thirty nine.'

Addie shook her head and spooned some more rice on to her plate.

'He was divorced. We weren't hurting anyone. Though Sarah would be horrified. She hates him. He looks a lot like Jeffrey. I thought I was getting the original back. It went on for two or three months. The sex was good. I was very uninhibited. I cringe about it now. I kept expecting him to make one of Jeffrey's comments. He didn't. He didn't have Jeff's sense of humour; didn't really joke at all. He took advantage of me, of course. He knew how vulnerable I was. He never was one to miss an opportunity. That was the worst of it, really. He simply didn't have Jeff's ethics. He was quite

302

devious and dishonest over trivial things. It fizzled out - I see him as little as I can now - too embarrassing.' She took some wine, her hand shaking a little as she lifted the glass. 'I grieved all over again, you know - it was realising that I wasn't going to replace Jeff - not ever. Jonathan was wonderful. Of course he was around - Sarah was back at Uni by then. We spent a lot of time talking about how Jeff and I first met and what he was like when he was young, and we both talked about the day it happened and how it had affected us.' She put down her fork, her eyes moving away from Addie into the middle distance. 'I shall never forget. Bruce rang from the office and said Jeff had collapsed and he'd sent for an ambulance. Jonathan didn't work with them then, but he was nearby. We both raced to the hospital and sat with him. Wires and things attached to him. We both held his hands. One on either side. They couldn't save him.'

Tears streamed down her face unashamedly.

'I keep thinking the well's nearly dried up. But it hasn't.'

'Sarah was a bit left out of this, wasn't she?'

'She came the next day. Jonathan couldn't get hold of her that night. Jeff was dead by the time she got home. She was very brave, very strong. Kept patting my arm and saying, "It's all right, Mummy. We're here." I couldn't hurt her feelings. I wanted to say, "I don't give a damn who's here. Why don't you stop the clichés and cry with me?" But she couldn't. Not then and it seems, not now.'

They ordered coffee and the waiter brought them a pot and small cups and a couple of fortune cookies. Addie poured the coffee.

'You know, I didn't mean to come out with all this. I only wanted to tell you not to mind Sarah. You must still come and visit. I enjoy having you. It's like having another daughter. And you mustn't let her spoil your relationship with Jonathan.'

'It's not that fragile,' Addie commented. 'And I'm not that

easily put off. I'm just sorry I didn't tell her as soon as it happened. It just took us both a bit by storm.' Literally, she thought.

'I don't think it would have made any difference. I just wish all this silliness would come to an end. I don't know how to get through this barrier.'

Addie summoned the waiter and signed the credit slip. She refused Helen's invitation to lunch on Sunday. 'Let's give it a rest for a few days. Maybe Sarah will calm down.'

She treated Sunday like the rest of the week - read, wrote and ran and, at the end of the day, lay in the empty bed, missing Jonathan and thinking with some heat and with pleasurable anticipation of the next time he would be there with his arms around her.

Chapter 26: Dirty Weekend

Jonathan came back from the conference midweek, and arrived at *Tamar* like a worn out minor executive who has been standing on the tube for the last hour. His briefcase was bulging with documents and the paper he'd been reading was crumpled.

'The seminar was boring and work's been uninspiring. Or the other way round. I didn't go home and I've brought two dirty shirts. Do you think I could use your washing machine?'

He looked like a man who needed a tot of whisky. She took the shirts and brought him a drink.

'Jonathan, I want to go away at the weekend.'

He looked alarmed. She sat on his lap and stroked his face, the end of the day's stubble rough on her fingers.

'Will you come with me?'

'To the end of the earth. Can I commute to the firm?'

'Only to Long Barton, Jonathan. And just for the weekend - not for life.'

'This is not because of Sarah, is it? You're not trying to avoid her?'

'I've seen her. She wasn't happy. But your mom said I shouldn't worry about it. We got together while you were away.'

'She was an absolute pain about Tabitha, too. Even in the days when things were going well. Why do you want to lure me away for a dirty weekend, then? All the facilities are here.'

'It'll be great to be away together.'

Jonathan put down his glass and stopped jesting. 'To be honest, Addie, I'd much rather stay here. I was looking forward to a few quiet days with you - here, just the two of us. Can't you put off your research?'

Addie was dismayed at his lack of enthusiasm. She got up

and paced the room. 'It's true I have loose ends to tie up. But I thought we'd both enjoy it. No chance of the Graingers arriving on the doorstep, for one. Look, I've got to make more trips to Long Barton. It's not just Dorothy - it's the whole of my family. I don't want to be there without you.'

'I understand that, Addie. But so soon. Couldn't you leave it a week or two?'

'Jonathan, my family's important to me. You know that. I need to feel I can close the book on Dorothy and move on. The most important person now - since I've read the diary - is Richard, my father. I had hoped that finding out about Dorothy might lead me to him.'

Jonathan looked sceptical.

'Okay. Perhaps I'm being too optimistic. To be honest, I don't know where to begin, but I can't believe I'm going to find out anything unless I go there. That's the starting point. And there's another thing. I want you to meet Ada, my great-grandmother. I got a call from Veronica Daborn that she's had her operation and she can see clearly out of the good eye. She's an old lady. She hasn't got all the time in the world, you know.'

Jonathan sighed in resignation. 'All right, I'll come. I'll do it for Ada's sake, if nothing else. What's she like? Will I like her?'

'She's a bit more crabby than me.'

Jonathan got up and pulled her towards him again. 'Well, if I can put up with you … Promise me there'll be some time for just the two of us.'

It was so good to have him back. And for Addie, the thought of the weekend ahead with Jonathan at her side gave it an extra dimension.

'I'll give you my undivided attention.' She buried her face in his neck. 'I might even start now.'

'Well, in that case,' Jonathan said, 'it might be an idea to have an early night.'

'Don't you think six-thirty is a little too early?'

'Not for what I have in mind.'

They drove down first thing on Friday, so that Addie could meet Sue Hawthorne, the archivist at Dorothy's school. On the journey, Addie reminded Jonathan of what she'd already found out. Jonathan had previously only heard sketchy details. Somehow, in their discovery of each other, external events had been pushed to one side. Addie only now remembered to ask why he hadn't gone home after the Conference.

'I visited Tabitha,' he said challengingly.

There was a few seconds in which they fought a silent duel.

'Why?'

'There's someone interested in the flat. He wanted to negotiate directly with me. In fact he wanted to by-pass the agent. Tabitha didn't know if that was okay.'

'And is it?'

'No. I had to tell him it was out of the question.'

She rested her hand on his leg. The car shuddered slightly, veered to the edge of its lane, then returned to its former calm cruising along the motorway.

'Thanks.'

'What for?'

'For telling me.'

He glanced in her direction with a smile. Removing the hand and squeezing it slightly, he said, 'You're welcome.'

They booked into The Stonemason's Arms. Addie just didn't feel able to share a bed with Jonathan in the intimate atmosphere of Mrs Simpson's B & B. Then they drove immediately to Long Barton Girls' School.

Sue Hawthorne led them to a tiny room.

'There's quite a lot of enthusiasm for collecting up old records, now,' she told them. 'In fact, I've been given a sabbatical from normal duties, in order to do as much work with these records as possible.'

Addie felt the chill as she entered the room. 'You must

have a ghost in here. There's quite a drop in temperature.'

'Yes, we said that it had to be dry and cool to keep the papers in the best condition possible. They went rather overboard on the "cool". It can be absolutely freezing in the winter months.'

'Can I take anything away with me?'

'I'm afraid not - but if there's anything you want to photocopy, just let me know.'

'Thanks,' Addie said. 'I'll get started.'

Sue Hawthorne squeezed out, so that Jonathan could get in. 'I hope you can both fit in here.' But he eyed the small room, and said, 'Look Addie, I think this is something you should do on your own. I've got my mobile with me, so I'll go back to the hotel and spend a couple of hours making some phone calls and reading over papers. Just give me a ring when you're ready to come back.'

Again Addie felt a moment of disappointment that Jonathan did not want to share her discoveries. Still, he was here. That was the main thing. 'I'm bound to get engrossed,' she said. 'You come and get me when you're hungry.'

Sue Hawthorne had arranged files in years, as far as she could. She pointed out two or three log books which contained information on the period when Dorothy would have been at the school. In addition to that, there was a collection of poems written by the girls, dating back to the twenties. There were school magazines surviving from some years, and a history of the school written about fifteen years before.

But disappointingly, the information in the log books was sparse. It gave only the barest details of examination results and other successes. Looking through the lists of girls' names and dates, Addie eventually found the entry for Dorothy Heron. Apart from the examinations she had passed, it mentioned that she was in the Long Barton School Choir. Other than that, there was nothing surprising or interesting in the list of achievements.

Searching for another mention of Dorothy, Addie painstakingly read articles in the school magazines that had survived. Finally, her perseverance paid off. First, in 1931, there was a report of a performance by the choir at the local church. The members of the choir were mentioned by name and Dorothy was amongst them. And in the following year, there was a long article describing the choir's achievements, written by Margaret Holbrook the choir mistress, in which she mentioned Dorothy as one of their most promising soloists. On the strength of her talent, Dorothy, at that time fifteen, had been awarded a bursary, which would enable her to stay on at school until she was seventeen.

Addie turned to the poetry collection, a set of stapled photocopies, and skimmed through it. The original book was there, but faded and yellowing and Addie felt safer reading the photocopies. Dated 1929, it held groups of poems, remarkably similar in style, suggesting that the girls had been prompted in a particular direction. Nevertheless, some of them were quite skilfully written, and a few of the most gifted girls were featured several times. Suddenly, in a batch of poems, all entitled The Sun, she saw Dorothy's name. But whereas most of the poems had treated the subject as one which was likely to bring them pleasure, Dorothy's poem was in a different vein.

> Bereft of love, I stare.
> I feel the sun's harsh glare.
> Somehow I learn to bear
> What life holds for me.
>
> My body feels its burn.
> For peace of mind I yearn.
> How can I bear to learn
> What life holds for me.

There were more verses, along similar lines. It was a disturbing piece of work to have been written by a child of twelve or thirteen. Addie felt quite chilled, and was aware this was only partly to do with the temperature of the room. The strangely adult attitude seemed to hold prescience of what was to come. Somehow Dorothy had learned to bear her existence with Rodney Heron. But in addition, the simple verse suggested that life had been unkind to Dorothy, even at the threshold of her teens.

Addie was quiet all through lunch. Now she lay on the bed at The Stonemason's Arms, resting on her elbows, the folder of photocopies in front of her.

'I want you to look at this, Jonathan.'

'I am looking,' he said from a chair at the window, surveying her rear end.

She aimed a paperclip at him.

'Come and look.'

He joined her on the bed and looked over her shoulder, his hand resting on the small of her back.

'This poem,' Addie said. 'Just read it, will you? It confirms to me what I've felt for a long time. It says to me that Dorothy was on the receiving end of violence even then. I don't know whether it was physical or verbal, but I somehow feel that "the sun" is a euphemism for a person, someone powerful - almost certainly her grandfather, since he was probably the only man in her life.'

'I suppose it would have been unthinkable to be any more direct than that.'

'Jonathan,' Addie said. 'What makes men hit women?'

'Anger, sometimes, I suppose. Frustration. An expression of power. Sometimes women hit men too.'

'Yes, but sometimes men hit women because they enjoy it.'

'Yes.'

'Sometimes, it's sexy.'

'Yes.'

'I don't know what happened to Dorothy when she was young, but I suspect she escaped from one unhappy situation into another. Rodney got his sexual kicks from violence. She never learned how not to be a victim.'

'I'm sorry, Addie. I'm not responsible for the entire race of males.'

'Jonathan.'

'Yes?'

'Did you ever hit Tabitha?'

'No.'

'Did she ever slap you?'

'Yes.'

'But you still didn't hit her? What did you do?'

'I walked out and left her to it.'

Addie got up, took the photocopies and put them on the dressing table. Then she got back on to the bed and climbed into Jonathan's arms. 'Make love to me. I need to be reminded that you're not like them.'

It was not until eleven am on Saturday that they visited Ada Seccombe. As Addie walked past the door marked *Margaret Holbrook; do not disturb*, she caught her breath.

'Margaret Holbrook,' she murmured to herself. She must try to speak to her again.

Jonathan's mobile rang, a thin but piercing sound in the corridor.

'Hallo.'

'Oh, Tabitha.' Pause. Addie glared at the phone.

'Can you speak up. I can hardly hear?' He moved around, searching for a better signal. 'I see. I'll talk to him. I'll take it outside.'

As Jonathan walked towards the front door, Addie glanced at the closed door to Veronica Daborn's office and, without knocking, made a hurried entrance into Margaret Holbrook's room.

'Mrs Holbrook. Do you remember me? Please don't throw

me out.'

The woman turned her head to follow the sound of the voice.

'Ah yes. The desperate American.'

'I know I offended you - the way I spoke about Dorothy Heron. I was upset. My mother died when I was a baby. I never knew her. Nor my father. It's so important to me to understand who I am. Will you please help me?'

'What is it you want to know?' the woman said stiffly.

'I started off thinking that Dorothy was uncaring, because she rejected me. But gradually I've come to be more and more interested in her and fond of her. I know now she was a tragic figure. A desperately unhappy woman. Even her childhood seems a sad time.'

Remembering the photocopy she had taken from the school, she drew it from her bag. 'Can I read you this poem that she wrote? I just wonder if you could throw some light on it.'

Without waiting, she started to read:

> Bereft of love, I stare.
> I feel the sun's harsh glare.
> Somehow I learn to bear
> What life holds for me.
>
> My body feels its burn.
> For peace of mind I yearn.
> How can I bear to learn
> What life holds for me.

Margaret Holbrook listened, her mouth set. 'It's hard for me to admit to myself that I failed her,' she said finally. 'There can be no doubt that her grandfather was a tyrant, the way he treated that child.'

'What did he do?'

'Oh, nothing unusual. He beat her. As I recall, he told me quite proudly that he beat her to keep her on the path of righteousness.'

'Couldn't you put a stop to it?'

'Don't you understand? It was not unusual at that time. We could do nothing. Generally, one didn't even comment on it. Some of the children would come to school almost in rags, with bruises all over them, and still cheeking, bouncing back, almost asking for another thrashing.' Addie did not interrupt her. At last she was talking freely.

'But Dorothy was not remotely naughty, and we - I discussed it with one or two teachers - we felt that it was almost a ritual in her household that she should be beaten for no good reason. Her grandfather was obsessively narrow-minded. I remember to this day - and it chills me still - when I told him that I felt sure Dorothy would bring credit to the family, he said, "Dorothy is a bastard. Her presence never ceases to bring shame on a God-fearing household." Then he said to me, "Fortunately with regular chastisement, I believe I have kept her from further shame." If I could have seized a strap and beaten him myself at that moment, it would have given me great satisfaction.' She wiped her eyes. 'I was very fond of Dorothy. It was appalling to me that she appeared to be resigned to this treatment. And for a child of that age to be resigned is a bad thing.'

Feeling the locker beside her, she took a glass in a shaking hand, and drank some water before continuing.

'I did what I could to help. Dorothy had a good ear for music and I helped her with pronunciation and elocution and included her in the choir, too. Little enough. But it meant I could keep her under my wing, to a certain extent.'

A voice sounded in the corridor. Addie realised that Jonathan had no idea where she was, but she had to hear what this woman had to say.

'Later, the old man wanted to take Dorothy out of school,

so that she could work. She would either go into service or into a factory. It was an appalling waste. We wanted her to have a better future. We managed to arrange a bursary from school funds. We had one or two local benefactors. Her grandfather was greedy. He regarded himself as deeply religious and moral, but he was not averse to bribery.'

The door opened and Veronica Daborn walked in. Her normally amiable face was frosty.

'You had no right to come in here, Miss Russell.'

Margaret Holbrook smiled. 'Let the girl stay. One should always resist the power of others, as I have been telling her.' Her mouth compressed in an angry line. 'I am imprisoned here in my chair. A cripple, ninety-five years old and blind. But I am not resigned. I am angry at this fate. I am as bloody-minded as I can be. As long as I am angry and bloody-minded, I will stay alive - that is, my spirit will stay alive. I can no longer vouch for the body. But once I become resigned, there will be nothing left for me.'

She turned her head back towards Addie. 'If only Dorothy had fought. But she seemed to have no fight in her. She just accepted, as if she had no right to decent treatment or dignity.'

The matron left the room, quietly closing the door behind her.

'The grandfather's one thought was that Dorothy would become pregnant at a young age - like her mother, I gather, who had died in childbirth.'

Addie did not correct her.

'Consequently, I managed to alarm him by saying that sometimes girls in service were seduced by the master of the house. That she would meet girls who were more knowing and sophisticated, in the factories. He found these arguments persuasive - together with the bursary.'

She paused for a moment.

'We managed to buy her another couple of years at school. She helped with some of the younger ones and I hoped she would train as a teacher. But then she met Dr Heron and suddenly, she told us she was marrying him. I could not understand it at first; he was so much older than she was, and, in any case, she was naïve - young for her years. I felt that there must have been some pressure placed upon her from her grandfather. Financial security. Respectability, becoming a schoolmaster's wife. But mainly removing her from the prospect of premature sexual adventures.' She sighed. 'I was very much against the idea, as you can imagine; I even tried to dissuade her, but she would not discuss it. Nevertheless, here you are, young lady, the eventual progeny of this union - the no doubt delightful product of a happy relationship - so my judgement must have been at fault.'

'My grandmother had a brief affair with someone else - an officer she fell in love with - he was my grandfather.'

'So she had some little happiness?'

'Yes. And she did at least see my mother grow into adulthood. But you were right to be concerned for her, because her marriage was unhappy and, to be honest, I don't know how she survived it.'

'Well, as to that,' Margaret Holbrook said. 'What I said about Dorothy being resigned - I realise that perhaps, as a result of that - she had an unusual ability. I saw that she was able to escape into books and music, and somehow distance herself from what was going on around her. I felt that when she was badly treated, she would somehow leave her body and take her mind to another place. I think it was this quality of detachment that might have helped her to survive seemingly unbearable circumstances.'

'Mrs Holbrook,' Addie said. 'I want to thank you. I felt that no-one cared what happened to Dorothy, and now I know that's not so. Much of her life seems to have been quite dreadful, but she must have gained a great deal from being in your care.'

'It is important to have someone to love. I lost my young

315

husband in the Great War, but I loved my girls. They became my family. Alas, I have outlived or lost touch with all those I cared for.'

On an impulse, Addie said, 'Mrs Holbrook - I met the ex-headmistress of Long Barton School. She is so very intelligent and articulate. May I tell her you are here? She is a widow too, and you would have so much in common.'

'I appreciate your kindness,' the woman said. She smiled in the direction of Addie's voice and held out a thin fleshless hand in dismissal.

Jonathan was waiting in the corridor, looking perplexed. He glanced at her face and said nothing. She took his hand, paused for a moment, absorbing its warmth and strength; then they walked together to Ada's room.

Chapter 27: Exits and Entrances

Ada was sitting in front of the television, watching snooker.

'Hi, Ada. Do you remember me?'

Ada recognised the voice without moving her head. 'It's my little girl.'

'Your great-granddaughter, Addie.'

She turned round slowly, as if to savour the moment.

'You're very pretty. Are you like her?'

'I'm sorry, Ada, I don't know. But I know she had brown eyes.'

The old lady stared at her for a few minutes, saying nothing. Then she looked back at the television.

'It's that Steve Davis. He gets them in the holes all the time. I always used to watch him when my eyes were going. He's still the best.' She turned back to Addie. 'Is that your young man?'

'This is Jonathan,' Addie said by way of an answer.

Jonathan smiled and put out a hand, but Ada ignored him and turned back to Addie.

'Nice looking boy. He reminds me of my Perce. He was skinny too.' She beckoned Addie closer. 'I don't think I'm going back to my little house, now. You can have it if you want it. You and him could get married and live in it. You could come and see me regular, like, then.'

'That's very sweet of you, Ada,' Addie said, touched. 'But I may not stay in this country. I may go back to America.'

'I suppose the house would belong to you, anyway, if something happened to her,' Jonathan said later, when they had left the room. 'I imagine you're her only relative.'

Out of curiosity, she asked Veronica Daborn about it.

'Ada's paid for by the social services, and they can use their discretionary powers to sell a property when they're funding residential care. Ada doesn't really understand that - she's not very knowledgeable about property and money. But in any case, I have a feeling that the property belonged to the other old lady, or her family. So I'm afraid she's nothing to leave you.'

'I've already been left one property,' Addie said. 'I'd rather have living relations than dead ones.'

When they arrived back at The Stonemason's Arms, Addie suddenly remembered Chris Templeman. Fuelled by an impish desire to see Jonathan's reaction, as well as genuine curiosity, she said, 'I wonder if Chris will still be at his office.'

'Who?'

'Chris Templeman - the guy I met last time I was here. I'm writing some stuff for him. And he's going to see if he can find out anything about my folks here.'

'You're insatiable, Addie.'

'I want to find out as much as I can.'

'I meant the number of men it takes to satisfy you. Chris, Julian, me. Is there no limit? Well, go on, why don't you phone him?'

You're very sure of me now, aren't you? she thought, keying in the number.

The phone rang only twice, 'Chris Templeman, Hampton & Barton Gazette.'

'Hi, Chris, how are you?' She noticed her voice had moved up half an octave. Why do women always do that when they're flirting, she thought.

'Hallo, Addie. Back again from the commuter heartland, eh? Thanks for your articles. I've passed them for payment and they'll be going in, in the next few weeks.'

'That's really sweet of you, Chris,' she said in the same voice. Jonathan looked up and stared at her.

'I've got something really interesting to show you. Something I found in the archives. Why don't you meet me for a meal? I've got nothing to do tonight.'

318

'I'm here with a friend, Chris.'

'Well, bring her along.'

'Perhaps we could just meet for a drink,' she said without clarification, not really wanting to have a polite threesome, when she could have Jonathan to herself. They had sat in the restaurant last night, eating their meal, their eyes meeting and their fingers touching periodically. Then Jonathan had suddenly downed his coffee, grabbed her hand, pulled her to her feet and said, 'Did you ever see the famous scene in *Tom Jones*?'

The bar was crowded when Chris arrived. He looked with surprise at Jonathan, but shook his hand enthusiastically.

'Addie, I've brought some cuttings to show you, well, photocopies, but I can hardly hear myself think in this din. Could we go somewhere else?'

To her surprise, Jonathan suddenly backed off. 'Addie, I'm tired.' He looked straight at her. 'I haven't had enough sleep, the last couple of nights. Why don't you two go off and look at the cuttings and meet me back here when you're ready for a meal? I'm going to have a sleep.'

She looked to see if he was sulking. He moved towards the stairs and she followed him, turning to Chris, 'I'll be with you in a second.'

'What is it?' she said as they reached the staircase together. He turned round and cupped her face in his hands. 'It's okay, Addie.' He kissed her. 'You've just worn me out, woman. See you later.'

They drove for about half an hour with Chris giving her a running commentary on the country outside, though the daylight was fading quickly. Addie started to tell him about finding her father's first name in the diary, and he promised to give some thought about how she might find out more about him. Chris didn't comment on Jonathan at all. Eventually, he pulled up at 'The Cider Apple', a quiet country pub in the

319

middle of nowhere, and they went into the Saloon Bar.

Chris had made no comment about Jonathan until now.

'Tell me about your new man,' he said, getting her a lager and escorting her to a seat.

'How did you know?'

'Addie, I'm a newspaper man. But if I'd been a dustman, I would have still picked up the vibes.'

Addie laughed. 'Okay. You're right. It all happened since I last saw you.' She saw a wistful look on his face. 'But you don't really want to hear about my boyfriend, Chris. Where are these photocopies you were going to show me?'

Chris had found another clipping from the social column of the Gazette. Addie's eyes turned immediately to the familiar names:

September 1934: The bride, Miss Dorothy Ann Seccombe wore a simple dress of white satin and a bouquet of fresh flowers. The groom, Dr Rodney Heron, is senior housemaster and classics master at Marsh House School, and owner of the Orchard Farm Estate, left to him by his late parents. The young bride announced her engagement when she was still a pupil at the Long Barton School for girls, and continued her education until the end of term. The bride and groom share an interest in books and choral music.

Drawn to the names, Addie had not noticed the photograph alongside the text. Now for the first time, in the indistinct photocopy, she saw Dorothy - solemn features, a smile, but not rapture on the face; a quiet dignity - a bit like Olivia de Havilland in *Gone with the Wind,* Addie thought, with the same dark hair and brown eyes. And next to her the man who had eventually driven Dorothy to suicide. He too was dark, with a thin face, a moustache and a sadistic mouth. He was smiling - a smile of triumph.

'Not exactly a suitable match. He looks twice her age,' commented Chris.

'What's the Orchard Farm Estate?' Addie asked.

'Doesn't exist any more as such. A farm, a few farm cottages, all split up and sold now. Some have had planning permission and have had extensions added. Others are just as they were a hundred years ago - probably with a more sophisticated plumbing system.'

'Do you know Appletree Cottage, where Dorothy was born?'

'Yes, that's part of the estate.'

'So Rodney was their landlord.'

'Do you think that Dr Rodney put some pressure on the family? Like in the old silent movies? He looks a nasty piece of work. But why would he do that?'

Addie shrugged. 'He must have been really taken with her,' she said. But she could envisage the scenario - Dorothy, wretched, eager to escape her grandfather at any price - constantly abused as being of no worth because of her illegitimacy - presented with the prospect of a marriage to an educated schoolmaster - an escape to someone who might offer her cultured conversation and who shared her interest in music and literature. Addie could see how, despite the age difference, despite the lack of romantic love, Dorothy could regard marriage with Rodney as a heaven-sent escape. And if she was as naive as Margaret Holbrook had implied, she would have little idea of the physical relationship between man and wife.

And Rodney, what did he stand to gain? It could be that he was genuinely charmed by Dorothy's quiet good looks, her dignity, modesty and intelligence; but no doubt he was also gaining a cloak of respectability to cover his unpleasant sexual preferences. And, eventually, an available victim, when there was no other.

For a few moments, Addie was lost in her reverie. This was the nearest she would get to an explanation of Dorothy's decision. With George, Rodney and both Dorothys dead now, the full truth would never be known. But she had a fair picture; as clear a view of the situation as she was likely to get.

'There's another one,' Chris said, bringing her back to reality.

This clipping was earlier and dated July 1933.

On 20th July, at the end of their summer term, the girls of Long Barton School Choir performed at Marsh House School. Staff and boys were entertained by a performance of lays and madrigals performed by the twenty strong choir, after which senior members of the choir were introduced to the staff of Marsh House school.

'That was pretty observant of you to spot that,' Addie commented.

'I wouldn't have, but for the photo,' Chris replied. 'I did a search for the names. In fact Rodney came up a few more times but on matters purely related to school. There was one report about a boy who claimed he'd been assaulted, but then confessed he'd made it up - storm in a teacup - but that probably wouldn't have interested you.'

'No,' Addie agreed without comment. She hadn't told Chris anything of Rodney's abuse of the boys at the school, nor of his violence towards Dorothy. Dorothy herself had tried so hard to keep those matters private - who was she to reveal them to all and sundry - to the press, no less?

She glanced at the photograph, adjacent to the report. *Head girl of Long Barton School, Dorothy Seccombe, meets Dr Rodney Heron at the end of term entertainment at Marsh House School.*

Dorothy's dark good looks were again apparent from the photo, while Rodney was almost obscured by his billowing academic gown.

'Could I keep this? I'd like to give it to Ada.'

'Of course. I expected you to keep them anyway. I'll do you another photocopy, if you like. Oh and there's another thing.'

'About Dorothy?'

322

'No. I was just thinking about your father. You could try going to the university and looking at the students for that year.'

'That's a good idea,' Addie said. 'Though he was older than Adrienne. He was already in Bristol when she arrived. I have to look at the diary again, and see how old he was.'

'What was he reading?'

'I don't know,' Addie admitted. 'But not just a straight degree. He wasn't going to finish at the same time as Adrienne.' She sighed. 'It'll be hard work, won't it? But I've got to find him.'

They finished their drinks and returned to the car. Jonathan should by now have recharged his batteries and be ready for a meal. Addie's natural sociability had overridden passion for now.

'Are you doing anything tonight, Chris?'

'Going home to fish and chips and cocoa.'

'Care to join us for a meal?'

'How about Jonathan?'

'He'll expect you to come.'

His pleasure was obvious. He didn't even go through the motions of refusing.

'How long is it since you broke up with your girl?'

'It's about three years, I suppose.'

'Time you got yourself a life, Chris.'

'Funny you should say that. As a matter of fact, I'm thinking about moving on. I'm going to a job interview on Monday. On one of the London papers.'

They walked into the bar at The Stonemason's Arms. Addie said, 'I'll go upstairs and get Jonathan, if you wait here.'

She ran up the carpeted staircase to the bedroom. The door was locked. She tapped. No reply. She banged more loudly and called through the door, 'Jonathan. Johnny.' That would annoy him. There was no answer.

Worried, she went downstairs and caught the barman's

eye. 'Do you have a pass key for the bedrooms upstairs?'

'The gentleman left his key at the bar, with Debbie, when he left.'

Addie stared at him in astonishment. 'Left? What do you mean? Has he gone out?'

'He's gone, miss. I thought he said he'd leave a note with the key.'

She couldn't take it in. Chris saw her puzzlement and came over, hearing the tail end of the conversation.

'Why would he go?' she said. Surely he wasn't jealous. He couldn't really have been that small-minded.

Chris turned to the barman, who was pouring a measure of Martini into a glass and taking another order at the same time. Saturday night was a busy night at The Stonemason's Arms.

'Didn't he say anything? What actually happened?'

The barman turned to a young woman also serving. 'You spoke to the young man - what did he say?'

She spoke with the soft local burr.

'He came down here and asked where the telephone was. Said he'd had a call on his mobile and could hardly hear what she was saying.'

'She?' Addie said.

The woman paused for a minute. 'Yes, he definitely said "she" because I remember thinking to myself, no sooner was one young lady out the door, then another one was ringing him.'

Addie felt her polite expression freeze on her face.

'But then of course, you were off with the other young gentleman … I couldn't really sort it out.' The woman reddened and stopped talking abruptly. The barman glared at her and said, 'Get on with it.'

'Then he came back again after a bit, and said he had to leave and could he pay the bill and give me a note. I was a bit busy at the time and I said to see Debbie on the till, and he could leave the key with her as well.'

'Well let's have a word with Debbie,' Chris said. But Debbie had left at seven o'clock and though her replacement, Rosa, was as helpful as she could be, finding the room key in the cash till, and establishing that Jonathan had settled the bill for the whole weekend, she could see no sign of a note.

How could he, Addie thought? What could be so important that it wouldn't wait an hour? She thought of her ultimatum to him, 'I won't share you, Jonathan.' If he had gone back at the beck and call of Tabitha Plowright, their relationship had ended almost as soon as it had begun.

* * *

When Addie awoke the following morning, for a moment she couldn't remember why she was there. She had thrashed around during the night and thrown off the duvet. Now, her shoulder felt cold, and at the dawn of wakefulness, she felt for the warmth of Jonathan in the empty area beside her. Then she remembered. Jonathan was back in Surrey, no doubt pandering to the spoiled Tabitha. For a moment, she felt a strong desire to go to the telephone and call him, even in spite of her irritation. She had a momentary vision then of his business card, still sitting in a drawer or on the mantelpiece, back at *Tamar*. The change in their relationship had been so sudden, so fast, and she had no idea of his mobile number, nor the number of his bachelor pad. A stupid and serious omission she now realised. She glanced at the time. Eight-forty-five on a Sunday morning. If she tried the Amery family number, she would simply disturb Sarah or Helen. As her mind went through the options, the telephone rang.

'Addie Russell.'

'Oh, Miss Russell. This is Veronica Daborn.'

Addie was immediately alert. 'Is something wrong?'

'Yes. I'm sorry to disturb you so early. I'm afraid Ada has had a fall. Being able to see again made her a little over-confident. She tripped over a footstool on her way to the loo,

325

this morning - we always tell them to ring if they need any help - and I've sent for Dr Morgan, her GP. She's in a lot of pain and I'm worried that it's something serious.'

'I really appreciate your calling me,' Addie said.

She was at the residential home by nine. Veronica Daborn shook hands with her. 'Doctor's with her now. I've told her you're a relative.'

Addie stood looking at the fish tank in Veronica's office. The door clicked.

'Miss Russell?'

She turned. A middle aged woman with greyish hair stood in front of her, a doctor's bag in her hand. She seemed about to speak, but something about Addie's face caused her to draw in her breath. 'Adrienne!' she said in a shocked voice.

Addie stared.

'I'm sorry,' the woman said. 'You are so like - someone.' She recovered her professional manner. 'You are Miss Russell? Ada's next of kin?'

Addie nodded.

'I've arranged for an ambulance to come. I'm afraid she may have broken her hip.'

'That's fairly serious at her age, isn't it?'

'I'm afraid that it can be.'

'Dr - Morgan, is it?'

The doctor nodded. Some caution still prompted Addie to hold back the full information.

'I am related to Adrienne Heron.'

The woman looked at her with dawning enlightenment. 'You're the girl who rang my mother - about family research. You're a cousin or niece or something.'

'Your mother?' Addie said.

'Yes - Elizabeth Charlton - she's my mother.'

Addie took in the information.

'I'm Patricia Morgan - Charlton's my single name. I knew Adrienne very well. I was quite shocked at the likeness.'

326

Addie tried to remember a mention of Patricia in the diary, but failed. Obviously she had not been an important figure in Adrienne's life.

Veronica Daborn came into the room. 'The ambulance is here.'

'I'll go to the hospital with Ada,' Addie said.

'Not in the ambulance, I'm afraid, but I'll drop you off there,' the doctor said. 'It's not very far and it's on my way.'

Addie said very little on the journey. She was wondering how much the dragon of a mother had said to her daughter, and if it would be insensitive to bring up the subject of Dorothy. But if Dr Morgan, like her mother, felt that Dorothy and her problems had contributed to her father's death, perhaps she too would be reluctant to talk about it. On the other hand, the doctor might simply be trying to be tactful by keeping off the subject.

They pulled into the hospital area and the car slowed to a halt. Patricia Morgan got out and opened the car door on Addie's side. They stood in an area slightly above the hospital.

'The ambulance will have taken Ada through that entrance,' she said, gesticulating with a finger. 'But if you walk down those steps and check in at the main entrance, over there, they'll be able to help you.'

She started to move away, then turned. 'They'll let me know what's happening,' she said. 'I hope things go well for her. Life hasn't dealt her the best of hands.' She gave Addie a sympathetic smile.

'You don't know the half of it,' Addie said. Her desire to see the doctor's reaction finally overrode her original doubts. 'You know, I must tell you. I'm Adrienne's daughter. You're the first person I've met with who knew her.'

The doctor stared at her, the smile on her lips ebbing away. 'Adrienne's daughter? But she didn't - we didn't know she ...'

'She died when I was born,' Addie said, bemused by the other woman's reaction. 'She didn't send out birth announcement cards.'

The doctor said nothing. Her face was a mask of concealed emotions. Addie couldn't fathom out if she was surprised, embarrassed or simply shocked at Addie's flippant comment.

'I have to go. I'm on call,' she said and turned back to the car.

Inside the hospital, Addie was directed to the casualty doctor in charge of Ada.

'Fortunately, she hasn't eaten this morning. We can operate very soon. I understand you're the next of kin. If you'd like to pop in before the pre-med, you can have a little chat with her.'

Ada was lying down in the admissions area.

'How are you feeling?' Addie asked quietly.

The old lady looked tearful. 'Silly old fool. Fancy tripping over me own feet like that.'

'I've got something for you, Ada,' Addie said, fishing in her bag. 'This is a picture of Dorothy, when she was about sixteen.'

Ada looked long and hard at the photocopy, putting it close to her good eye. Tears ran down her face and she murmured, 'My little girl - my lovely girl.'

'You'll have to go now, miss,' a nurse said, coming into the cubicled area.

Addie bent and kissed the wet cheek. 'Good luck, Ada.'

As she walked away she saw that the old lady was still clutching the picture tightly in her hand. Addie wiped a tear from her face. She wasn't quite sure if it was Ada's or her own.

Chapter 28: Family Business

Addie took a taxi back to The Stonemason's Arms, and went to the bar. A solitary coin-operated Cona machine and crockery awaited her. She helped herself to coffee, feeling in rather a state of limbo, and tried to figure out what to do next. She was suddenly aware that she felt sticky, and knew that she needed the shower she'd missed earlier.

As she made her way to the stairs, she heard a voice behind her.

'Oh, miss.'

'Yes?'

'There's been a call for you. Oh, and a note as well.'

'A note?'

'Yes, sorry, someone slipped it in with the early morning tea orders. They only found it this morning.'

She unfolded the flimsy piece of paper, right away, not moving from where she stood. The note, obviously written in a rush on an order docket, was brief.

Addie, Uncle Bruce collapsed and seriously ill. Couldn't wait for you. Forgive me love, Jonathan.

Mixed emotions crowded in on her. Two tragedies had occurred in a twenty four hour period. Ada seriously at risk in hospital here; Bruce Amery seriously ill in Surrey. Poor Jonathan. He must have been out of his mind with worry, receiving such an unexpected call. Yet for a moment, she could not help focusing on one thing. Jonathan had not abandoned her for some trivial reason. The brief sentence 'Forgive me love' seemed to express more than an outsider might imagine was contained in those three words. She shook herself out of this selfish mode. Uncle Bruce seriously ill. All sorts of repercussions for Jonathan. He would wonder why he hadn't heard from her.

She went to the room and dialled the Amerys' number. Sarah answered.

'Sarah. It's Addie. Did Jonathan get back all right? How is your uncle?'

'He's dead. Jonathan was too late.'

'Oh, Sarah. I'm so sorry. Is there anything I can do?'

'Not a lot.'

'Is Jonathan there? Can I talk with him?'

'He's gone out. There are things to arrange. Family matters.'

Her manner was short. Sarah was still cold - deliberately excluding her.

'He tried to call me earlier.'

'No. *I* tried to ring you earlier. It doesn't matter now.'

'But what ..?' Addie started, but Sarah had put the phone down.

It was mid-afternoon before Addie left Long Barton. The Sunday train service back to Surrey was poor, but in the end she did not have to worry about that. For when Chris telephoned to find out what had happened to Jonathan, he offered to drive her to Surrey.

'I couldn't let you do that, Chris,' she said, but he reminded her that he was going to a job interview in London on the following day.

'If you could put me up overnight, I could get into London tomorrow morning without having to leave here at the crack of dawn, and without spending a fortune on a hotel. It would be a very fair exchange.'

'Well, in that case, that would be great,' Addie said. 'But not till I've checked up on Ada.'

She telephoned after lunch, when she knew the operation would have taken place. Once she heard that it was successful, she took a taxi to the hospital and looked in on Ada, who was sleeping off the anaesthetic, but who opened her eyes to say blearily, 'Oh, it's you, dearie.'

'I have to go to Jonathan,' Addie told her.

'Nice boy - like my Perce,' Ada said. 'You hang on to him, m'dear.'

Addie was careful not to mention the family bereavement. In this hospital, with its infinite potential for imminent death, it seemed tactless to bring it into the conversation. In any case, Ada understood about young men. Hadn't her whole life been shaped by an illicit encounter with one?

It was a couple of hours before they got back to *Tamar*, and she left Chris there, making some changes to his CV on his laptop. He brushed aside her apologies; he understood her concern, and her desire to commiserate with the Amery family and Jonathan in particular. But when she arrived at the Amerys' house, there was just one car - a familiar bright red one - in the drive.

Sarah opened the door, stony-faced.

'Oh, so you're back.'

'I came back with Chris. He's staying at my place tonight.'

Sarah turned away abruptly from the open doorway. Addie followed her inside. 'What is it with you?' she said.

Sarah glared at Addie, her face red and angry. 'I don't know how you could do this to Jonathan. I knew you'd hurt him. Just when he needs all the support he can get.'

'What do you mean?'

'You were off with that Chris the minute Jon's back was turned. You were with him last night.'

'Yes, we had a meal when I found that Jonathan had left the hotel.'

'You were too busy to phone.'

'I didn't know about your uncle. They didn't find the note till this morning. I had no idea why Jonathan had left. I was quite mad - angry.' Yes, she had been angry. Angry and hurt. It was a credit to Chris that he had managed to take the heat out of her anger, to take the sting out of her pain, by his calm, unemotional conversation.

'So angry that you slept with this guy Chris.'

'What, are you crazy? I didn't sleep with him. He's a nice guy, but he's not my type.'

'Come off it. You weren't at the hotel last night and you weren't there at nine this morning.'

'Sarah. The reason I wasn't there this morning was because I received a call that Ada - my great-grandmother - had an accident and broke her hip. I went to the hospital.'

'Oh.' Sarah's lip quivered.

'And Chris is going to an interview in London tomorrow, and he said he'd drop me off, and we agreed he should stay the night at *Tamar*, rather than pay out for a London hotel.'

'Oh,' Sarah said again.

'Now let's talk about the important stuff. Tell me what happened.'

'They called me from the hospital. My aunt - his ex-wife - didn't want to come. We were the only relatives. Mum had gone to the ballet - I couldn't even remember what show. I got Jon on the mobile, and he said he'd leave straight away. Then I went to the hospital myself. I sat with him and watched the monitor. He had these breathing tubes and things. Suddenly the monitor started to go wild and the nurse chucked me out. Ten minutes later, she came out and said they couldn't save him.'

'It must have been awful for you, Sarah.'

'You know I didn't give a shit about him. But he looked so vulnerable lying there. Sort of innocent. All his nastiness erased. The worst thing was - he looked like Dad. That's what really got to me. It was like watching Dad die. I kept getting mixed up and thinking that if he didn't die, we'd have Dad back. And also I felt guilty because when Dad died, I thought, why wasn't it Uncle Bruce? And now it's come true.'

'You know it doesn't work that way.'

'When they came and said he was dead, I just broke up. I just couldn't stop crying. The nurse went and got me a cup of tea. She said, "I'm sure you loved him very much," and I said, "Yes," though, of course, I meant Dad and she meant Uncle Bruce. I still miss him. You must think I'm mad after all this time.'

'How could I think that, Sarah? How could I think the loss of your father is unimportant? I lost my parents twenty-six years ago, and I'm still searching for them. But your mom's grieving too. Maybe you could help each other.'

'We can't. At the beginning, when we first started talking about it, she'd start crying and then I'd feel I had to be brave. To be honest, if there was a stranger I could have talked to, I would. But when I went back to Uni, it was a different life. As long as I was there, I could pretend that nothing had changed - home was exactly as I'd left it. You end up going along with everything that's happening at Uni. You think you're making a new life. And then you come home and it's all there waiting for you again. Anyway, there were some things I couldn't say.'

'Like what?'

'Like - I was Daddy's girl. I had a special relationship with him. And it's the same with Jonathan and Mum. If I said something about it, she'd think she was failing in some way - it's not a criticism - or she'd think I was jealous.'

'Aren't you?'

'I suppose I am. Sometimes I feel left out. Specially now. It worked out okay when Dad was alive.'

'Sometimes people just click. Maybe you need to find someone special yourself. Then you'd be a little less possessive.'

She shouldn't have made the last comment, but Sarah took it.

'I've been stupid about Jonathan. He's really keen on you, you know.'

'He's a very special guy,' Addie said, deliberately trying to understate her feelings, but yet leave Sarah in no doubt of her sincerity about Jonathan. 'I wish you could meet someone like

333

him - have you tried talking to Trevor?'

Sarah looked at her silently for a moment.

'Addie, you and I both know what Trevor's good for. Trevor's not one of the world's great talkers. Or rather he talks, but what comes out most of the time is, frankly, trivial drivel.'

'Oh, Sarah,' Addie said. 'Why don't you stop wasting your time with him?'

Tears started up suddenly in Sarah's eyes. 'Because when we're in bed, he loves me. I want to be loved. I miss being cuddled by my dad.' She sobbed then, noisily and childishly and Addie put her arms round her and held her till the sobs subsided.

Afterwards, Sarah put the kettle on and made some coffee. They were both happier and more comfortable at the resumption of good relations, though Addie soon started to feel guilty about leaving Chris on his own.

'Perhaps I should go back and be a good hostess,' she said. 'I didn't think I'd be so long.'

'Bring him over here. You want to see Jonathan, don't you?'

'Your mom and Jonathan are out a long time,' Addie commented. 'I guess there's a lot of things to deal with.'

'They had to go to collect the death certificate from the hospital and organise the undertaker. And Jonathan said something about going to the office.'

'But it's Sunday.'

'Not to work, Addie. He was worried about the paperwork Uncle Bruce left. To be honest, he's worried about finding "something nasty in the woodshed," you could say.'

'What does that mean?'

'Well, I probably shouldn't say this. I mean you're a client and I don't want to get you worried, but recently Jonathan's been saying that Uncle Bruce may have had some little scams going on. He kept some private files that Jonathan never saw. And Jon didn't trust him.'

'He as good as said that to me.'

'So he wants to get started right away in checking that everything's above board. He tried to ring you last night to make sure you got his message, but you were out then and he asked me to try this morning. He didn't know whether you'd stay down there or not.'

'Sarah, to be honest, I should have stayed on at Long Barton. I *am* worried about Ada, and I'll have to go back. Finding you've got family means you have obligations too.'

Sarah nodded.

'But when I heard about your uncle, I was concerned about Jonathan - about all of you, in fact. Blood isn't everything. My mom and pop have proved that. I feel really close to the three of you - you're also a family that I'm part of now.'

'Sorry I was such a bitch.'

'Even the best of families have squabbles, I guess.'

It was nearly six when Jonathan and Helen got back. They had obviously seen Addie's car in the driveway, because when Jonathan opened the door, he walked straight up to her and took her in his arms. He didn't kiss her, and his manner was of a weary traveller stopping for a moment to receive relief and sustenance. As he sat down at the kitchen table, and Sarah leapt up to make yet another cup of coffee, Addie saw his face was grey and strained with tension and worry.

He started when he saw Chris, also sitting quietly at the table. Chris leaned across and offered his hand, 'Sorry to hear about your uncle.' Jonathan accepted the hand and the sentiments, but Addie saw he was not happy at the apparent intrusion. She started to explain how Chris had driven her back from Long Barton, how she had dropped him off at *Tamar*, how she had stayed so long talking with Sarah that she had finally gone to collect him. She saw he was not appeased, and so obviously did Chris, for he said, 'Time's getting on a bit now, so if you don't mind, Addie, perhaps I can take myself off for a meal. I have an early appointment in London.'

Addie noticed that Sarah looked quite disappointed. She seemed about to suggest rustling up something there, but stopped when she caught the look in Jonathan's eye. To help things along, Addie said, 'I'll take Chris for a meal. I think you've got family business to sort out. We'll see you later,' and Sarah said weakly, 'Family business - sounds like *The Godfather*.' But no-one laughed and no-one suggested that Addie and Chris should remain.

Addie made up the bed in the little room that Nora used when she stayed. It was odd, she thought, that Nora gave such a strong impression of being dour, and yet had such a deft hand at making a room welcoming and attractive.

Addie had no compunctions about having Chris to stay. He knew the score. Though he was a nice looking guy, she just didn't fancy him. They were both outgoing, untemperamental people and perhaps that explained the lack of magnetism, on her side, at any rate - what was it about unlike poles attracting? But they had an easy, comfortable relationship that ensured she made him a welcome guest in her home. She felt grateful, too, that he had put himself out to bring her back to Surrey. Much as she wanted to be with the Amerys, she could not have abandoned him to his own devices, though she felt that, without him, she would not have been excluded from the family conference.

She made a light meal, and they talked about the potential job that had arisen in Canary Wharf.

'I always wanted to work in Fleet Street and now I'm too late,' Chris said a trifle sadly.

It seemed he had realised he had become stuck in a backwater, both from the career point of view and in terms of relationships. The interview had been arranged a few weeks ago, and it was just lucky that it was organised for this particular weekend.

He left early the next morning, and Addie rang the Amerys

as soon as she decently could. Helen answered. She sounded sombre.

'Hallo, Addie. I'm sorry about last night. Normally we would have made your friend welcome.'

'I'm sure you would, Helen. It was dumb of me not to realise we'd be intruding.'

'Not you, Addie. But a stranger - particularly in view of ... I mean we wanted you there. Jonathan was really glad you'd come back, especially after Sarah told us about the mix up with the note, and your great-grandmother too. But there was a private matter - we couldn't have talked about it in front of your friend.'

'Naturally I understand, Helen. And I didn't want to intrude on private grief. It must have been awful for you - to relive your husband's ...'

'No, you don't understand. Well, in some respects, of course - yes, it was like a terrible action replay of what had happened before. Except of course that ... But it wasn't that. I mean this directly affects you, Addie. Jonathan's gone back to the office - I think he'd appreciate it if you telephoned or popped in. He really does want to talk to you.'

Her voice filled Addie with foreboding. What could possibly affect her? What did Helen's concerned tones mean? Something very serious had happened in the family. A congenital illness that ran through the males - Jonathan seriously ill with the same complaint? Her heart stopped for a moment. Don't be ridiculous, said her head. It was a coronary, plain and simple. She'd put Jonathan on a fish and chicken diet for life, if it was necessary to avert that. Given the chance of course. But now he was the main representative of Palfrey, Willow and Amery. 'Addie, my dear, I have summoned you here because, much as I have enjoyed our little interlude, I now have weightier things on my mind.' No, Helen wouldn't be delivering messages in a worried voice about Jonathan's love life.

She got in the car and drove to the office. She recognised the receptionist from her first visit - a blonde, rather supercilious girl. She recalled speaking to her on the telephone.

'Will you tell Mr Amery that Miss Russell would like a word with him.'

'Mr Amery Senior or Ju...' The girl checked herself. Addie waited.

'Mr Amery's very busy this morning, on account of ...'

'I know. Just tell him I'm here, would you?'

The blonde phoned through, then waved towards the doorway, where Addie had previously met Uncle Bruce.

'He'll see you now.'

He was not standing on the threshold of the room, meeting a valued client, as Uncle Bruce had been. He remained at his desk, his face so careworn that she went over to him and cradled him to her breast. Grief on its own was not this bad.

He put his arms round her waist and stayed there unmoving for a moment.

'For God's sake, what is it?'

'Uncle Bruce has been embezzling clients.'

'Oh, Jonathan.' Even as she exclaimed in sympathy, she was aware of a sense of relief. It mattered, of course, to Jonathan. For someone with his nature, it was hugely upsetting. But it was not to do with the two of them. That was the important thing.

'He used his position as executor to try to benefit himself - set up a separate company to buy and sell properties from estates he was supposed to be administering.'

She sat down. He looked at her, waiting for a reaction. She thought suddenly of the house.

'Do I still own *Tamar*?'

'Yes.'

'Oh, that's good. I love my little house.'

'It does affect James's estate though.'

Once again, she felt him looking at her.

'Jonathan. This has nothing to do with you and me. This is facts and figures and money. Will you please just get on and tell me the worst.'

'As far as I can see, he sold a flat in London that belonged to your grandfather. Sold it at the peak, as it later turned out, and bought the freehold of the Graingers' property - as James instructed.'

'Why would he do that?'

'Your grandfather wanted to present the Graingers with their own home on his death.'

'Well, that's great. That would make up for them not having my place.'

'It's not as simple as that, Addie. My uncle put the property into his company, but he didn't transfer it into the Graingers' names. I suspect that the 'further instructions after six months' was his idea - a delaying tactic, should he need it. Your grandfather was very vulnerable at that time. In fact, he drafted another will later, in which he recognises that Adrienne is dead. This one was much clearer and in it, he leaves *Tamar* and the money to Adrienne's child, and tells the Graingers of their bequest, without any six months' delay. But my uncle chose to ignore that copy and use the older one. Presumably so that he could use the Graingers' property as security for some other deal.'

'And?' said Addie anxiously, for it was no longer her own property being discussed, and she was concerned for the Graingers.

'I think he started to lose money when the property market fell flat, and it looks to me as if the assets - the Graingers' property and one or two other properties - represent less in money terms than the liabilities. In other words, in order to give the Graingers the house that's rightfully theirs, we - the firm, that is - have to find a way of redeeming the deeds from the bank they're now with. Something tells me that if you hadn't come along when you did, *Tamar* would have been moved into the company and possibly lost to you.'

'We could mortgage it and give the Graingers their house,' Addie suggested.

He took her hand and kissed her fingertips and said gravely, 'This is my problem, Addie. I just wanted you to know the score.'

She felt a chill run through her again, for a moment, as if the problem which was not of their making was going to drive a wedge between them.

Chapter 29: Orphan in a Storm

In the end, returning home so speedily had been rather a wasted effort. Except for the important interview with Jonathan and the curative conversation with Sarah, she could almost have remained in Long Barton during the week that led up to the funeral. Helen and Sarah were both badly upset, the painful wounds of the previous Amery death re-opened once again. And Jonathan was quiet, remote and concerned, his pain more directly connected to his fears for the Amery name and the firm's reputation.

When, after three days, he still had not called in to *Tamar*, Addie telephoned.

'I know you're busy, but why don't you come over this evening for a quiet meal. Maybe you'll feel better for it.'

'It's difficult at the moment, Addie. I'm trying to speak to all our clients, to tell them about Uncle Bruce - to prepare them for what might happen.'

'What do you mean?'

' The Law Society will probably close the firm, when I contact them.'

'You mean they don't know he's dead.'

'Of course they do. I told them that straight away. He'd nominated me as the person to take over the partnership. I need that now like a hole in the head.'

'Then …'

'I'm still trying to check through files in case there can be any doubt about what he's done. I'm just hoping I'll find some evidence that he put things straight. I'll give myself till after the funeral - then I've got to let the Law Society investigate. I dare not leave it any longer.'

'Then what will happen to you?'

'I'll be out of work.'

'Jonathan, please come over. Just for a little while. I miss you so much.'

He gave in the end. He arrived at the door and Addie ran to hug him. She felt his body tense up instead of responding and she stepped back bewildered.

They sat at the kitchen table eating steak and salad, and the conversation was stilted. She was reminded of their first meetings when she had found him cold and unfriendly.

'What's wrong, Jonny?' she said, teasing to get some response. He didn't smile.

'When I think of my Dad - and how absolutely straight he was. It kills me to think of what Uncle Bruce has done to the firm - to our name. My father's name. Who knows? Maybe Dad suspected something. Maybe the stress aggravated his heart condition and caused his death.'

'I know you're upset. But it doesn't have to affect us, does it? I want to help you get through this.'

'It's just taking me so much time to look at all the paperwork - to deal with everything. I can't stay tonight. I really can't. And there's something else, Addie. What will it look like when the Law Society see that your grandfather is one of the clients my uncle has swindled?' He paused and looked at her with that bleak expression she had come to dread. 'I need time to work things out.'

Time. What did he mean? Two weeks? Two years? Her visa would expire in three months. Would she have to return to the States with a distant memory of a brief love affair?

He got up to leave after the meal and, when she kissed him, he barely responded. It was as if he had been turned to stone. It was torture to have loved him so completely, only to lose him again behind his stiff English facade.

During the week, Addie telephoned Chris to find out how he'd got on. He did not yet know the result of the interview, but he sounded very optimistic. Nevertheless, work at the *Hampton & Barton Gazette* was continuing as usual.

'Do you think I could have a photo of you, Addie?'

Addie was startled. Perhaps she had made more of an impression on him than she realised.

'A passport size will do. I'm publishing your first article this week, and I'd like a photo at the head, with your by-line. You know what they say - "a picture's worth a thousand words." Not that I'm implying there's anything wrong with your thousand words.'

She asked Sarah on the phone where the nearest photo booth was. It was important to keep lines of communication open, even with trivialities. Sarah said she'd come round with her Polaroid - if Addie's face was going to be exhibited, she might at least have a better image than the average photo booth could produce. She arranged the background quite carefully and produced a few surprisingly good shots.

'That's great, Sarah. Did I tell you Chris is going to put a little piece in with my article?'

'What sort of piece?'

'Something about me being over here to find my family.'

'Oh maybe they'll all come out of the woodwork,' Sarah said, adding suddenly, 'He was quite nice, your friend, Chris.'

'Mm. You could do worse.'

'I wanted to tell you something. Trevor and I have finished.'

'Oh, Sarah, I'm sorry. Are you upset?'

'Only in the way that you miss a piece of furniture you've got used to. And if things go on too long, I'll start getting the hots for more unsuitable men. But it had to end.'

'Did you have a row?'

'He was so completely inadequate at talking about *real* things. You know how we - you and I - talked about Uncle Bruce and my dad - I couldn't talk properly to him. And I just kept getting more angry with him for not being what I wanted. I was an absolute cow. You know how nasty I can be sometimes.'

Addie smiled but said nothing.

'Suddenly he just stopped taking it. He said, " This isn't working, is it, Sarah?" I was surprised that he'd noticed. I expected to keep dishing it out and he'd keep taking it. He said, "Jumping into bed isn't everything. Other things count too." I said I was sorry. I was ashamed, actually. I'd thought he was so insensitive I could say anything to him. I hadn't respected him as a person at all. I was being totally insensitive myself.'

Sarah didn't stay long that evening, because the funeral was the next day. Knowing that she too would be occupied, Addie rang the hospital to check up on Ada's progress, as she had every day since leaving Long Barton. She particularly wanted to be with the Amerys at the funeral and was glad to be reassured that there was no reason for her to rush back.

The funeral itself was quiet and modest, attended, surprisingly, by the ex-wife, who talked at length to Helen. It seemed she had come more out of respect for the Amerys, with whom she had a good relationship, than out of affection for her ex-husband.

The situation changed the day after the funeral. Addie had only just risen, when the phone rang and Ada's GP, Dr Morgan, spoke at the other end, her voice serious and sympathetic.

'I'm afraid I'm rather concerned about Ada. She was doing extremely well, but she's developed pneumonia. We have her on antibiotics, of course, but there's no saying how things will go. I thought you would want to know.'

'I'll come down today,' Addie said immediately. She was thankful that she now felt no conflict - there was no reason not to go. She was performing no useful function here. Sarah had gone back to her data entry job, and would soon be preparing to return to university. And as for Jonathan - she knew of no way to break down the barrier that he'd put between them.

She rang Helen and told her of her departure. Helen

offered to drive her to the station, but Addie had already organised a taxi.

She took enough clothes for a few days' stay, and when she arrived in Long Barton, she went immediately to the hospital, where a nurse directed her to Ada's room. When she went in, she saw that Ada was having difficulty in breathing. Her face looked almost yellow behind the oxygen mask, but her eyes were open and they followed Addie as she walked into the room. On an impulse, Addie took one of the photos from her bag and showed it to Ada; she saw a small smile on the old lady's face. She placed it on the locker, with the photocopy of Dorothy, which was already there, held into position by an empty vase. Then she sat at the bedside and took Ada's veined hand. She wished she had stopped to buy a few flowers. The emptiness of the fruit bowl and the vase seemed to reflect the emptiness of Ada's life.

She stayed a while, just sitting with Ada's hand in hers. Her mind drifted and, eventually, she noticed that Ada was sleeping. Addie unclasped her hand from Ada's unresponsive one and quietly got up.

As she walked into the corridor, she met the nurse on duty, who said, 'I was just about to pop in to Ada.'

'How do you think she's getting on?' Addie asked, when she emerged.

'The doctor's prescribed antibiotics,' the woman said, 'but so far, there hasn't been much of an improvement. She is quite old, after all. Did you want to go off for a little while - just to stretch your legs? I'm sure it'll be all right?'

She's not going to die yet, Addie translated to herself, but she is preparing me - it's not going to be very long.

She had a coffee in the canteen and sought out the hospital shop. There she found a florist, where she bought some roses - the bright red colour that she always saw in the dreams about her mother - and some fruit from a shop manned by volunteers.

345

When she returned to Ada, she saw that she was awake once again. A faint smile appeared on the old lady's face, and she watched as Addie put the flowers into a vase and filled the fruit bowl with oranges and apples. Ada was not eating; she was being fed intravenously, but the gesture succeeded in giving her the look of someone who has family. Addie was intrigued to notice that Ada was now holding the photos of Dorothy and herself, clutched in one hand. As she took the other hand, Addie felt a little squeeze; she was in no doubt that Ada welcomed the visit and gifts and was glad to be in the company of her only relation.

She sat quietly for an hour or so, and the weak pressure of the old lady's hand gradually diminished. After a while the hand went completely limp and Addie, her thoughts far away, glanced at Ada to see if she was asleep. The face had lost its yellowness and become more translucent. The faint movements of the mouth as Ada had passed in and out of sleep had ceased. Addie withdrew her hand and looked carefully at Ada's face in repose. There was a lifelessness there that had not been present before. She summoned the duty nurse, who bustled in and felt for the pulse.

'I'm afraid it's over, Miss Russell. She didn't really make a fight of it. But I'm sure she was comforted by your being here.'

As next of kin, there were formalities to be dealt with but, for the moment, Addie wanted a little time to herself. She had found almost no point of contact with this old lady, whose life had been so different from her own. And yet to her surprise, she felt a sense of emptiness and loss.

As she walked out into the corridor, she met Dr Morgan on her way in. 'I've just finished my calls and I thought I'd check up on Ada before I go home.' She looked at Addie's face and said gently, 'I'm sorry. Poor Ada.'

'I'll pay for her funeral,' Addie said fiercely. 'At least she can go with dignity, though she had very little of that, shut up in an institution for the best part of her life.'

'I know you must feel very upset about what happened to her - it made me angry too when I read it in her case notes - but she and her companion did have a reasonably comfortable life, for twenty years or so. Mrs Horrocks' daughter was aware of their importance to each other, and provided a little money, and though their lives were quiet, they were completely independent.'

Addie smiled, grateful for the woman's attempt to comfort her. She started to move off again, when Dr Morgan's hand resting lightly on her arm restrained her.

'Perhaps now is not the best time to mention it, but I would like a chat with you before you go back to Surrey. I was intending to ring you.'

Addie hesitated, surprised for the moment - the illness, and now death, of an elderly woman was commonplace after all - then realised that there was more to this proposed discussion than concern about her recent bereavement. Remembering suddenly that Dr Morgan knew her mother, she felt her heart beat a little faster.

'I expect I'll need two or three days to tie up loose ends,' she said, aware that she had no idea of procedures in this country . 'So we can get together as soon as you want. I guess you're a lot busier than me, so why don't you give me a call? I'm staying with Mrs Simpson at the B & B in Long Barton.'

Addie was in fact fully occupied during the next couple of days. A form had to be obtained from the hospital. The death certificate had to be taken to the undertaker, and a simple funeral arranged. She had almost forgotten about the doctor's suggestion but, on Thursday morning, Mrs Simpson relayed a message that Dr Morgan would meet her at the hospital entrance at lunch time.

Addie arrived by taxi and the doctor hurried up almost immediately afterwards. They shook hands at the entrance. 'Do you mind if we walk into the town centre?' the doctor

347

asked. 'I see quite enough hospitals and the like.'

'Have you finished your calls?'

'Yes, unless there are any emergencies - and I have my bleeper.'

They went out together through the car-park and towards the town. Dr Morgan did not broach the topic of family, choosing instead to talk about the facade of the hospital, built in the local stone. Addie recognised that no real discussion was to take place until they had arrived at the café, and she went along with the convention, as if it were a Chinese-style meeting, and they must first have ritual small talk and tea before commencing the business of the day.

When they were seated with sandwiches and drinks in front of them, Addie felt the ritual had gone on long enough.

'Perhaps you could tell me what you know,' she said.

Dr Morgan drew in a deep breath. 'I was very shocked when I saw you the other day. You perhaps realised that I couldn't talk to you.'

'Your mother had explained about your father's death, Dr Morgan,' Addie said, always ready to be generous in letting people off the hook. She saw that the other woman's lips were trembling. 'I want to assure you that there was no improper relationship between your father and my grandmother, Dorothy Heron. Please reassure your mother that Dorothy loved someone else - but she regarded your father as the kindest of friends.'

'Thank you for saying that, Addie - you don't mind the informality - and please call me Pat. After all ...' She hesitated, then continued. 'It was not that, Addie. It was not to do with Dorothy. It was seeing you there - a replica of Adrienne - almost exactly as I last saw her - with just a slight difference in colouring. Like a photo that comes back from the developers incorrectly processed. You see, Adrienne and I were very good friends.'

Addie looked at her slightly puzzled - reluctant to confess

that there was no mention of her in Adrienne's diary. It seemed a bit of a slap in the face to say that Adrienne had not had the same regard for Pat Morgan.

She approached the subject tentatively, 'When exactly were you and my mother friends? I am reading her diary - perhaps I'll come upon a mention of you.'

'So you've got the famous diary!' Pat exclaimed. 'We used to laugh about that. She always kept that little gold key round her neck - she was determined that no-one would be able to read it without her permission. Even though we knew each other's every secret. When I heard she was dead, it was the most terrible moment - up to then - because afterwards things got so much worse. I'd never lost anyone close before and Adrienne and I were like sisters. And for Richard ...'

'Richard?' Addie repeated, suddenly alert.

'My brother, Richard. You see, Addie ...'

She stopped, looking at Addie's face.

'Dr Morgan,' Addie said. 'Who was Charlie?'

'Well, that was me. Patricia Charlton. Charlton abbreviated to Charlie. I didn't like my name - Patricia - when I was ten or so and the nickname stuck. No-one calls me that now.'

Addie had stopped listening. She felt the hairs on the back of her neck standing up, as if she had seen a ghost. Automatically, she put her hand out for the cup of tea, but it was shaking so much, she put it down again.

'You know, don't you?' Pat Morgan said. 'About Richard. I wondered if there could be any doubt.'

'He's my father,' Addie said. She looked at the face opposite and she recognised, in the older woman, facets of herself. The same green eyes looked back at her. 'Your brother is my father. No doubt at all.'

Chapter 30: Survivors

Afterwards, Addie would always remember those moments in the café, staring at Pat, waiting for a reaction.

The older woman sat, her face serious, for a moment before she spoke. 'I don't want to offend you, Addie. But isn't it possible that your father is an American that Adrienne met, once she arrived there?'

'You wouldn't say that if you read her diary,' Addie replied. 'She loved Richard so much.'

'But she stopped writing to him after barely two months. After that, he only received the briefest of postcards. When he tried to get hold of her, they told him she'd moved on and left no forwarding address. And the same with her job. He was sure she'd met someone else – or had a breakdown.'

'She was already pregnant. The dates tie up. I can give you all the details and my Mom and Pop will confirm it. She told them my father was English and she didn't want him to find out.'

Pat continued, her voice now accusing. 'She disrupted his studies. He was training to be a doctor at the Bristol Royal Infirmary. How could she hurt him like that?'

'I didn't know he was studying medicine,' Addie said. 'But I know that Adrienne thought she was doing it for the best.' Her voice shook and she tried to control her emotion. 'She left England, so she *wouldn't* distract him from his studies. Your mother told Adrienne to back off – and she did. She loved him. That's why she did it.' She paused. 'Pat, I just know I'm Richard's daughter. I'll go for any genetic tests, if you like.'

Pat looked down and, in a voice that sounded resigned rather than reassured, said, 'That won't be necessary. Let me tell you about what happened here.'

Speaking quietly, she started to describe to Addie the effect of Adrienne's disappearance and subsequent death on those left behind.

Richard, tense and angry, had turned to Dorothy. Though he tried to keep his mind on his studies at the hospital, he took to ringing Dorothy frequently. She too was worried; she had received cards - no address - almost no information - and could not help him. Once, near the end of that time, she rang him. Adrienne had just sent another card. Perhaps with some premonition, she had written, 'Tell Richard I love him.'

Briefly, they became conspirators - confidants - finding no support from anyone else. Richard's mother, particularly, seemed unsurprised by Adrienne's apparent unpredictability and offered little sympathy for the pain Richard was experiencing. He could not face his family's disapproval of Adrienne and similarly, Dorothy could not discuss the daughter she loved with the husband that did not share her feelings.

Then the terrible day arrived. Pat Morgan's face looked gaunt as she described it to Addie. Richard on the telephone to Pat, his voice strange and unlike itself. 'Adrienne is dead. Food poisoning they say. I'm going home. I have to find out what happened.' He went home, but learned nothing. The Heron home became a fortress. Rodney allowed almost no contact with his wife. Dr Charlton - Richard's and Pat's father - saw her once and gave her sleeping pills and sedatives. Richard was grief-stricken, incapable of returning to his studies. Pat - Charlie - overcome with sorrow, but working on, to try and blot the loss of her friend from her mind. Then Dorothy's suicide and the virtual collapse of the Charlton family. Dr Charlton - racked with guilt for prescribing the pills; for failing to visit again; guilty too that he had been unable to protect a woman who had suffered obvious abuse - all this ending up with his breakdown. Pat's mother torturing herself with the possibility that her husband had been in love with Dorothy Heron and blaming her. Finally the father's sudden death from a heart attack. A family in devastation -

three people, all distraught, all powerless to help each other.

'Richard's married now,' Pat had said finally. 'He's happily married - and they have three children.

'It almost ruined his life, losing Adrienne. I've talked about it to mother. We don't think he should be told about you.'

And Addie, tears running down her cheeks as she listened, turned to her in total disbelief. 'After all these years, I've found my father and you don't want me to contact him. I can't believe what you're saying.'

'We wanted to be fair to you. We thought you had a right to know.'

'So has he. You mean *she* thought it would be a way of stopping me from digging any further.'

'Addie, you could damage the lives of five people. They're a nice family. He has one daughter - his second child - she's called Adele.'

And that's when Addie had said, in a moment of deep bitterness, 'Did you ever train to be a surgeon? You're so good with the knife.'

* * *

Now she was back at *Tamar* - her mind in turmoil. Even thoughts of Jonathan held no comfort, for he seemed to think, quite misguidedly, that it was right and proper that he should put her out of his life because of their professional association. She tried to remind herself that he was not deliberately setting out to hurt her; all along she had tried to be patient, for undoubtedly he was suffering himself; but it wasn't working any more. It felt like she wanted him, but he didn't want her.

She'd have to go; leave it all behind; the pain and anguish - the rejection by Pat Morgan, and Jonathan's retreat to somewhere where she could not reach him. Yes, after Ada's funeral, she would do that. It had all been a mistake.

But the Amerys had meant a lot to her; Sarah and Helen had been good friends. She would at least put them in the picture.

352

She dialled the Amery number and her voice was flat, fighting off tears, as she spoke.

'Sarah, hi, it's Addie.'

Sarah yawned. 'Hi. What *are* you? The dawn chorus. One of my few days of rest, and you get me out of bed.'

'Sarah. I wanted to talk with you. I'm thinking of going back to the States. I'll organise the sale of the house from there.'

Sarah's voice at the other end was suddenly wide awake and incredulous. 'Go? What are you talking about? What's happened?'

'Ada's dead. The funeral's tomorrow.'

'Oh Addie, I'm sorry. But that's no reason …'

'And my fa…' She stopped, unable to go on.

'Addie, don't do anything. I'm coming over.'

Addie was rummaging though the wardrobe when Sarah arrived. She had bought quite a few clothes now, and was looking for a suitably modest skirt for Ada's funeral, to team with a white blouse. She had to make a good showing, if she was to be the only mourner. The tears that had brought an end to her conversation with Sarah had dried on her face. Now as she let Sarah in the house, her lips were tightly compressed in restrained anger.

'When did you get back?'

'Last night.'

'Have you eaten?'

'I've had coffee.'

'We'll have some cereal. I haven't had breakfast yet.'

Addie didn't look at her. She was breathing fast, pacing up and down the small kitchen. She let Sarah find the cornflakes, milk and bowls.

'This isn't just about Ada, is it?'

Addie opened the cutlery drawer, and took out two spoons. She banged one down in front of Sarah. 'No.'

'Jonathan?'

353

Her voice quivering with anger, Addie said, 'First I lose my only living relative. My lover has more or less dumped me because he's so conventional and correct. Then I find my father and he doesn't want to know me. I find three people who matter to me - and now I've lost them - in one week - that's not bad going.'

Sarah had never seen her like this. Addie could see the fear in her eyes. She hardly recognised herself - it was so rare for her to feel this level of anger. All her instincts told her to get away from these cold English people who had the capacity to hurt her so badly - to go back to Mom and Pop - to Joan and Tony, whose warmth had sustained her all her life.

'Addie, you mustn't go back. Please, sit down. Eat something. Please. You mustn't just walk out on Jonathan. It isn't all black. Just give him time to sort things out. Why, he'd be over like a shot, except ...'

'Well, where is he?'

Sarah looked embarrassed and said, 'Sorry, I can't tell you. I expect he'll tell you himself. But anyway, there's some very good news. He and Tabitha have sold the flat. So he'll have a bit of money if the business goes pear-shaped. That's something, isn't it? Please tell me what happened to you. You know it's no good bottling it up.'

Addie sat down. She put the spoon into the bowl of cornflakes, and left it there. She felt her mouth distorting into tears. She was not reassured by Sarah's secrecy, and, even if it was linked to the sale of the flat, the mention of Tabitha did nothing to comfort her.

'Tell me about Ada.'

Sarah had judged correctly. It was the least painful part of the story for Addie. Ada had not rejected her. Addie had, in fact, gained satisfaction from the knowledge that she had brought comfort to the old lady. The tears that ran down her cheeks were calmer now, as she described Ada still clinging, in death, to the photos of her daughter and great-granddaughter.

The rest was harder. Piece by piece, Addie revealed the story to Sarah. At first almost incoherently but, as she became more composed, in a more clipped, detached manner.

When Sarah finally left, Addie was calm, with the kind of calmness that stems from exhaustion and resignation. When the telephone rang, she was simply sitting staring out of the window, and she got up, like an automaton, to answer it.

Because her rejection by the Charlton family had illogically become entwined with Jonathan's aloofness, she had somehow felt they had come to the end of their relationship. She was quite surprised to hear Jonathan's voice on the phone, and surprised too by his anger.

'I hear you're going back,' he said. 'I hope you enjoyed your little fling. Just a holiday romance, was it? Something to enhance your stay, or so you can tell your friends the English make lousy lovers.'

'What right have you got to shout at me? You've ignored me. You've neglected me. You've pushed me out. You've shown me I'm not wanted here. That's why I'm going back.'

'You know full well what I've had on my plate. You know how worried I've been these last few weeks. All I wanted was a little patience. A little loyalty. After all it's your grandfather's estate, I'm trying to protect.'

'I don't give a damn about the estate. If you had problems, why didn't you share them with me? You know I would have backed you to the hilt, whatever you did. But no, you pushed me away from you. You rejected me. But whenever Tabitha called, you were always at her beck and call.'

'You're paranoid about Tabitha. You've never even seen her, yet you're insanely jealous.'

'Jealous. You're one to talk. The look on your face, when I talked to Chris.'

'Flirted, you mean. Flirted outrageously. No wonder Julian thought you were giving him the come on, if that's the way you behaved. I don't blame him.'

355

They were both shouting now. There was no way out of this. It was simply going to get more abusive.

Addie said, 'I don't have to put up with this. To think I thought I loved you.'

She slammed down the phone.

She should not have come back. She should have stayed in Long Barton until the funeral had taken place. She had behaved like a hurt animal running for cover and, instead of finding a refuge, there was more pain. What should she do? Go back to Long Barton, book a hotel; go to the funeral. Yes, that's what she would do. And after that …? The phone rang again.

She drew in a deep breath, ready to tell Jonathan to go to hell.

'Yes?'

'Is that Addie Russell?'

'Yes. Who is this, please?'

'I'm a stranger to you. But I knew your mother. My name is Valerie ...'

'Valerie. Of course. You shared a flat with her.'

'I'd very much like to talk to you.'

'That would be marvellous. Are you anywhere near Surrey?'

'No. I live near Long Barton. I saw your photograph in the Hampton & Barton Gazette. It shook me to the core, because of the likeness to Adrienne. I had absolutely no idea there was a child.' The woman sounded breathless, unable to stop the flow of excited speech, 'I might have thought it was coincidence, but for seeing the Herons mentioned in the article.'

'I would really love to talk to someone who knew my mother so well. I can't tell you how wonderful that is. I've read all about you in her diary, and I know you were a real good friend. But how did you get my number?'

'I rang someone at the Gazette - Chris Templeman - and he told me where to find you, because you see ...'

356

'I have to be in Long Barton tomorrow afternoon. I would really love to meet you. Could we make it tomorrow morning? Or even later today?'

'I wasn't expecting ... Are you sure you want to come down so ...?'

'I have to come back for my great-grandmother's funeral tomorrow.'

'Oh, I see, I'm so sorry. Well, tomorrow then, if that isn't too much in one day.'

'No. In fact, I was already thinking of travelling back today.' Her voice shook slightly as she added, 'I have nothing to keep me here.'

She collected up the clothes she would need for the funeral, and a smart, casual outfit to meet her mother's old friend. The thought of this meeting gave her a lift - a feeling of the old excitement that she had at the beginning of this journey. She brought her suitcase down from the bedroom, found her house keys, and called a taxi. She was standing at the door, waiting, when the phone rang again. She was tempted to ignore it, but she didn't.

'Hallo.'

'Addie, is that you, honey?'

'Oh Mom, it's you.'

'We haven't heard from you in a few days. Is everything all right?'

'Well ...'

'You don't sound happy, honey. When you told me about the lawyer, it sounded as if things were going well. He sounded a nice guy.'

'Things have gotten complicated, Mom. Sometimes these people are difficult to figure out.'

'Addie, I don't mind telling you that I was kinda upset when you told me about this Jonathan guy. I thought, we're going to lose her. She's going to stay in England.'

'Look, Mom ...' Addie interrupted.

'Just let me speak, honey. I was thinking about when your dad and I met up. And I left my home and followed him here. You know it's a culture shock, moving from the South to the East Coast. Not so very different from moving from the States to England, I guess. At first, I couldn't settle down with these people here. But after a while, they warmed up, and I thought, when you scratch people, they're all the same under the skin. You just have to work at it a bit, sometimes. So if he's worth it, you stick it out, honey. Your dad and I - we'll be over to visit - why on Concorde, it's not much different to a ride on the subway.'

'I don't know how things are going to work out, Mom. It's not just one thing. I can't explain, now, but I'll call you in a few days. When I've sorted things out. I'm just off somewhere, and the cab's on its way. Did you call for anything special?'

'Sometimes you just get a feeling about family. That something's wrong and they need you. Maybe it's telepathy; maybe it's sixth sense.'

'You were right, Mom. I was feeling very low. I did need you. I always will.'

'Oh, honey. You take care, now.'

'Love you, Mom.'

The train was slow to Reading station. She picked up her book and started to read. It was useless. She could not concentrate. She remembered how she had sat and thought of Lloyd, on an earlier journey to Bath. Strange, he had no power over her any longer. He's all technique, she thought. Plenty of passion, but no emotion. I wonder what I saw in him. Perhaps after all, I was looking for a father figure - the sort of person I envisioned as my real father. Or maybe everyone goes through that stage. After all, he was the sexiest of men, but so empty, so completely cynical. And now Jonathan came into her mind. She thought of the storm, and she remembered how he had wrapped her in James's robe when she was soaked to the skin. He'd even let her make the first move. She

358

would be crazy to let him go; surely she hadn't really lost him.

She was weary when she arrived at Long Barton. Everything looked familiar, like a second home though, for the moment, she could harbour no good thoughts about the place. She didn't feel able to cope with Mrs Simpson's chat, and booked into The Stonemason's Arms. She had a quick meal, talked to no-one, and took herself off to bed with a stiff martini. She fell into a troubled sleep.

The dream when it came was vivid. It started off in familiar manner, with her idealised mother walking into the garden with her basket on her arm. Then, her long robes sweeping behind her, she walked into the kitchen. The kitchen at *Tamar*, as it happened. There, Joan was making waffles and setting them down on kitchen paper to absorb the grease. She said, 'Hi, honey. We just flew in on Concorde.' The dream mother took the basket and placed it on the kitchen worktop. 'This is for you,' she said. 'I have to go. I won't be coming back.' Joan stopped cooking, her face aghast and said, 'No. Please. Please don't go.' But Adrienne turned away and disappeared. Joan looked in the basket, carefully took out the roses and saw the baby that nestled there. Then she just lifted the baby out and held it close to her heart.

Addie woke with a start. For a moment the dream stayed with her. Then she looked at her watch. If she didn't hurry, she would miss breakfast and her appointment with Valerie.

She was in the bar when Valerie walked in. She was a pleasant looking woman of forty-something, with brown hair framing her face. She was well groomed and smart, but not in an unapproachable way. She looked at Addie, who was sitting on one of the armchairs skimming through the pages of the current week's Gazette, and walked towards her smiling.

'It's so wonderful to meet you. It was such a tragedy that Adrienne died. The death of someone young is such a terrible waste - and she was so vibrant, so lively! To know that, after all, part of her is still alive is just unbelievable.' She

359

surreptitiously wiped away a tear. 'Sorry - seeing you - I feel I've stepped back in time. It makes me feel as if I'm young again myself. I know I'm being very sentimental. But it's so amazing to see the likeness. I would have known you anywhere - and to see Richard in you too. The eyes are his.'

'Of course, you knew them both.'

Valerie glanced at her, her brow furrowed. 'Have any of the family been in touch? I was going to say ...'

'Yes. I've spoken to Pat Charlton - that is - Morgan. I'm sorry. I'm being very bad-mannered. Let me get you a coffee. I am so very grateful to you for contacting me.' Addie leapt up, anxious to move the conversation away from the family, and to get back to the subject of the young lovers as soon as possible. She returned with more coffee from the bar.

'Please tell me about them. I've read the diary. I've read about them. But I want them to come alive for me. Am I asking too much?'

'They were very much in love,' Valerie said, her eyes far away. 'There was no doubt about that. But in a way they were a bit too similar. They both used to get very excited, very passionate about things - though not necessarily the same things. I always felt that there was some danger that they would burn each other out. Had things continued, I mean.'

'In the diary, it implied that Adrienne stopped Richard from studying. Was that true?'

'Yes I think there was some truth in that. Adrienne could be self-centred sometimes. I know Richard's mother got very angry about it. And she was right in some ways. Richard's medical training was all important to him. Romance could have come later. Or he could have had more casual relationships. But it didn't happen that way. Neither Richard nor Adrienne were casual about things. She was in a terrible state when she left for America; she didn't seem to know what she was doing. She hardly said goodbye to anyone; she left her diary behind, as if there wasn't going to be a life to record.

360

That frightened me somehow.'

She shivered slightly, before carrying on.

'I even wrote saying I'd send it on, but she said in her letter, "You keep it for now. Nothing is going to happen to me without Richard. I'm putting life on hold till I get back to him." I wrote back to her, "You must enjoy yourself while you're out there. You can't waste the year," and she said that she'd enjoy the sight seeing and write letters to us instead of her diary. Then suddenly the letters stopped. Just occasional postcards, but no addresses. It was very hurtful. To me - and I know Charlie - Pat - felt the same way. But most of all to Richard.'

'She was trying to protect him,' Addie said rushing to the defence of her mother. 'She didn't want to trap him into marriage. Not after the miscarriage she'd already had. She really didn't mean to be selfish. It's quite clear from her diary that she only went away because Mrs Charlton said she was damaging his studies.'

'When I heard she was dead, I sent the diary to her parents. It never occurred to me it might have helped Richard to know what she was thinking. In any case, I felt it was theirs by right. None of us believed she died of food poisoning. It seemed so unlikely. We all thought she'd committed suicide. It seemed to link up with her breaking off contact with us. You can imagine that Richard felt he was in some way to blame. It took him years to let himself off the hook. That's another reason why I'm so glad you've come here.'

'I'm sorry, I don't follow you.'

'Yes. It's wonderful that he'll meet you and understand at last that she was just covering up the pregnancy. Perhaps my mother-in-law won't feel the same way. She seemed to feel very bitter about the whole Heron family. And she can be dogmatic at times. I don't know if you've met her too. But she must put her own feelings aside. He must meet you. Just give me a little time to prepare him. I destroyed the newspaper. I

361

didn't want him to get the same shock that I did.'

'I don't understand what you're saying.'

'I'm sorry. You said you spoke to Pat. I thought she would have explained.' She paused again, to look at Addie. 'You don't know then. I married him. I married Richard. I always loved him - from the very beginning.'

* * *

Addie arrived at the church an hour before the service was due to start. Not that there was much to prepare but, in her present state, she hardly knew what to do or how to behave.

The low sun of autumn was shining, and the trees in the churchyard were turning to golds and browns. Addie felt strange, drugged, cut off from what was going on around her. One thing only stood out in her mind. She would meet her father, Richard Charlton, with the blessing of his wife; she would see her half brothers and half sister. She could not anticipate what that would feel like.

It was amazing that Valerie had managed to arrange their first meeting, now, even before the funeral. Somehow, Addie had briefly thought there would have to be some formal gathering. The matriarch glowering at her, Valerie with a teapot in her hands and the children clustered around. There would have been time for her to take in what had happened. But against all the odds, Valerie had organised this other meeting.

She glanced down at her watch. What time had they agreed? She looked up again, and saw a couple walking towards her hand in hand. As they got nearer, the woman, Valerie, dropped her hand, and the man walked forwards on his own. He was about fifty, with thinning, reddish hair. She remembered Adrienne describing his odd, bony face. She stood, not moving, as he walked towards her. She felt tears running down her cheeks and, as he came closer, she saw that his cheeks were wet too.

The looked at each other for a moment, then he caught hold of her and hugged her. She was aware of the scent of pipe tobacco on his skin and the roughness of his jacket against her cheek.

'It's Richard, isn't it?' she said ridiculously, when he released her.

'And you're ... Addie.' He paused before he said her name, and she knew he'd wanted to call her 'Adrienne'.

He caught her by the shoulders again, and held her at arm's length. 'Let me look at you,' he said, and they stood and looked at each other, both laughing, both crying and unable to speak.

'Have we got a few moments?' he said, finally, and she nodded.

They started to walk away from the church entrance, and he took her arm as she stumbled on the gravel path.

'You're not a replacement for my father,' she said suddenly.

'Of course not.'

'I love my Dad.'

'And I love Valerie and my children, and I loved Adrienne, and part of me still does. There's always room to love more people.'

'I'm so glad I've found you,' she said, barely able to keep her voice from shaking. 'I'm very, very happy. I haven't been unhappy, but I wanted so much to know where I came from.'

'I'm just a country doctor - a bit like my father - nothing special.'

'Yes, you are,' she said.

'I want you to meet the family - your brothers and sister. Will you? Is that all right? Can you cope with all this?'

She nodded, not trusting her voice any longer.

'We're not going to stay now. You mustn't be late for the funeral. But I wanted so much to see you - to have these few minutes.'

'Yes,' she said, finding her voice again. Then she

363

remembered something she wanted to say.

'I'm not another Adrienne. I'm not like her - only in looks. You won't be disappointed with me, will you?'

He smiled a lopsided, shaky smile and rested his hand on her shoulder. 'No. Of course not. You're her legacy. You're the best thing she ever did.'

'Come on,' he said, and once more guided her back to the church entrance.

She had composed herself by the time the mourners arrived, and she stood at the entrance to the church. She was not, after all, on her own. Veronica Daborn was there, and one or two other members of the staff of the home. Lily Horrocks' daughter too had come, preceded by a beautiful sheaf of flowers. A few minutes before the funeral was due to start, Patricia Morgan also appeared. She gave Addie a brief smile of acknowledgement and then, after a moment, approached, looking embarrassed.

'I'm sorry. Valerie has convinced me that I was wrong. I shouldn't have been influenced by Mother.'

Addie half turned to avoid the sun.

'You did what you thought was best.'

'He is a grown man. I should have some faith in his ability to cope. He did cope in the end with everything that happened, after all. I hope we can still be friends.'

'I hope so too,' Addie replied. She needed time to forget the hurt that Pat Morgan had inflicted.

Pat's eyes moved away from her face. 'I think someone's looking for you.'

She turned again. A long shadow was blotting out the sun. 'I nearly didn't make it. The coffin's just arriving.'

'Oh, Jonathan. You came all this way.'

'She was a nice old lady. A lot less crabby than you.'

'Forgive me,' Addie whispered.

'Me too. When I spoke to you, Sarah had only told me half

364

the story. I didn't give her the chance to tell me about Ada. Nor about the other thing. I just slammed the phone down on her. I'm sorry.'

Addie reached out and touched his arm. 'Don't worry, Jonathan.'

'When I heard, I thought you might need some support.' He glanced at Pat Morgan, who had discreetly moved a step away. 'Afterwards I understood why you were so upset.'

'It's all okay now. It's all wonderful.'

Jonathan turned back to her, questions in his eyes.

'My father. But I can't talk about it yet. It's all too new.'

She moved towards Pat Morgan to include her once again. 'This lady is my aunt, Jonathan.'

They shook hands, and Pat disappeared to take up her place.

'I've just come from *my* aunt,' Jonathan said, and she could tell that he was keeping the conversation low key, while she recovered herself. 'I've been with her for the last couple of days. In Watford.'

'I thought …' Addie started, but tailed off.

'She was a signatory to an account that Uncle Bruce put money in. He was trying to hide the money, using her name, but she wouldn't release it to him when he wanted it. Now she's going to.'

'Doesn't she stand to lose a lot of money herself?'

'Yes, she does. But we had a great deal of discussion about it. She doesn't want to make money dishonestly or to have some financial gain at the expense of other people. If I can arrange for at least some of those people who have lost out to be compensated, she's happy with that. And it may help to maintain our family's good name. It was very decent of her - she did it for me and my father as well.'

'Oh Jonathan. I'm so glad.'

'And there's been some other progress. Good news and bad news, as they say.'

'What's the good news?'

'Now that Uncle Bruce has gone, Meera's uncle has asked me to join her in a new firm of solicitors. That's a wonderful vote of confidence. And also, while you were down here we exchanged contracts on the flat. The buyer finally made a firm offer and, in another couple of months, with a bit of luck, we'll be rid of the place, and I'll cease to be encumbered with either the flat or Tabitha.'

'What's the bad news?'

'There won't be any money left from the sale, after we've paid off the mortgage.'

'You could come and live with me. Until my visa expires and I have to go back.'

'Addie. You don't really want to go back, do you? I know I have no right to ask you to stay. I have very little to offer you, now.'

'Jonathan,' Addie said. 'I don't want to lose you. I love you.'

They paused at the church door.

He put his hands on her shoulders for a moment, his face serious. He said quietly, 'I love you too, Addie - very much.'

Then he relaxed again, and something of his old self re-emerged.

'I've heard some girls will say almost anything to get British citizenship.'

They sat in silence together through the brief service, then led the mourners into the September sunshine. Addie threw a single red rose on to the coffin, as it was lowered into the grave.

Then as the other mourners dispersed, they walked, hand in hand, across the village to The Stonemason's Arms. He turned to her.

'I can't offer you special effects today. No lights, no music. No lightning and thunder. No dramatic incidents.'

'I don't care,' she said. 'I just want you, Jonathan.'

They walked into the bar entrance. The barman was polishing glasses, ready for the evening rush.

'Oh, so you two found each other again, did you?'

Jonathan smiled. 'Yes. We've found each other again. Not a moment too soon.'

Acknowledgements

I should like to thank the many people who have encouraged me in the writing and editing of Tainted Tree, in particular, members of Guildford Writers and my editors at Goldenford. In addition, I am most grateful to Adrienne Dines for her support, Janice Windle for the creation of her much-admired cover painting, and my husband, for giving me space when necessary. My thanks, too, to Tormead School, Guildford, who allowed me access to their archivist and to old records, which I used to create a scene in the book.

I would also like to thank the members of The Round Table Reading Group for constantly expanding my knowledge of and interest in other people's books.

Coming Soon from Goldenford

Jay Margrave – *Luther's Ambassadors*

In the second of Jay Margrave's exciting trilogy of mystoricals, Priedeux becomes the companion and mentor of the scheming Anne Boleyn in *Luther's Ambassadors*. In the third novel, jumping through history, as a fictional character is allowed to do, Priedeux travels with Christopher Marlowe through Europe, after his supposed death in Deptford, in *The Nine Lives of Kit Marlowe*.

Irene Black – *Darshan*

A young woman staggers through a morass of unsuitable relationships, involving betrayal, danger and heartbreak, in order to find her cultural identity. Her journey takes her from India to Britain to America and back to India. Is she destined to live her life on the fringes of the communities where she grew up? Or will she finally come to terms with who she is?

Also Available from Goldenford

Esmé Ashford – *On the Edge*

Tramps with bad feet, a sheep rustler, a busker invited to dinner; a weird monster who devours a nasty husband and a child who learns from a visit to the fun fair; limericks and blank verse; it is all here.

Irene Black – *The Moon's Complexion*

Bangalore, India 1991. Ashok Rao, a young doctor, has returned home from England to choose a bride.

But who is the intriguing Englishwoman who seeks him out? Why is she afraid and what is the secret that binds them together? The lives of two strangers are turned upside down when they meet and the past comes to haunt them. The Moon's Complexion is a tale of love across cultural boundaries. It is also a breath-taking adventure tale played out in the mystical lands of Southern India and Sri Lanka and in the icy countryside of winter England.

Irene Black – *Sold ... to the Lady with the Lime-Green Laptop*

The author, based in the UK, has used the experience gained over five years of trading on eBay to describe one hundred of her most interesting, entertaining, sometimes lucrative and occasionally disastrous sales. Each page is devoted to one item and carries a photograph, a description, the purchase and sale price, and, as the author says in her foreword "some additional trivia". The "trivia" consists of hilarious, fascinating and sometimes useful observations.

Anne Brooke – *Thorn in the Flesh*

Kate Harris, a lecturer in her late thirties, is attacked in her Surrey home and left for dead. Continuing threats hinder her recovery, and these life changing events force her to journey into her past to search for the child she gave away. Can she overcome the demons of her own personal history before time runs out?

Anne Brooke – *Pink Champagne and Apple Juice*

Angie Howard has one ambition - to escape from her home in the idyllic Essex countryside and set up her own café in London. Once there, she seeks out her long-lost Uncle John, whose lifestyle is not at all what she expected.

Before she can achieve her goal, she has to juggle the needs of a glamorous French waiter, a grouchy German chef and her exuberant, transvestite Uncle John.

What's more, if she manages to keep the lid on all that, what will she do about the other hidden secrets of her family?

Jacquelynn Luben – *A Bottle of Plonk*

It's 1989 – a time when Liebfraumilch, Black Forest gateau and avocado bathrooms are all the rage, and nobody uses mobile phones.

When Julie Stanton moves in with Richard Webb one Saturday night in May, she doesn't expect their romantic evening together to end with her walking out of the flat clutching the bottle of wine with which they were to toast their new relationship.

But then Julie and the wine part company, and the bottle takes the reader on a journey through a series of life situations revealing love, laughter and conflict.

Jay Margrave - *The Gawain Quest*

In *The Gawain Quest*, Priedeux is a medieval hitman. He is sent to kill the writer of the poem, *Gawain and the Green Knight*, to stop rebellion against the King, Richard II. As he follows the clues in the poem, Priedeux finds himself questioning the very purpose of his vocation.

Can he act in time? And what will he report to his master, John of Gaunt?

info@goldenford.co.uk
www.goldenford.co.uk